TONY TORZILLO

Children of the Yew

GERONIMO
PRESS

To my loving wife, Alaina, who encouraged me to keep writing the book I started long before we met, and gave me the courage and strength to finish. You have been my muse and my light in the darkness.

Acknowledgement

There are many people that I worked with to make this book happen. As I learned more of the writing craft, the book changed and developed over time. Many people contributed along the way. My beta readers, Kim Napolitano, Dr. Donna Birdwell, John Howell, Michael Britt, Dr. Dustin Miller, Brad Davis, and Darran Walker gave me immensely useful feedback. My editors, Kevin Anderson, Josephine Hao, and Rebecca Brewer were instrumental in shaping the book into what it is today with their developmental editing expertise. Leonora Bulbeck did an outstanding job with copy editing. My cover artist, Laercio Messias, did a great job with the artwork. My chief medical consultant, beta reader, and developmental editor who provided an enormous amount of advice and loving support along the way was my wife, Alaina Torzillo.

Chapter 1

The manila envelope lay on the table unopened. It had come by mail—a rare thing to receive correspondence in such a fashion—and it was addressed to Vance Malloy, a name Wesley O'Keefe hadn't used in over forty years. He'd left that identity and life behind, like he had so many others. Wesley picked up the envelope with a shaky hand, then returned it to the desk in his den. Perhaps the letter should stay there, and he could continue to remain ignorant.

As he walked to the arched veranda overlooking his garden, the scent of blooming lilacs filled his nostrils. A horseshoe pattern of gray clouds had formed in the sky, and dark tendrils reached like gripping fingers toward the barely visible sun. Wesley's cat, Hunter, swished his tail and made a chittering noise as he watched a small bird perched in the branches of a Japanese maple. The scrawny kitten that had appeared at Wesley's front door ten years ago had since evolved into a healthy, furniture-shredding menace under his loving care.

A large Douglas fir stood among the other sentinels framing his five-acre estate. How long had it been there? A hundred years? He envied the tree. It could stand in one place and live its life without having to hide its identity. Wesley had lived many different lives, always hiding the truth of his longevity, though he didn't know its origin.

He spoke to his cat as he bent down to stroke his fur. "I'm going to open the envelope, Hunter."

Hunter positioned himself to receive a scratch under the chin, unimpressed by the droning noises Wesley made. "More scratching, less talking" might have been his reply if he could speak.

He returned to his den and retrieved the envelope. Using an ornate brass paper knife, he sliced open the envelope and retrieved the contents. He held on to the table with one hand to steady himself as he stared at the picture of him and a former business partner named Jonathan Moore, with Jonathan's five-year-old niece standing next to them. The photo must have been taken forty years ago, in the year 2002. The other picture showed him and a woman he'd been dating at the time, Beth Norbeck.

Wesley dropped the pictures onto the table and poured himself a Scotch. The malty liquid warmed his gullet as the smoky overtones developed on his tongue. He reveled in it, closing his eyes to forget about the images. Though his hands were cold, the Scotch warmed his stomach during his brief reprieve.

Perhaps Beth had found him. A woman scorned, especially if she now knew he wasn't dead, could be spiteful, but why? He'd broken off relations with her long before faking his death. Wesley did a web search for her and found an obituary from April of 2021. He let out a long breath and rubbed his chin. Not her, then.

After a considerable amount of time searching the internet, Wesley found that Jonathan now lived in a retirement home in Seattle named Sunset Towers. It would be a quick drive across the Evergreen Point Floating Bridge to get there from his house, in Medina. He also found that the young girl in the photo was now a forty-five-year-old woman named Dr. Candace Rosenbach, a research microbiologist at the University of Washington.

Though Wesley hadn't spoken with Jonathan in decades, he hoped Jonathan could offer an explanation for the photo. Changing identities and starting a new life would no longer be practical in this modern world, with smart cars, smartphones, DNA databases, and everything else that made it impossible to disappear into anonymity.

Wesley drove across the bridge to Seattle and parked in the garage for

Sunset Towers. He rode the parking elevator to the lobby and entered the building, and the smell of urine and sanitizer assaulted him. A man in a wheelchair drooled as his head lolled to the side while the screen in front of him blared out entertainment videos. Holograms danced in front of a woman who appeared heedless of their presence as she stared off into space. Wesley bit his lip. Surely Jonathan wouldn't be that bad, would he?

The young woman at the counter smiled, showing perfect white teeth. Her unblemished skin provided a stark contrast to the wrinkled leather that covered the surrounding residents. "Hello. Welcome to Sunset Towers. Who would you like to visit?"

Wesley brandished what he hoped was a warm smile. "I'm here to visit Jonathan Moore."

She swiped her hand across a screen. "ID, please."

What an unnecessary gesture. The facial-recognition system must have identified him already. He slid his identity chip across the counter.

"Mr. Wesley O'Keefe?"

"Yes, but can you please tell him that Vance is calling?"

The receptionist stared at him, perplexed.

"I'm sorry. Vance was my nickname. Tell him Vance is here to see him."

She shook her head. "You're a real peach, aren't you? The computer says your name is Wesley. I can't introduce you as Vance."

He breathed in, trying to remain patient. "I changed my name long ago. If you don't tell him Vance Malloy is here, he won't know who you're talking about." He leaned in close and lowered his voice. "He might not even know who I am anyway, but humor me. Please."

She narrowed her eyes in thought for a few moments. "Okay, but I warn you that if Mr. Moore doesn't recognize you, I'm going to have security escort you out of the building."

A massive security guard stopped watching various monitors and trained his gaze on Wesley. He had the look of a bulldog waiting for an intruder to make a sudden move. Wesley smiled back at the man until he broke his stare. Wesley tried to remain hopeful. Would Jonathan remember him? They'd spent years working together, but time stole men's memories as they aged.

The receptionist swiped a few more screen items. By now, there would be a 3D image of Wesley in Jonathan's room, with a text description that said *Vance*.

A small hologram of Jonathan appeared on the desk. "Vance, you old rascal. Where've you been getting your plastic surgery? Come on up."

"A word of warning," the receptionist said. "Mr. Moore is a sundowner, so he may not be lucid in the afternoon or evening." She smiled at Wesley and gestured toward the elevator. "Room 4002. Elevator K."

Relief filled him. Perhaps he would get some answers. Wesley bade her a good day, then walked into elevator K.

Moments later it opened, and he entered the bright hallway, where illuminated arrows on the floor pointed the way to Jonathan's room. Cameras in domes stared down at him from the ceiling with their ubiquitous eyes.

The door slid open as Wesley approached. Jonathan sat in a wheelchair, with small oxygen tubes coming out of his nostrils and an IV attached to his arm. A little robot checked his vitals, then zoomed past Wesley into the hallway to assist the next individual staving off death.

With bright lighting, plants, and stylish furniture, the well-appointed room bore little in common with the hopeless scene forty floors below. Jonathan's money allowed him to spend his final moments in comparative luxury, though he would someday rot in the same ground as everyone else.

Jonathan stared at Wesley with bloodshot eyes and a smile with too few teeth. Pallid skin with small splotches of purple covered his face. "Vance, you don't look a day over thirty. How? What's it been? Forty years since I last saw you?" He narrowed his eyes. "Are you here for money?"

Forty years sounded right. Good, Jonathan was more lucid than Wesley had hoped. "I've got plenty of that. You should know—you helped me grow my portfolio. What do you remember?"

Jonathan nodded. "I remember." He narrowed his eyes and stared off into space for a long moment. "I remember helping you create a new identity and faking your death." He shook his head. "Why come back now, forty years later?"

4

Wesley bit his lip. "I got two photos in the mail. One of you and me with your niece, and another of Beth and me."

Jonathan furrowed his brows. "Beth?"

Heat rose in Wesley's cheeks. He hadn't shared much with Jonathan about Beth. "Yes. She was a woman I dated briefly, but she died twenty years ago, so it wasn't her. I'm trying to figure out who sent me the letter and why."

Jonathan gestured to the tubes behind him. "So you think I might have sent it? I've got a lot more to worry about than digging up skeletons from my past. We haven't talked in forty years, and I didn't know you were dating anyone named Beth. It wasn't me."

"The letter was addressed to Vance Malloy, to my home in Medina. How thorough a job did your guy do changing my identity?" Wesley asked.

"He was a consummate professional, and I'm offended you'd think otherwise. You really shouldn't be in Seattle, you know. You paid me a lot of money to make sure no one would ever find you. I thought you were moving to another country."

Wesley smiled as he thought of the good times he'd had in Portugal. "Yes, I did. Had a great time of it, then moved back here ten years ago. I could only spend so many years making love to beautiful women and surfing."

Jonathan let out a long breath. "Forgive me if I don't feel sorry for you. I don't understand it, though. Why do you look so young? I know there's no plastic surgery that good. You never told me why you wanted to start a new life, and I never asked. You could have at least sent me a postcard or something. I thought we were friends."

Wesley had grown weary of watching those he loved wither and die around him. Keeping his agelessness a secret had made sense for the longest time, and now it no longer did. He'd never fake his death again. He wanted so much to figure out why he didn't age, to live a life where he could grow close to others. Even if nobody would believe an old sundowner like Jonathan, Wesley would feel some sense of relief. He'd reveal himself to Jonathan and take the hand fate dealt him. He'd grown tired of the hiding, and it wouldn't be possible in this modern world to continue changing identities.

Wesley wrung his hands. "I'm sorry for that. Every time I started a new life, I never looked back." He waited for Jonathan to say something, but he only stared back in confusion. Wesley let out a long breath. "I don't know why, Jonathan, but I don't age."

Jonathan raised his eyebrows. "Are you trying to tell me you're immortal?"

Wesley held up a hand. "No, not immortal. I came near death about a decade ago. I saw the light, saw my first wife, Samantha, beckoning me forward to heaven. It was a swimming accident, and the paramedics did CPR on me in time. It's why I left my new life behind and came back. I can die, but I don't age."

Jonathan pursed his lips. "So why hide it? Why not share it with your friends?"

"I always thought I was being punished by God for my past sins. I thought He wanted to keep me alive to make me remember the anguish I had caused others. I was born in a time when I would have been burned at the stake if people had known my nature. On the drive over here, I realized something."

"Sins?" Jonathan asked.

Wesley admired the majestic peak of Mount Rainier through the window. He closed his eyes, and images of the fire filled his mind, and the awful smell of burning flesh came back to him. "I burned down my aunt's house in Ireland by accident when I was fourteen, and I ran away on a ship to the Colonies. I never looked back." He forced himself to swallow as he looked into Jonathan's eyes.

Jonathan motioned for him to continue with a slight nod of his head.

"I can no longer hide from my past. I run and change identities because I can't bear the notion of losing everyone I love, over and over again. I've given up on the idea that God wants to punish me. There must be something unique about my biology. I mean to find out what it is and share it with others. I researched your niece, Dr. Candace Rosenbach, from the photo. Maybe she can help me discover my true nature, or she must know someone who can. I can't run anymore, Jonathan. I can't. I may not be aging, but a piece of me dies every time I need to leave the people I love behind." He took in a long, deep breath. "Jonathan, I'm sorry I left so abruptly. I never got a chance to spend some of my life with you. I deeply regret that."

A look of anguish came over Jonathan. "Yes, I've lost many people myself. I don't even know who I am at night, or so they tell me. I don't remember the episodes. I wouldn't believe it if you weren't here before me, looking young. You could have trusted me, you know?"

A lump grew in Wesley's throat. Guilt filled him, regret that he'd allowed his friend to suffer the effects of aging while he had managed to escape them. "I'm sorry. Starting over was always easier, until it wasn't."

Jonathan sniffed. "It's probably too late for me, but I'm sure Candace can help you. I'll call her." He pressed some buttons on his watch and left a message. "Hey, Candy Bear. It's your uncle. I have a friend that needs your help. Please come visit me as soon as you can, and I'll fill you in. Love you."

Wesley's mind raced as he listened to Jonathan leave the message for his niece. Who had sent the photo? He couldn't think of anyone that made any sense at all.

A strange look came over Jonathan's face when he turned to Wesley. "Hey, are you mad I beat you? Is that why you're here?"

Wesley's watch read 4 p.m. This must be the "sundowner" effect the receptionist had warned him about. "Jonathan, I told you why I've come to visit you."

A long pause. Did Jonathan even recall the previous conversation?

"Oh, you're fine," Jonathan said. "I figured you were tired of me beating you at golf."

Wesley laughed, but he'd never played golf with Jonathan. "I wanted to start a new life where no one knew me. I go by Wesley O'Keefe now. My original name."

"Really? Isn't that something? Did I tell you I got Harriett a Cadillac? I brought that Caddy home, and she beamed. You should've seen that smile. She loved it."

Wesley remembered Harriett. She'd been at several of the company parties they'd hosted. In his web search for Jonathan, Wesley had seen that Jonathan's wife, Harriett, had died of cancer twenty years ago. Dread washed over him as an ache grew in the back of his throat. "I'll bet she did."

"You know, life isn't as great if you don't have someone to share it with.

I'm glad I have my Harriett. I don't know what I'd do without her. Are you married, Vance?"

Wesley bit his lip. Thoughts of Samantha came pouring into his head. Those last gasping, wheezing noises she'd made, and he had never forgotten. He stared into Jonathan's eyes before he answered. "No. She passed away."

A strange look drifted over Jonathan's face as though he'd realized something awful. Then his face changed, and he smiled. "You need to get you a Harriett—not my Harriett, mind you, but someone you can spend your life with." Jonathan broke into a coughing fit and hacked up something into a tissue. He fumbled around in his pockets and couldn't find anything. "They won't let me smoke in here. Why am I paying them so much damn money?"

Why indeed? The man didn't need to live in such luxury at this late stage of his life. "Because you're a rich old fart and don't want to share a room with someone else that's at death's door, Jonathan."

Jonathan attempted to stand and almost fell forward. Wesley caught him and kept him from falling any further. "I'm in the prime of my youth. Ask Harriett. Where did she get off to? You know I had a robot checking my medicine. A robot. Can you believe that?"

He could. Robots performed more and more tasks. He would call his car a robot, though no one else would. Wesley replied with mock incredulity. "No. Personally, I'd prefer a human nurse."

A deliberate, quiet exhalation escaped Wesley's lips, and his shoulders relaxed as the tension left him. Jonathan was incoherent at the moment and likely wouldn't be intelligible until tomorrow. He may not even know his name from one minute to the next, but Wesley could seek help from his niece.

Technology ruled the world now, not superstition and fear. People didn't get burned at the stake as witches. Wesley imagined a world where he wouldn't have to watch the people he loved disappear from old age. He could share the secret, once he found it, with others. He desperately hoped Jonathan's niece could help him.

Wesley's confession had given him some small measure of relief. Still, too many years had passed, and he'd lost the opportunity to make a meaningful connection with an old friend, even if he'd had a fleeting moment of precious lucidity.

Wesley placed a hand on Jonathan's frail shoulder. Jonathan was a man who had once captured the attention of all when he'd entered a room. This wisp of a person was but a shadow of the giant Wesley had once called his best friend. Wesley forced a swallow down his dry throat. "Goodbye, Jonathan. Until we meet again, may God hold you in the palm of His hand."

As he turned to walk away, Jonathan cried out. "Wait. Why don't you leave me a card?"

Wesley smiled. No one used business cards anymore, but they were one of the old-fashioned habits Wesley had never shaken, and he placed one on the tray next to Jonathan's hand.

Jonathan looked tired. "I'm not sure what the hell meds they have me on here, but I can't stay awake for long."

Jonathan's eyes closed as Wesley watched him. Loud snores followed, and Jonathan's mouth hung agape as he drew in ragged breaths.

Gratefulness filled Wesley as he considered that fate had spared him such a life. "Next time, old friend." He patted Jonathan's shoulder and walked away.

The elevator whisked him to the ground floor, and he swiped his watch to call for his car to return him to his beautiful waterfront home in Medina.

The twenty-minute drive barely registered, and he left his car and smiled at his expansive, immaculate garden. He marveled at how a man who had once been a poor Irish boy living on the outskirts of Oxmantown Green could live in such a place as this.

He opened the door to his waiting companion. Hunter's tail stood erect as he rubbed against Wesley's leg, and Wesley reached down to scratch him behind the ear. An extra-thick, long layer of fur around the tabby's neck made him look like a fifteen-pound lion. "You're nothing but a mangy, old, good-for-nothing cat. Don't you have some mice to catch?"

Hunter purred and rubbed against his pant leg. Wesley tried to scowl but couldn't keep from laughing.

They ate dinner together, as was their daily custom. "I met with my friend Jonathan today. I don't think he remembered anything I'd said to him. Can you fathom such a thing?"

Hunter looked up from his crystal bowl filled with turkey pieces and licked his paw. He wiped his face without any concern for what the human in the room was saying.

"I guess you're right. It doesn't matter much. There are more important matters to attend to, like licking paws and cleaning fur. If only I had a life as simple as yours."

Hunter turned his back to Wesley and swished his tail from side to side as he looked out at a finch. Lucky cat. When Wesley had been young, people had stood and watched birds and talked without care for much else. Of course, a bad winter or a failed crop had meant death, so not everything had been perfect, but people had savored things more. Perhaps he was getting too old. The nostalgic pull of yesteryear beckoned him. He was out of place in this modern world, like a feather quill in a room full of computers.

A call appeared on his watch.

"Hello?"

"Hello. Is this Mr. Wesley O'Keefe?"

"Yes."

"I'm Candace Rosenbach. I found your card in my uncle Jonathan's room. How did you know him?"

Wesley paused. Why was she using the past tense? "I'm an old friend."

Several seconds of silence passed. "I'm at Sunset Towers. I'm sorry to be the one to tell you this, but Jonathan passed away in his sleep."

Too late. "I see. Thank you. Sorry for your loss." His hand shook as he tried to hold it steady. "Why did you call me?"

Another long silence. "Jonathan left me a message to visit him, saying a friend needed help. I assume he was talking about you?"

Wesley shut his eyes tight as the grief welled up inside him, then cleared his throat. "Yes, that was me. I visited him for the first time in forty years today. I caught him while he was still lucid, and then he checked out. I'm glad I got to see him. He didn't seem on the verge of death, though. What happened?"

The line was quiet, with only the sound of controlled breathing on the other end. "Uncle Jonathan has been fighting this for a long time." A few moments of silence passed. "What can I help you with, Mr. O'Keefe?"

"I need some research help. Can we meet to talk about it in a week or so?"

"That's vague, but I'll help, only because Uncle Jonathan wanted me to. If this is some sort of investment scam or something, you better tell me now, because I don't have time for that crap."

Wesley drew in a long breath. "No, not a scam. I appreciate your time, Dr. Rosenbach. Your uncle meant a great deal to me, but not as much as he must have meant to you. Please let me know if you need anything at all. I'd be happy to help."

"I will. Goodbye."

Wesley disconnected the call, then placed his face in his hands to rub his eyes. Too late for him to save Jonathan, but not too late for all the others he could help.

Chapter 2

Candace replayed Jonathan's last voice message again as she stared ahead in shock. "Hey, Candy Bear. It's your uncle. I have a friend that needs your help. Please come visit me as soon as you can, and I'll fill you in. Love you." She listened to the message several more times, then put her hands over her face. She had ignored the call while she had focused on her lab research. Her quest to stop cancer wouldn't have been impacted if she'd taken a five-minute break to talk to her uncle. He'd put his life on hold to raise her. If only she could have spoken to him one last time before he had died. If only she could have said "I love you" back to him. She played those words again and mouthed her response back in silence as she stared through the windows of Jonathan's condo at the looming skyscrapers.

Jonathan didn't sound like a man who was about to die. Candace stared down at her hands. She needed to get out of this place to focus on saving the people that she could help.

Candace shambled over to the bed and held Jonathan's cold white hand. Now he lay there in peaceful repose, like a porcelain doll. "I'm sorry I didn't answer."

A tall blond nurse with striking green eyes entered the room and glided toward her with poise. She placed her hand on Candace's shoulder. "I'm sorry for your loss. Do you need anything?"

The nurse sounded so genuine in her concern. Candace lost the bearing she'd struggled so hard to maintain as her whole body shook with sobs. She wailed as the nurse held on to her, and tears streamed forth, wetting the nurse's shoulder.

The nurse held her for several minutes before Candace regained her composure.

"I'm sorry," Candace said. "I'm not usually this emotional."

The nurse smiled. "It's okay. I've seen several lifetimes of grief working here. Are any more family members coming to see your uncle?"

Candace shook her head.

The nurse nodded and patted Candace on the shoulder again. "He had a visitor here earlier, a Mr. Wesley O'Keefe. Should I ask him to come?"

"No. I called him and let him know Uncle Jonathan passed away, but I have no idea who he is. He said he was an old friend." She stared out the window for a few moments. "Can I see what he looked like?"

The nurse pulled a small tablet from her pocket and showed Candace a video of Mr. O'Keefe walking into the room.

She stared at the images of Wesley, a tall man with blond hair and green eyes, for a long time. He appeared familiar, and she tried to remember why, but the memory wouldn't come to her. "I expected someone older. He looks barely thirty, if that. How could he be an old friend?"

The nurse smiled. "A wonder what the right cosmetics can do. I suspect if he's your uncle's friend, he's a man of means. Do you recognize him?"

No plastic surgery would be good enough to make a man who should be in his seventies seem that young. Candace opened her mouth and stared at the image for a long time. A memory filled her mind—a dinner party with that man talking with her uncle, with lots of other people in suits walking around, laughing. She'd only been five years old. She remembered those eyes now, and she remembered thinking of the eyes of the lions at Woodland Park Zoo. "I do. He was friends with my uncle when I was a young girl. He hasn't changed."

The nurse was shocked but then returned to her calm demeanor. A microexpression. "Odd. Perhaps that was his father."

"No. It was him. I'd remember those eyes anywhere." Eyes like the

13

nurse's eyes, which stared at her now. Why was this woman so interested in knowing if she recognized Wesley? "I didn't catch your name."

The nurse straightened herself. "I'm Anne. If you need anything, please let me know. I'll call the funeral home for you if there are no more guests. Please take your time. I know how hard it is to say goodbye. I'm sorry, I need to get to a patient." She rushed out of the room.

Candace grabbed Jonathan's hand once more and grasped it to her chest. "Goodbye, Uncle Jonathan." She kissed him on the forehead and left.

She stopped to talk to the receptionist on the way out. "Please tell that nurse Anne that I appreciate her being there for me."

The receptionist shook her head. "We don't have an Anne working here."

Odd. Maybe she'd heard her wrong. "Okay. Please tell the nurse attending to Jonathan Moore thanks for me."

She nodded, and Candace left.

*

Candace approached her lab at the university, determined to throw herself back into her work. Trudy stood on the sidewalk, staring ahead.

"Trudy, are you okay?"

Trudy shook her head and motioned toward the entrance. "They've blockaded the entire Department of Microbiology."

There was a massive wave of young students wearing red shirts with stop signs on them that read stop vivisection. Some of them held photos of animals with their bellies splayed open. Another sign read animal experimentation is scientific fraud.

Are you kidding? She did not have time for this crap. She stormed forward.

Trudy tried to grab her arm to restrain her. "Dr. Rosenbach, don't provoke them, please."

Heat filled Candace's body as the anger welled inside her. She shrugged off Trudy's grasp and ran toward the protestors. They shouted, "One, two, three, four, open up the cage doors! Five, six, seven, eight, snatch the locks and liberate!" She hardly heard them as ringing filled her ears.

Candace made for the door of the building. "Out of my way! Now!" She grabbed a sign from a large young man blocking the door and smacked him in the face with it. He recoiled in horror. "Would you rather I tested on humans?"

Several of the people answered yes in unison.

Candace couldn't take it anymore. "If anyone wants to volunteer to be my subject, please step forward."

No one stepped forward, and everyone remained silent.

"How many of you hypocrites ate bacon this morning? I may harm some rats, but I'm finding a way to save people from dying of cancer. Two thousand people will die today from cancer. And tomorrow. And the day after that. Do you want those deaths on your conscience?" No one said anything. *"Do you?"*

Candace stormed through the door and up to her lab, leaving a stunned crowd of students behind her. Her hand shook as she held it in front of the biometric scanner, and the heavy door to her lab clicked and opened. She locked the door behind her.

She tried to focus on checking the quantum model of the cancer cells she'd scanned in a few days ago. The model appeared to be progressing nicely. She needed some good news. A video call request from the Department of Microbiology chair, Dr. Michael Hermann, popped onto her monitor. Was he calling to check on her progress? She pressed the accept button.

Dr. Hermann's face appeared. His flaring nostrils and raised eyebrows, along with his red face, gave Candace a slight hint that he wasn't calling to wish her good morning and to check her progress. *Damn it.*

"Dr. Rosenbach, would you care to explain what just happened?"

She let out a long-held breath. "They were blocking me from conducting important research, Dr. Hermann." She tried to keep her tone flat but winced at the anger in her voice. She sounded like an unruly teenager protesting her parents grounding her.

A video of Candace swinging a sign and hitting the student, along with her tirade, played in a small window next to the chair's face. "When has it ever been okay to assault a student, Dr. Rosenbach?"

For a few moments, she maintained her composure. Awkward silence stretched on as she stared at the glaring face of Dr. Hermann. By keeping to her routine, she'd hoped to keep herself from feeling the grief that now welled inside her. *Push it down. Don't let him see you get weak—you're a scientist, damn it!* She closed her eyes tight and pinched the bridge of her nose, straining to keep the mounting tears from falling.

"Dr. Rosenbach, is everything okay?"

Maybe it was the sound of genuine concern in his voice or seeing herself go postal on the student in the video that would now go viral. Maybe it was neither of those things, but she lost her composure and cried in front of her department chair.

After several minutes of crying, she wiped her eyes with the sleeve of her shirt. "I'm sorry." This time the words sounded contrite. She'd lost it, and some students had filmed her doing so. Now the video would be plastered all over various social media. She could see the headlines now: crazy professor loses it in front of animal rights protestors. "My uncle died today. I came here from his nursing home."

Dr. Hermann breathed out, and some of the anger, only some, left his face. "Candace, you're a valuable asset to the research we do here. Take some time off and mourn your uncle; the university will release a statement on your behalf."

How much time off was he expecting her to take? She couldn't be alone with her thoughts. She had to work with the experiments so close to bearing success. She folded her arms and tried to keep the anger from her voice. "I'll be fine, Dr. Hermann. I need to work on this."

He pursed his lips. "It's not a request. Go home. Now."

She nodded and disconnected the call.

What the hell was she supposed to do now?

Chapter 3

Wesley drove his Mercedes to the office in downtown Bellevue, a cosmopolitan city across Lake Washington from Seattle. The facial-recognition system granted him access to the garage, and he rode the elevator to the thirtieth floor. He worked his way to his office, waved his smart card through his desktop reader, and peered into the camera that allowed the software to recognize him.

"Good morning, Wesley," said the computer.

"Please tell Jake to get in here with the latest reports," Wesley said.

"Sent message to Jake," it replied.

What amazing technology. Sure did beat an old Dictaphone. A real secretary would be lovely, but nobody did that job nowadays. The era of humans making him coffee when he got into his office was long past. Robots and computers did it all now. When would Wesley need to start making the robot coffee?

Jake arrived in his office ten minutes later. "Hey. You'll find some interesting stuff here," Jake said as he placed the memory stick in Wesley's hand. Jake was paranoid about using email and advised him to save sensitive data to an encrypted drive and never to send files to anyone over the network.

"Thanks. Give me a bit to read through these." He liked to peruse the reports on his own and then ask questions.

Jake's mouth twitched slightly at the right corner, and his left eye opened and closed spasmodically in its customary manner. "Right. See you soon." He turned around, ran his fingers through his thinning red hair, and exited through the office door.

Wesley regarded Jake as an invaluable employee, but Wesley liked to keep him in his place. He smiled inwardly whenever Jake's mouth started to twitch, never showing his amusement.

Wesley grew more pleased as he read through the reports, finding information to make him even wealthier. He spoke to his computer. "Send a message to Jake. 'Could you please come up here?'"

The computer replied in its usual friendly female voice. "Message sent."

Jake appeared five minutes later. "Happy?"

How could he not be pleased with so much profit made? "Yes. Good work, Jake. Thank you."

Wesley stood and exited, seeing an incredulous expression on Jake's face as he left. Jake had probably been expecting Wesley to ask lots of additional questions, as he usually did, but he didn't need to this time. His portfolio had increased in value by five million dollars in the last week thanks to Jake's work, and while only a small percentage of his holdings, it was still cause for celebration. Perhaps he could invite Jake to go out. He'd never done that before. He returned to the office.

When Wesley came back, Jake gave him a quizzical look.

"Hey, Jake, you have a small son, right?"

Jake frowned back at him. "Yes. His name is Zach. Why do you ask?"

"I thought we could go out for dinner. My treat. A way of saying thank you for all the hard work you've done."

Jake's mouth opened and closed a few times before he said anything in response. "That's gracious, but he's with my ex-wife tonight."

"You and I, then?"

A long pause, then a quick shake of the head. "Sorry. I have to meet someone tonight."

Wesley nodded. "Another time, then." He smiled and left.

He really didn't want to be alone with his thoughts, so Jake's refusal stung.

Jonathan had been his last good friend. He hadn't spoken to him for forty years, and rekindling the friendship, even if only for a few hours, had filled him with joy. Now a hollowness remained where the joy had been. He covered his eyes with his hand, and his throat tightened. An old wound once again torn asunder. He should have tried to find a way to help Jonathan sooner. He closed his eyes. The lump in his throat continued to grow, and he could hardly swallow.

He dashed off to a nightclub, hoping to find someone who would help him forget about his troubles.

*

Wesley awoke the next morning in the condo of a woman he'd met the night before.

Her full lips smiled as her brown hair fell forward. "Feeling better?"

With a dry throat, he opened his mouth, and a pounding started in his head. How much had he drunk last night? "A bit. Could I have some water, please?"

She returned with a glass. "Here you go." She watched him drink the water. "You never did tell me why you were so down."

No, he hadn't. He let out a long sigh. "Sorry. I had a friend pass away a few days ago. Thanks for helping me forget about him."

She narrowed her eyes. "Is that all this was? A way to help you forget?" She stormed out of the bedroom.

Shower noises started, so he put his clothes on and ran out of the door. With any luck, he'd never see her again.

On the way home, Wesley's watch buzzed a few times—calls from that woman. He ignored them.

*

A few weeks passed, and Wesley managed to avoid any further conversations with the woman he'd slept with, though she messaged him a few times.

With the hope that Candace had had enough space and time to grieve for her uncle, Wesley called her.

After a few rings, a hoarse voice answered. "Hello?"

"Is this Candace?"

A pause. "Yes. How can I help you, Mr. O'Keefe?"

She must have saved his contact information. That was a good sign, wasn't it? He cleared his throat. "I wonder if you could meet me for coffee. I'd like to talk more about why I met with your uncle." He didn't drink coffee, but Americans found it odd if you asked them for tea.

"Can we talk over the phone?"

He cleared his throat. "It's a delicate matter and would best be discussed in person."

The silence stretched on for several moments. "Okay. I'll send you a place. Give me an hour. Say, ten thirty?"

Relief filled him. He needed this meeting to work. "Thank you. I'll see you then."

*

Wesley sipped his tea as he caught up with the latest news. miners extract water from an asteroid in kuiper belt. He shook his head as he read the article. He'd invested millions in the company, PRI, that had finally managed to get a small mining rig into space, and the only thing they had to show for it was a few liters of water. He'd hoped they'd be mining platinum by now.

"Mr. O'Keefe?"

A tall woman with red hair and blue eyes stood before him. He swallowed and rubbed the back of his neck. He stood and took her hand to kiss it. "My apologies. You must be Candace. I'm sorry, I got wrapped up in this news article. Please have a seat. What can I get you?"

Candace smiled, though the expression didn't touch her eyes. She looked like she hadn't slept for some time, and her face was red. She stared at him before she said anything. "I'm sorry, I'm a fright. I'll take a quadruple skinny almond milk macchiato with sugar-free hazelnut, please."

"Sorry, can you say that again?"

"It's fine." She pointed at the small robot whizzing past the table. "The bot heard me." She gave him a funny look. "You weren't planning to walk to the counter and ask for it, were you?"

He nodded and sat down. "I'm sorry about your uncle Jonathan. He was someone I called a dear friend for many years."

A robot that looked like an upside-down trash can with wheels rolled toward them with Candace's drink on a tray. Candace grabbed the cup and sipped at it for a few long moments. The soft whine of the robot's electric motor sounded as it wheeled away to the next patron.

Candace narrowed her eyes and set the cup down. "Help me understand that, Mr. O'Keefe. I recognize you. I saw you forty years ago, when I was only five years old. You haven't changed."

Wesley choked on his tea and wiped his lips. He considered his standard line about Botox and the wonders of modern medicine. Telling Jonathan had been less difficult—after all, no one would believe a man so old and senile. How was Wesley supposed to let this beautiful young woman know? "I may not have changed, but you've grown gorgeous."

Candace took another sip from her coffee, then set it down on the table. She looked less than amused. "I'm forty-five years old now. You should be at least seventy by now, yet you look thirty. Who are you?"

Wesley took a long sip of his tea before answering. "I invested with your uncle. I convinced him after the tech sector collapsed in 2000 that we should buy as many tech stocks as possible. He thought me mad, but I convinced him. We made a lot of money after waiting for a while. I've learned in my long life that patience always serves one well in investing. At the time, I went by the name of Vance Malloy. I knew your aunt Harriett. You know me, and you know that you know me."

She frowned and tapped the side of her coffee cup. "I was five years old. I researched you on the internet. I didn't find a single social media post for you. Nothing."

Social media. Wesley had never understood the urge to share personal details that advertisers would sell—only another way for them to know his business, which he wanted to keep to himself. His chest tightened. "I was born in 1710, the year the British captured the capital of Acadia from the French—"

Candace's eyes widened, and she stood up. "Listen, I don't have time for this. You're crazy."

He stood and motioned for her to lower her voice. "Please sit down. I need your help. Please. Your uncle told me you're a researcher and might be able to help me. Was he right, or was he having some sort of senile breakdown?"

She glared at him, but she sat down. "Yes, I have a doctorate in quantum genetic applications and do microbiology research at the University of Washington. I'll listen to you, but only because you say my uncle asked for it. You must be the reason he sounded so excited when he left me a voice message."

Wesley sat back in his chair and sipped his tea. He remained still as he let the relief sink in. "Have you heard of progeria? The disease that causes kids to die of old age when they're about thirteen?"

She rubbed her chin with her hand. "Yes, a genetic disorder. I know of it."

Candace hadn't stormed away yet—that was a plus. "Maybe I have something like that, but the opposite."

She shook her head. "Hmm. If such a condition were possible, I find it highly improbable that you'd be the only one to have ever had it."

Wesley remembered when sixty-five was considered old. Anyone that lived into their eighties was doing well. People were living to over a hundred and thirty now, and thanks to modern medicine, it wouldn't be much longer before they could live as long as him. "Perhaps I'm the first. I don't get sick. I haven't had a cold since I was fourteen." Wesley thought about the fever and strange dreams he'd had then and was glad for having never been ill again. "Maybe that has something to do with it. I've hidden my identity for years. Other people with my 'condition,' as you called it, might also have kept it a secret."

"If you've hidden it for so long, why tell me now?" she asked.

Why indeed? Wesley carried on like a lone evergreen tree in a deserted field, surrounded by grass. "I want to figure out why I don't age and then share it with the rest of the world."

Candace's cheeks turned red, and her nostrils flared. "Incredible. You actually believe whatever this crock of crap is you're trying to tell me."

Wesley's hand shook, and he found it hard to breathe. "You're a microbiologist. I was hoping you'd help me. I'm convinced there's something unique about my cells. If I'm telling the truth, there's a unique research opportunity in this for you. For me, it's a chance to learn the truth about myself and to help others."

Her expression softened. "I'm skeptical, but if you're telling the truth, it would certainly be an incredible research opportunity. I'll concede that it's possible, though not likely."

He smiled. "I've heard worse odds."

Candace stared at him as he talked. "I think you believe you're telling the truth." She gulped down the rest of her coffee and threw the cup into the trash. "Have a good day, Mr. O'Keefe."

Wesley watched Dr. Rosenbach walk away, and his hopes traveled with her. He sipped his tea. Whom would he ask for help now?

Chapter 4

The funeral director handed Candace an urn containing her uncle's ashes, and she stared at it for a long time before she looked up at him. "Thank you."

He gave what must have been a well-practiced smile of sympathy. "You're welcome, and my deepest condolences for your loss. Are you certain we can't do a ceremony to honor your loved one?"

"Yes. He explicitly said in his will that he didn't want a funeral. He wants me to put his ashes in my garden."

The funeral director tried to hide what must have been disappointment, then spread his hands and turned his gaze to the heavens. "I'm sure he knows those who loved him will mourn his loss. Have a good day."

She held the urn to her chest and walked away. A thought nagged at her as she drove home. Who had been the nurse in Jonathan's room? Why had she been so interested in Wesley? Candace redirected her car to Sunset Towers. She needed some answers.

*

The receptionist scowled at Candace. "I'm sorry, but I can't give you any feeds from your uncle's room."

Candace calmed herself before responding. "Look, I was in there with him. It's not a privacy violation if I was in there. Not to mention he was dead."

A more senior resident looked up from her food tray to see what all the fuss was about, then returned her attention to the food. The receptionist gave the other onlookers an apologetic smile. Her cheeks reddened; then she lowered her voice. "You're asking only to see the video feed from the room when you were there?"

Candace nodded. "Yes, please. I need to see the nurse that was in there."

The receptionist pursed her lips. "We've been over this. You haven't given me a good reason. Saying that you want to thank her isn't enough. We're busy."

Candace raised her voice. "A nurse who doesn't work here was in my uncle's room, and I need to know what the hell she was doing there. Is that clear? How do I know she didn't kill him?"

A large security guard lumbered over to Candace, the palm of his hand resting on his baton. She narrowed her eyes at him. He puffed out his chest. "You need to leave."

The gap between them narrowed as she approached the guard, holding her index finger toward him. "I'm not leaving until I get some answers. Who was the nurse in my uncle's room? Surely your security systems identified her. Is your security so bad that you don't know who goes into the rooms of vulnerable residents?"

The guard seemed to take her statement as a personal affront. "I'm sure there's a reasonable explanation."

The receptionist typed furiously on her keyboard, and a hologram of a female nurse with blond hair and green eyes floated above the desk. "I found the nurse. Her name is Anne O'Keefe. She was visiting a fellow RN friend and did her the favor of covering for her for a few minutes. Now, can you please leave, or do I need to call the police?"

The guard gave Candace a smug grin and raised his eyebrows, daring her to ever challenge the security systems of Sunset Towers again.

Candace stood in silence as she stared ahead. She shook herself out of the shock. "Thank you. Is her friend here?"

"No. She's off today. She does per diem work."

"Can I have Anne's contact info?"

"I'm sorry. I don't have that info," she said with an apologetic shake of her head.

Candace stomped out of the building. At least she had the nurse's name.

On the way to the university, Candace tried to find information on Anne O'Keefe. She searched the Washington State Department of Health website and found the following:

Credential Information for: O'Keefe, Anne E.
   Credential Type: Registered Nurse License
   First Issue Date: 03/01/2024
   Last Issue Date: 01/23/2042
   Expiration Date: 03/01/2043

A little more searching, and she discovered that the expiration date for a nursing license was the nurse's birthday. With that information, she searched for any Anne E. O'Keefe with a birthday on March 1. After paying thirty dollars, Candace had her phone number. She dialed it.

"Hello?"

Candace gathered her thoughts. "Yes, may I speak with Anne O'Keefe?"

"This is she. Who's this?"

"Dr. Candace Rosenbach. You were there for me when my uncle, Jonathan Moore, passed. Do you have a minute?"

A few seconds of silence. "I suppose so. How can I help you?"

"Why were you in my uncle's room?"

More silence. "I was visiting a friend who works at Sunset Towers. She wanted to take a break, so I covered for her. Is there a problem?"

"Not a problem per se. I'm more interested in knowing why you were so curious about Wesley. He has the same last name as you. Are you related?"

Anne laughed. "There are a lot of Americans with that last name. I doubt we're related."

"Then why the interest?"

Anne let out a long breath. "I only wanted to know if you needed to call someone else. I thought he may have been someone you'd like to notify. Listen, I've seen a lot of family members go through grief. People don't always have the presence of mind to think of calling others. I was only trying to help."

Candace noticed the car was nearing the university parking lot. She rubbed the back of her neck. "Where do you get your makeup?"

"Excuse me?"

"Well, I noticed you got your RN license in 2024. You must have been at least twenty-two. You don't look forty. I'd like to shop wherever you do for my makeup from now on."

Several seconds passed. "I'm not sure where this is leading, but I need to go. My condolences for your loss, Dr. Rosenbach. God be with you."

The call disconnected.

As the car parked, Candace dialed her friend Professor Dianne Erdlen. They'd been friends for years, and Dianne taught European folklore and mythology. If Wesley was telling the truth, there had to be some mythology related to it. The most persistent folklore tended to be rooted in reality at some level.

Dianne answered. "Candace. It's been a while."

"Yeah, it has. Sorry. Can we meet at the Burke for some coffee?"

Dianne agreed, and they met at a small table at a café inside the Burke Museum. Candace caught her up on everything that had happened with her uncle. Dianne munched on a little fry bread taco as she listened.

"I'm so sorry about Jonathan."

"Thank you." Candace cleared her throat. "He hardly knew who I was half the time. At least he's not suffering anymore."

Dianne nodded and nibbled on her taco some more.

Candace watched her eat for a while before she broke the silence. "Hey, have you heard any folklore about Irish people that didn't age?"

Dianne laughed. "We're the ones that don't age."

"Who?"

Dianne motioned to herself with a sweeping gesture. "Well, I'm fifty-eight, and a lot of people think I'm forty." She raised her eyebrows.

Was she really that much older than Candace? "Okay, I'm talking about mythology here, not your beautiful black skin."

Dianne gave her long brown curls a flip with her hand. "Don't hate me because I'm beautiful."

Candace didn't want to encourage her, but she laughed anyway. "Are there any myths about ageless people in Ireland?"

Dianne took a long draw from her cappuccino and smiled. "You know, this place does these right. I haven't found any place better other than a café I went to in Venice. I'm going back there." She shook her head. "Sorry—Ireland. Yes. You know, Ireland has a fascinating history—"

Candace cut her off, knowing they'd be here all day while Dianne caught her up on everything that had happened in the country since the Stone Age. Candace loved Dianne and all the knowledge she had in that big brain of hers, but right now, she didn't feel like spending that much time here. "I really only want to know about the mythology concerning anyone ageless."

Dianne gave her a hurt look. Was it feigned or serious? "Well. Some other time, then. Yes, the Tuatha Dé Danann, or 'the folk of the goddess Danu,' were descended from Nemed, who came to Ireland by ship with thousands of people. Some stories have them coming from the heavens, and others by sea. Anu was the mother of the Irish gods. The Tuatha Dé Danann were immortals that taught science, architecture, and art to the people of Ireland."

"I've never heard of such a thing. What happened to them?"

Dianne took another sip of her cappuccino and closed her eyes. She opened them again with a wide smile. "Sorry, I love these. Well, what happened to them in mythology? They were the rulers of Ireland. Nothing more about them after about 1200 BC. In truth, whatever stories they had were likely lost during the many invasions or deaths that occurred after that. Take your pick: famine, plague, Viking raids, the English, the Normans. Ireland has been through a lot. Archaeological records show widespread deaths occurring at various times ever since people first arrived there. Now, what makes you so interested in this topic? I've never known you to be interested in folklore, or history for that matter."

That was true. In fact, she and Dianne didn't have much in common academically, but they enjoyed spending time with each other despite that.

"I met an Irish guy."

Dianne gave her a sidelong glance.

"It's not like that. He was a friend of my uncle. I think he might be into that stuff." She wasn't sure she wanted to tell Dianne much more about Wesley—not yet.

"Hmm." Dianne gave a coy smile, broke off a piece of her fry bread taco, and handed it to Candace. "Try it. You'll like it."

Candace bit into the fry bread taco and savored the morsel. Avocado, tomato, cheese, and puffy fry bread mixed together to create a savory delight for her taste buds. "It's good. Thank you. Sorry, I need to get going."

"Stay in touch. I expect to hear more from you." Candace gave Dianne a hug before she left.

A thousand ideas sparked in Candace's mind as she walked to her lab. She needed to call Wesley.

When she arrived at her lab, her grad student Trudy was waiting for her. "Dr. Rosenbach, can we go over the findings from the virus classification research project?"

Candace did her best to act enthusiastic when she replied. "Sure, Trudy." It was going to be a long day.

Chapter 5

Wesley's office window gave him a magnificent view of the Bellevue skyline. They'd built several new skyscrapers over the last few decades, but he could still see an outline of the Olympics among them.

A call came in.

"Hello?"

"Hello, Wesley. This is Dr. Rosenbach. Do you remember me?"

She had called back. Wesley secured his earpiece, fearing it might fall out somehow and disconnect the call. Excitement filled him. "Yes, of course I remember you. You aren't someone anyone could easily forget. I wasn't sure if I'd hear from you after what you said, but I'm glad you're calling."

"Yeah."

Her flat tone didn't sound promising, and his heart sank. "So, what do you have in mind, Dr. Rosenbach?"

"I got interested when you said you haven't gotten sick since you were a child. I'm doing a research project on immune system and would like to know if you'd participate in a study. I'll pay you for your time."

Pay him. Wesley laughed. "Your help is payment enough. I don't imagine you'd pay me enough to make it worth my time if I didn't think you could assist me. Long ago, I discovered the power of compounding of interest. I have plenty of money. That isn't what motivates me."

"Listen, we're on a university budget, so I'd have to agree with you.

However, this is in the interest of science that will benefit humanity. You interested or not?"

"Can we also work on the stuff we talked about over coffee?"

"I may be able to help you figure out why you're as old as you claim to be, even though I don't believe it. Can you come to the University of Washington right away? We can meet at the Husky Union Building."

Wesley tried to contain his excitement as he nearly tripped over Hunter on the way out the door. "Yes. I'll see you soon."

*

Wesley crossed the 520 Bridge to get to the UW. When he arrived at the HUB, Candace stood near the doorway in a lab coat, smiling at him.

"Thank you, Wesley, for coming on such short notice," she said. "Follow me."

They came to a large glass building with a row of greenhouses surrounding the outside.

Candace leaned in toward him and said, "I'm fascinated with the idea of negligible senescence in humans. If there's any truth to your claim, it will revolutionize multiple fields in biology."

Good sign. Warmth filled Wesley's stomach. "Negligible senescence?"

"Sorry. It's a term for organisms that don't show evidence of aging. Examples are rockfish, some species of tortoises, aspen trees, et cetera."

"So, how would you figure out the age of a rockfish?" Wesley asked.

"The otolith is an ear bone, and you can count the number of rings in it, like in a tree trunk. I'm planning to extract a core sample from your ear today."

Wesley stopped. "No. No way. I'm rather attached to my ear bones."

"I'm messing with you. I'm pretty sure it doesn't work in humans." She said this as they got into an elevator and rode to the fourth floor.

When they arrived at Candace's office, she stood in front of a biometric scanner for a retinal scan. The door clicked open.

"Is this level of security necessary?"

"I wish it weren't, but it is. We have lots of protests from animal rights activists, who aren't fond of my experiments on rats." Her face contorted in palpable anger.

"Aren't you saving human lives?"

"Yes, but that doesn't matter to them. Anyway, let's go in and get started."

Several Petri dishes lined the shelves next to a large transparent box with inverted gloves. Wesley started to reach toward it, and Candace called out, "Watch it. That's where I do my anthrax experiments."

Wesley jerked his hand back to see her laughing at him.

"Ha! I love to pull that one on grad students. Gets them every time."

He didn't see what was so funny. "What is it?"

"It's called a glove box. It's a contained system. We have to work in a sterile environment, so it's the only way to manipulate the microorganisms we work with."

Rats in labeled cages lined one wall, next to a large oven-like apparatus. A sinking feeling overcame Wesley, and he licked his dry lips. "That's not a gas chamber for the rats, is it?"

"Ha! No. That's my autoclave. I need to sterilize lots of equipment for my experiments, and this kills all the nasty bugs."

"Oh, good. I wouldn't want the activists to have another reason to cause trouble for you. What's the plan?" Thank goodness she wasn't gassing rats.

"I'd like to take a few blood samples. Can you please sit down?"

Queasiness filled Wesley. Was she planning to take them from him right now? "Did they teach you how to draw blood in doctorate school?"

"Of course not! I'm winging it. Find a vein and poke, right?"

Wesley started to get up to leave. "Seriously? Find a vein and poke?"

"Relax. I'm kidding. I took an eight-week phlebotomy course during a summer at MIT. I drew blood for the Red Cross as a part-time job to help pay for the things my scholarship didn't."

Wesley stuffed his shaking hand into his pocket to hide it. He focused on a calm lake and tried to think of anything besides watching the blood leaving his arm into a tube. He sat. Perhaps this was a bad idea. He'd seen too many men die from bloodlettings administered by people who had called themselves doctors.

No. Candace wasn't some quack from the eighteenth century. Wesley gulped, trying to force saliva down a dry throat. He looked to the side, away from where she'd be drawing blood. Did those rats feel the same about having their blood drawn?

The cold rubber tourniquet snapped onto his skin, and a sudden poke of pain seared through his arm and then subsided. A quick peek showed him several small tubes filled with blood. Had she noticed how nervous he was? If so, she was kind enough not to mention it.

A small strand of Candace's red hair fell to the front of her lab coat. She placed the tubes full of his precious blood into a small rack. That part was over. Good.

She turned toward him. "When's the last time you remember being sick, Wesley?"

"I was fourteen, in 1724, before I left for the Colonies. I got sick and then had a fever the next day. I haven't taken ill since."

"Were you sick as a child before that?" she asked.

Thoughts of his mother ladling warm broth into a cup filled Wesley's head. How she would run her fingers through his hair as he coughed and make him drink the broth. He missed her so much. "Yes, I had the usual colds and coughs. Never again after the fever."

"Was there any event that precipitated the fever?"

Nausea overtook him as he tried to recall what had happened. "I have a fuzzy memory of my ma handing me some smelly concoction."

"Did you see what she put in it?"

What had it been? Wesley hadn't seen her put anything into the cup. "No. It had a bitter taste. After I drank it, I got sleepy and had a strange dream."

"Interesting." Candace typed something on her tablet. "When did you first notice you weren't aging?"

A pang of heartbreak filled him. "I didn't notice until I was forty, though people had often remarked on my youthful appearance. I noticed one day when my wife, Samantha, told me I looked so much younger than her. I hadn't noticed how old she was until that day. It was on my birthday, so it must have been May of 1750. Others started to notice as well, and it progressed from joking to feeling uneasy around me. When I was older, I would put flour in my hair, but it didn't help."

"Any children? Did they exhibit any signs of not aging?"

"I had a son, yes, Jared. He died of a heart attack when he was fifty-five, and he looked old. My wife was sixty-five when she died of pneumonia." The rasping sounds of her ragged breathing filled his mind as he swallowed hard at the memory.

Candace typed some more on her tablet. "What about your parents? How old were they when they died?"

Regret filled Wesley. Why hadn't he sent any of those letters he'd written? Surely, they would have forgiven him for the fire. He bit his lip. "I'm not sure. I left for the Colonies and never saw them again."

"You never tried to contact them?"

He remembered flames, soot, and ash. The fear on his cousin Billy's face as he had melted like a candle. Wesley winced. "It's a long story. When I last saw my parents, they were in their thirties, and I don't know when they passed away."

Candace's long, delicate fingers tapped at the tablet as she took more notes. "Any siblings?"

"None when I left."

She gave him a funny look. "Have you done any DNA testing for your heritage to see if you have any relatives?"

Wesley shook his head. "No. I don't trust those things."

"Hmm. We don't have enough data to rule out genetics. It didn't manifest in your son, so perhaps it's a recessive gene." She tapped her finger on her tablet. "Any history of cancer?"

How had he avoided lung cancer with all those smoke-filled bars he'd frequented? The offices in the sixties, where everyone was smoking throughout the day. "No. I've been disease-free for over three hundred years. No cancer."

Candace keyed in a code on a small cabinet, placed her fingers on the biometric sensor, and the door opened, revealing several rows of Petri dishes. She pulled one filled with gelatinous goo labeled *BxPC-3 human cell line*. She fussed around and found a few others, then placed them inside the glove box and flipped a switch that turned on a loud fan.

"What are you doing?"

"I need to use a HEPA filter to remove contaminants from the glove box. I'm planning to inject a small portion of your blood into each of these." Candace maneuvered a tube of his blood into a small compartment on the side and donned a surgical mask before putting her hands into the gloves. She moved the tube from the side chamber into the main one and filled several small syringes with his blood. She then lined up the Petri dishes and injected each of them with a small amount.

She placed a tube into a little device, which started to spin. "This centrifuge is going to do a full-spectrum analysis on your blood after separating it into its constituent parts. It would've taken a few days twenty years ago. Now we'll have the results in minutes with quantum spectral analysis."

"What are you hoping to find?"

"Oh. When you told me you haven't gotten sick since childhood, I was interested in analyzing your leukocytes. Also, I'm going to look at red blood cell count, platelets, and electrolytes to see if there is anything of interest. Most of all, I want to make sure you aren't a vampire before we get too far into this research."

That sort of assumption was the reason Wesley had kept this hidden. They both laughed.

"I can assure you I don't have fangs," Wesley said.

"Hey, that reminds me. What about your teeth? Mind if I take a look?" She put on some latex gloves as she asked this.

"Sure, but I'm afraid you'll be disappointed. I have a few fake ones, since the real ones got knocked out. I've been wearing those since about 1820. You'll be disgusted to know that back then they were made from ivory and actual human teeth—usually from dead soldiers."

Candace recoiled a bit in revulsion. "Is that what you have now?"

"Oh, no. These are permanent modern dental implants. Feel free to take a look if you like."

Candace lifted his lips with her thumb and forefinger and felt around, poking at his gums. "No signs of gingivitis or gum loss. Remarkable. These are beautiful implants, by the way. No vampire fangs either, I'm glad to see."

She swiped some more items on her tablet. "When did you last receive the bundle shot?"

The bundle shot protected everyone from colds, influenza, coronaviruses, and practically any other malignant virus. Wesley had wanted to buy stock in the company that made it, Immunitrex, but it was a privately funded venture. Because some viruses, like the cold virus, mutated so frequently, the vaccine had to be given every quarter. Almost no one got the common cold nowadays, because of the quarterly injections.

"I've never had one."

Candace narrowed her eyes and stared at him. "It's required by law every three months. Do you want a repeat of the pandemics from recent decades?"

Wesley licked his dry lips. "I told you, I haven't been sick for centuries. I didn't know if the shot would have unintended side effects."

Candace stared back at him, looking angrier than he thought the situation warranted. "How did you avoid the fines?"

Wesley squared his shoulders and raised his chin. "I paid someone to say they had given it to me. Enough money that they never asked questions."

She stared at him for a long moment. "Weren't you worried you'd give something to someone?"

"I didn't get sick in the 2020s. I didn't get sick during the Spanish flu in the 1920s, nor during any of the numerous epidemics in Ireland or anywhere else. I don't think I can give anything to anyone. I don't know why."

Candace's mouth formed a tight line, and she said nothing. Her cheeks flushed and her nostrils flared.

The spinning device stopped whirring, and a green light flashed. The anger dissipated from her face as Candace made a few swipes on her tablet and studied the data. "Wow."

The rate at which technology had improved over the last few decades continued to astound Wesley. "What?"

"White blood cell count's a little high, but within normal limits. Not remarkable. What is fascinating is all of the cells show no telomere shortening."

36

He'd heard of telomeres. They were like little caps at the end of a chromosome that maintained the chromosome's integrity. "Why don't mine shorten?"

"Normally, each time a cell divides, those telomeres shorten. Your cells don't have this problem. There may be no limit to the number of times they could divide."

That could explain his continued youth. But why? "Is that why I don't age?"

Candace held up a hand as she read some more data on her tablet. She swiped at various menus and nodded, then held her chin in her hand for a while, then continued reading. She turned to face him with an expression of awe. Her mouth hung agape as she held his gaze with a wide-eyed stare. "I'm sorry. I didn't believe you, but this … well, this changes everything."

"Can you please tell me what 'this' is? What are you seeing?"

"Your mitochondria show additional RNA patterns beyond what I'd expect. I'll do a detailed quantum analysis on these RNA patterns and run them through a database. It might take a few days."

Due to an interest in investing in the technology, Wesley knew a bit about quantum analysis. The technology had come of age in the late 2030s and allowed analysis of the subatomic structure of particles in such a way that they could be modeled exactly by a quantum computer. The quantum model could be used for pharmaceuticals and genetics to know exactly what the interactions would be with other things, like the human body.

"Tell me more about this database."

Candace smiled. "Well, we've done a good job in the past of classifying plants and animals. Part of my research efforts has been focused on the taxonomy of viruses. We still don't know for sure if viruses came before more complex life or if more complex life created viruses. We've partnered with multiple universities to scan as many viruses as possible and put their complete RNA and DNA makeup into a database."

"What does that have to do with my mitochondria? Those are the parts of a cell that produce energy, right?"

She leaned toward him and nodded her head. "That's right, and we've now cataloged and scanned so many human bodies that we can simulate interactions with any cellular structure. You have unexpected RNA in your mitochondria that doesn't match anything we've seen before."

Wesley nodded. She'd probably figure out a way to model this RNA pattern and figure out what it did.

Candace studied the tablet more, then stopped and stared at him. "Wait … oh my God."

He drummed his fingers on the table. "What?"

Candace pointed to a monitor with a magnified view of the Petri dishes. She zoomed in on the one labeled *BxPC-3*. Small cells darted around a large mass of reddish cells. The whole cluster of red cells shrank as the small ones zipped into them.

The battle wasn't going well for the red cells, whatever they were. "What is it?"

"The Petri dish you see here is a cell line from a sixty-one-year-old female with primary adenocarcinoma of the pancreas."

What was Candace talking about? Wesley stared at her. "Sorry, I don't follow."

"Pancreatic cancer cells. Your white blood cells are eating the cancer cells at an extremely high rate. I've never seen anything this effective."

The other dishes had similar battles in play, with cells darting around, eating others, like piranhas eating some poor animal that had fallen into the water.

"What about the other Petri dishes?" Wesley asked.

"Various types of viruses, such as the cold virus, along with a few bacteria, one of which is pneumonia. All of them are getting eaten alive by your blood cells."

Guilt filled him. Pneumonia. Could he have saved Samantha somehow by giving her his blood? If so, he could have helped a lot of people. People like Jonathan, for whom it was too late. "So, do you believe me now?"

Candace looked to be in shock as she stared forward, and her lips moved a few times without producing any words. She shook her head. "I'm sorry. I can't believe what I'm seeing. It shouldn't be possible. But yes, I believe you."

Chapter 6

Trudy needed to talk about her virus classification study findings, so Candace asked her to meet in the lab to discuss them.

"Dr. Rosenbach, I'm telling you, it's a new microorganism."

Candace stared at the data, and she couldn't argue against it suggesting the notion of a novel virus. "What does the computer model suggest?"

"It behaves like a retrovirus, but it doesn't seem to have any real impact, deleterious or otherwise. It's interesting because we haven't seen it in any of the databases."

Candace stared at a 3D image of the virion. The outer protein shell was thicker than the shells on other viruses. "How many of the tested subjects had this virus?"

"Every one of them. I'm surprised we've never seen it before. We must have missed it."

Candace drummed her fingers on her desk, then rubbed her chin. "Perhaps. Can you gather some historical samples and analyze those?"

Trudy's cheeks reddened a little. She was likely embarrassed that she hadn't thought to do so. They often kept refrigerated samples from test subjects in cases like this, where they needed to test historical trends. "We'll get to work on that."

As Trudy made to leave, Candace bit her lip. Should she include Trudy in her research with Wesley? "Trudy, one more thing."

Trudy turned. "Yes?"

"You're doing great work. You should be ready to defend your dissertation soon, right?"

Trudy beamed. "Yes, though depending on our findings here, I may need to change my thesis a little."

Candace smiled. "Great. Thanks, Trudy."

Candace waited for her to leave, then ran a viral spectral analysis of Wesley's blood.

The average human body had about thirty-eight trillion bacteria and over three hundred and eighty trillion viruses. Recent advances in quantum computing and spectral analysis had made the research project her graduate students were doing possible—they would classify and analyze those trillions of viruses in multiple test subjects and define the entire virome. Many of those viruses, called phages, were busy attacking various bacteria, including harmful pathogens. One of the study goals was to find and classify the viruses that destroyed the pathogens and find ways to reduce the ones that attacked the beneficial bacteria.

The quantum particle analyzer whirred as the centrifuge separated the sample into smaller and smaller components. The process would take a while, so Candace called Dianne to meet for a quick lunch.

Dianne gave Candace a warm hug when she arrived at the café. Candace gestured to the front. "You know there are a lot of coffee places around here, right? We don't have to keep coming to the Burke."

Dianne smiled. "Yes, but none of them can make a cappuccino like this place. You should try one, and the fry bread taco."

"Okay. Why not? I'll get both."

In moments, the small robot delivered their meals, and Dianne raised an eyebrow. "So? Tell me more about this Irish guy."

Candace felt a little heat in her cheeks. "He's more of a research subject. He's a tall blond guy with green eyes. Not my type."

Dianne nodded. "Mmm. I see." She looked away. "Reminds me of a guy I met in Venice—Puccio. He wasn't my type either—tall, blond, muscular. All he wanted to do was make sure I was satisfied. Horrible guy."

Candace sniffed. "Your sarcasm is noted. Okay, I won't say that I don't find him attractive. It's just … well, complicated."

Dianne laughed. "Isn't it always complicated with men? I've found them to be simple creatures, though. Show them some admiration and physical affection, and they're happy."

"Isn't that a bit reductive, Dianne?"

Dianne shrugged. "Maybe. What can I say? I'm a child of the eighties. Things were different back then."

"Please, you were *born* in 1984. I thought you millennials were supposed to be less gender biased."

Dianne raised her eyebrows. "We got older; things changed. What can I say?"

Candace bit her lip. "That's part of the issue. He's quite a bit older than me."

"Please. Older men have shorter memories and newer money." Dianne gave her a questioning look. "As long as he's still *healthy*." She put a special emphasis on the last word.

Candace's face flushed a little. "He's in good health, but I couldn't tell you if he is 'healthy,' as you put it. We aren't dating."

Dianne narrowed her eyes. "Honey, he isn't married, is he?"

"Oh, no. He's a widower. His wife died a long time ago." Candace sipped her cappuccino. The sweet foam contrasted sharply with the pungent, bittersweet espresso, producing a melody of flavors upon her tongue. The rich, earthy aroma enhanced the experience. "Do you believe that mythology is rooted in reality?"

Dianne took a bite from her taco before she answered. "An interesting question. I've been doing a lot of work in comparative mythology lately—looking at the shared themes and stories from a wide variety of cultures. I could easily spend the next several hours discussing my thoughts on your question. I'd say that mythology reflects what a culture values, and some myths are inspired by actual events in history. I can think of several examples of that."

"No. I'm asking if you think some myths were true. Do you believe the

Tuatha Dé Danann existed, for example?"

Dianne gave Candace a long, hard look. "Back to that again. What is it you're not telling me?"

Candace sipped her cappuccino, allowing the flavor to fully develop on her tongue before she swallowed. She rubbed her chin in thought for a few moments, then let out a long breath. She lowered her voice to a murmur and leaned in close to Dianne. "My Irish guy claims to be over three hundred years old." She leaned back and waited.

Dianne almost spat out her taco but managed to gulp it down before she laughed. "Honey, that's ridiculous." She waited for Candace to say something. "Wait, you're serious? How is that possible?"

"I'm not sure. I only asked about the Tuatha Dé Danann because if there's enough folklore from the region, perhaps there were others like him. Maybe it could explain his condition." Candace chewed on the side of her lip. "I didn't believe him, but I've done some tests in my lab, and without getting into all the science of it, let me say that there's good reason to believe him."

Dianne leaned in and lowered her voice to a near whisper. "Listen, I may not be a microbiologist, but I need you to break this down for me. What tests?"

"Every human cell has chromosomes with repetitive nucleotide sequences at the end called telomeres. They shorten with age every time a cell divides. Eventually, the cells can't divide anymore. In my analysis of his cells, I found that his telomeres aren't decreasing in length."

Dianne raised an eyebrow. "Honey, I need some of whatever he's having. Keep me apprised of whatever you find out. I'll be your guinea pig if you need one." She held a hand out in front of her. "I'd love to be able to stare at twenty-year-old fingers again."

"I'm not sure it works that way. I don't know anything about the mechanism. All I know is that he has some unrecognized RNA patterns in his mitochondria—"

"Hey, you figure out the microbiology stuff and get back to me."

"Would you really want to live without aging?"

"Of course. You're too young to know what it feels like to be scared you'll break something going to the bathroom."

"Oh, please. You're not that old."

Dianne grabbed Candace by the hand. "I may not have broken anything yet, but I'm old enough to be scared."

Candace nodded and took another draw from her cappuccino. "Listen, you can't discuss this with anyone yet. I need to confirm these findings first."

Dianne made a zipping gesture with her fingers across her lips. "So when will you know, and when will you make me look twenty-three again?"

"I'll know soon, once my genome sequencing is done."

Dianne drew her lips into a thin line. "So, are you going to be hanging out with this guy much?" She gave a coy smile and batted her eyelashes.

Candace waved a hand. "I don't know. I need to figure out first if this is all true. If he's lying or delusional, then no. I'll be filing a restraining order."

"What if it's true?"

Candace tapped a finger on the side of her mug and took another sip. "Then our world as we know it will never be the same again."

Dianne nodded, then fished through her purse, pulled out a small plastic capsule, and handed it to her. "Here. A gift from me."

Candace eyed the capsule and opened it to find two small and smooth spherical objects. "Okay, what are these?"

Dianne sniffed. "My mom gave me several of those. They are little tracking devices you put in your bra strap. They send the data to a third-party site."

"And you just happen to have some on you? Why?"

"Oh, I'll be traveling soon, and I want to put them in all my luggage. I have plenty."

Candace held a tracker up to the light to get a better view of it. The thing was barely larger than a pinhead. "And you think I need this?"

"If this guy is crazy, you'll need it. If you find the secret to eternal youth, you'll still need it. I wear mine to keep my mom happy and to let her know I'm safe. She worries about me. I'm worried about you and would like you to wear one. For me."

Candace nodded. "If it makes you feel better. Do I need to charge it or something?"

"No. It gets its electricity through you moving around. Don't ask me how. I do mythology, remember? It might as well be magic, for what I understand of it. Just punch the little code from the capsule into the app, and it works. Try it. You can add me."

Candace spent a few minutes downloading the app and setting up the device. Then she sent the information to Dianne. "Great. Now you can see how boring my life is. Home, lab, home, lab. Honestly, you're the only social life I have right now."

"About that. I'm going to Venice the day after tomorrow. I'm hoping to rekindle an old flame. Sorry I won't be around for the summer quarter. I need a break."

Candace took in a breath and let it out. "Well, at least I can live vicariously through you."

Dianne smiled. "I don't know, honey. It sounds like you and I will have to keep track of each other. Things sound like they're about to get exciting for you."

Candace stared at her plate, then back at Dianne. "They might." She received a notification on her smartwatch that the sequencing was done. "Looks like I'm about to find out what makes my Irish friend special."

Dianne gave a sideways grin, then hugged her. "Listen. You take care of yourself. I'll let you know when I get to Venice."

"You too. Have fun."

*

Candace studied the sequencing results. With several hundred trillion viruses making up the virome in any person's body, most viromes had a diverse number of viral species. In the case of Wesley, there was one virus type, and this virus wasn't like anything in any database. To say it was novel would have been an understatement, because it differed markedly from any other classification. If viruses were like different types of fish, this one would be more like an elephant in comparison.

Next, she input the viral genome sequence into her quantum-modeling software. Due to the wonders of modern quantum computing, she'd get results in a few minutes. The program would simulate the impact on a varied population of virtual human bodies. Because it was done at a quantum level, it was as close to doing testing on actual human subjects as she could get. The modeling also had the advantage of allowing the interactions to take place in a few seconds, rather than the inordinate amount of time and hassle it would take with real people.

The progress bar crept forward as Candace waited to see what would happen. When it finished, she frowned as she read the result.

All human subjects are immune to viral contamination.

She scratched her head as she reread the findings, slowly forming words with her mouth. So Wesley had a virus in his system, only one virus, and every human subject was immune to it already? Strange.

She tweaked the model, giving the human subjects suppressed immune systems, then reran the quantum simulation with the new data. With little patience, she watched the progress bar. Was it her imagination, or was it moving even more slowly than the last time?

After an eternity, the simulation finished, and Candace perused the results. Only subjects that had suppressed immune systems in the model got the virus. This finding only created more questions. How did anyone get the virus?

She analyzed the data some more and determined that Wesley was infected with a retrovirus that inserted beneficial genes into his cells, and these genes augmented his immune system and kept him from aging. She drummed her fingers on her desk. How would such a retrovirus evolve? What environmental pressures would cause natural selection to allow these features?

Candace needed more data to make sense of this. The information she had now would be enough to allow groundbreaking advances in medicine and microbiology. She'd need to do a lot more work before releasing any information to the public. Using her quantum encryption key, she uploaded all the data to the cloud, then gave Wesley a call and invited him to her lab. He agreed, and she waited, lost in thought.

Chapter 7

Wesley watched as Candace typed away on her keyboard. She'd invited him to her lab and asked him for saliva samples, then tried to explain to him that he had a retrovirus that stopped him from aging. She had also launched into some discussion about another virus her graduate students had found as part of a research project.

Candace's information still didn't make a lot of sense. Something about a graduate student of hers who had found engineered RNA in several sample subjects. Wesley didn't want to look stupid, but microbiology wasn't exactly his area of expertise. "So every one of your tested subjects had this RNA signature? Why is it special?"

Candace let out a long breath. How had she become a teacher with the lack of patience she exhibited? Her face contorted into that look someone would get when they wanted to appear calm and collected but were bursting with impatience. "We're sampling and cataloging viruses we find in volunteer test subjects. We're building what you might call a family tree."

Wesley understood that part of it. The unclear part was the other stuff. "I get that. What about this RNA construct, or whatever you called it?"

She walked over to a virtual whiteboard and drew a large ring with another inside it. She colored in the outer ring in black and then wrote many letters in the small circle. "This big circle is the outer ring of the virus—think of it like a rubber tire. The inside wheel is a real virus. As it runs down the road, it burns away rubber over time. Eventually, the interior piece is released, and the host is infected with the inner virus."

The whole analogy reminded Wesley of one of those suckers with a chocolate center. "But it still makes copies of itself? With the outer part intact?"

Her arms moved about in giddy animation. "Yes. This RNA pattern isn't something we've ever seen before. Someone engineered this. I can't think of any other explanation that makes sense. If not, we're looking at a whole new type of microorganism."

Fear rose within Wesley. Did he have something to do with it? "Did you find this thing in my blood?"

Candace shook her head. "No. I don't think it relates to you in any way. I only brought it up because I wanted you to understand why I ran an additional analysis of your blood as well."

Wesley bit his lip. "Did you analyze the virus inside the smaller circle?"

Frustration played across her face. "No. I'm not sure it's a good idea yet. My modeling suggests the outer barrier may take about four months to wear away on its own. I'm having new subjects brought in because I'm not sure my grad students didn't make an error. Quantum spectral analysis has been accurate so far, but I need more data to come to any meaningful conclusions."

Wesley nodded, though he wasn't sure he truly understood all that she had said. The significance was clear. If the findings were correct, many people had some sort of microorganism with unknown properties running through their bodies.

Wesley waited in the lab as Candace typed on her keyboard and studied the images from her microscope. His watch buzzed to tell him someone was at his door at home. "Excuse me," he said as he walked out of the lab and into the hallway. He pressed a button to view the door camera feed, revealing a young woman in scrubs holding herself with an air of authority.

Wesley spoke into his earpiece. "Hello?"

"Yes, I hope I have the right address. Were you friends with the late Jonathan Moore?" she asked.

He steeled himself as a chill filled him. She stood there with a businesslike smile on her face, with her fierce green eyes staring into the camera lens. She looked familiar, though he couldn't place the face. "I was, but I'm not home right now. How did you find me?"

"Oh, I'm sorry. I looked you up, since you'd come to visit Mr. Moore."

Where was this conversation leading? Wesley looked at the time: twelve thirty. He looked at her through the camera again. She wore her long blond hair in a simple ponytail. "I'm still mourning his passing. Who are you, exactly?"

"I do per diem nursing work at Sunset Towers. I asked Mr. Moore about you, and he had nice things to say. I think he held you in high regard."

Had Jonathan been lucid enough to give this woman some details? Wesley struggled to keep his hand from shaking. He tried to sound calm and unconcerned when he replied. "Sorry to see his mind go the way it did. I hope he didn't tell you anything too crazy. What do you want? Did he make me so intriguing that you had to meet me for yourself?"

She frowned. "Perhaps. Listen, my name is Anne O'Keefe. Could you meet me later tonight, at my condo? I want to ask you some questions about a story he told me."

At her condo? What sort of woman would feel comfortable with a man she didn't know coming to her home? She was either self-assured in her ability to protect herself or crazy, or maybe both. Wesley's muscles went rigid. Who was this woman? "Yes, I can meet you. I'm not sure if tonight works. Give me your contact info, and we can arrange something, though I'd ask you not to put much stock in the musings of a demented man in his final days."

He received her address and went back into the lab.

"Who was that?" Candace asked.

Wesley took in a deep breath and struggled to calm his nerves. What should he tell her? "Someone from Sunset Towers. She wants to tell me about something Jonathan told her."

She glanced at him with concern. "Is there something I should know?"

"Your uncle may have shared a little too much with her."

Candace frowned.

"I may have shared a little too much with him."

She nodded, though she didn't seem convinced. She fiddled with her lab equipment. "Do you like being as old as you are? Don't you feel out of place?"

To Wesley, she was asking if a fish liked being wet. That was the nature of the fish if it wanted to live. Sometimes he'd feel a pull of nostalgia so strong it was like a giant ocean wave trying to reclaim the sand on the beach. "I do. I've watched others grow old and feel pain, and I've always wanted to help them. I've been running from the pain of losing people I grow close to for years." He recalled being in bed next to Samantha, holding her close to him as he had kissed her aged hand. The hopeless feeling that had overwhelmed him as she'd coughed. He had comforted her but had been helpless to ease her pain. She had deserved to live a long and healthy life more than he did.

He tried to force a swallow down his dry throat. "I've never wanted to die, and I've never wanted to feel the pain of aging. My one regret is not being able to help anyone. I hope you can change that for me."

A wan smile crossed Candace's face. "I'm struggling with the idea of making everyone ageless. Once we figure this out, everything changes. Perhaps you were right to keep it to yourself."

Not the answer he had expected. "It's an easy thing to say for someone who hasn't watched the people they love slip away from them."

Candace wheeled her chair around and stood, then closed the distance between them to poke a finger into his chest. "Listen here. I've lost plenty of people I loved. My parents. My husband. My aunt, and now Uncle Jonathan. Who are you to presume to know anything about my experiences?"

Wesley held up his hands. "You're right. I'm sorry." He pressed a fist to his chest. "I've seen a lot of people age, and it was never fun. I'm over seven times older than you. Let that sink in. I'd rather give people a choice. That's all. There are plenty of ways for anyone to die, whether they age or not."

She relaxed a little and sat back down to cover her face with her hands. "I'm sorry. I guess part of me knows how you might feel. No one I loved is still alive."

A smile came to his lips. "There's a chance for that still."

Candace lowered her hands and stared at him with narrowed eyes. "You're right, but I feel there is little hope for you. No one in their right mind would date a crusty old man like you."

They both shared a much-needed laugh at that statement, and Wesley prepared to leave. "I need to go grab lunch. You want anything?"

Candace shook her head and turned back to her computer. "No. You go. I have a lot to do here. I'll call you later."

"Sure," he said, still feeling wooden from the conversation with Anne.

She bore a striking resemblance to his father.

Chapter 8

As Candace continued her research, she thought of Wesley, with his cropped blond hair, striking green eyes, and tall, muscular build. Not the typical kind of guy she found attractive, but she couldn't get him out of her head. Did he have a romantic interest in her, or was he only using her? She pushed the thoughts away to focus on her work.

She attempted to further isolate the properties of the retrovirus inside Wesley's cells. She knew it kept him from aging, but she needed to figure out how.

"Why are humans already immune to you?" she asked the retrovirus. She didn't expect an answer, and none came. There was a missing piece to the puzzle. How anyone would have gotten the retrovirus in the eighteenth century was a mystery that remained unsolved. How had it infected Wesley?

She created quantum models of the human immune system and experimented with simulated viruses. Quantum prototyping had advanced so many fields. Doing this with traditional cultures would have taken years and still would never have produced these results. The models showed that the virus only spread via the blood and required a wholly suppressed immune system. How would such a thing have happened in the eighteenth century? She'd already tried modeling various diseases that would have been prevalent at the time. None yielded infection with the retrovirus as a result. What was she missing?

Perhaps it had been deliberate. What if someone had intentionally given it to him? What if it required human intervention? Wesley had told her about his mother, making him drink something at the age of fourteen. That was when he said he had stopped being sick. There was an apparent temporal correlation.

What would someone in that time frame have done if they had wanted to suppress the immune system and give someone a blood-borne virus? People of the time had often believed plants and animals that exhibited certain traits could pass those traits on when eaten. Eat a strong animal, and it would give you strength. Eat a long-lived plant, and maybe it would help you live longer. Was there a plant that suppressed the immune system?

Candace's watch read well past six. She needed to take a break and grab some dinner, so she called Wesley and asked if he'd like to join her. She still wasn't sure she wanted to discuss the matter over the phone. He quickly agreed to meet her.

She continued searching for methods that might have been used to propagate the virus. Something bugged her, though. How would the virus ever have come to be if such great lengths were required to spread it? What specific environmental pressures had led to its development? More questions than answers, and that was something she did not like.

A knock sounded at the door, and relief filled her. She needed to eat.

Why hadn't Wesley said anything when he'd knocked?

The feed from the door camera showed several men in suits.

Her pulse quickened, and her fingers trembled as she reached for her smartphone. She called one of her grad students and kept her voice down. "Trudy, are you still on campus?"

"Yes, I'm down the hall. Why?"

"Some men in suits are here, and I need you to get over here. Call Dr. Hermann and tell him what's happening. Hurry," she said before terminating the call.

Candace hammered at the keyboard, saving her results and uploading them to a cloud server. The knocking persisted, followed by a loud kick, and the door flew open.

She calmed her rapid breathing. "Who the hell are you? Activists dressed like FBI agents?"

"We're not activists. I'm Special Agent Ahad Atenoud, with the FBI. You, Dr. Candace Rosenbach, are under arrest for bioterrorism."

Her hands shook under the desk as she kept her face placid. "Bioterrorism? What are you talking about?"

"You have the right to remain silent. Anything you say can and will be used against you in a court of law. You have the right to speak to an attorney, and to have an attorney present during any questioning. Is that clear?"

She nodded.

"Good. Now, I'd like to know with whom you've shared your research."

How did he know anything about her research, and why did he want to know that? Did it have anything to do with Wesley? She hadn't told anyone about it yet. There must be an explanation. "I have the right to remain silent, and I intend to do so," she replied. "Why are you here? It should be obvious that I'm not a bioterrorist. I'm researching microbiology for the university."

The man shrugged. "I see. I'm here, Dr. Rosenbach, to keep people like you from stopping people like me from making the world a better place."

"What are you talking about?"

His eyes narrowed. "We'll discuss this later. I need you to remain silent, like you said you would." He looked around at the other agents. "Take the data storage units. And bring the vials and cultures."

He lowered his face to her ear, close enough that she could feel his hot breath and smell his teak aftershave. "I have great plans for you, and I've devised a much better plan for humanity," he said.

What did he mean?

The men scurried about like ants. Despair filled Candace as she watched them placing everything from her lab into evidence bags.

Trudy ran down the hallway toward them, but one of the FBI men stopped her. She watched in confusion as they led Candace away.

Candace struggled against the cold bite of the handcuffs but found them and the grip of the FBI agent that shoved her forward to be unyielding. The men rushed her to a long black sedan with tinted windows, opened the door, and shoved her in. A woman with olive skin entered the car, and one large man held Candace in place while the woman pulled out a syringe and injected something into her arm. A few seconds later, all went dark.

Chapter 9

A young woman stood in the hallway when Wesley arrived at the lab to meet Candace. A shorter girl with brown hair in a ponytail. A lab coat covered her large frame. The lab door lay in ruins on the floor, with splinters strewn about.

"Can I help you?" the girl asked, her voice wavering.

"Yes. What happened to the door? Where's Candace?"

"I called facilities to repair it. The FBI arrested Dr. Rosenbach. I don't have any details. What did she do?"

Wesley licked his dry lips. Why would they arrest Candace? If it had anything to do with him, how did they know? "I have no idea. Did she tell you anything about what she was working on?"

The young woman gave him a suspicious glance. "I can't discuss her research. Who are you?"

"Wesley O'Keefe. I was working with Candace on one of her projects."

Her expression softened a little. "Oh. Yes, she might have mentioned that."

"What did she say?"

The girl stared at the floor, and her face reddened a little. "She was going to involve me in her project but hadn't provided any details, other than it involved a test subject named Wesley. She called me when the FBI agents were arresting her. They took her away in handcuffs." She paused and gave Wesley an awkward smile. "I'm Trudy."

Wesley had to get to the bottom of this. "Thank you, Trudy. Can you please call me if you get any word?"

She nodded, and he pressed a button on his watch to send her his contact information, then received a message with her details.

"Please let me know if you hear anything too. To put it mildly, we were all shocked by the news."

"Of course." Wesley rushed toward the exit and called his lawyer, Gordon Weinberg.

"Wesley, how's it going, buddy?"

"Not well. The FBI arrested my friend. Can you please investigate and find a way to help her out?"

"Tell me more about this friend of yours. How did you meet her?"

"Dr. Candace Rosenbach is her name. What can you tell me?"

"Rosenbach, huh? Sure, I'll look into it. I'll call when I have something. Take care."

Wesley left the building and made his way to the street near the university known as "The Ave." He meandered without purpose as he waited for some word from Gordon.

After he'd ambled for twenty minutes, a call came in.

"Hey, buddy. Listen, the FBI has charged this friend Candace of yours with bioterrorism. I couldn't get any more details."

Bioterrorism? Wesley tasted bile in his mouth. Did this have something to do with him? "Well, where the hell is she, and how do we get her out?"

"Yeah, that's the problem. They've got seventy-two hours to hold Candace until they need to show probable cause. I can't do anything until then, and they aren't required to disclose her location."

Three days? How was that possible? "That's not helpful. I need results, damn it. There has to be someone you can call. How much am I paying you for this, anyway?"

"Ha! You don't even want to know. Trust me. I'll be billing you. I'll see what I can do, but until the seventy-two hours have passed, I can't do much. Terrorism prevention acts and all that."

"What can I do?"

"Write your congressperson and ask them to change the laws. Until then, you wait."

"Thanks, Gordon. Very helpful," Wesley said with more than a touch of anger as he disconnected the call.

The arrest must be related to the help she had been giving him. How did anyone, especially the FBI, know anything about it?

He should go and meet this Anne character—maybe she had something to do with Candace's arrest. Whoever she was, he couldn't do anything about Candace right now, and he needed to find out what this woman was all about. At least he'd have something constructive to do while he waited for Gordon. She'd given him the address of her condo in Ballard. He made his way to his car and punched in the address.

*

Wesley rode the elevator to the fifth floor of the condo building and knocked on the door marked 504. After a few moments, scuffling and rummaging noises ensued, and the door opened a crack with the chain still engaged.

"Hello?" she said, sounding as though she'd just woken up.

"Yes, it's Wesley O'Keefe."

"Sorry. I do shift work. I was taking a nap. Thought you weren't coming tonight, or I would have had some tea ready. Come in, please." She ushered him in.

Why was she so confident about letting a stranger into her place? Wesley entered the well-lit condo. Through the window, a balcony overlooked Shilshole Bay. The lights of several boats were sprinkled about on the water. She probably had a great view of the Olympic Mountains during the day. The maple floors gleamed. White marble countertops reflected light onto spotless stainless-steel appliances in the kitchen. How did she afford such a marvelous place on her salary?

"Impressive. Nice place you have here."

Anne gave a tired smile. "Thank you."

Time to figure out what she wanted. No sense exchanging pleasantries. "So, what did Mr. Moore tell you?"

"It wasn't what he told me that got me interested in you, per se. You look like my father, Kyle O'Keefe. I asked Jonathan about you, and he told me that you burned down your aunt's house in Ireland when you were a child. I'd like to hear this story for myself."

Kyle. That was *his* father's name as well. Wesley waited before answering, staring at her. Fierce green eyes stared back at him, unwavering. "Not sure what he was talking about. He was a demented old man."

"My brother died in a fire. Much like the one Mr. Moore described to me. Over three hundred years ago. It so happens that his name was also Wesley. I need some answers. Now, will you tell me this story or not?" Her fierce gaze pierced him.

He returned her stare. She had his father's eyes and his mother's fierceness. "I haven't a clue what you're talking about. How could your brother die over three hundred years ago?"

She folded her arms and waited for his answer.

Wesley steeled himself. Perhaps telling her would provide some measure of relief. "Very well. I will summarize. There was a fire at Aunt Elizabeth's house. You didn't know her, but she was a prim and proper woman. She forgot she was Irish when she married Uncle Owen. Ma loved her, though, and she brought me there. I still don't know why. I got into a fight with my cousin Billy and knocked over an oil lamp. I fled through the window and went to find Ma, but she was gone. I sailed on a ship to the Colonies to find Da."

"Who was your childhood friend that lived near you?" she asked.

"Aye, Patrick Adrian. Did you know him?" Wesley asked.

Anne smiled, a sad smile, then gazed into the distance. "Aye. I did. I married him."

"Married him? Oh, that's wonderful. Is he still alive?" Had she given the gift of long life to his beloved childhood friend?

"He passed away long ago, maybe thirty years after we were married. 'Twas a horrible carriage accident. He was a sweet and dear man. The love we had was true and blessed. I miss him so." Anne stood silently as she stared at the wall. Then she rounded on Wesley. "How is it that you burned in a fire in July of 1724, yet here you are, standing in front of me? How is it that our father grieved for you my entire childhood, and how is it that Patrick himself grieved for you, yet here you are? Tell me!"

Wesley balled his fists. "I told you what happened. I was but fourteen years old when I left. I found a leather pouch buried in some leaves near Aunt Elizabeth's house with a letter and a ticket to the Colonies. When the fire happened, I fled on foot. I tried to find Ma at our house, but she wasn't there. I left on a ship, thinking Da could help me. On the ship, many people fell ill, including a man named Quinn. He encouraged me before he died to take on his identity when I arrived, and I became an indentured servant working for the timber industry."

Anne drew in a long breath. "They found the whistle Da gave you in the ashes and assumed you were among them."

A wan smile played across Wesley's face. "I remember that whistle. Da made it for me and fashioned a small metal necklace for it. He told me to blow it whenever I missed him, and he would hear it. I blew it every day for months."

Anne nodded.

Guilt filled Wesley as he thought of the pain he'd caused his family, leaving them to believe him dead. "How did he find out? About me."

"Da got a letter from Ma telling him what had happened. He returned to Ireland earlier than he'd planned, just in time for me to be born."

Wesley stared at the wall for a while. "We may have passed each other on the voyage."

Anne stared at him with tear-filled eyes. Her nostrils flared, and her cheeks burned red. "Why didn't you go back to the house and wait for Ma?"

"I did go back to the house, and she wasn't there. I wanted to find Da. I told you that."

"You didn't think it a good idea to wait around and tell Ma? Maybe tell some neighbors or something? Seek out Patrick? What the hell was running through your head?"

"I was fourteen. I was worried that I'd burned everyone in the fire and would get hanged at the gallows."

"Fourteen. It was a bloody lousy idea to come to the Colonies. And then to never write a letter to let anyone know you were alive? What the hell? Why did you let them suffer believing you dead? For the love of Pete, Wesley, don't you have a heart?" She was shaking, and tears ran down her face.

Wesley glared back at her for a few moments before responding. Heat ran through his cheeks. "I thought it easier to run away and start a new life. I went to find Da. And I did write letters, but I never sent any of them."

"You have to send the bloody letter for it to do any bloody good. It doesn't do a damn bit of bloody good to write something and then let it sit. The road to hell is paved with good intentions, and from what I'm hearing, you paved a road straight to it."

Wesley choked up before speaking. "Listen, I can't take back the past. I'm not proud of it."

"Bollocks. You never tried."

Wesley raised his voice. "I was trying to survive; I didn't know what to say. I guess I thought someone would come find me."

"Only a twit would have such a notion. We thought you dead. One letter would have remedied that. One."

Wesley wanted to disappear and let the earth consume him. Why hadn't he reached out to his family? He needed a Scotch. Perhaps he should leave. "You're right. What I did, it shames me. It was easier to run and try to forget about it."

Anne folded her arms and glared at him. "I never even got to know you. I only heard stories from Patrick. Da rarely spoke of you. When I asked, he'd get a hurt look in his eyes and couldn't speak of you. I never met you, and yet even I grieved for you, for the brother I never got to meet, because he died in a fire. I prayed to God every day for years that my brother would come back. I saw the hole in Da's heart that you left. A hole that I tried to fill myself but could not. Have you ever thought of him? Of any of us?"

Wesley winced as he recalled the smell of the fire, the burning of human flesh. It was a scent he would never forget. He heard the screams as he had run through the field with no shoes, and he felt the fear of his mother's judgment. All these things came to him, as they did most days. "Aye, I have.

I'd do anything to see them again."

Anne's glare softened a bit, and her arms went to her sides. "Da is still alive. He lives in San Jose. He still wears the whistle he gave you around his neck."

Sunshine flooded Wesley's soul, and he wanted to dance a jig. Then a realization hit him, and his heart sank. He tried to swallow, but the lump in his throat made it difficult. "What of Ma?"

Anne stared back with moist eyes. "She died giving birth to me."

The room whirled around him as his thoughts became a disjointed jumble. His parents had been like Schrödinger's cat, neither alive nor dead, because he'd never opened the box. Some part of his imagination had always placed them alive and well somewhere in Ireland. Now he knew his mother was gone. "I see. I'm sorry."

Anne wiped tears from her eyes with a tissue. "What was she like? Ma."

"She was beautiful. She had this stare she would give that would make the devil himself confess his sins. You have her eyes. You have the look of Da but the piercing gaze of our mother."

She gave a sobbing laugh. "Patrick often told me how intimidating I was. If only I could have seen that stare."

Wesley smiled. "Look in the mirror, and you'll see it." He waited, thinking more of his mother. "I remember when she brought chickens to the neighbor's house. They'd lost a child, and she brought them new gifts every week. When I asked her about it, she said it was what neighbors should do."

"Da said she had a kind heart. That was one bit he managed to share."

Warmth filled Wesley as another memory came to him. "I saw an exchange with a merchant once where he tried to give Ma less money for some toys Da had made. Da tried to calm her, but she launched into him with a fury of words that left the merchant's ears burning. He gave her the money, and never again did he give Da less."

Anne laughed. "Patrick may have seen my temper a time or two."

Wesley closed his eyes. Tears threatened to fall, but he managed to keep them in. "You remind me of her. Though I won't see her again, I'm glad I got to see you. But tell me, how is any of this possible? How are you still alive?"

"A retrovirus. Grandda calls it 'the Raven's Kiss.' He says powerful people will seek us out if we reveal it."

Cold seeped through Wesley's body as his pulse quickened. What would happen to Candace? Who were these "powerful people"? Any doubt that Candace's arrest was unrelated to him left in an instant, like a puff of smoke in a strong wind.

"I met with a microbiology researcher named Dr. Candace Rosenbach," Wesley said. "I let her take a sample of my blood for a research project. I wanted answers. I thought she'd help me discover why I don't age so I could share it with the world." He paused. "I'm tired of being alone in this world full of people."

The color drained from Anne's face. "How did you meet this Candace woman?"

"I received a forty-year-old photo in the mail of myself, Candace, and her uncle, Jonathan Moore. Candace was only five years old. The letter was addressed to my previous fake identity, Vance Malloy, which I haven't used in forty years. There was also a photo of a woman I dated at the time, named Beth Norbeck. I suspected her of sending it, only to find she died twenty years ago."

Anne turned from pale to green. "Who sent the photos?"

Wesley shrugged his shoulders. "I don't know, but I thought Jonathan might help me figure that out. In the process, I discovered that Candace is now a microbiologist. She is Jonathan's niece, and I was searching for answers. She didn't believe me when I told her that I was three hundred and thirty-two."

Anne shook her head. "Fancy that!"

Easy for her to sit on her high horse and judge him. She hadn't lived his life. Wesley balled up his fist and clenched his jaw a few times as he glared at her. "I wanted to try telling someone the truth. I tried to be okay with being alone and making lots of money and moving on to live new lives. But it's become impossible to change identities now with all the technology—smartphones, smart cars, smartwatches—and I was tired. I hadn't been given any direction in these matters. As far as I knew, I was the only one experiencing this. What harm could come of it? I wanted to keep other people from getting sick. I wanted to know why I haven't aged. Do you understand that I've lived like this, with this guilt, surviving while those I loved perished around me?"

Anne raised her eyebrows, then spoke. "Are you done with your tirade?"

What an infuriating woman! Wesley rushed to the door and turned the doorknob.

"Don't leave."

He whirled to face her as tears streamed down her face. "Why shouldn't I? Do you want to berate me further?"

She put a hand on his shoulder. "Please, sit down."

Wesley dropped onto the couch. His hands shook as he regarded Anne, sitting next to him with her head cocked to the side, face red from tears.

"I'm not entirely without understanding in this matter, brother. I do have our family, who I can share this with, and that's been a blessing. Had you not run off, you would've had the same."

More judgment. He clenched his jaw and began to stand, but Anne firmly pushed him on the shoulder, urging him to stay. She held his hand. The warmth of it filled him, and he smiled at her.

"I've passed up many a relationship because it wasn't possible to be sincere," Anne said. "If I told a person I was dating about the retrovirus, we would have to be partners for life, which puts a tough expectation on any budding relationship. I don't understand how you could so blithely tell someone you don't even know about this, and give her samples of your blood to boot. A daft and impulsive move at best. Did you consider the long-term implications?"

Was it possible for Anne to not give constant judgment? Wesley breathed slowly, forcing himself to be calm. Perhaps she meant well. "I did. I wanted to help people. My friend Jonathan died, and it was more than I could bear to see another friend die of old age while I am blessed with agelessness. Why should we be the only ones to have this gift? Why should we continue to hide it from the world? What's the harm in revealing it?"

Anne sat in silence for several long moments. "In principle, I might agree with you, but we have powerful foes. I don't know much—Grandda doesn't like to talk about it."

"Is Grandda Emmitt still alive?"

"Yes. He and Grandma Alomena live in Mexico City."

Excitement filled Wesley. He hadn't seen either of them since he had been four years old, when they had left for the Colonies. Fuzzy images came to him, but he couldn't discern them. Too long ago to remember their faces. Too many other memories of so many other people in the way.

What about Candace and the FBI? Wesley had to tell her. His breath quickened. "I need to tell you something."

Concern covered Anne's face, but she motioned for him to continue.

How much would she chide him now? Maybe she could do something to help. He had to tell her, despite the risk of more tongue-lashings. "An FBI agent named Ahad Atenoud accused Candace of bioterrorism and arrested her today. My lawyer, Gordon Weinberg, is trying to get more information."

"Bloody hell," Anne said before standing and pacing back and forth. "I need to talk to Da, and I'm sure there will be some damage control. The fact that the FBI has already become involved makes me think they've been following you. It could be too late. You've already opened Pandora's box."

"How can you compare this to Pandora's box? What evils am I unleashing upon the world? We can only help the world with this information. There's no reason we should be keeping it to ourselves. I thought for the longest time that keeping it a secret was the right thing to do, but it isn't."

She narrowed her eyes at him. "These are powerful people, and we aren't ready to fight them. Not yet."

Wesley drummed his fingers on the couch. "What do you propose we do?"

"Da's working on something. I would have thought you'd learned patience by now. I need to call and talk to him. In the interim, I'll see if there's anything we can do to help your friend. I suggest you refrain from talking to her or anyone else about this again."

"Very well. I shall leave you to it." Wesley made for the door.

"Wait," she said as she hugged him and wept. "I'm sorry. It's a lifetime of wondering why you had to die and watching Da grieve. I'm happy you're alive, and I want to get to know you better. I'm sorry I was harsh with you."

Anger melted away as warmth filled him. "Listen, Anne. I'm glad to have met you too. You were right. I thought I could keep going to new places to start a new life. But I was always running from the things I'd done."

She smiled. "Take good care of yourself."

Chapter 10

A portly man with thick glasses sat in a chair next to Candace's bed. She was in some sort of hospital gown, and when she tried to move her hands, they wouldn't respond the way she expected. Her brain didn't seem to be in synch with her muscles for some reason. What sort of drug had they given her?

The man stared down his long nose at her. "Hello. I have some questions for you. I'd like to know the last thing you remember."

She tried to shake her head, but she got an odd feeling of disorientation as she did so. "Where the heck am I, and who are you?"

When the man smiled, his rotund face became even larger. "You're in an FBI facility. Who I am isn't particularly germane to our conversation. Can you please answer my question?"

"I'm not saying a thing until you get me a lawyer, for whatever it is you think I—" Candace broke off as pain seared through her teeth, like a jolt of electricity from her jawline to her tongue. A pain squeezed her temples like a vise. Pain like she'd never felt in her life. Her lungs burned, and parts of her body that she didn't know could hurt blazed. She wanted to scream, but her body was paralyzed by the utter physical agony.

The man sniffed. "I see you're not planning to make this easy. Now, I'm going to ask the question again. If you choose not to answer, the pain will be much, much worse."

Oh God! How would that be possible?

The pain subsided, and she breathed rapidly, sucking in sweet air. The man raised an eyebrow, and Candace held up her hands. "Okay, okay. Don't hurt me again. Give me a moment to get my bearings, please!"

She shook, and her teeth clacked together. Fear gripped her—fear of feeling those sensations that no one should ever have to feel. How had they caused her so much pain? There was nothing attached to her body, not even handcuffs. Maybe she should run through the door.

She turned her attention back to the man, wincing as she thought of what he might do to her. "I ... I remember being in my lab, working on a project. I'd just eaten lunch with my friend."

The man nodded and signaled for her to continue. A wave of pleasure coursed through her body, like the sensation of tasting chocolate and being hugged at the same time. Her breathing eased.

"I was reviewing the data from an experiment in my lab when FBI agents came in and accused me of bioterrorism. Someone injected me with something."

The man showed his gleaming white teeth when he gave a broad smile. "Good. Can you tell me your first memory?"

The words came out in a rush. "I remember my older brother, Andy, showing me how to play *Super Smash Bros.* I played Rosalina, and he was Donkey Kong. I was four. My dad came in and played with us. I think he played Link. Andy got mad that Dad was helping me win." It was one of her first and last memories of her father before the car accident.

The man rubbed his chin. "You left something out. At the end there. What was it?"

Shock filled her. How did he possibly know that? Fearing more pain, she told him. "I was thinking how it was one of the last times I saw my dad before he died in a car accident."

The man wore a smug grin, pleased with himself. "I'm going to ask you a few baseline questions." He knitted his eyebrows as he focused on something. "Are you familiar with the concept of a subatomic neurological-state storage array?"

"No. I've never heard of such a thing, but based on the name, I might guess what it is."

He raised his hand and waved away her idea. "No need. I'm not asking for supposition." He stared at something again, but there was nothing on the wall where his eyes focused. "Have you ever engineered a deadly virus?"

Candace's stomach churned. Would they coerce her into a confession with more pain? She closed her eyes in anticipation of the agony as she answered. "No."

Much to her relief, the man nodded again. "What is the nature of the virus classification project you have your grad students performing?"

She took in a few deep breaths, forcing herself to relax. Her hand trembled in anticipation of another jolt of the suffering they might inflict. "The goal is to classify viruses in a sample population, enough to characterize what we call a virome. We want to identify the relationships between various microorganisms and how they evolve over time. We hope to also identify opportunities for phage classifications."

Again the man stared at something, then continued. "Have you collaborated with anyone beyond your grad students?"

She shook her head. "No."

A wave of pleasure washed over her again, and she breathed in rapidly several times before she noted the man staring at her with a strange look on his face. The man cleared his throat. "With whom did you share information about the retrovirus you found in Wesley O'Keefe?"

Candace bit her lip. "No one." A jolt of pain seared through her body, forcing her back to arch and her head to whip back. She tried to raise an arm to ask them to stop. She tried to scream. But she couldn't move anything. When the sensations subsided, she sucked in several rapid breaths and waited for the room and the man to come back into focus.

He made a tsking noise. "I'm afraid we need you to tell the truth, Dr. Rosenbach." He gave her what was probably meant to be a smile of sympathy, but the way it revealed his teeth made it seem sinister, like the smile on an evil clown.

Candace grabbed one shaking hand with one that trembled and forced her mouth to move so she could speak. She tasted the salt of her tears as she licked her lips. Somehow they knew when she was leaving out information or lying. "I talked to my friend Professor Dianne Erdlen about Wesley. I told her that he said he was over three hundred years old. I didn't tell her about the retrovirus at the time, because I didn't know about it. My lab analysis wasn't done by then. I swear."

The man stared at something again, then nodded. "I believe you." He waited. "Now, what do you know about this new virus you've found in all the test subjects?"

Was there a way to defeat whatever trick they used to observe when she left something out or lied? She could perform lots of mathematical calculations as she talked. The awful memory of the torture she'd endured kept her from conducting such an experiment. No, she would cooperate, do whatever they needed.

"We don't know much yet. We suspect it's an engineered delivery mechanism, because the models show that it has no impact."

The man raised an eyebrow. "Why would you come to such a conclusion? Aren't there millions of undiscovered viruses? Isn't that the point of your study?"

This man knew more than an average FBI agent. If someone was feeding him questions, that person had done their homework.

"Lots of experiments have been done in the last few years to sort and classify viruses," Candace replied. "We've found millions of beneficial viruses, and only a tiny percentage are harmful—or pathogenic. All our recent research leads us to believe that life as we know it would be impossible without viruses. I theorized that it was bioengineered, because it was present in every subject and it does nothing, even though it has a thick protein shell. We think there may be another virus inside the one we found."

The man shifted in his seat. "Don't you feel that is a rather bold intuitive leap? Did you actually determine the properties of this 'inner virus,' or is this wild speculation?"

Despite the threat of more pain, she gave the man a look of utter indignation. "I'd hardly call it 'wild speculation.' I'm a scientist, and I know how to view the data objectively. I always fall back on natural selection. I find it unlikely that such a mechanism would have developed without giving an organism more chance of survival. I always ask the question 'How does it help it survive?' If I can't answer that, I know I need to do more digging. In this case, it feels like something bioengineered and not something that would develop in nature. I'll admit it is only a hunch at this point, but I object to you calling it wild speculation."

The man waved his hand in dismissal. "So you haven't found anything to support your wild theory?"

"No." A wave of pleasure passed through her body as she said this. Again the taste of chocolate in her mouth and a feeling like she'd been given a warm hug.

"How did you meet Wesley O'Keefe?"

"He came to visit my uncle, Jonathan Moore, and left his business card there. My uncle left me a voicemail saying Wesley could help with my research."

The man gave a wan smile. "What aren't you telling me?"

Somehow she would need to find a way to guard her thoughts. She narrowed her eyes at the man. "When I was in the room after Jonathan died, a nurse named Anne O'Keefe was there. She showed me a video of Wesley entering earlier and wanted to know more about him. I wouldn't have found it too odd, but when I asked the receptionist about her, she said they didn't have an Anne that worked there." Candace focused her breathing and pictured herself on Lake Chelan when she was sixteen, waterskiing with her friends.

"Let's go back to something. Did you upload any information about the viruses you sequenced to a cloud system, or did you keep it all on local file systems?"

She was on the lake, enjoying her time with friends. She wasn't here. *Keep thinking about the lake.* "I kept it local."

Searing pain, like her skin was burning across her entire body, lanced through her. All thoughts beyond the agony left her. She writhed helplessly on the bed until the pain finally stopped.

"Care to revise your response?"

Her mental trick didn't work. They knew she was lying. "I uploaded all the information to a cloud system."

The man nodded. "I'm going to need the credentials for your password safe. Once we verify we can access your cloud data, we'll leave you alone and let you get some rest. Do we have a deal?"

A sick feeling rose in Candace's stomach. They'd delete everything. "This isn't legal. You can't torture American citizens like this. Even if you suspect bioterrorism. I have rights. I want a lawyer."

The man shook his head. "You'd be correct if you were real. Fortunately for us, digital entities don't have any rights. I can make the pain last for much, much longer. Are you going to cooperate?"

"What are you talking about?"

"We scanned your neural state into a quantum storage array. Your body, and everything you experience, is provided by simulated sensory interfaces. It's the reason why I can cause you pain or pleasure at will. The real Candace is back home right now." He waited for a few moments. "Now, about that password."

Chapter 11

A wave of nausea threatened to make Candace run to the bathroom again. Fuzzy memories of being carried by men in suits to her doorstep as a black sedan sped away. The smell of bile assaulted her senses, and the wall to her living room came into focus as she stared at it. What exactly had happened?

Candace stared at her watch. June 9. When she'd been arrested, it had been June 6. She didn't remember anything of the last three days.

The men had come into her lab and told her she was under arrest. Then what?

A wave of pressure around her skull made her feel like she'd worn a too-small bicycle helmet for days. *Focus.* She recalled the sting of the needle as it had poked into her flesh. They must have arrested her and drugged her. *Those bastards.* How did they think they would get away with that?

Delirium gave way to anger as the heat rose within her. She reached into her bra, looking for the small tracking device Dianne had given her. It was still there. She ran to her computer and opened the tracker program, but the data made no sense. The app showed she had been in a place about forty miles northeast of her house for the last three days. She zoomed in on the satellite location, only to see a small shack surrounded by a field of grass with several pine trees reaching toward the sky. Would there be an FBI facility there, amid a rural backdrop of agrarian houses? Not likely.

Candace took a long shower. The hot water warmed her skin, and the steam filled her lungs with moisture. A towel hung over the curtain rod, and she dried herself off quickly before she put on some comfortable clothes. She pulled a hoodie on and donned some sunglasses that covered her face. Sure, it was cloudy, but like most people in Seattle, she wore them anyway in case there was a sudden cloud break.

Her hands shook as she called Dianne, but the call went straight to voicemail. Dianne must be on a plane. Would her location tracker show her somewhere over the Atlantic Ocean right now? Candace pulled up the app, fully expecting to see Dianne on the way to Europe. Instead, she found that Dianne was at the same location she'd just left.

Candace searched her medicine cabinet for an antiemetic to help with her nausea. She found a Zofran and let it dissolve under her tongue as she thought about what to do. She envisioned any conversation she might have with the police or the FBI: "So, you're telling me that someone took you somewhere for three days, claimed to be from the FBI, and now they have your friend there? Okay. We'll be right over."

Instead, she called Wesley.

"Candace? Are you all right?"

Touched by the concern in his voice, she gulped before responding. "Yeah. Can you meet me somewhere? I'll give you the address of a coffee shop up in Everett. I need your help."

"Everett? Why so far?"

She pinched the bridge of her nose. Her head continued to throb. "I can't explain right now. Not on the phone. Can you meet me?"

"Sure. I'll be there."

*

Candace hardly noticed the trendy decor of the coffee shop, which had skylights and plants hanging from the ceiling, and several rows of wooden benches framing large tables with hanging lights above them. She'd only picked the place because of its proximity to I-5. A young man came to take her order. *An actual person—how retro.*

"May I get you something to drink?"

Candace nodded. She probably wouldn't touch it, though her nausea seemed to be passing. *Thank goodness for Zofran.* "I'll take a cappuccino and a tea with some milk."

The man gave a polite nod and smiled.

She checked her watch. How long would Wesley take to get here? A woman at another table gawked at her, and Candace realized she'd been drumming her fingers loudly on the surface of the bench. She tried to smile, but her facial muscles were too tense. She squeaked out a pitiful-sounding word of apology.

Wesley entered the café, and when Candace stood, he embraced her. She found herself hugging him back. As she pressed herself to him, she smelled his cologne, with soft hints of sandalwood and fresh cedar. She felt comfort in his arms and held the embrace until she could pull herself together.

Wesley stepped back. "On the way here, my lawyer told me the FBI had released you." His brows furrowed as he took in the sight of her. She must look a fright. "What happened?"

They sat, and Candace gathered her thoughts.

The server arrived with their drinks, and she held the warm cappuccino cup to her chest like a person lost in the cold woods might grab an offered blanket. She stared out the window before returning her gaze to Wesley.

"I can't remember what happened to me. I think they drugged me. I should probably go to the doctor and get a toxicology report."

"Did they tell you why you were there? What did they ask you?"

Candace shook her head. "I don't know. I remember when they arrested me, and I remember them dropping me off at my house. Everything else is gone. Three days. Gone."

Wesley hadn't touched the tea. He rubbed his chin. "Why? My lawyer told me they could hold you for up to seventy-two hours before charging you when they suspect bioterrorism." He narrowed his eyes. "You know how much that man charged me, only to call me on the way here to tell me you'd been released?"

She raised an eyebrow. "You paid to find out what was happening to me?"

He waved his hand. "Yes. Sorry. I was worried about you." He took a slow sip of his tea, then nodded in appreciation of the brew. "I tried to get him to have you released, but he said that you'd been charged with bioterrorism, and you didn't have any rights for three days. I've been a wreck. Oh, something else happened while you were gone." He glanced around the coffee shop, then leaned forward in a conspiratorial manner. He whispered, "I met with my sister."

Wesley told her details about their meeting at her condo, and everything they had discussed.

"She invited you into her condo, someone she didn't know?" Candace asked.

"I know. My sister's a tough woman. Reminds me of my mother. Few dared to cross her, and those that did never forgot it." He bit his lip. "My mom died giving birth to my sister, Anne."

"Anne? That woman in Jonathan's room was your sister?"

Wesley furrowed his brows. "Come again?"

Candace recounted her meeting with Anne and how she had called her.

Wesley fidgeted with his watch for a second before answering. "She didn't mention that to me. I get the feeling Anne has been following me for a while. I don't think she was in Jonathan's room by happenstance. Oh, she told me that we've lived long lives because of a retrovirus my grandfather calls 'the Raven's Kiss'—whatever that means."

Perhaps it was the shock, or maybe the drugs they'd given her, but Candace suddenly realized the urgency of her situation. The blood drained from her cheeks. "I'm sorry, but we'll need to discuss this on the way to save my friend Dianne." She gathered her purse and stood to leave.

Wesley motioned for her to sit. "What are you talking about, please? You look like you've had a bad dose of it."

She spoke in rapid fire. "My friend Professor Dianne Erdlen gave me some micro tracking devices. I have one in my bra strap, as does she. We shared our locations on the app. It shows that I was in what looks on satellite photos like a small shack in farmland northwest of here for the last three days. She was supposed to be heading to Venice today for summer vacation. The app shows that she is there at the facility."

Wesley shook his head. "Are you sure? I don't place much stock in these apps. Most of them want to sell your data to someone."

Candace crossed her arms. He sounded like her uncle. Had he not evolved with the times? "Dianne is a trustworthy friend and I believe it. I called you because I need your help going to this place and finding Dianne. Will you help me, or should I call someone else?"

Wesley looked both bewildered and hurt. "I'll help you, but we should start by calling the police."

She smacked her fist on the table. "No!"

One of the other customers looked over at her, then looked away.

Wesley shook his head. "Sorry, but I don't think we should do this ourselves."

Candace lowered her voice. "Wesley, this was the FBI! How are the local police going to help?" She tried to lift the cappuccino to her mouth, but her hand shook so much that she had to set it down.

Wesley rubbed his chin. "Yes, and I know that it was the FBI, because my lawyer verified they had arrested you. I don't believe what they are doing is legal."

"Yet here I am, proof that the FBI is able to do whatever the hell they want if they can pin a terrorist label on someone. Will you go with me or not? Because I'm afraid of what they might do to Dianne."

Wesley bit his lip, lost in thought. Then he sprang into action. "How did you get here?"

"I drove my car. Why?"

"I'm sure the FBI must be following you. They may be following me too. I have an idea. Can you give me your car access card and your tracking device?"

"I can, but why?"

"I'm going to talk a few people into driving our cars back to our houses, and we're going to get a taxi up to this farm place to get your friend."

"Who would do that?"

Wesley smirked. "Would you do it if I offered you four hundred dollars?"

"What? That's a lot of money. I might if I thought I'd be safe."

"I'll tell them it's part of a social media prank. I hear kids like to do that."

Wesley approached a man and negotiated with him. Much to her surprise, the man nodded, took the money, and left the coffee shop. He brokered a similar deal with a young woman. He handed her more money and winked back at Candace.

In short order, they were in a self-driving taxi on their way to the location. Candace turned to him. "That was impressive. Thank you for doing this."

He nodded and smiled. "Anytime."

"What of this Raven's Kiss? Did Anne explain how you got this retrovirus when no one else did? I ran models, and they suggest that the human immune system prevents viral insertion."

Wesley gave her an apologetic shrug. "No. I'm sorry, I didn't ask. I was too upset by the other news that she delivered."

Candace placed a hand on his shoulder. "Oh. What did she say?"

"My mother." He let out a long sigh. "It hit me hard. She died giving birth to Anne over three hundred years ago. I know it shouldn't bother me now, but it does." He drew in a breath. "I suppose my ignorance was bliss."

They rode in silence for a while. Then Wesley spoke again. "I told Anne of your arrest, and she said that powerful people would try to stop me if I revealed the existence of the retrovirus."

"I wonder if the man who arrested me is one of them." Candace told him of Agent Atenoud.

He tugged at his ear. "The man sounds dangerous."

Candace nodded and stared out the window, lost in thought. Anger at being arrested and abducted without probable cause propelled her forward. She flexed her fists, perturbed by the gall of that FBI agent, calling her a bioterrorist when she'd done everything in her power to prevent diseases.

Twenty minutes passed as the urban landscape gave way to one-lane roads bordered by pines and fields of grass and scarred with long tracts of electrical wire stretched taut between wooden utility poles. One of the houses they passed even had an old, rusted-out pickup with an internal combustion engine. Candace shook her head—why would anyone have one of those nowadays? They weren't even legal to drive anymore.

As she neared the location, her breaths became more rapid. What was she doing coming out here? Perhaps Wesley was right about having the police deal with the situation, but how would the authorities help her with this problem when they were the ones that had gotten her into it? No. She'd lost three days of her life and wasn't looking for some bullshit answer from another bureaucrat. The empty feeling in the pit of her stomach urged her to turn the car around, to go back home, to enjoy the safety and warmth of her house and a nice cup of coffee. But she had to find out who had taken her and why.

The taxi pulled into the location, onto a long dirt road leading into a field surrounded by pine trees. They exited the vehicle and watched it leave down the country road.

Wesley surveyed the area, then whispered to Candace. "This is nothing but a tin-roof-covered shack in the middle of the country. Are you sure this isn't a giant mistake?"

She tried to project confidence when she answered, though she didn't feel it. "Yes. Let's go."

Candace motioned for Wesley to follow, and they skulked along the tree line at the edge of the property, then made their way to the ramshackle shed. She jiggled the door handle and found it locked. *Now what?*

The loud whine of an electric engine accelerating from the road sounded, and they sprinted for the tall evergreens surrounding the clearing. Candace gave a silent thanks to her aunt for making her join track in high school. Though that had been nearly thirty years ago, it had made her develop the habit of running three times a week to stay in shape. Panting, she risked a peek at the driveway, where a large black SUV sped toward the shed.

Two burly men in suits stepped out of the vehicle. Candace froze as one stared in their direction. She remained motionless and silent, thankful that it was too cloudy for sunshine to reflect off her large sunglasses. The man looked away, and both of them moved to the trunk, where they lifted out a limp man and carried him into the shed. Several minutes passed with no movement.

Candace rose to move toward the shed, but Wesley placed his hand on her shoulder. "I'll go. If it's clear, I'll signal you. If it's not, call the police."

She nodded, a bit relieved. He disappeared, and her heart thumped in her chest as she waited.

Several minutes passed. Where was he?

Wesley became visible again and motioned for her to come to the shed.

Adrenaline coursed through her veins as she sprinted to the shack.

"The door's open now. There's an access hatch in the floor in there."

Candace steeled herself. "Let's go."

She followed him inside. The interior was much like what she would expect in a derelict storage shed, with some rusted farm implements on shelves. The floor was made of concrete, and a rug had been moved aside to reveal a large metal access hatch. When Wesley opened it, the grating of metal on metal caused a loud creaking sound. Several lights along the wall below revealed a long metal stairwell. Candace winced, and her rapid heartbeat pounded in her ears.

Wesley whispered again. "I'll climb in first. If something happens—"

"I know—call the cops. Let's get on with it. Dianne is in there somewhere."

He gave a quick nod and shimmied down the stairs. Through the dim light, he held up a thumb, and she followed.

They continued the strategy of Wesley going in first, with Candace following after he gestured.

They reached a long hallway with many doors. Wesley turned to her. "Now what?"

Candace shrugged. Then a noise at the end of the hallway made her jump. She opened the door closest to her, ignoring their protocol.

Wesley rushed in after her and shut the door.

The room was sparsely decorated with a small desk, two chairs, and a strange helmet with a thick cable attached to it. When voices echoed down the hallway, they dashed into a small utility closet.

Wesley's hot breath warmed her neck as the two of them pressed together in the small space. Her chest heaved like that of a frightened rabbit. She closed her eyes and struggled to stay calm, and then a door creaked open.

There was rustling in the room, then a man's voice. "Why do these scans take so long?"

A woman answered. "With the number of qubits and scanners we have, we can scan about six hundred thousand neurons per second. We have one hundred billion neurons to replicate. If you do the math, that takes about two days."

An angry voice replied. "My statement was rhetorical. I know why it takes so long. I only wish it were faster."

Candace recognized the man's voice. A cold shock went through her body. *Ahad!* She wrapped her arms around her legs and rocked back a little, trying to keep her foot from falling asleep.

Ahad spoke, this time with more authority and less anger. "Time to talk with Dr. Rosenbach. Let's see what she has to say."

Oh no! They knew she was in the closet. She readied her nails, the only weapon she had, and hoped Wesley was ready to pitch in. She probably should have thought to at least bring some Mace. She turned to face the door. At the very least, she'd give Ahad a solid kick to his groin. She steeled herself and braced for the fight.

Ahad spoke. "Please bring me out of the simulation in fifteen minutes."

The simulation?

For what felt like hours, the only sound she heard was the occasional typing on a keyboard. Simulation? What the hell was going on? Candace continued to shift and made a small bump. She froze and waited in panic for someone to open the closet door. No one came. Her legs and arms fell asleep as the minutes passed by. Her heart thumped in her ears as she took careful breaths.

Ahad's voice broke the silence. "The scan appears to have been successful." He laughed. "Dr. Rosenbach wasn't pleased with me. Congratulations. Now, let's go to Seattle. There's someone we need to meet."

"I know what I'm doing," replied the woman. "Of course it worked. How long will we be gone? I have much to do."

Ahad laughed. "Always the industrious one. A few hours. Relax. These digital entities aren't going anywhere."

"We only have four months to finish everything. We don't have a lot of time."

"You're right. We'll get it done. We haven't much choice."

More rustling noises, then the sound of a door opening and closing.

A long-held breath escaped Candace's burning lungs. She inhaled several times, then opened the closet door.

She pointed at the helmet on the desk. "I need to put this on and see what they're doing."

Wesley shook his head. "No way. We need to find your friend and get the hell out of here. Ahad may work for the FBI, but he is doing something very illegal here. We should call the authorities. Now."

Candace grabbed the helmet and stared at it as she talked. "They said they only had four months. Whatever they're doing, we need to figure it out and stop them. We won't know what it is if the police come here. I'm sure Ahad has figured out a way to make whatever all of this is look legitimate."

Wesley paced the floor. "Okay. Put that thing on and see what happens. I'm pulling it off your head in five minutes."

Candace sat in the chair and placed the bulky helmet on her head.

A sound like a torrent of water rushing into a bucket filled her ears, and her vision went blank. She found herself in a small room with white walls and a single door. She turned the doorknob and gasped when she saw the person sitting on a small cot. She was staring at herself.

The other Candace must have seen the look of surprise on her face. "What's the matter, Doctor? Did you forget your stethoscope?"

Candace looked down at her hands. A man's hands. She rubbed one wrist with the other, and her curly hair produced an odd sensation. She gasped. She felt it, as though she were touching it in real life. The simulated Candace stared at her with mouth agape.

"Sorry," Candace said to her double. "Listen, I don't have much time. I'm not who you think I am. I'm you, and you aren't you. Does that make sense?"

The simulated Candace folded her arms. "Is this another cruel trick? I've suffered your abuse and torture long enough. Now this? You told me I was in some sort of accident. The last thing I remember is being in my lab at the university, doing research. Now you sound crazy. Who the hell are you, anyway?"

Candace struggled to find a memory to use, then blurted out what came to mind. "When Aunt Harriett was dying, we whispered into her ear a promise that we would find a way to cure cancer, or we'd die trying. Do you remember that?"

The other Candace grimaced. "I'm sure you could've found that out from anyone. Most of my grad students know why I'm so adamant about finding a cure. If you're me, you'd know something else. Where did I put the ten-dollar bill from Andy's piggy bank?"

Candace had never told anyone about that. She remembered hiding the ten dollars in the back of a photo frame. Then she'd forgotten about it. The money had fallen out of the picture frame when she'd hung it on her wall at her MIT dorm. She had thought about calling Andy to tell him about it at the time but never had. How did this thing, whatever it was, have all her memories? "*I* put it behind a picture frame when I was eight years old. Aunt Harriet gave it to him for doing chores, and I was jealous."

Her simulated version covered her mouth with her palm and stared for several moments. Her face showed shock. She shook her head. "I thought they were messing with me. I thought somehow I was still real, and that I would wake up from whatever drug-induced psychosis they'd created. I'd hoped it wasn't true."

Candace wished it weren't true herself. How and why had they done this to her? Stripped her of her privacy and made a copy of her like this. How was any of this technology even possible? She shook Sim Candace's shoulders. "Listen to me, and listen carefully. I don't have much time. I was arrested and drugged by the FBI, by a man named Ahad Atenoud. I can't remember anything that has happened over the last three days. I don't know what he wants, but I suspect it has something to do with the research we were doing with Wesley O'Keefe. No matter what he does to you, don't tell him or anyone else that comes in here about our research. I overheard Ahad and some woman talking about doing a neural scan. These people aren't who you think, no matter what they say or do. This place is somewhere in the middle of farm country by a small town called Lochsloy, near Marysville. We're in some kind of underground facility."

Sim Candace's eyes darted back and forth, and she shook her head more. Her mouth opened and closed a few times, but no words came out. "I ..." She touched her hands to her face, then covered her eyes. She removed her hands and stared back. "I already told them everything. They've caused me more pain than I've ever felt in my entire life. They also have a way of making me feel ..." She paused and grimaced, then swallowed hard. Her lips curled into a snarl. "They make me feel pleasure. It sickens me. It's like they're raping me mentally. I know they're doing operant conditioning. But—"

"So you told them about Wesley and Dianne?"

She nodded. "Yes. I also gave them access to your cloud server. They can connect me to the internet from here. There seems to be an interface between this and the real world. Please get me out of here. Nothing you know or have done is safe. I can't withstand the torture. Because I don't have a physical body, they can give me a sensation of pain for longer than I think would be possible in real life before I fainted." She shook her head and covered her face. "You can't possibly imagine how horrible it is. Please, I need your help."

Candace walked to her and hugged her, then sat beside her and held her hand. "I don't know what this is or how they did it, but I promise I will get you out of here somehow. The thought of these assholes having access to all my memories is unnerving beyond measure."

Sim Candace nodded, then stared at the wall for a long time before she spoke. "I'll find out what they want, and I'll find a way to reach you. I know all your email addresses." She laughed, though there wasn't much joy in it. "I feel real. I wonder if you're the one in the simulation. You don't exactly look like me."

They both shared a laugh at that. "This technology fascinates me. I put a large helmet on. There was a loud whooshing noise, and then I was here. The helmet seems to have intercepted the neural sensory interfaces in my brain and put me in this simulation. I can't imagine what they are doing here."

A tear formed in Sim Candace's eye. "I'm scared."

84

Candace stroked her hair in sympathy. "Me too. These people have a lot of resources. I—"

Everything blurred around her, and then all went dark as the strange static sound filled her ears.

Wesley stood there, holding the helmet in his hands. "Did it work? You twitched a little, but other than that, you didn't respond to anything I said. When I tapped you on the shoulder, you didn't react."

"Yes. I've never experienced anything like it. I felt everything with my hands. I touched things. *I* was in there, copied and digitized. I talked to myself. They're torturing me in there."

Wesley bit his lip and rubbed his chin. "Let's get your friend. We need to leave."

"Hold on, please."

Candace poked around the monitor and keyboard, then got into an interface where she would be able to write some code. Her fingers flew across the keys as she typed. Wesley tapped his fingers as the minutes passed by, and she continued writing code. She composed a message and, after a minute, received a reply: *Thank you.*

Wesley stared at her with his mouth open. "What did you do?"

"I gave Candace a way to contact me, and hopefully a way to keep them from hurting her." She closed the programs and made for the door. "Let's find Dianne."

Wesley didn't move; he pointed at the keyboard. "But how? How did you know what to do there?"

"I studied physics at MIT, but I spent a lot of time in the computer labs and participating in hackathons. Call it a hobby."

He gave her an appraising look but said nothing more as he followed her out of the room.

It took some searching, but they found the room with Dianne. She had an IV attached to her, a device similar to the helmet attached to her head. Vital signs flashed on screens, and a percentage bar displayed five percent.

"What do they possibly want with Dianne? She's done nothing other than listen to me talk briefly about you."

Wesley raised his eyebrows. "Perhaps that's everything that was needed. Listen, I sent the info about this place and Dianne to my lawyer, Gordon, on the way here. He got back to me and said there's no record of her being arrested."

"What? So where does that leave us?"

He gave a small shrug. "I believe it means that while you were arrested by the FBI, they brought you to a place that isn't under their control. All the more reason for us to call the police."

"Wait, are you getting a signal down here and actively talking with someone?"

"Yes. I've been messaging with Gordon. He's worried about me, probably because he wants to make sure he gets paid." Wesley pointed to Dianne, attached to what had to be scanning equipment. "What should we do with her?"

Dianne had a tube coming out of her throat. They'd intubated her. Candace touched her own throat. "We can't disconnect her. The machine is doing the breathing for her."

The door opened, and a man sauntered into the room. He started when he saw the two of them and made for the exit, but Wesley forced him to the floor, then held his hand over his mouth.

"Scream or call out, and you'll regret it." Wesley motioned to the man's watch, and Candace took the hint and removed it.

"What did you do to her?" Candace asked.

Wesley put the man in a chokehold.

The man growled at them. "Piss off."

Wesley tightened his grip, and his face turned red. "Answer the question, please." He let up, and the man coughed.

"I'm a CRNA, all right? They paid me a shitload of money to do this job, as long as I never talk about it. I've got bills to pay."

"How much are they paying you?" Wesley asked.

"Two hundred thousand. So please, leave, and I won't say anything."

Wesley whistled. "That's a lot of money. What sort of bills do you have?"

The man licked his lips. "Let's just say I lost a lot of money gambling. But

I could lose my CRNA license for this. Look, man, I spent years in medical school to become a CRNA. Any less money wouldn't have been worth the risk."

"I'm going to reach into your pocket and grab your wallet. If you try something, I'll make you regret it," Wesley said, and he gave the man's wrist a twist.

The man yelped. "Okay, fine! You won't find anything valuable in there."

"I beg to differ. I've found your identity chip." He handed the chip to Candace.

She scanned the chip with her smartphone. "Sebastian Worthington. Maybe I could call the Department of Health."

"Okay, okay. I'll help you two out, but I need to get the hell out of here. Can you get me to Canada?"

"Yes. I'll get you there," Wesley said. "Now wake her up." He released his grip on the man, and they both stood, with Wesley staring Sebastian down. "Don't try anything, or we'll hook you up to one of these IVs and see what happens."

The color left Sebastian's face. Then he nodded and licked his lips. "Okay. This shouldn't take long." He looked at both of them, and his eyes darted to the doorway. He lowered his voice. "Listen. Once we revive her, it's going to stop the neural scan. They need the patients to be in a coma to do them, because it won't work when the brain is active. The state changes more quickly than they can track it. Or something. Don't ask me—I'm not a neurobiologist or anything. The point is, we'll need to leave. Fast."

Candace glared at the man. "How do you live with yourself, working for these assholes? Are you the one that drugged me?"

The man looked down. "Sorry. It was nothing personal. I owe the wrong people a lot of money. Hey, if it hadn't been me, they would have found someone else. At least I'm good at my job. You're lucky."

Candace didn't feel lucky. She let out a long breath. "How long is this going to take?"

"About thirty minutes, maybe less. It depends on how the patient here responds."

"Her name is Dianne Erdlen, and she's my friend. She's not a patient. Nothing was wrong with her until you people brought her here."

He winced a little. "Look, I'm sorry. Like I said, nothing personal."

Sebastian continued to work, injecting something into the IV and closely monitoring Dianne.

Candace surveyed the computer equipment in the room. Some quantum-computing gear, heavily shielded, and standard computer systems next to that. She sat down and began typing at the console.

Wesley hissed, "What are you doing?"

She held up a hand for him to shush. The security of the control systems was laughable at best. They must have relied on being in a secure location. Using obscurity to keep information safe was the weakest form of protection and the easiest to defeat.

After about ten minutes of hacking around and modifying source code, Candace raised her head to speak. "The scanner has a feedback loop to report progress. Anyone checking on this will see the progress continuing to rise at a steady rate. Also, I see that our friend here did periodic progress reports. I've set up a cron job to make it look like he's still doing that. It might be a while before they figure out she's gone."

Sebastian looked to the ceiling and let out a breath. "Man, that's a relief."

Wesley stared at Candace in wide-eyed disbelief, but he was smart enough not to say anything. If he'd made some sort of comment about being surprised that a woman had the technical aptitude to hack the computers, she would have lost it.

Suddenly Dianne started flailing and making choking noises.

Candace yelled out, "Help her, damn you!"

Sebastian raised a hand to calm Candace. "It's normal. It's called bucking the vent. Her body is trying to breathe on its own. Now let me do my job, and we'll be out of here soon, okay?"

He removed the tubes and disconnected all the scanning gear.

Dianne opened her eyes and looked around. "Candace? What's going on? Where am I?"

Candace ran to her and held her hand. "It's okay. You're safe. We're going to get you out of here. I'll explain later."

Sebastian opened a cabinet and pulled out a suitcase. "Her personal effects. I suspect she'll be needing her passport."

Candace supported Dianne from one side, and Wesley supported her from the other. They helped her get up the stairs and out of the underground building. They made their way along the tree line to the road, where a taxi waited. They all managed to get into the cab.

Candace turned to Wesley. "Where are we headed?"

"First, we'll head to Boeing Field. Then we're taking a plane to Abbotsford, in British Columbia."

On the way down to the airport, a video call request came in from Dr. Hermann. Despair filled Candace before she even pressed the button to accept the conversation.

Dr. Hermann's face showed all the signs of someone trying hard to keep their anger under control yet failing. "Dr. Rosenbach. Where do I begin?"

She thought of several responses, including a quip that would attempt to lighten the mood, but settled on an apologetic smile and a shrug. She had little humor left herself.

He narrowed his eyes. "We think we've managed to get the charges leveled against you by the FBI dropped. I don't understand this research project for which we have received a cease-and-desist order from a federal court. What is it, and why don't I know about it?"

Candace's mind raced with possibilities. Which one was Dr. Hermann talking about? She wasn't required to get approval for every research project, as long as they utilized existing resources. "I'm sorry, can you please elaborate?"

He raised his eyebrows, no longer attempting to hide his anger. "Something about the classification of various viruses based on blood samples from several volunteers."

Why was the FBI trying to block that? "We received approval for that project. One of my graduate students is pursuing it as a way of identifying the taxonomy of various microorganisms."

"The FBI says the research jeopardizes national security. Our lawyers will fight this, but I need you to take a two-week leave of absence. Dr. Melville will oversee your graduate students' work."

Melville? He would have them all writing useless academic essays. *Argh.* "Very well."

Dr. Hermann glared at her. "No research project work. I already told you to take time off. This time, if I catch you back here or working on anything at all over the next two weeks, I'll be forced to fire you. Is that clear?"

All too clear. "Yes, sir."

"Good day."

She nodded, and he ended the call.

Candace turned to Dianne. "Can you believe Dr. Hermann? He's making me take a two-week leave of absence."

Dianne held her hand. "Those men pulled me over on the way to the airport. They injected me with something. Who the hell were they?"

Heat rushed to Candace's cheeks. "People who want to keep something to themselves, I'm afraid. Listen, what do you want to do after we go to Canada?"

Dianne frowned. "Honey, I'm not going to let them ruin my vacation. I'm going to Venice." She lowered her voice and leaned in to whisper in Candace's ear. "Is this Wesley guy the one we were talking about at the café?"

Candace nodded, then whispered back. "Yes, and he's probably also the reason they kidnapped you. I suspect they don't want anyone to find out about him. I'm not sure what they have planned."

Dianne whispered back. "Honey, you don't go for simple, do you?"

Candace managed a chuckle. "I suppose I don't."

Chapter 12

Wesley did all the preflight checks on the plane. He'd upload the passenger manifest once they were near the border, because he didn't want to take any chances and risk getting intercepted on the way.

The news that Candace had to take a forced two-week vacation was great. He'd take her up to the cabin he'd built if she'd agree to it.

Sebastian and Dianne sat in the back, out of earshot. Wesley had asked Candace to sit near him, in the copilot seat, though she knew nothing about flying planes.

He turned to her. "I have a cabin in a remote area of Canada where the two of us could go for a few days. What do you say?"

"Are you asking me on a date?"

"I like you. You're beautiful, but I'm sure you knew that already, because I know I'm not the first man to have told you that. You're the first woman I've met in a long time that I actually want to spend time with. I deeply admire your conviction. Your hacking skills are impressive as well. What if it were a date?"

Candace gave him a calm, measured look. Had he gone too far? She crossed her arms. "You're not my type."

Wesley's cheeks flushed with heat. He needed to escape. Not for good, like he had in the past, but for a week or two. "I'd like your company, and it sounds like you could use a break. Please. I need to get away for a while. I'm worried the FBI may come for me next. All this work will still be waiting for you when you get back. Plus, what else would you do for the next two weeks while you can't work?"

Candace pursed her lips. "How remote are we talking?"

No one else would be there. The muscles in Wesley's jaw relaxed at the notion, and he dropped his balled fist to the side. He hadn't realized he'd balled it up, and sweat covered his hand. "Very remote. We'd be the only humans for miles."

Candace's expression softened. "So we drop off Sebastian and Dianne in Abbotsford, then head up there?"

He nodded. "Sure. We can go shopping for clothes and toiletries. This mess will be waiting for us when we get back."

She contorted her face in disbelief. "I can't leave with no notice like that." She gave him a sidelong glance. "What are you expecting from me?"

Candace wanted to know if he expected her to get intimate with him. He could keep it platonic if required. Maybe she'd change her mind about him, but if she didn't, at least they'd have engaging conversations. "Nothing. Listen, I have a spare bedroom. We'll get to know each other. I'm not expecting anything other than companionship."

She rubbed her hands together for a few moments. "Getting away does sound good. I need to make it clear this doesn't mean anything between us. I do like you, but I'm not ready to date you yet."

The "I do like you" part was encouraging. He'd work on the other part later. "Very well, it's a date. I mean, it's a plan, not a date."

Wesley sent a message to his pet sitter, Natalia, letting her know he'd be at his cabin for a while and asking her to please feed Hunter.

A response from Natalia came in: *Have a good trip.*

Candace fidgeted. She must have been upset after everything she'd been through.

Wesley put a hand on hers. "Listen, you'll feel a lot better when we get out by the lake and can soak in nature."

She nodded, then took off the pilot headset he'd given her. "Sorry, I need to go talk to Dianne. Also, does this plane have a bathroom?"

"Yes, it does. This model has a—"

She cut him off. "I'm sorry, but I have to go. We'll talk about it later."

Wesley checked the navigation systems and found everything to be in order. Candace and Dianne talked in low whispers and looked his way periodically.

*

After they landed, Wesley taxied to his hangar.

Dianne spoke. "Don't we need to check in or something?"

Wesley shook his head. "No. I submitted your information to border control. They know you'll be taking a flight from here to Vancouver and then to Venice. I sent your flight information to your watch."

She raised her eyebrows. "Impressive." She winked at Candace. "I'm sorry we didn't get to chat much, but I think you'll take good care of my friend." She glared at him. "You better, anyway."

Wesley raised his hands. "I will. I promise."

He opened the door and rolled out the stairs. The air had a pleasant warmth with the afternoon sun shining across the expansive horizon. Massive mountains framed the patches of farmland, with small pine groves sprinkled throughout the landscape like clumps of green fabric.

Sebastian had been sitting in the rear of the small plane, near the bathroom. Now he walked to the front. "So, I'm good, then?"

Wesley nodded. "Yes. Make your way out the gate, over there." He pointed to the exit gate at the airport. "Your paperwork is done."

"Cool." He sauntered away, looking back a few times before he left through the exit.

Dianne stared at Wesley. "I've got a lot of questions, but I'll save them for when I get back from Venice. Thank you both for saving me."

She hugged the two of them in turn, then left through the airport exit.

Candace disembarked, and he guided her to another hangar, which contained the plane they'd be taking to his cabin.

Candace shook her head. "How rich are you, anyway?"

Wesley chuckled. "I've been fortunate to have made several good investments and also to have learned the lesson that compounding of interest allows my money to work for me, rather than me working for it. I'm comfortable."

They moved over to his other plane, which had a large glass canopy and floats for water landings.

Candace stretched her legs. "That's a beautiful-looking plane. I admittedly don't know much about airplanes, but it looks nice. How old is it?"

"About two years—"

"Hands in the air!" shouted a voice from behind them.

Wesley raised his hands and turned around slowly. A male and female Canadian Mountie rushed toward them with two large police robots in tow, stun guns at the ready. The robots had four legs with inverted knee joints, and two large arms holding two foot-long Tasers. The monocular camera eye they each had made them seem like a cross between a cyclops and a centaur. Were these what the Canadian Mounties used instead of horses now?

Wesley's hands trembled as he leaned back. Now what? If he got arrested, there was no telling how he would get help. He had come here to get away from this. *Damn it!* He couldn't run, and he didn't want to be arrested. Perhaps he could talk their way out of it. "There must be a mistake. What's this about?"

The tall female Mountie, in the RCMP's traditional immaculate red serge, with three chevrons below a small crown on her sleeve, spoke. "This woman on your manifest is on an FBI watch list."

The hair on Wesley's arms and neck lifted. FBI watch list? "I don't understand."

The sergeant pressed her lips together, shuffled her feet, and looked sidelong at her partner before addressing Wesley. "Cameras identified her as Candace Rosenbach. Accused of bioterrorism and plotting to overthrow the US government. Sounds pretty serious. You know anything about this?"

Wesley squeezed his eyes shut, and bile burned in the back of his throat. He focused on his breathing for a few moments. What now? They would arrest them both, and then he'd be held in Canada for aiding and abetting a terrorist. He had to find another way. Their government was harassing them. "The US government has framed her for a crime she didn't commit. She's seeking asylum here in Canada."

The male Mountie frowned, and the female Mountie rubbed her chin. They stared at each other, and the female Mountie finally shrugged. "We'll have to take her in for processing. This could take a while."

The tightness in Wesley's chest relaxed. He held still for a few moments as the Mounties moved toward them. The robots lowered their weapons. He really wanted to run with Candace back to the plane. But those robots could probably outpace him in mere seconds, and the stun guns they held looked menacing. Great way to end up in a Canadian prison for a long time. "Can I call my lawyer? He specializes in these sorts of things."

The female Mountie shook her head. "Not yet."

She motioned to her partner, and he put Candace in handcuffs. Then Wesley felt the cold bite of the metal as the Mountie enclosed his wrists in handcuffs. With all this technology, couldn't they have designed some restraints that weren't so damn uncomfortable?

"You'll both get a chance to make a phone call when we get to the station," the sergeant said. "Read them their rights, Robby."

One of the robots faced them, and a monitor displayed the statement, which it also read aloud: "You do not have to say anything unless you wish to do so. You have nothing to hope from any promise of favor and nothing to fear from any threat whether or not you say anything. Anything you say may be used as evidence.

"It is my duty to inform you that you have the right to retain and instruct counsel of your choice in private and without delay. Before you decide to answer any question concerning this investigation, you may call a lawyer of your choice or get free advice from Duty Counsel. If you wish to contact Legal Aid duty counsel, I can provide you with a telephone number, and a telephone will be made available to you."

After that, they were pushed into the back of a large SUV. The robots folded themselves up and mounted into the trunk at the rear of the vehicle.

Wesley chanced a glance at Candace, but her lips were pursed, and she stared straight ahead, saying nothing.

They heard nothing other than the whine of the electric motor as the SUV sped across the airport tarmac to a small building.

"You okay?" Wesley asked Candace.

She took in a deep breath and held it for a bit before she answered. "I'm fine."

"We'll be fine. I'll call my lawyer and get us out of this. He's expensive, but he's worth every penny."

She nodded.

They led them into separate rooms. The Mountie freed Wesley's right hand and secured him to the table with the handcuffs. "Make your call now."

Wesley nodded and quickly dialed Gordon's number. *Please answer, Gordon. Please, please.*

Just as he thought the voicemail message would come on, Gordon answered. "Hello?"

"Hey. Candace Rosenbach and I are at an airport in Abbotsford. The RCMP are arresting her for being on the FBI watch list for bioterrorism. We've asked for asylum. Can you help?"

Gordon whistled. "You feeling charitable or something? Wanting to help pay for my yacht?" The wretched man laughed. He actually laughed.

Heat rose within Wesley's abdomen. He clenched his jaw. "Damn it, Gordon! I don't have time for jokes. This is serious. Can you help me or not?"

"Sorry, sorry. Just trying to lighten the mood. I can help. Listen, an asylum case in Canada can take well over a year. It's not a slam dunk. If you were south of the border, I'd have you out of there in short order, but those Canucks can't be bribed. That said, all charges against Dr. Rosenbach were dropped. I'll get the system updated, have them check again in ten minutes."

"Listen, Gordon, if this works, I won't feel so bad about paying for your yacht. Thank you." Wesley disconnected the call.

The female Mountie looked at him with raised eyebrows. "A yacht? Are you bribing someone?"

Wesley shook his head. "No, not at all. My lawyer charges exorbitant fees. He said the US government has dropped all charges against Dr. Rosenbach, and the system needs to be updated. He said it should be done in ten minutes."

She gave him a sidelong glance. "If you say so."

She motioned for his watch, which he removed and handed to her. Then she cuffed his hand again.

Wesley let out a long breath. Things should be fine now, he hoped. The Mounties didn't believe him, but if Gordon did his part, it wouldn't matter. Wesley crossed his fingers. There wasn't much he could do now other than wait.

*

Twenty minutes later, the female Mountie came back. "You're both free to go. You Yanks need to get your shit together. Honestly, this is more paperwork today than I've had to do for a month."

Gordon had updated the database as promised, though it had taken longer than Wesley would have liked. At least they were free again.

They took a taxi to a large store and quickly grabbed what they'd need for a few days in the wilderness. Wesley admired Candace's efficiency in picking out clothes in minutes. Her mood seemed to be better. She talked a bit about how much she had loved camping with her uncle when she had been younger. Then she got quiet again.

Candace was silent on the ride back from shopping. When they made it to the plane, she stared at the ground. Her face turned pale. Was she going to vomit?

Wesley frowned, and his stomach quivered. "Are you okay? You haven't said anything. You're a little green."

She reached out with her hand and put it on his shoulder. "I'll be fine. Maybe we should go back home."

Not now—they were free to get away from everything for a while. If he took Candace home, he doubted she would get much relaxation. "We need to take a deserved rest. You've been through a lot. I'll make a fire for you and some tea, and you'll feel a lot better."

Candace stared at him. Was she going to say yes? She narrowed her eyes. Her shoulders relaxed, and she let out a long breath. "Okay. But I sure hope you have more than tea."

Wesley's whole body warmed. A nice Scotch would be welcome after this. "Aye, I bought the good stuff. We need something to add to the water to make it drinkable, don't we?"

She smiled and laughed.

Were things finally going to get better?

"Where is this place, anyway?" Candace asked as they taxied out to the runway.

Truly, it was in the arse-end of nowhere. "Near Stoyoma Mountain. Not near any town. The closest town would be Lower Nicola or Merritt."

Candace gazed out the window.

Off to the left, Harrison Lake came into view, a long lake that stretched like a bony finger past the snowcapped majesty of Mount Breakenridge.

"You can see Harrison Hot Springs out your window there. We'll be passing the Hell's Gate Airtram soon."

"Hmm," she said.

His stomach tensed. She must be deep in contemplation. It hadn't sounded like a promising "hmm," more like an "I'm ignoring what you said because I'm trying to figure out if this is a bad idea" sort of "hmm."

She continued to stare out the window.

"Once we figure out how to do so, do you think we should share my agelessness with the world?"

Candace drummed her fingers on the dash in front of her for a long while before responding. "There are two ways to answer: as Dr. Rosenbach, the pragmatic scientist, or with my own emotions and feelings. Which answer do you want?"

"I'd like both. Start with the human answer."

She nodded and pursed her lips. "Well. I think we should let people die, like they are supposed to. I wouldn't want to live as long as you have."

Not the answer he had been hoping to hear. How could anyone feel that way? How should he respond to that? "Why wouldn't you want to live as long as you can?"

"Everything has an end. Even our universe will eventually decay into complete entropy—if you're like me and subscribe to that theory of the future of the universe."

A horrid vision at best. "Surely it can't be all that bleak. Besides, if you don't age, you'd still end. You'd still die."

She tapped her finger on her cheek a few times. "True. But think about it this way. How many assholes are out there? There are some stupid people I wouldn't want to be around forever. Things are easier to deal with when they are temporary. I'd like to know that some grumpy old asshat that I know would be dead someday. Easier for me to think of. If I knew that he'd be around for a few hundred years, well, that wouldn't be so easy. He'd keep putting his bad DNA into the gene pool for hundreds, maybe thousands of years. He might even carry those bad genes to some other planet and create a whole world full of jerks like him."

Some people Wesley had known would have fit into that category. Things had always been more manageable knowing that he would outlive those types. "I see your point. I've experienced that in ways you couldn't imagine. But you brought up other planets. If we don't age, it would be more practical to consider a thousand-year journey to one."

She snorted. "We have a lot of other technical considerations to overcome before that's a factor. Radiation, propulsion systems, having enough food, et cetera."

Why did he always like the stubborn ones? "I want to give people a choice. If they don't want to age, they don't have to. If they want to age, by all means, go ahead. You've not gotten to the point in your life where everything hurts, where walking, even breathing, becomes a real struggle. I've seen too many people go through that. I don't want to see it anymore, and I don't want to die." He said all this a little louder and angrier than he'd intended.

Candace's face reddened, and she cleared her throat. "You haven't heard Dr. Rosenbach's opinion on the matter."

Wesley resisted the urge to shake his head. "Yes, by all means, Dr. Rosenbach. Please share your opinion." He winced a little. He hadn't meant that to sound condescending. Had it seemed as cordial as he hoped? The woman had him twisted in knots.

She smiled. Was she being gracious or hiding her displeasure? "I feel that we have outgrown our need for aging and evolution. As a society, we need to develop and grow. Our biggest threat right now is other humans. By not aging, it's conceivable our social development will stagnate, or we might somehow create a society where everyone thinks far into the future. Why bother to care for a planet you won't be around to see in fifty years? If we have to stick around for the consequences of our actions, maybe we'd plan ahead more."

Wesley scratched at his temple. How did one person have such divergent opinions on a matter? "I'm sorry if I sounded upset. In truth, I hoped you would feel differently. I have lost so many people I cared for to aging, and I couldn't do anything about it. I hoped you would want to live a life of agelessness, so I'd have someone to share my life with besides my cat."

A relaxed smile crossed Candace's face as she looked into his eyes. She placed her hand over her mouth. When she put her hand down, the smile was gone, but her eyes twinkled. She held his hand. "Wesley, I'm touched. Truly. You're a remarkable man. I'm not at that stage yet, but it was sweet of you to say that."

Wesley came from a different age, when a man pledged his fealty to a woman in the initial stages of courting. Candace wanted to take things slow, but she liked him. Didn't she? Why else would she smile so? Warmth filled his chest, and his muscles relaxed as he looked at her fondly. The corners of his lips twitched upward. "Thank you. We should be getting there soon." He paused. "To the lake, I mean, not to the stage."

She laughed. "Of course, to the lake."

Wesley pointed out several landmarks, like the Hell's Gate Airtram and some logging areas. Candace looked out the window with evident interest now.

The remote lake near Stoyoma Mountain grew closer. A sufficient amount of twilight remained to see it clearly, surrounded by pine-covered mountains capped with snow. Wesley would have to adjust his approach to allow for a good flyby. He kicked himself for getting here this late. Another half hour, and visibility would have been too limited to land on the lake safely. He remembered the old saying "There are old pilots and bold pilots, but no old bold pilots."

"Wow, look at all that snow," Candace said. "I see how the lake got here. It's beautiful, but I don't suppose there is a living soul for many miles. The water is so clear."

Wesley studied the lake and the surrounding area, and all was clear for a landing. He did a box pattern starting on the southern side of the lake and got ready for a gentle touchdown from the eastern side. The water was as smooth as glass. He glided onto the lake surface, turned the plane around, and headed for the dock, pushing a button to retract the canopy. Crisp mountain air washed over him, carrying the fresh scent of pine trees.

Candace let out a relieved breath. "Nice landing. How long have you been flying?"

Hot-air balloons probably didn't count. He'd flown his first real plane around 1940, and he'd been hooked ever since. "Over one hundred years."

Candace stared at him, then shrugged.

Was she getting used to the idea of him being as old as he was? Did she believe him? At least she was receptive to the idea now.

Wesley steered the plane toward the dock, then applied thrust in the opposite direction to slow them down, gliding in next to the wharf with a few feet to spare. He threw a rope down, shut off the engine, and jumped out to secure the plane to the moorings. A few logs floated in the distance. If he'd hit one of those during landing, they would have died quickly. He shook his head as he kicked himself for taking the risk of landing in the lake this late.

"I built this dock myself, even cut the wood," he said. Pride surged through him as he surveyed the dock. Still in great shape. The trick was to shear off the bark and let the wood weather for a year before staining it. It had taken him a year to make the dock, but he had learned how to do it a long time ago, when men had used simple tools to accomplish such things.

"Impressive," Candace said, and she raised an eyebrow. "You're a man of many prodigious talents. I'm glad we met."

"Me too." He offered her a hand as she jumped down, and they both set to unloading the luggage.

Candace folded her arms. "Where's your cabin?"

Wesley pointed to the top of a mountain. "You see that ridge up there, past all the pine trees and covered in snow?"

She stared at him with raised eyebrows. "Yes."

"Okay. It's on the other side of that. Don't worry. I brought an extra set of snowshoes."

She gave him a light punch on the shoulder. "Ha ha. Very funny. Where is it, wise guy?"

Wesley smiled as he led her onto a narrow dirt path with steps made from hewn logs. Once they made it past the steps and through some pines, the cabin came into view. He'd used several grand fir trees and timber-framed the entire structure using the old joinery methods.

Candace's eyebrows rose. "It's beautiful. Don't tell me you built this."

Wesley expanded his lungs as he puffed out his chest. "I had some help. Don't forget I was in the timber industry when we built these things without all the tools and machinery people use today. There are no roads to this area, so I couldn't bring tractors or backhoes in here for this. All the solar panels and batteries were brought up here by a large helicopter that dropped a floating pallet onto the lake. It took a long time and a lot of money to build, and the labor wasn't cheap."

They stepped onto the cedar porch, covered with a wooden awning to keep the snow away from the entry. A clunk sounded when Wesley unlocked the large wooden doorway and opened the door. Large logs stretched from one side to the other across the vaulted ceiling, and the walls were adorned with polished pine.

Candace's eyes widened as she took a few steps back and slowly shook her head. "Well done."

A large fireplace made from local stones adorned the far end of the cabin. Granite countertops and stainless-steel appliances made for a well-appointed kitchen. The polished pine of the cabinets gleamed.

"This is incredible. Wow. I would never have believed a place like this could exist way out here. I'm even more impressed now than when I saw it from the outside."

He smiled. "Wait until you see the bedroom."

Wesley led Candace to his bedroom. The side walls were made of hewn logs, and the other walls from tongue-and-groove cedar. A real bearskin rug decorated the floor. A massive king-size bed frame made from pine logs held a mattress topped with rustic blankets. Rock walls in the bathroom surrounded a sizable soaking bathtub large enough to accommodate two people, with a separate standing shower surrounded by glass block.

Candace stood speechless with her mouth agape. "How in the world did you get all of this stuff out here?"

He hooked his thumbs into his belt loops as he thrust his pelvis forward. "Oh, it took a lot of time, a lot of money, a lot of planning, and a lot of patience. I'm glad you like it. Let me show you the guest room."

Wesley led her to a second bedroom, and Candace sniffed. "This is nice. Is it where you'll be sleeping?"

He chuckled. "Ha! You're funny, but no, this will be your room, unless you get cold and want to come into mine."

She gave him a sidelong glance before she dropped her bag in the room and followed him outside, where he started cleaving some logs with an ax. Though he pretended not to notice, Candace watched him as he worked. When he chanced a direct look back, she averted her gaze. He continued chopping logs until the pile was big enough for a fire.

She licked her lips and cleared her throat. "Do you have a carbon permit for that?"

Carbon taxes. Seemed excessive way out here, but he'd gotten a permit from the Canadian government with the understanding the fireplace was only to be used for "occasional and infrequent entertainment purposes" and not as a primary source of heating. Most of the house ran on solar power and batteries. "Yes, I have a permit. The fire is for entertainment. I use quadricyclane to bottle solar energy and convert it back to heat."

Candace tilted her head. "I'm familiar with the quadricyclane–norbornadiene cycle. The norbornadiene passes through a cobalt-based catalyst, which converts it to heat, and the sunlight converts it back to quadricyclane.

Too bad people didn't start using it when they invented it twenty years ago."

What was he going to say? His thoughts had escaped him. Who was this amazing woman? He moved closer to her as he gave an appreciative smile. "Wow."

She folded her arms across her chest and stepped back. "What? Because I studied physics and microbiology, I don't know chemistry?"

Oops. Wesley wasn't trying to anger her. He held his hands in front of him in a placating gesture. "No. Sorry. I guess most people don't know that."

A wide grin formed on her face, and she gave him a playful punch on the shoulder. She snorted and laughed. "I'm messing with you. I took some extra chemistry classes in college. I enjoyed it. I'm a nerd at heart. You're right. Most people don't understand it. Maybe even you."

No, he didn't know how it worked. Heat rushed through his face and ears. "I was smart enough to hire people who understood it well enough to install it for me. I knew how it worked. I didn't remember the names of the chemicals. Most people call it quad-nor heating. The guy that installed the system said it would last forever. Keeps the place warm even when I'm not here in the winter."

Candace smiled wistfully and stared toward the lake. "Yes, he's right. The cycle can continue to repeat. If I ever build an android, it will use some sort of quad-nor power system." She snorted and laughed. "Hey, don't you ever get worried about vandalism or theft out here?"

"There isn't a road nearby for miles. The closest thing is a hiking trail, but it's several miles away. They'd have to trek through brambles and thickets to get close. That's a sturdy lock over there." Wesley pointed at the large deadbolt. He'd reinforced the door with iron bars. An intruder would need a battering ram to take it down.

Candace put her hand on his chest and fell in toward him. "I feel pretty safe here."

Wesley's pulse quickened. Light hints of perfume and lotion-kissed skin filled his nostrils. He put his arms around her, and her chest rose and fell.

Candace helped him bring in a few logs, and he soon had roaring flames burning in the fireplace. The fire warmed him as he held her gaze. He took her hand, and she smiled. They leaned against each other and stared into the dancing light, the crackling of flames the only sound to interrupt their solitude.

Candace turned to Wesley and smiled. "After all that's happened this last week, I'm glad to have this moment. I want you to know that I believe how old you are now. The evidence is irrefutable."

A wide grin crossed his face. "Great. Am I still not your type?"

She raised her eyebrows, then sighed. "Not really. I might find a way to tolerate you, though."

They laughed and stared into the fire. Euphoria and energy filled Wesley as they held hands. This woman had found her way into his heart. Would she ever let him into hers?

Chapter 13

Anne looked over the chart of a ninety-two-year-old woman with emphysema. The patient took in several deep breaths, then several shallow ones. Occasionally she would cough. Anne pushed the painkiller meds the chart called for into her IV.

She held the patient's hand. "May the Lord protect you and lead you to eternal life."

Anne found the charge nurse outside and said, "The woman in room ten only has a few hours left before she passes. She is Cheyne–Stoking, so I strongly suggest we call her family and have them here to say goodbye. No one should die alone."

The charge nurse gave a half-hearted shrug and shambled off to make the call. Anne had once been ninety-two, but that had been over two centuries ago.

She was on break when her phone rang with a number from Mexico.

"Hello. I'm Morgan Thorsen, from TTF Security Systems. We were hired by Emmitt O'Keefe to protect him and his wife, Alomena. He listed you as his emergency contact. Are you Anne O'Keefe?"

Anne's stomach dropped, and her fingers grew cold. Her hands and her voice wavered. "Yes, I am. Are they okay?"

A long pause on the other end stretched on for several seconds. Anne clenched and unclenched her fists. "No. I'm sorry to report that Emmitt was shot and that Alomena was kidnapped by the same people that killed him," Morgan said.

Killed? *No, no.* She reached for the table in front of her and sat down. The room spun about her. She clutched her shoulders to still her quaking body. As a nurse, she dealt with people dying every day, but she'd never expected her grandfather to die. How long had it been since she'd seen him? Too long. She'd just talked to him on the phone the other day. "How? How can he be dead? Are you sure?"

"Yes, ma'am. The police carried him away in a body bag."

Who was this man calling her? Was this a sick joke? Nausea clawed at her stomach, threatening to make her retch. It wasn't possible. He couldn't be dead. "I don't believe he's dead. There must be a mistake."

"I watched them carry him away, ma'am."

She tasted bile in her throat. "I'd like you to verify it, please. I'm going to come down there. Please do whatever you can to find my grandmother."

"I will, and I'm sorry for your loss."

He couldn't be dead. Grief shook Anne, overwhelming her, and she started crying, racked with sobs in the break room.

The charge nurse entered. "Is everything okay?" she asked.

Anne wiped the tears away with the sleeves of her scrubs and sniffed. "No. I just received word of my grandfather's death. I need to leave."

The charge nurse put a hand on Anne's shoulder. "Please, Anne, take as much time as you need."

She had to find Wesley. He needed to know. She called his phone, but he didn't answer. She found her car and drove to his house, trying to call a few more times on the way. Probably better that he didn't answer the phone, so she could tell him in person.

Anne called her dad. Her voice trembled as she spoke. "Grandda's been shot, and they kidnapped Grandma Alomena."

"Shot? Is he okay?"

She bit her lip and squeezed her eyes shut. "No. They took him away in a body bag. He's gone."

"Oh my God. I need you to come down here now, please."

"I can't, Da. I need to find Wesley and tell him first."

"Do you believe it's him?"

"I've been following him for quite a while now—on your advice, I might add. Yes, I think it's him."

She relayed the details of her meeting with Wesley and everything he had said.

"Send him to me, this man who claims to be Wesley," her father said.

A cold chill went through Anne's body. If the car hadn't been driving itself, she would have driven it off the road. Her hands were shaking too much to drive. "It's him, Da. I met him. I know. He knew about Patrick and Aunt Elizabeth. Who else could it be?"

"Listen, this makes it all the more important for you to come here. Once you find Wesley, please, get down here. We'll find your grandma. I love you."

She wiped her face with a tissue and choked as she tried to swallow with her constricted throat. "Love you too, Da. See you soon."

Anne passed several palatial mansions on the way to Wesley's house. He'd done well for himself. She parked at the end of a long marbled-stone pathway and passed several Japanese maples on the way to the door. She passed a small van with a picture of a large cat and the words *Karen's Smiling Kitties*. She rang the doorbell and waited, still dressed in her scrubs and ID badge.

A small older woman answered the door and stared at Anne.

Was she going to say anything? Or stand there and gawk at her?

"Hello. I'm here for Wesley," Anne said.

"He is on vacation. I feed his cat," the woman replied with a heavy Russian accent.

So much for client security. Maybe she'd tell her where he had gone. "Yes, that's right. My brother mentioned he was going on vacation, but I thought it was tomorrow. I need to find him. It's urgent family news. Did he say where he was going?"

"He said he would go to cabin. No internet there. Two weeks gone. Better tell him news when he is back." She started to shut the door.

Anne pushed on the door firmly. "Listen. Our grandfather died. I need to let him know. Please. Let me at least come in."

"No. How I know you aren't thief? Not allowed to let people in."

Anne bit the inside of her cheek. Foul woman. "What's your name?"

The woman glared and narrowed her eyes, standing in silence for several uncomfortable moments. "Natalia."

Anne clenched her jaw. "Natalia, call his cell phone. You'll see that he doesn't answer."

Natalia folded her arms and gave her a challenging stare. "Yes, maybe no signal. He never give permission for sister to come in."

Anne brought forth a practiced calm, one she'd learned after so many years of dealing with difficult people. "Right. Which is why I need to go to him. Take a picture of me and check my ID badge. We have the same last name. My brother and I look very much alike. Wouldn't you agree?"

Natalia stared at her for a while, then took her picture. "You do look much alike. I need your phone number and address. Also need you to sign paper."

Anne bit her lip and blinked rapidly. She relaxed her balled fists and took a deep breath. "What sort of paper?"

Natalia pointed a menacing finger at her. "Paper saying if he fire me, you pay money I make from him for year. Good client. You sign?"

Anne doubted Wesley would fire her once he found out about everything. "I agree."

They exchanged information, and the insufferable woman made her sign a contract that she wrote up on the spot. The ridiculous document contained many misspellings and wouldn't likely be taken seriously by a court, but she signed it anyway.

Natalia looked her tablet over, scrutinizing the signature. "Okay. Come in, then."

A cat ate from a crystal bowl and ignored the two of them. Anne passed the cat and found a study and went in, closing the door behind her. She searched through the drawers, each of which contained actual file folders with labeled tabs. She laughed in appreciation—she still used many old artifacts like file folders herself, though most people in modern times would not. She found a folder labeled *Cabin* and used her phone to take pictures of all the pages, one of which contained latitude and longitude coordinates and a legal description of the property. She put the folder back, then left the study.

She went into the nearby bathroom, flushed the toilet, and washed her hands to keep from arousing Natalia's suspicions.

"Thank you," she said to Natalia as she was leaving.

Natalia grabbed her by the shoulder and blocked her exit. "Stop. Let me check you."

Anne was tempted to grab Natalia's arm and throw her to the floor, but she restrained herself. "Check me? For what?"

The wretched woman pointed at Anne's pants. "Make sure not steal anything. Empty pockets."

This was easy. Anne didn't have her purse or anything other than her phone. She pulled out the pockets of her scrubs and showed Natalia that she didn't have anything.

"Okay. Sorry about grandpa. Lost my *babushka* long time ago. Aging is not fair," she said. "I miss her."

"Thank you," Anne said, then walked to her car.

With trembling hands, she opened the door, barely able to keep it together. How could Grandda Emmitt be dead? For now, Wesley would need to be her focus. The map photo she stared at didn't have many landmarks. No way to drive. How the heck was she supposed to get the cabin? Could she ride a horse from a nearby town? No. Today's horses wouldn't be as rugged as the ones that used to be able to make a trip like that—not to mention it would take days.

After some more searching, she found a floatplane charter company in Vancouver, British Columbia. She called them and asked if they'd fly her to the cabin.

"You want us to fly you out to a remote lake with no facilities?" the man asked.

"Yes. Is that a problem?" she asked.

"We can do it, but it's going to cost you a lot of money. Do you want us to drop you off or, like, stay there with you or what?" he asked.

"I'd like to stay for a few hours, and then go back. Can you do it?"

"Are you telling me you want to pay a few thousand dollars to fly God knows where, and then you want to leave right away?"

Anne gathered her wits before responding. "Listen, I don't lecture you on how to spend your time. Do you want my money or not?"

"Hold on a minute." Muffled voices spoke in the background for a moment. Then he continued. "Sure, we'll take your money. When did you want to leave?"

She punched in the coordinates for Vancouver and ordered the car to drive her there. "Three hours from now."

"All right. We're going to need a little extra for an expedited flight."

"Fine." Anne disconnected the call, then received a message asking to authorize a charge from the charter company, to which she replied yes.

*

Anne had been crying for so long that she was a complete mess when she went through the border crossing. They didn't seem to mind, since they waved her through.

She arrived at the floatplane charter company and must have been a real sight, because the person at the counter stared at her. What was the receptionist thinking of her with her scrubs and puffy eyes?

The receptionist asked, "Do you have a backpack or anything you need to get? Some supplies?"

Anne tried to manage a pleasant smile before responding. "No. I have what I need, thank you."

"Aren't you going to get hungry? You should take some food or something."

Why did these people think they knew what she needed better than she did? She managed to stifle a sigh. "I'm fine. Let's go."

Anne had to sign several waivers before getting into the plane, along with a document that made her acknowledge that they were not providing any provisions, and if she starved to death, it was her fault. She didn't care—eating was the least of her concerns.

A long and noisy two hours followed before the pilot pointed down at a small lake. He circled it a few times before they landed on the water. The plane bounced as they sped toward a dock at the end of the lake. As they neared the dock, a large plane with a propeller on the top came into view.

The pilot pointed at the docked plane. "That's a nice Seawind over there. Your friends must have some money, eh?"

Based on what she'd seen of her brother's estate and how he carried on, she figured he had a great deal of it. "Oh, yes, I suppose they do."

As she walked up the steps, she held out her hand to stop the pilot. "Can you please wait here?"

The pilot looked dismayed. "What, you aren't going to invite me in for a beer after flying all this way?"

She hadn't the patience to be courteous to him. "I'm sorry. I need to have a difficult conversation with someone."

"Oh, no, I'm kidding. I can't drink alcohol before flying, unless your friends want to invite me to stay overnight, maybe."

Anne glared at him, and he stopped talking as she walked away from the dock toward what she hoped would be her brother's cabin.

Chapter 14

Snow-kissed mountains framed the lake as tendrils of sunshine peeked out above the horizon, casting welcome warmth upon them. Wesley and Candace held their mugs as they stared out in silence. They were surrounded by several large pines, each of them reaching high into the air to be bathed in the sun's glorious rays. The scents of sunbaked earth and evergreen sap flooded Wesley's nostrils. Wisps of vapor rose from their mugs, and Candace sipped at her coffee as Wesley enjoyed his tea.

She smiled at him. "What are you thinking about?"

"I'm thinking about how great it is to be here with you. Thanks for coming. Sometimes you need to get away, and I couldn't ask for better company than yours."

She smiled and reached over to squeeze his hand, but the moment was interrupted by what sounded like a small aircraft. A floatplane came into view and began a landing pattern around the lake.

Wesley's heart raced. "Shit," he said as he stood and ran for the cabin with a startled Candace in tow. He ran into his bedroom and slid open a panel where he hid his Winchester Model 70 rifle.

"What in the hell are you doing with a rifle?"

"We're quite isolated. We can't call for help out here. I need this in case whoever it is in that plane means to do us any harm."

"Where did you even learn to shoot one?"

A funny question, and he didn't have a short answer. He had learned to shoot well in boot camp during World War II, though he had served as a supply officer at a Marine motor detachment in Camp Lejeune throughout the war. Back then, learning to shoot had been a normal part of life in the US. "I took some shooting classes when I was younger. Listen, we need to get out there and figure out who is here. I need you to hide in the trees until I give you an all clear. Can you do that?"

He said the last statement a little more forcefully than he'd intended. Judging by the frown on Candace's face, it hadn't been well received. She grabbed a knife from the kitchen, stormed out of the cabin, and hid behind a tree. Wesley waited in tense silence for several heartbeats, watching as the plane glided across the water toward the dock.

A man and woman disembarked, and the woman marched toward the cabin. As she got closer, he saw her blond hair. *Anne!* What the hell was she doing here?

Wesley waited in shock as she made her way along the path toward the cabin. "What are you doing here, and how the hell did you find me?" he asked.

"Your pet sitter, Natalia, let me into the house. She was accommodating once I told her that I was your sister. I found some papers in your office in a file folder that mentioned a cabin you own. Would you please stop pointing that gun at me so we can go inside?" she asked, admirably calm for someone with a rifle aimed at her.

Wesley lowered his rifle and engaged the safety, then beckoned Candace to come out from hiding.

Candace gaped at Anne and brandished the knife in front of her. "You. What are you doing here?"

Anne stood with hands on her hips. "I'm his sister. I recognize you from the nursing home. Candace, right?"

Candace rounded on Anne. "What exactly were you doing in my uncle's room?"

Anne sniffed. "I was getting information about Wesley. I had to make sure that he was who I thought he was."

Anne's cheeks turned red, and her nostrils flared as she confronted Wesley. "I thought you weren't going to see Candace anymore."

His voice rose as the heat in his cheeks grew. "Listen. This will revolutionize medicine. Why keep it a secret?"

Anne looked at him, then at Candace. "I swore an oath. Let's not pretend you're seeing her because you want to revolutionize medicine. You want to make a bunch of money and get into her pants."

Wesley glared at Anne. "I won't have you talk about her that way. I want to share this with the world, but not to make money. I'm tired of watching my loved ones age and die. I also want a lot more from Candace than to get into her pants." He winced as he said those last words. They hadn't come out in the eloquent form he'd intended.

Candace folded her arms and narrowed her eyes. The knife she clenched in her hand accented the tone. "Is that all I am? A means to an end for you?"

Wesley shook his head. "No. That didn't come out how I wanted. I meant to say that I'd like to have a relationship with you. I enjoy spending time with you. The world feels like a better place with you in it, and I can't imagine my world without you."

Candace still looked hurt and angry, but her expression softened a little. "I don't understand what she's doing here. How does a sister you claim to have never met until recently show up at your remote cabin?"

Anne interrupted. "Listen, as much as I'd love to hear you two carry on and profess your feelings for one another, I'm here with urgent family news. Can we talk inside?"

Wesley opened the cabin door and motioned for Anne to enter.

Candace made for the door, but Anne said, "If you please, I'd like to have this discussion alone with him."

"I don't see why I can't be a party to this conversation. It's odd for you to show up like this, and how do I know that you don't mean Wesley any harm?"

"Look, we both know I'm not here to harm anyone. I need to talk with my brother. Alone. Please."

The two women stared each other down, with Anne's calm glare and

Candace's furious gaze, until Candace broke the stare and stormed away. She threw the knife to the ground, and it plunged into the earth and flopped back and forth a few times.

Now that Wesley had a chance to take a breath, he realized how crazy Anne must be. "I don't understand. Why the hell are you here?"

Anne invited herself into the dining room and sat down. "You have any whiskey?"

"Aye. You sure you wouldn't prefer some tea?"

"This is a whiskey conversation, brother, not a tea conversation."

He placed two glasses on the table and poured them both a measure. He sipped the drink slowly, feeling his belly warm. Anne wore nursing scrubs and looked like she hadn't slept for a while. She drank the whiskey and stared off into space as she did so. Wesley watched her in silence, waiting for her to speak as she continued to drink.

"Thank you. I needed that," Anne said at last. "A man named Morgan Thorsen called me to tell me that someone shot Grandda and kidnapped Grandma. He is looking for them now."

Wesley hardly remembered his grandparents but was still shocked at the news. "Shot? Is he okay?"

Anne shook her head slowly. "No. Mr. Thorsen told me that he watched them take Grandda Emmitt away in a body bag. I'm having a hard time believing he is dead."

Wesley tried to process the news and let it sink in. "I get the feeling it has something to do with the FBI agent that arrested Candace."

"Damn it, Wesley. I believe they've been spying on you for a while now. Is there anything you've done that would cause them to have an interest in you?"

"No. Everything I do is legal. I've too much at stake to jeopardize it by doing something stupid. I know you think me impulsive, but I'm not rash enough to ever do something that would make the FBI have an interest in me."

Anne regarded him. "Perhaps it isn't something you did. Maybe it is who you are. We need to see Da as soon as possible. He may have a better idea as to why there is such an interest in you. Though I'm not sure Da believes that you are still alive, he wants to meet you as soon as possible."

"We've evaded aging for years, Anne, and hidden it from the rest of society. Maybe someone figured it out. Perhaps I should never have said anything to Candace about it ... I'm sorry. I feel like this is my fault."

Anne finished the rest of her whiskey in a long draw, slammed the glass on the table, and stood up. "I don't know whose fault this is. All I know is that you better go to San Jose and visit Da now. We need your help."

She hugged him and left through the front door.

*

Wesley found himself dumbfounded by the sudden arrival of his sister and the news of his grandparents.

Candace rounded on him. "What in the hell was she doing here?"

Wesley summarized the details of their conversation.

Candace regarded him for a few uncomfortable moments before responding. "I'm sorry to hear about your grandparents. Listen, you should see your dad. I'll be fine. I still have a lot of research to do."

"Do you believe me?"

"Yes. Your sister looks a lot like you."

"She does, doesn't she?"

Wesley drew closer to her and held her hands in his. Part of her hair fell into her face, and he gently brushed the strands away and traced his fingers along her cheek.

Candace reached up to hold his hand. "Thank you for trying to make me feel better. We should pack."

Wesley took in a deep breath. "Is everything okay?"

Candace stared at the wall. "I feel like I should be doing more to save her."

Wesley frowned. "Who?"

"The digital me."

"What? She's merely a simulation of your brain. Not something real."

Candace shook her head. "You weren't there. She knows everything about me. She can *feel*, Wesley. She said they were torturing her. What is anyone but an amalgamation of their experience of sensory inputs?" She pursed her lips. "We need to find a way to save her. I felt a kinship to her—like a sister. Seeing your sister reminded me of her."

Wesley nodded. "Okay. We'll figure something out. I'll contact Gordon and see what we can do. There has to be some legal recourse available."

Candace gave a half smile and a nod that suggested she didn't believe that there would be any legal recourse.

*

They made their way home after several hours of flying.

Wesley directed his car to the university.

"Let's head to the Fremont neighborhood," Candace said.

"What's in Fremont?"

"My house."

"I thought you only took guys you were dating to your house."

She narrowed her eyes at him. "My mistake. You want to send me home in a self-driving taxi?"

"No, no. I can take you. I'm sure you must be exhausted. You've been through a lot."

They continued the drive and pulled up to a tall three-story house near the University District on Forty-Second Street. Wesley parked and carried her luggage onto a small porch. He leaned in to kiss Candace, but she hugged him instead.

"Are you sure you don't want me to come in?" he asked.

"I don't think that's a good idea right now. Good luck, Wesley."

Good luck? Was she interested in him or not? "Goodbye. If you don't hear from me, let's hope it doesn't mean the FBI has arrested me."

She raised her eyebrows. "Same."

He kissed her on the hand before getting in his car to make his way to the airport. She didn't seem to share his feelings of admiration. A shame—he found himself thinking about her the entire day.

Chapter 15

Nervous fingers tapped on the kitchen table as Candace waited for Trudy to arrive. She'd had grad students to her place before but usually to celebrate some milestone. Not one-on-one time. Trudy hadn't hesitated when Candace had asked her to come, hadn't even asked why. She narrowed her eyes. Why not? She'd have to ruminate on that later.

Thoughts of Wesley also distracted her. What had she been thinking, going with him to his cabin? Everything was moving too fast. She released a long-held breath. In truth, she had enjoyed the brief break, though it hadn't ended well, with the news of Wesley's grandparents. She liked him, but would he stick around after he got what he wanted? Was she only a distraction to him?

Now a new focus plagued her mind—the words of the woman at that strange facility. *We only have four months to finish everything. We don't have a lot of time.* The significance of the time frame hadn't hit her until a few moments earlier. Four months. The strange microorganism her grad student had found in her quantum spectral analysis had an outer coating that her models showed would break down over four months. The FBI had issued a cease-and-desist order for that research, and now she was barred from her lab.

An alert on her watch indicated Trudy was at the front door. Candace reviewed the camera first—Trudy was alone and didn't look overly distressed.

Good. A wave of Candace's finger caused the front door to open, and Trudy walked in.

Candace tried to put on her warmest smile. "Thanks for coming, Trudy. I'm sure you're wondering why I asked you here."

Trudy stared at her. Her cheeks reddened, and she gave a quick nod.

"Can you do me a favor and put your smartwatch and any other transmitting devices on the coffee table here?" She motioned toward the table in the center of the living room.

Trudy shrugged and placed the items on the table.

Candace led Trudy to a small guest room with no electronics in it. Was she being too paranoid?

No. The people harassing her had far too many resources at their disposal.

Trudy looked around when Candace motioned for her to sit in a chair. "Dr. Rosenbach? What's all this about?"

Candace gathered her thoughts. "You might know I've been barred from any research for the next two weeks. I'm not allowed to go anywhere near the lab."

Trudy nodded. "We all got a briefing from Dr. Hermann." She paused, her rosy cheeks reddening further. "I have to say I've never seen him that angry. I thought the veins were going to bulge out of his forehead."

A briefing? Wonder what he said. She tried for an air of nonchalance. "Oh?"

Trudy nodded quickly, then began a rapid discourse. "He said you couldn't come anywhere near campus and to contact him right away if you reached out to any of us—"

Candace drew in a quick breath. "Did you tell him I asked you to come here?"

She shook her head. "No, I didn't. I didn't tell anyone."

Relief filled Candace. "Good. What else?"

"He said we had to cease all work on the viral spectral-analysis project and destroy any data we had related to it. Any failure to do so would result in immediate expulsion and would subject us to civil and criminal penalties." She paused to catch her breath from talking so fast. "We asked why but didn't get any answers, other than we were obligated to do so under federal law."

Damn it. How would Candace get anything done? She tried to swallow but couldn't shake the sinking feeling in the pit of her stomach. She lowered her voice, though no one else was in the house. "Trudy, I need to ask you a favor. I wouldn't ask if I didn't think it extremely urgent. I need you to collect more samples and get the spectral analysis. We need to find a way to continue the research."

Trudy stared at the floor. What was she hiding? "I don't think we need to do that." She winced as she looked back up.

The heat rose in Candace's cheeks. What was Trudy doing? She paused, gathering as much calm as she could muster. "I know this is risky, but we stumbled onto something significant, and we need to find out what. I also don't think we have the luxury of time."

"I know. Listen, can I tell you something? In complete confidence?" Trudy waited until Candace nodded, then continued. "We realized we were doing something important if the government didn't want us to do it. I mean, they *arrested* you. We didn't hear anything about you for three days, and then we heard you were suspended. We knew something was up. That's when we decided to … well …"

Candace lost her patience. "To do what? What did you guys decide to do?"

"Okay, okay. Promise you won't be mad?"

Candace made a dismissive hand gesture. "No. Out with it. I won't be mad."

"You know those quantum-computer cloud resources we garnered a few months ago, where we do modeling in the public cloud with quantum encryption keys?" She continued after getting a quick nod from Candace. "Well, we uploaded all the data from the spectral-analysis experiment, along with the lab data you were working on in secret with Wesley."

Candace laughed. Their act of defiance and initiative had saved her weeks of research time. Ahad and his goons had deleted all her cloud data. "Oh, Trudy, I could kiss you right now."

Trudy looked around the guest bedroom, and her cheeks grew red again.

She cleared her throat. "So, you're not mad?"

Candace smiled, and for the first time after getting back from the trip, warmth filled her whole body. "No." She laughed again. "I'm not mad."

The tension left Trudy's shoulders. "Good. Then I'll tell you the second part. We used the cloud resources to do more quantum modeling of the data and emulated the impact of the corvid virus—"

Corvid? "Sorry. Come again? What do you mean?"

Trudy gave a nervous laugh. "Oh, I'm sorry. You know what a dark sense of humor John has. He said the virus, with its outer layer, was like a crow carrying something in its beak. A crow is a corvid, you know from the Corvidae family. He thought it was funny because it sounded like the old COVID-19 virus from the twenties."

Candace sighed. These students had been very young when that pandemic was happening. She found no humor in it. "Let's call it the Crow virus for now. I don't like the ring of calling it corvid."

Trudy nodded and looked away for a moment as her face flushed.

"What was the impact of this Crow virus in the quantum model?" Candace asked.

"We had to simulate the passage of time to model the breakdown of the outer layer. The inner layer—you're not going to believe this, Dr. Rosenbach."

Candace's body grew cold as she considered the implications. "Try me."

Trudy bit her lip. "The inner layer is a highly virulent species of virus, similar to Ebola in nature, but more deadly. The whole thing is fascinating—the outer shell replicates, with all the RNA from the inner virus intact. John said it was like a Trojan horse program on a computer."

Candace's breathing quickened for multiple reasons. One, this was new scientific ground, and the implications for microbiology and genetic engineering were enormous. Two, the danger to the world was dire. "Fascinating. Did you examine the outer shell from the various samples to determine the date of infection?"

Trudy beamed with pride, like a kid that had come home with a report card full of As. "Yes. We reviewed the intake questionnaires and did a great deal of quantitative correlation analysis. Everyone that has the virus received the most recent bundle vaccine. They show an infection time of two weeks. About ten percent of the subjects never received the bundle. They said they'd been too busy. All of them also had the Crow virus, but the age of the outer shell indicated they had only had the infection for a few days."

Candace gave a long whistle. She swallowed hard. "Oh my God."

Ahad's conversation made sense now. *We only have four months*, he'd said. Somehow Ahad had found a way to insert a new deadly virus into the bundle shot, one that infected the host without causing any symptoms for four months. The hosts then infected people who hadn't received the booster with the deadly virus, also without showing any signs of infection. Her disdain for the man grew. The bastard had used the bundle vaccine, the very thing that kept everyone from experiencing sickness, against the world.

"Listen, keep this to yourselves," Candace instructed. "You were never here. Don't do any more research, but give me access to your cloud data."

Trudy smiled, and her eyes twinkled. "I have your quantum key right here." She handed a small cube to Candace. "I forked the model, so you have your own copy of it now. You can do whatever tests or simulations you like. There might be a small problem, though."

Oh no. What now? "And what might that be?"

"Heh, well, the university might get a rather large bill from the public cloud providers."

Candace laughed, with some relief, though in truth part of her wanted to cry. "If anyone is still around in four months to chide us for running up the cloud compute bill, I'll count my blessings."

The color left Trudy's face, and her lip trembled a little. "What are we going to do?"

Candace stood. "For now, sit tight for a few days. If you don't hear from me by Saturday, get this information to the CDC, though I don't know if anyone will listen. I'm going to San Jose."

Chapter 16

Wesley stared at the slip of paper containing his father's address, which Anne had given him. His dad lived in the Silver Creek Valley area, in the southeastern section of San Jose—most assuredly an affluent area, and Wesley was glad to see that his father was doing well for himself. Wesley had flown down from Seattle right after dropping Candace off at her house.

He made his way to the rental agency and picked up his car, rushing onto Airport Parkway and then 101 south toward the Yerba Buena Road exit. Forty miles an hour felt too slow as his vehicle sped along the exit ramp and onto Yerba Buena, then Silver Creek Valley Road. Several opulent houses overlooked the greens of a beautiful country club.

He parked on the curb, walked to the door, and rang the doorbell. Only then did he realize the rashness of his behavior, and how shocked his father was going to be.

His dad appeared young and weathered at the same time. His fierce green eyes regarded Wesley with scrutiny, surveying him. Wesley noted the brown mark below his dad's right ear, a prominent birthmark he remembered well. "How may I help you?" he asked.

"Kyle O'Keefe, my name is Wesley O'Keefe. I thought I might come in and have a word or two. If I may." His dad regarded him with a scowl. He shook his head and began to close the door. Wesley slipped on his Irish brogue, something he didn't often do, except when the occasion called for it. "Da, I would blow me whistle, but I lost it in July of 1724, during the fire at Aunt Elizabeth's house. I trust Anne told you that I spoke with her today."

Tears welled up in his dad's eyes. Kyle pulled a necklace from under his shirt with a small metal whistle attached to it. That was the whistle his father had handed him before he'd left for the Colonies. The one that had snagged on the window catch on the way out of his aunt's burning house and fallen to the ground. His dad blew it, and a shrill note escaped. Wesley rushed forward to hug his dad.

"I came home, and Ma was gone, so I found a timber boat going to the Colonies. I meant to find you. Where did you go?"

"Wesley, your mother sent me a letter. 'Twas the worst thing I'd ever read, what happened to her. When she returned to her sister, or the ashes of her sister, and found you gone, it nearly destroyed her. She barely managed to get the words together for the letter. I found it a most gruesome way to find out I'd lost my son, but we had no other way to communicate. I rushed onto the first ship to Ireland. I paid handsomely for it, but there was little choice but to return as swiftly as I could. I didn't believe you were dead until I found the whistle I gave you among the ashes. I've worn it every day since that time." Kyle laid his hand on Wesley's shoulder, tears streaming down his face. He handed the whistle to Wesley.

Wesley put the whistle around his neck once again and cleared his throat. "And what of Ma? Why did she leave me as she did?"

His dad nodded. "That day, when you were out with your friend Patrick—" He looked away and grew silent. He narrowed his eyes, then continued. "Wesley, your ma was raped that day. She took you to your aunt so she could see one of the medicine women to prevent any seed from taking root in her womb." For a long time, he said nothing more. "When she arrived, the healer told her she was already with child."

Wesley didn't ask the question in his mind. Was Anne the daughter of a rapist? His dad had left maybe a month before the incident. No, she looked too much like their dad. He cleared his throat again and tried to swallow but found it hard with the lump in his throat. "I see."

They remained in silence with one another for a long time. Now more than the guilt of the fire bore down upon Wesley's conscience—now the burden of his mother's rape and subsequent death during childbirth weighed down his heavy heart. What if he had been there? No one would have raped her, and she wouldn't have died.

Wesley licked his dry lips. "How is it that I'm still alive? It can't be genetic. I watched my son grow old and die while I still lived. What is it? How am I still here?"

His father nodded. "Most people that received the gift had it explained to them beforehand. Your mother didn't follow protocol, but after what happened to her, I agree with what she did. She was worried that you would be taken ill with the plague. Aging is programmed into a person's cells. With each division, the telomeres shorten, and over time, they shorten to a point where the cell can no longer replicate. There are, however, many complex animals that don't age."

"Yes, I spoke with a woman named Dr. Candace Rosenbach about that the other day. Anne told me that she'd informed you of the research Dr. Rosenbach was doing with my cells."

"Yes, and I also understand the FBI arrested her. I want to speak to her as soon as I can. We must let her know not to release her findings prematurely."

They were too far past that point, but Wesley nodded anyway. "What were you saying about the gift, as you called it?"

"You are infected with a special sort of retrovirus. We refer to it as the Raven's Kiss."

"How is the retrovirus that I have special? And why don't other people have it?"

"I've done a lot of research over the last few decades on that subject. I started a company called Immunitrex. Have you heard of it?"

Of course. Who didn't know the company that had invented and provided the quarterly bundle shot to billions of people worldwide? But Wesley had never heard his dad's name mentioned in any of it. "Yes. I didn't realize that it was your company."

Kyle smiled. "Let's say that I created it through a few proxies." He took in a long breath. "A virus first has to get into a cell. The human immune system is already immune to the virus that you have. The immune system already recognizes the retrovirus as an attacker and does the normal things the immune system would do to prevent it from entering the cells. Although we didn't understand why at the time, we were giving the people that we wanted to receive the virus a special tea made from yew bark and the blood of someone that already had the virus. Yew bark acts as a natural immunosuppressant. It's also a poison, so we had to get the dosage correct. The virus can't enter a cell to infect it without something suppressing the immune system. Does that make sense so far?"

Old Celtic folklore praised the yew tree as a symbol of immortality. "Yes, it does. The yew bark weakened the immune system long enough for this special retrovirus to enter the cells. What happens after that?"

"Next, the virus inserts its genome. Typically, the genome contains the genes necessary to transcribe and translate to create another virus. In the case of the special type of retrovirus that we have, that our ancestors called the Raven's Kiss, it also confers genes that are beneficial to the host. These useful genes are the ones that are responsible for repairing the telomeres and preventing them from shortening, as well as creating the enzymes that boost the immune system."

Wesley shook his head. A helpful virus? "So the virus has an extra payload of beneficial genes? How did that happen?"

Kyle frowned. "That is something I am currently researching. I haven't come up with any theories that aren't completely crazy. It seems there must have been some unique environmental pressure to have such a virus evolve. In a way, it is a symbiotic relationship. The virus extends its host's life, and in turn, the host lives indefinitely until they are killed. Consider the virus as a genetic engineer that rewrites the genes that cause aging and makes new genes that boost the immune system and further protect against aging."

Wesley had heard of beneficial bacteria, like those in the gut, but never a helpful virus. "Is this the only virus that provides benefit?"

"Oh, no. There are plenty of examples in nature of viral symbiosis." Kyle explained many examples of viruses that helped plants and how viruses likely shaped the evolution of mammals.

Wesley finally interrupted his dad. What didn't make sense was how the Druids had known long ago how to infect people. "How did you figure this out so many hundreds of years ago?"

Kyle smiled. "We didn't. We thought we were doing magic. You may know that in Celtic religion, slips of yew bark were cut at the eclipse of the moon and used to convey powers of healing and to preserve a dead body for everlasting life. Do you know why many English churches have yew trees planted in front of them?"

Old folklore came to mind, though Wesley didn't know what was relevant. "I suppose they were there already."

His dad nodded. "Yes. The Druids planted them long ago, and the English kept them when they invaded. The yew became a symbol in every graveyard." He gave Wesley a wistful smile that didn't touch his eyes. "Your grandfather did lots of experimenting before finding a method that worked consistently. The Druids would create a mixture, primarily consisting of yew bark, to suppress the immune response. The poison made it risky, and we had to do it in a way that ensured success. The ancient Druids referred to it as the Raven's Kiss because the raven was a symbol of rebirth and regeneration. We later referred to ourselves as 'the Children of the Yew.' We agreed to keep our longevity a secret."

"Then how did I get it? I don't recall anyone weakening my immune system …" Wesley's voice trailed off as he recalled the night that his mother had given him a vial of burning liquid, followed by strange dreams and fever.

How different might his choices in life have been if he'd known all of this? What if he'd given his wife, Samantha, the virus, so she hadn't aged? Knowing this could be shared with anyone was hard to hear. What of his son? Why couldn't Wesley have known this when he had been married, in 1734? Questions reeled through his head. Heat rose in his cheeks. "Why haven't we shared this with the world? All the people I've lost would have been alive now."

Kyle stared off into the distance for a long time before he replied. "Mayhap. Age isn't the only arrow in Arawn's quiver." A hint of tears formed in his eyes as he stared out again. "Your grandfather said we had to keep the group small. He claimed powerful people would stop us if we tried to share it. And now he is gone."

Wesley tried to swallow past the lump in his throat. "Anne told me. Who did it?"

Kyle braced himself against a chair with an agonized look on his face. "I'm sorry. I've been in denial this whole time. I didn't believe the news." He reeled, clutching the chair, and his knuckles turned white as he gripped it. "I don't know, and I've lots of questions for you, and perhaps some answers for you as well, but for now, we need to get out of here."

"Get out of where?" someone said from the doorway. Wesley turned to see a tall man with olive skin and piercing green eyes brandishing a pistol. Several men in flak jackets stood behind him. They wore caps and jackets that displayed *FBI* in large white letters. "Kyle O'Keefe?" he said, with the corners of his lips turned into a snarling smile.

Kyle puffed out his chest and stood tall. "You know who I am."

"I'm Special Agent Ahad Atenoud, head of the regional Anti-Terrorism Task Force. I have a few questions for the two of you."

"Am I under arrest? If so, I'd like you to address all your questions to my lawyer. What's the charge?" Kyle had an air of calm, but the pale color of his face betrayed how nervous he must have been.

"The charges"—Ahad emphasized the plurality of the word as he said it—"are as follows: income tax evasion, identity theft, falsifying passports, embezzlement, bioterrorism, and insider trading."

Wesley pressed his watch to call Gordon. As he touched the call button, an agent snatched the device and, in a swift motion, pushed him to the floor and handcuffed him, knocking over a chair in the living room as he did so.

A sadistic grin played upon Ahad's face. "Oh, and one more thing. You're being charged with bioterrorism and plotting to overthrow the US government. Since you're now considered terrorists and enemies of the state, you won't reach out to any lawyers. You'll only be talking to me." He paused. "You may not enjoy the talk, but I'm certain I'll enjoy it very much."

Nausea rose within Wesley as the bleakness of his situation became more apparent. He looked at his dad for reassurance. Kyle's expression of dread did little to provide Wesley with a reprieve. He wasn't sure what shocked him most—that his dad, whom he hadn't seen in three centuries, was alive and standing next to him, or that he was now under arrest by the FBI.

Agents shoved Wesley and his father into the back of a black sedan with government plates and tinted windows. The vehicle sped away.

Kyle whispered to him, "This can't possibly be a coincidence, and I can't believe that the Constitution or any other established right will apply to us, though exercising our right to remain silent may be the wisest course to follow."

Silence consumed Wesley. He had little he would like to say.

Chapter 17

After not hearing from her dad and Wesley for several hours, Anne took a flight to San Jose. She drummed her fingers on her seat arm as she waited for her turn to get up. When would the passengers in front of her move? With a fist clenching her carry-on bag, she felt relief fill her when she left the plane, and at last she hopped into the rental car.

Thirty minutes later, she arrived at her dad's house, punched in the entry code, and didn't find anyone inside. A tipped-over chair in the living room caught her attention. Her dad's car remained in the garage. Wherever he was, he hadn't taken it with him.

Anne struggled to keep her emotions in check. She needed to stay calm if she was to help this situation.

She turned on her dad's computer in the living room and stood in front of the camera. The facial-recognition software allowed her to log on—nothing in the browser history file, and nothing about any directions or maps.

The blinds on the house across the street were open. She walked out of her father's house and knocked on the neighbor's door.

A woman answered, short with thick glasses and a simple dress.

Anne tried her friendliest voice. "Hello, Mrs. Kensington. How've you been?"

Mrs. Kensington scowled up at Anne. She stood for a bit, staring, until recognition dawned on her face. "Well, hello, young lady. It's been a while since I saw you. No Girl Scout cookies for me this time, I see." She cackled and wiped some spittle from her mouth with her leathery hand. She spoke with a London accent, softened by several decades of living in California.

Anne bit her lip, as it seemed that Mrs. Kensington was having some memory problems. Anne had never given her Girl Scout cookies.

She cackled again. "Oh, I'm kidding, Anne. I recognized you. Come on in and sit down, and I will brew you a cup of tea." She hobbled forward and gave Anne a big hug, then shuffled off to the kitchen.

Anne sat on the sofa in the sitting room, waiting for her host to return. "Can I help you out at all, Mrs. Kensington?"

"No, dear. I'm fine. Please relax. How many lumps of sugar?"

"None, thank you. I'm watching my figure."

"I haven't heard that expression in years, dear. Mr. Kensington used to like to watch my figure. Now he only cares about golf."

Mrs. Kensington came in holding two cups of tea and sat across from her in a small armchair, setting the two cups on the coffee table. She smiled warmly as she took her cup and motioned for Anne to take hers.

Anne tried to keep her anxiety under control and not act too worried—Mrs. Kensington had always been one for formalities. Anne smiled and said, "It seems you've had nice weather here lately."

One couldn't start a proper conversation with an Englishwoman without first discussing the weather, as Anne well knew, and Mrs. Kensington seemed happy that Anne was playing along. "Why, yes, it has been wonderful. Mr. Kensington is out playing golf again today, though I'm sure he'll find a way to blame the wind for his game. Golf seems like a clever excuse for a long walk, if you ask me." She laughed, a much softer laugh than the unpleasant cackle she'd produced earlier, likely because she was annoyed by her husband's golf habit. "Are you house-sitting for your father?"

"I came down from Seattle. Why do you ask if I'm house-sitting?"

"I noticed a few men in suits arrive in a long black car with tinted windows. Your father and some other man got into the car with them and left. The other man left his car parked in front of your dad's house. I assumed they were going on a fancy vacation."

Anne hoped Mrs. Kensington didn't notice the frown that crossed her face. She tried to smile, but the tightness of her lips must have made it look fake, so she told the truth. "To be honest, he didn't tell me where he was going, but I did come down to make sure everything was going well. Have you noticed anyone trying to break in or anything?"

Mrs. Kensington shook her head. "There haven't been any prowlers. It's a safe neighborhood. You needn't worry."

They chatted idly for another ten minutes. Not much had happened with Mrs. Kensington since they had last talked. She had lost a cat but gained another one. Her husband had gout. Her husband played golf too often. They needed a vacation. She had found a lovely new hairdresser, but she charged far too much.

Anne excused herself and hurried across the street. She left her phone on the computer desk, went into the garage, and got into her dad's car. She pulled a smartphone from the glove compartment and opened it, searching through the contacts for Valerie Lundstrom.

She dialed the number, and someone answered.

"Hello?"

"Yes, is this Special Agent Valerie Lundstrom with the FBI Office of Professional Responsibility?"

"Speaking. This doesn't sound like Kyle. Who is this?"

"I'm Kyle's daughter, Anne O'Keefe. Listen, can you get over here to my dad's place right away? It's urgent."

"Of course. I owe your father a few favors. I'm in Oakland, so I'll be there in an hour," she said.

Anne thanked her and disconnected the call.

She paced the room, wondering where Wesley and her dad could be.

A message popped up on her smartwatch: *Please call Sunset Towers regarding resident family member issue. Urgent.*

What did they possibly need? She worked per diem. Why would any family member need to talk to her? She called.

"Sorry to bother you. A woman named Candace Rosenbach keeps calling. She says she needs you to call her about an issue with her uncle, Mr. Jonathan

Moore. He passed recently. She said you were the only person that could help her."

Anne balled her fists. Not good timing for whatever this woman wanted. "I'm familiar with the case and the resident. Thank you. Did she leave a number?"

"Yes. I've sent it to you. Sorry to bother you during your time off, but she's called us at least fifty times. We weren't sure if we should get an anti-harassment order or call you. I hope we did the right thing."

Anne sighed. "Yes, I think you did. Have a good day." She disconnected and dialed the number.

Candace answered. "Anne? I need to talk to you as soon as possible. I'm in San Jose. Where can we meet?"

Anne bit her lip. "I'm right in the middle of an urgent matter. Can it wait?"

Quiet on the other end of the line. "I can't reach your brother. Is he okay?"

Anne wasn't sure how much she should say over the phone. "I'm not sure. I haven't seen him or my dad. Is that why you called?"

Hesitation on the other end. "No. There is something important I need to discuss with you, but not on the phone. A matter of extreme urgency." She paused. "A matter of life and death—for a lot of people."

Candace wasn't making much sense. What sort of person was her brother dating? "I'll send you my dad's address."

Anne hung up. She held her face in her hands as she considered how her life was spiraling out of control.

*

Anne's stomach grumbled. She'd ordered teriyaki from a local restaurant and opted to pick it up herself rather than have it delivered, because she needed to clear her head. When she entered the restaurant, a camera recognized her, and a green light flashed before a door opened with her food in a small paper bag. The smells of grilled chicken and soy sauce greeted her. The pain in her stomach grew as the scents overpowered her other senses. She ate a few bites in the car before she placed the tray on the seat beside her. Her hands trembled, and she was grateful that the car drove itself.

Anne returned with her food and came back through the garage. She headed toward the front door.

"Hands up and don't move," said the voice of a man behind her.

The hairs on the back of Anne's neck stood on end as she raised her hands and stole a glance back to get a glimpse of a balding, red-haired, middle-aged man with glasses, wearing a brown sports jacket.

"Keep your eyes forward."

Anne tried to stay calm but failed. "Where is my dad?"

"How should I know where he is?" said the man as he walked in front of her, brandishing his small pistol. "The less you know, the better it'll be for you, Anne. Got that?"

She gave him a cold stare. "Yes."

"It turns out I'm in a talkative mood, so I'll tell you where your dad and your brother are. The FBI is holding them as terrorists. How does that sound?"

She hadn't mentioned a brother. Whoever he was, he knew that Wesley was her brother, something she hadn't told anyone. Anne snorted. "You're not with the FBI. If you were, you'd be wearing a suit. You'd have shown me your badge. How did you know my name?"

He nodded. "Let's say that I've been following you for a while. You're correct, Anne. I'm not with the FBI. Call me a freelance agent, doing some contract work for them. Either way, you're going to come with me."

Anne looked out the window toward the driveway and said, "Who's that pulling up in the black sedan? Your friends at the FBI?"

The man held the weapon in front of him with his right hand, facing Anne as he turned to look out the window. Anne swept her left arm in an arc toward the pistol, causing it to fly from his hands and onto the floor. She followed with a knee to his groin and came down hard with a blow to his neck as he doubled over from the pain. He fell forward, and Anne placed a knee on his lower spine and snatched the pistol from the floor. She smacked him on the back of the head hard enough that he fell unconscious.

Anne rushed off to find some rope but only found duct tape. She shrugged and ran back into the room and bound his legs and arms with it. She looped the tape around and around, not worrying about how tight it would be.

Children of the Yew

Soon she'd completely encased the man in duct tape, with his mouth covered and his legs bound together, bowed upward and taped to his hands. She dragged him into the garage. She retrieved the pistol and noted that it was a 9 mm Beretta—a fine choice.

The man started to stir and tried to struggle free, but she'd done an excellent job securing him. She shouted down at him as she poked the pistol in his face. "I want to know who you are and why you're involved with the FBI, and why they have my dad in custody." She fired a round into the ceiling to emphasize her point.

He made some noises, and Anne ripped a piece of tape off his mouth so he could speak, not worrying if it hurt.

"My name is Jake Rivers. I'm supposed to bring you to the FBI. I don't know anything beyond that."

"You're lying. Why would the FBI want me in their custody? And why wouldn't they send their agents?"

Jake shrugged. "I'm not sure. Maybe they were too busy."

Anne grew weary talking to him and secured another piece of duct tape to his mouth. She then stepped back and trained the Beretta on him. "Don't move, or my finger might slip." She searched his pockets and found the chip for his car.

Anne walked outside and clicked the key fob. A distant beep sounded, and she walked toward the noise until she reached a gold BMW, older but still in decent shape. He must have parked the car away from the house to avoid anyone seeing it there. A quick search through the glove compartment revealed a digital recorder and a small device with antennae and headphones attached. In the trunk, she found a large duffel bag that contained a laptop, a few pairs of handcuffs, boxes of 9 mm ammunition, and several paper notebooks.

Anne returned to the garage with the device and the duffel bag, setting them on the table. She read through the materials, pausing every so often to eye Jake on the floor. She would grab the pistol and point it in his direction on occasion to remind him she still had it and knew how to use it.

"Interesting reading material I've found here. Let's see. Where do I start?

Yes, you were supposed to do industrial espionage on Immunitrex, which is where my dad works, by the way. Oh, look at that. Here's some account your boss, someone named Ahad Atenoud, is supposed to wire money to." Anne gave Jake a wan smile. "You better get comfortable, because you're going to be here for a while. I have a friend coming who will want to talk with you."

She walked out of the garage, leaving Jake inside.

*

Anne watched in anticipation as Candace exited the car in the driveway.

Anne opened the door and listened as Candace launched into an explanation of a virus that had already infected a large percentage of the world's population—one that threatened to kill over ninety percent of humanity in less than four months.

When she finished, Anne poured two whiskeys, not even caring if Candace would drink. She handed her one, then took a swig from her own. The warm rush of the alcohol heated her stomach. She stared at Candace. "I thought you were going to tell me a load of bollocks about how much you loved my brother or some such nonsense. Not this."

Candace drank the whiskey down. "I'm not sure how I feel about your brother yet. But I'm sure about this."

Anne laughed at Candace's remark. Maybe she'd like this woman after all. The full realization of what Candace had said hit her like a kick to the chest from a horse. *Ninety percent of humanity?*

Chapter 18

Jake remained on the garage floor in the O'Keefe house, wondering how he'd failed so miserably. Duct tape covered him from head to toe. Several times he tried to loosen its grip, to no avail. She must have used the entire roll on him. He imagined himself a silvery mummy lying on the floor, waiting for his sarcophagus. Despite how uncomfortable he was and how miserable the situation, Jake managed a chuckle at that idea. His laugh reverberated around the garage.

He'd overheard the conversation between Candace and Anne with his ear against the door. If it was true, what they had said about the deadly virus, he couldn't let Ahad get away with it. He had to save Zach. However, if so many people were already infected …

Candace had to be lying. Ahad wasn't the type of person to release a virus that would wipe out the population.

Jake could still get out of this mess. Anne would free him, and he would find a way to get her to Ahad. No, he had to get out of here now. Ahad wouldn't settle for tardiness.

Should he take Anne to Ahad? Wesley hadn't known Jake existed, so why should Jake continue to harbor anger for him? Ahad had his own vendetta against the O'Keefe family, so what would he do to Jake once he finished with them? He shuddered.

He rolled on the floor and bumped into the jagged corner of a small metal toolbox. He then sawed at the tape that bound his legs and hands together. A piece of metal punctured his skin and forced him to stifle a cry of pain. He continued moving back and forth, and after an eternity, his hands and feet were free.

He unwrapped himself and stood.

"Hands in the air. Special Agent Valerie Lundstrom, FBI," she said. The click of a gun hammer accented the command.

Jake slowly turned around to see an FBI agent standing with a pistol pointed at him. "Are you really with the FBI? How do I know this isn't Anne playing a trick?"

"I understand you've been working with Special Agent Ahad Atenoud. I just looked into your bank records and found that he's been paying you—for example, the ten thousand nine hundred and twenty-four dollars he deposited last week into your bank account."

The warmth left Jake's cheeks. He tried to stop his eye from twitching, but the unbidden spasms continued.

"I can offer you immunity in exchange for your cooperation, and you can help us stop Ahad from making a terrible mistake."

It seemed the game was up. He could find a way to Mexico and try to stay under the radar for a while, but he'd be doing so with no assets, as the FBI would freeze everything. He thought of his son, Zach. He couldn't abandon Zach like his own father, Wesley, had dumped him. "Listen. I need you to keep my son safe. He lives with my ex-wife. I need to ensure he'll be protected."

Lundstrom nodded. "We'll keep him safe. I'll make sure he and your ex go into protection right away."

Jake thought about Zach wondering where his dad was every day while he rotted in prison. "I need to ensure my immunity. I want a signed document absolving me of any charges in exchange for my cooperation. I need to be protected near my son and my ex."

Valerie held her chin high in the air. After a few moments, she nodded. "Agreed."

He nodded and closed his eyes. "Okay. What do you need from me?"

"I need you to follow me into the living room, sit down, and listen for a while. Can you do that, Mr. Rivers?"

Jake nodded and followed her to the living room, where Anne was standing off to the side. Candace Rosenbach stood near her. What was she doing here?

Jake found a seat. A few pieces of duct tape crunched into his rear as he did so. "Should I go ahead and call my lawyer before we start?"

Anne glared at him, and Valerie shook her head. "No need to call a lawyer yet. I want your assistance in apprehending Ahad for his crimes. I'm going to need you to take Anne to him and wear a wire."

A ringing filled Jake's ears, and a knot formed in his stomach. No way would he double-cross Ahad and live to tell anyone about it. "Are you kidding me? Do you know how powerful that man is? He has a lot of friends in a lot of places. You can't begin to understand what a horrible idea that is."

Valerie pursed her lips. "Are you aware that Ahad has apprehended individuals without probable cause?"

"No, he must have had cause."

"We suspect that Ahad has violated several laws that will justify his arrest. I need you to wear a wire, so we can catch him in the act and apprehend him."

Jake's stomach roiled at the thought of crossing Ahad, but he had little choice if he wanted to see his son grow up. "What do you need?"

Candace launched into an explanation of the virus she'd found and how she believed Ahad planned to use the virus to wipe out most of the human population. He thought back to watching Ahad invade Candace's lab with the nanobugs he'd planted. What was it Ahad had said? *I've devised a much better plan for humanity.* Everything clicked. A wave of nausea overcame Jake, and his face grew cold and clammy. He had chosen the wrong side.

He turned to Valerie. "Why don't you pretend to be Anne, and you wear the wire? After this, I can get busy disappearing into the witness protection program right away."

Valerie nodded. "I understand you've been spying on Ms. O'Keefe for some time now, so I'm sure Ahad knows what she looks like."

"I can change your appearance. My disguise kit will fool facial-recognition software. You two have similar facial structures and appearances already, so it won't take too much work. This will take about an hour, but it should be convincing."

The three of them talked over the plans. They would deliver the fake Anne—Special Agent Lundstrom—to Ahad, get him to confess his sins, and arrest him. That would be that. Jake got the uneasy feeling that he wasn't going to fool Ahad, since he'd been around the block more than a few times.

Jake spent the next hour applying makeup and contouring Valerie's face. As far as he knew, Ahad had only seen photos of Anne. Jake had learned some disguise techniques as a private investigator, and new waxes that could stick to and shape the face made the look more realistic. He continued working until his phone app identified Valerie as Anne.

Candace gasped when she saw Valerie. "Wow. That would fool me. The resemblance is uncanny. How did you learn to do that?"

Jake shrugged, though he was proud of his work. "Tricks of the trade. The app that comes with the disguise kit helps too." She really did resemble Anne. "You should change into her clothes too," he said to Valerie. "Sorry, but your outfit looks a little too FBI."

They agreed, and Anne gave Valerie some clothes from her suitcase. Valerie returned wearing the clothes, and now Jake would be hard-pressed to distinguish the two. They might be able to pull this off after all. The outfit and the makeup kit made everything very convincing. He breathed out a sigh of relief.

"Are you ready, Mr. Rivers?" Valerie asked.

"Ready as I'll ever be. Hey, listen, there's something I want to say to you, Anne, before I leave. We probably won't see each other anytime soon. I took a paternity test and determined that Wesley is my father. I never talked to him about it, and I'd like you to tell him I'm sorry that I let him down. I no longer believe that Ahad is the person I thought he was. I had a lot of anger toward Wesley for leaving my mom to raise me by herself, and I guess I acted out. I got to thinking while I was in the garage, and I realized that Wesley doesn't know that he has a son, so I shouldn't be so angry about it."

Anne rubbed her chin. "What was your mom's name?"

He sniffed. "Beth."

Anne narrowed her eyes. "Beth Norbeck?"

He nodded.

"So it was you that sent Wesley the photos? To what end?"

Anger welled up within Jake, and he balled his fists. "I wanted him to think about the woman he'd abandoned. He didn't even bother to find out she'd had a son. I'd hoped he would have."

Candace stared at him with her mouth agape, too stunned to say anything.

Anne looked at him in utter shock. "Are you trying to tell me that you tried to take your aunt, me, into custody to deliver to that bloody monster? What the hell is wrong with you?"

"I hope that I can make some amends for what I've done by bringing Ahad to justice."

"You're not the only one who's angry at him, trust me. I'm angry too, but delivering him, and me for that matter, into the hands of that monster … well, that's not easy to forgive. I do hope you can help turn this mess around. We'll talk again when this is over someday. May God help you, Jake."

Jake pulled at his collar. She wasn't wrong, and he wasn't going to deny it. "I'm sorry" was all he managed to squeak out before they left.

To keep up appearances, Valerie was handcuffed and blindfolded. Jake stuffed her into the back seat of his BMW, then drove away. Maybe he should leave for Mexico instead—that would be preferable to crossing Ahad. He could easily be in Tijuana in seven hours. Valerie wore a wire, though, and that meant someone would follow them. Jake spied a black sedan a few cars behind him, and another one in front of him. Yes, he was being followed and escorted by FBI agents, so even the notion of escaping to a foreign country was dispelled before it could take root. He couldn't leave Zach behind either. *Damn it.*

Chapter 19

Sleep wouldn't come. Wesley stared at the stark walls of his prison cell. Every time he drifted off, an anxious feeling would rise and force him to open his eyes. The cold permeated his bones, and a shiver ran up his spine as the severity of his situation became more evident. Wesley squeezed his pillow and flung it against the wall. He clenched his jaw a few times and stuck his head in his hands.

How was Candace doing? If only he had a chance to speak with her. He sincerely hoped she fared better than he.

Was the sitter taking good care of Hunter? He'd give anything to be at home playing a ditty on the piano for that mangy old cat.

The cell's bare walls loomed ominously, slabs of gray and lifeless concrete, cold like his bones. Could he escape? It was doubtful that he'd have any impact on the large steel door. Despair seeped in as he slumped onto the bed.

If only he could call Jake to help him. He'd always been there to help when Wesley needed it, and right now, he sorely missed him. Would he have the funds to afford an assistant after this? If the FBI marked him as a terrorist, they'd seize his assets and freeze his accounts. The burden of proof was on him, and it would be some time before he'd get the chance to defend himself in court.

He wanted to use the bed frame to break the wall, but heavy bolts held it securely to the floor. He might as well be a rat in a cage, with no hope of chewing his way out.

Wesley started doing push-ups. There wasn't much else to do in jail. After the second push-up, he decided there were lots of better things to do, like lying in bed while he contemplated how screwed he was.

Just as he finally managed to slip into a slumber, the door opened.

Ahad entered the room. "Wesley, I trust you are finding your accommodations satisfactory." He smiled with one side of his mouth and raised his eyebrows.

"I didn't get my complimentary water bottle, but other than that, I've found my accommodations to be quite lovely, thank you."

"We apologize for not bringing the water bottle. I'll get you a voucher for a free continental breakfast." Ahad steepled his hands and waited for Wesley's response.

Ahad was well dressed and held himself with a regal air. Wesley couldn't place his age. He didn't have wrinkles per se, but his skin had weathered like that of someone who spent a lot of time at the tanning salon.

"Instead of feeding me, I was wondering if you'd arrange to have someone feed my cat."

"Oh, you mean Hunter. Yes, of course. Jake mentioned what a lovely creature he was. Have you ever thought that perhaps cats are the more intelligent species? I mean, we do all the work, and they sit at home and wait for us to feed and entertain them."

It took a moment for the weight of what Ahad had said to sink in. Wesley's face must have blanched at that moment, for he lost any hope of respite from his plight. He tried to calm his voice and hide his shock. "You know Jake?"

"Ah yes, one of my best employees, and the funny thing is, he isn't even on my payroll. Not officially, anyway."

His smug smile made Wesley want to punch him, but he knew this would only make things worse. If what he said was true, all his business operations, his livelihood, and everything else were at risk. He tried to sound nonchalant as he replied. "Is that so? I'd have to agree. Jake's one of my best—although

I can't abide moonlighting, so I'm not sure how much longer he'll remain in my employ."

"It must have been difficult, living for so long without knowing anyone else that did so."

Wesley tried to suppress his surprise, but he couldn't stop his eyes from widening. He needed to work on his poker face. "What do you mean?"

"Well, by my estimation, you're well over three hundred years old. As far as I can tell, you had no idea why or how you have lived so long, while everyone you were with aged and died."

Wesley shook his head. "I've no idea what you're talking about."

"There's no need to play coy with me. I know the truth about you. I've been following you for a long time, as well as the others. I know most of the tricks. I've been alive for longer than most of you have."

This revelation surprised him. Who was this man, and why was he detaining him and his dad in cells as wanted terrorists? The possibilities were grim. "How's that possible? Are you one of the old Druids that called themselves the Children of the Yew?"

Ahad smirked and snorted. "Hardly. No, the 'Druids,' as they called themselves, were thieves who stole the technology from my people. The goddess Neith blessed us and bestowed her gifts upon us. We referred to this as Bot Akh. Your 'Druids' called this the Raven's Kiss, due to some mythology about the raven being the symbol of reincarnation. Bot Akh was vital to the Khemenu—it allowed us to live with the blessings of Neith without aging."

"Come again? The Khemenu?"

"It's what we called ourselves. Named after the original gods of Egypt."

Wesley raised his eyebrows. "That's incredible. So how many of you are there, and how old are you?"

"There are only eight of us, four men and four women. I am a little over a thousand years old. I was there before the barbarians came in and took over what you now call Egypt."

"Why bother with us? You must have better things to do than mess with a few people who reaped the benefits of your Bot Akh, don't you?"

A slow smile played across Ahad's face. "A promise I made long ago. I believe in keeping my word. The full story of it might be better for another day."

"I've nothing better to do right now. Tell it to me," Wesley said as he stared at Ahad and waited.

Ahad considered, then shrugged his shoulders. He collected his thoughts and then spoke. "Very well. The year was AD 1231. By this time, I was three hundred and thirty-one years old. I was given a creature known as an Akh Neith in AD 920. We only knew of eight of these creatures in existence, all of which were male. All the females were extinct by then, so the eight males that were still alive were very precious. Have you seen the Egyptian scarabs, with six legs?"

The image of a golden beetle with a ruby head came into Wesley's mind. "Yes. Is that what this Akh Neith looks like?"

"Yes, though an Akh Neith is about the size of a tick. A tick begins its life with six legs, but once it draws blood and matures, it grows two more, for a total of eight. None alive today know the significance of the scarab paintings, save for the other members of the Khemenu."

The thought of a tick-like creature crawling into his skin made Wesley shiver.

"An Akh Neith burrows into the skin and lives there in perpetuity, feeding off the blood of the host—"

Wesley interrupted him. "Is that what prevents you from aging?"

He nodded. "Yes. Your grandfather Emmitt stole it from me." Ahad stared off into the distance and frowned. "Would you like to know the story? If you aren't too busy, of course."

Wesley despised Ahad, but he had a magnetic quality to his voice that drew him in. Curiosity bested his misgivings, and Wesley nodded for him to continue.

"He betrayed his family."

Wesley folded his arms in front of him. "Why do you say 'his family'?"

A slow smile crossed Ahad's face but didn't touch his eyes. Emerald eyes, piercing and knowing, much like Wesley's father's eyes. "We'll get to that.

Shall I go on?"

Wesley's skin tingled with discomfort. What did he mean? He pursed his lips and nodded his acquiescence.

"On the day it happened, the warm, earthy smell of myrrh and the sweet, nutty smell of cardamom permeated the small temple. The priests prepared the room for Nenet's ceremony. Nenet's ancient relative Onofria had died from being attacked by Christian Crusaders. She was to receive Bot Akh that day, and we were to transfer the creature from Onofria's body to Nenet. I treasured Nenet as my eldest niece and knew of no one more deserving of receiving the gift we were to bestow upon her." Anger crossed Ahad's face as he stared off into the distance again. He balled his fists and released them a few times before continuing.

"We gathered in the temple, with myself and the other six members of the Khemenu in attendance. As the youngest among them, I was to cut open Onofria's shoulder and coax the Akh Neith out to place it upon Nenet. A man was lying on the rafters above us, watching us, though we did not know it at the time. I cut open her shoulder and watched the blood flow from it, and then the creature began to wiggle its way out. As it crawled toward me, I felt a calm peace and tranquility that was all-consuming." A strange smile full of rapture crossed his face, and he breathed in a few times before he returned to normal.

"I heard pounding at the door. The guards had been instructed not to let anyone enter. The pounding grew louder, and I was broken from my trance and ran with the others toward the door. At that moment, the man dropped down from the rafters. We opened the doors and screamed for the guards. As I surveyed the scene, I saw men in strange robes rushing down the hallway, men with white skin and reddish hair, bearing simple wooden staffs."

Ahad's face contorted in disgust for a few moments. "I still remember their smell. The barbarians must not have bathed the entire journey. Their pink skin reminded me of a pig's, though I would have found those creatures less foul." He shook his head in a quick motion, like someone shaking away the taste of sour lemon.

147

"They killed a number of the guards, and new guards ran up to destroy them. We were all busy surveying the battle results, and when I turned around to check on Nenet, a man with blond hair, dressed in a cloak similar to those of the others, ran toward me. I moved to intercept him, but he was too nimble. He dodged me and rolled to the floor. He yelled something in a language I'd never heard, which might have been Irish. We pursued the man, your grandfather Emmitt, but he managed to escape. I don't know how he made it out of our kingdom, but we never saw him again. I vowed to the others that I would find him and retrieve the Akh Neith."

Ahad balled his fists again a few more times before speaking. "I had to watch my niece Nenet grow old and die. He stole her chance at agelessness." He stood in silence for some time before he let out a long-held breath.

"There are no more than eight Akh Neith creatures in existence. The species has been otherwise extinct for over a millennium. I failed Nenet, but I did not fail my vow," he said with a self-satisfied grin.

The implications hit Wesley like a blow to the chest. Ahad meant that he was responsible for Emmitt's death. "What did you do with the creature and with my grandfather?"

Ahad rested his chin in his hand and stared at Wesley with those piercing green eyes. A long, considering pause, as though he was making a decision. "I haven't determined the final fate of your grandfather." He took in a long breath through his nose. "He lives. For now."

Wesley covered his mouth with his hands. Tension in his shoulders released for a brief moment. He let that subject drop, as he suspected no details would be forthcoming. Another issue nagged at him. "How did Emmitt know to go to Egypt? That's a long way for Druids from Ireland to travel."

"Yes. Another long story, but I will tell you a condensed version. Have you heard of the Lia Fáil?"

The name sounded familiar. "I don't recall the specifics. I've heard the name."

Ahad nodded. "It is the Stone of Destiny, a large stone, once surrounded by great monuments, which have long since crumbled to dust. Some in Ireland believe a divine race known as the Tuatha Dé Danann built the Lia Fáil. The truth is that our people once spanned the globe, creating monuments. My paternal line stems from my ancestors that once settled there, as does yours." He paused to glance at Wesley. "They were attacked and destroyed by barbarians, but not before my ancient grandfather returned to Egypt."

"How did my grandfather come to know this? What does this have to do with him?"

"Patience. I am getting to that. One of my ancient grandfather's sons opted to stay in Ireland in hiding. He passed on the story to his sons, who passed the story down to their sons. Many of the Druids' religious rituals were from the religion we had in Egypt at the same time. Emmitt O'Keefe knew of the Akh Neith because his father had told him about it. Do you know why it was easy to find you and the other Children of the Yew?"

A sick feeling overcame Wesley as the realization hit him, and he tasted bile in his throat. "You used DNA data. We're related to you through the Y chromosome of your ancient grandfather. The genetic marker would be strong. We're your distant paternal cousins."

Ahad sniffed. "The smelly side of the family, but yes." He smiled at his joke, but Wesley did not. He found little humor in it. "Emmitt betrayed his own family and a sacred vow. I am a man of my word, and I always keep it. I have pursued Emmitt for the last eight hundred years. Now I will have my revenge."

Wesley's mind raced. "Why punish me? I had no part in what my grandfather did. I didn't know any of them were alive until now."

"I may take pity on you and keep you alive, cousin." He let out a mirthless laugh. "For now, I plan to keep you and the rest of your family alive long enough to use you as scapegoats when things go badly for everyone. There may be survivors searching for answers, and if I can show them their villains, they will do the job for me. The new history books will show what you all did, so that my children and grandchildren won't think of me as a monster. I'm expecting your sister to join you soon."

What was he saying? *Survivors searching for answers?*

There was a quick knock at the door, and Ahad excused himself. He came back in a few minutes with a wide grin on his face. "It seems that Jake has your sister in his custody and is bringing her here now. I wondered what was taking him so long. It turns out your family reunion will happen soon."

Dread filled Wesley, and his hand trembled. "What now?"

"A decision for another day. For now, I need to go talk to your sister."

Wesley glared at Ahad as he exited the room and shut the door quietly behind him. Could things get much worse?

Chapter 20

Jake worried that Ahad wasn't going to believe that Valerie was Anne. He'd tested the disguise several times with facial-recognition software, and he couldn't discern any difference in eye color with the colored contacts Valerie wore. Anne and Valerie looked alike without a disguise—they wore their blond hair in ponytails and were nearly the same build and height. Nonetheless, he started to wonder about the wisdom of this idea.

Jake turned his head back to the blindfolded Valerie in the back seat. "Why did you agree to come and help Anne?"

"I'm a friend of the O'Keefe family. We've been investigating Ahad for some time. The most recent complaint about him detaining a research professor from a university in Seattle got the bureau interested in my investigation."

Of course. Candace. "Why not arrest him, then? Why put me at risk for this? Can't I testify about what he asked me to do?"

"It wouldn't be enough. We need to get Ahad on a wire, talking about what he's doing. Everything we have now is hearsay. We need to get solid evidence."

"I can show that he was paying me to investigate the O'Keefe family. Isn't that enough?"

"There's no law against him paying you to act as his investigator. He wasn't using bureau funds for that."

A hollowness filled Jake's chest. "What about the trading reports that he gave me to give to Wesley each week? Wouldn't that be insider trading?"

"There is nothing to tie those reports directly to Ahad. Only your testimony that he gave them to you. Again, not enough evidence to convict him, but plenty of evidence to convict you and Wesley. Is that what you want?"

"No, but I don't want this anymore. I don't see how the FBI can protect me from him. He's too well connected."

"I'm dedicating a lot of resources to this investigation, Jake. I need you to calm down and trust me. I can assure you that you'll be under the full protection of the FBI. We'll have several agents in place, ready to move in at the first sign of any trouble. You have my assurance that your safety will be one of our top priorities."

Jake didn't feel any more relieved by her promises. He found it hard to believe that someone like Ahad had achieved the position he had at the FBI. The checks and balances had failed, and those were the same mechanisms that they were asking him to rely upon for his safety.

"I hope you're right."

Jake wiped the sweat from his brow as they neared the building. He entered the underground garage. With shaking hands, he messaged Ahad that he was there with Anne.

Great was the reply that came back. He didn't call, out of fear that Ahad would sense something was wrong.

Now Jake's hands were shaking, and he was unable to stand without feeling dizzy. Ahad's cool demeanor was unsettling at best. Should he make a run for it? No, he needed to face this man and bring him to justice. The whole world counted on him now.

Jake moved to the back of the car and pulled on Valerie. She resisted him and kicked him. He imagined she was trying to keep up appearances, in case anyone was watching, but that kick had hurt. He grabbed her hands, rather uncivilly, and hauled her out of the car, forcing her forward. She cursed under the rag in her mouth.

He leaned in close to her so that no one would hear and whispered, "I don't think we should be doing this. I have a horrible feeling. We can't fool

Ahad this way. Let's get out of here."

Valerie shook her head and motioned forward with her chin.

Against his better judgment, he marched her to the parking elevators. Opening the door revealed Ahad's right-hand man, Syed, waiting for him. He nodded curtly to Syed and smiled.

"Well done, Jake. Let's go see what we can find out from her."

Syed's smile reminded Jake of a python before it swallowed a rat. The man motioned to the open elevator door, and they stepped in.

No turning back now.

Syed led them from the elevator to a holding cell for Wesley's father, Kyle. Jake had never seen Kyle in person, but in pictures, he looked a lot like Wesley and a little like himself. Kyle didn't have their full head of hair, and both of them appeared younger than him.

Ahad walked in and smiled at Jake. "Mr. Rivers."

Jake gulped and his eye twitched. "Ahad. Good to see you."

Ahad watched Kyle's face as Jake removed the blindfold from Valerie's head. Jake started to uncuff her but first said, "Anne, don't do anything stupid. I'm going to uncuff you. Sit down, and don't make any sudden moves." She sat as he finished removing the cuffs.

As soon as Valerie saw Kyle, she said, "Dad, it's you. I was so worried they'd done something to you. Are you okay?"

Kyle frowned in confusion. Jake hoped that Ahad hadn't noticed. He was still smiling and watching them both, so he must not have seen, but Jake didn't feel good about this exchange.

Kyle recovered from his confusion. "Anne, did they hurt you? I'm fine. Do whatever they ask you to."

"No, I'm not hurt. Where is Wesley?"

Jake wanted to wince but tried hard to control his facial expressions. Internal-affairs agents weren't good at acting, and this one was no different. Anyone would have seen by the way she acted that she was not Kyle's daughter. Kyle played along well, but was Ahad buying it?

Kyle shook his head. "I don't know. I haven't been allowed to see anyone. I suspect he is in a holding cell nearby, but I can't be sure."

153

Valerie glared at Ahad. "What did my dad do, and why did you bring me in?"

Ahad returned her look with an ice-cold stare before he spoke. "The charges are income tax evasion, identity theft, falsifying passports, embezzlement, bioterrorism, and insider trading. You have committed many of the same crimes, in addition to resisting arrest and murdering a government contractor."

Ahad turned to Jake. "Mr. Rivers, I told you the one thing I expect from any relationship is loyalty."

Ahad eyed Syed, who was against the wall next to the door. "I shouldn't have left my pistol on the desk like that in front of you, should I?" Ahad asked Valerie.

Oh no! God, no, please! Jake rushed for the door, and Syed pushed him back.

Ahad grabbed the pistol and shot Valerie in the forehead, then put the gun in her hand, placing her dead finger on the trigger as he squeezed a round into Jake's abdomen.

Jake screamed out in pain as he fell to his knees. Blood spilled onto the floor. The door slammed into his back as a stream of FBI agents flooded the room. Jake watched in horror as Ahad squeezed the dead finger of Special Agent Lundstrom again to shoot another round at his head.

Chapter 21

Wesley's stomach grumbled as he waited for lunch to arrive. Three gunshots rang out, a few seconds apart, followed by screaming and commotion down the hallway. He pounded on the solid steel door, demanding to know what was going on. No one answered. Why would gunshots go off in a secure FBI facility? He drummed his fingers on the bed frame. He held his stomach, unsure if the pain was from nervousness, hunger, or both.

The noise settled down, but lunch didn't come. His stomach grumbled in protest. Even though he had found the food here barely palatable, it did sate his hunger. Though he didn't know the time, it must have been many hours since he'd last broken his fast.

Wesley counted the number of tiles on the ceiling to entertain himself. One hundred forty-four, if he didn't count the partial tiles. He tried meditating, but he wasn't sure if he was doing it right. He pounded on the door a few more times and cried out but suspected that the thick door and walls prevented much noise from escaping. He waited, counted the floor tiles, then lay back and closed his eyes, hoping beyond reason that the solace of slumber would overtake him.

Commotion at the door. Would lunch be forthcoming?

"Mr. O'Keefe?" a young man in a suit said as he entered the room.

Wesley's stomach did a few somersaults—the young man didn't have any food in his hand. "The one and only. No lunch today?"

"You're free to have lunch wherever you choose, sir. We're releasing you. But first, I'd like to know if you'd please make a statement."

Wesley tried to maintain a measured response. "Can I call my lawyer first?"

"Yes, you can call an attorney. We'd like to know what Special Agent Atenoud said to you. We'll try not to take too much of your time. Please."

Now they wanted to be polite? After arresting him without cause? *Hell no.* "I want a lawyer for that. Can I have my stuff back?"

The young man nodded and motioned for Wesley to follow. They shuffled down the corridor, and as they did so, Wesley noticed a group of people wearing surgical masks and taking photos of one of the rooms, carefully picking up items with tweezers. Blood covered the walls and floor of the room. A gruesome sight at best.

"Who was in that room?" Wesley asked.

The young man winced. "I believe that was your father, sir."

Wesley's fingers grew cold as he stopped and took in the grisly scene. "My father? Oh God. Is he all right? That's a lot of blood."

"He's fine, though there is an active investigation, so I can't divulge much information concerning what transpired in that room—although, quite frankly, I don't know much myself, only that an FBI agent and another man were shot and killed, allegedly by Special Agent Ahad Atenoud."

The agent led Wesley to a room where his personal effects were waiting. "I suspect you want to make a few phone calls. All your stuff should be in there, but please take an inventory. We don't have all the normal paperwork. Ahad detained you and your family in a manner that was less than orthodox. I don't even have an inventory to tell me what should be in your box." He shook his head and sighed. "All the same, let me know if you find anything is missing."

Wesley rifled through the box, finding his wallet, keys, and smartphone. He didn't find anything missing. "Mind if I change out of this jumpsuit?"

"Of course. I'll wait outside," the agent said.

He left and closed the door behind him. Wesley removed the jumpsuit and put on his clothes. They weren't in the best shape, but it did feel good to be out of the jumpsuit.

Wesley's first call was to his lawyer, Gordon Weinberg. "Hey, Gordon. I'm in San Jose, in federal prison, and need some counsel."

"Jesus, Wesley! What did you do? Wait. Don't answer. Don't say anything, and hang tight. I can be there in four hours."

Relief filled Wesley to know that Gordon had his back. Only a few people in his life had earned such a high level of trust, and Gordon was one of them. "I'm afraid I don't have that much time. Do you have any friends down here? Or maybe a firm you partner with in San Jose? They're releasing me and want me to make a statement."

"Tell them you want to make a statement in Seattle with your lawyer present. If they give you any flak, have them call me. You can conference me in."

"Thanks, Gordon. I appreciate it."

"Hey, thank *you*. Once this is over, you need to take a vacation." Gordon laughed into the phone.

Wesley was glad he could be amused. A tropical island getaway did sound like a great idea, though. "Thanks. Have a wonderful day."

After a quick knock, a tall, attractive woman with ebony skin in a formfitting black suit dress rushed into the room. Tears covered her face. "My name is Special Agent Jane Higgins. My wife, Valerie, was shot by that fucker who brought you in here, along with your assistant, Jake Rivers. I believe that was his name."

What? Why would Jake have been here? The conversation with Ahad came into his mind: *He's one of my best employees.* Why would Ahad shoot him? "Jake? Is he okay?"

Special Agent Higgins looked at him with the sympathetic smile someone would give when they told him someone had died. Wesley had seen it far too many times in his life. She shook her head slowly. "I'm sorry, Mr. O'Keefe. Jake was shot and killed, along with my wife. Ahad tried to frame my wife for it."

Higgins leaned against the wall and pounded it with her fists. "Why the hell did she agree to this? She was supposed to be in the Office of Professional

Responsibility doing internal affairs work, not some undercover agent. She didn't train for this. Fuck!" She started crying, shaking visibly. Then after a few minutes, she pulled herself together and wiped her eyes. "I mean to get this fucker if it's the last thing I do. I haven't told my parents."

Wesley found himself speechless and distraught over Jake. After a few moments, he asked, "I can't believe he killed Jake. Are you sure?"

"Yes. He's dead. He double-crossed Ahad. Ahad must have meant to make an example of him."

Wesley shivered, unsure of what to believe. The room reeled around him. Everything was happening too fast. "Where's Ahad?"

"He's in a federal holding prison, one with excellent security. Listen, I know you want a lawyer, but I want to know what he said to you. That asshole killed my wife, and I want to see him fry for it."

Wesley told her right there, without a lawyer. Gordon would chide him for it later, but this woman wanted revenge on someone who had screwed him over. "Ahad said my assistant, Jake, was working for him. Jake was supposed to be bringing my sister here for him to question. Ahad was planning on pinning everything on my father and our family. He said something like 'I want your family alive long enough to use you as scapegoats when survivors are searching for answers.' I have no idea what he meant by that. I'll testify about all of this in return for immunity for any crimes the FBI thinks I've committed."

"Great. Start writing. We need your written statement now to keep this shithead locked away. I doubt the immunity will be a problem."

Wesley wrote down all the details, leaving out the parts about the Children of the Yew and the Khemenu. No need for that to be in any written record.

Wesley had to fill out lots of paperwork. He let Gordon review it all in a teleconference, but it was all boilerplate language. After what must have been an hour, he finished and met his dad.

His dad rocked to and fro without saying much. Kyle had the thousand-yard stare he'd seen from many men when they had returned from fighting in World War II. Wesley felt lucky he had never engaged in combat every time he saw that stare.

158

A lump formed in his throat. "Are you okay, Da?"

Kyle stared at Wesley for a while, like someone who hadn't understood the question. After a long moment of silence, he finally spoke. "Physically, yes. I watched a woman get shot. She was disguised as your sister. I knew it wasn't her, but the emotion of seeing someone who looks like your daughter die in front of you is hard to describe. I sat frozen and helpless while he shot your assistant." He shook his head and rocked back and forth some more. "I never should have helped that man."

What? Dizziness overcame Wesley, and he had to grab the back of a chair to keep his weak legs from buckling under him. He tried to move his mouth, but the words wouldn't quite form. Instead, he stood there opening and closing his lips like a fish gasping for air. His father must be delirious from shock. "Helped what man?"

Kyle rocked a few more times, then snapped out of the whole strange trance. "I'm sorry, son. Seeing people get shot right in front of me was a first for me. I've been lucky."

Wesley sniffed. He'd been lucky as well, though the men he knew that hadn't been so fortunate had never recovered completely from it. "I as well, Da. What of this man you helped?"

Kyle blinked a few times in apparent confusion. "I'm sorry. I don't know what I was saying. Please forget it."

Seeing his dad reduced to this pitiful state caused Wesley great distress. The pains in his stomach returned, likely a combination of nerves and hunger. He nodded to his dad and put a hand on his shoulder. "It's okay. Let's get you home."

Kyle winced. "About that. I'm going into protective custody. I won't be seeing you for a while. Can you do me a favor?"

"Sure. What is it?"

His wan smile held no joy. "I need you to find my dad's body in Mexico City. When you do, call me. Have Anne go with you. It's very important."

A strange request at best, though Wesley wouldn't need to fulfill it. "Ahad led me to believe that Grandda Emmitt may still be alive, though I'm not sure he'll stay that way."

"What? How?"

Wesley shrugged. "I don't know, but Ahad said he wasn't sure what he would do with him. Ahad also told me that his agelessness comes from a creature like a tick called an Akh Neith. He said Grandda stole it from them, and that's why he captured him. Do you know anything about this?"

Kyle narrowed his eyes. "Your grandfather never told me any of that. I wish he had. Why the hell did he keep it to himself? This knowledge could help explain the evolution of the virus. Listen, go to Mexico City. Find your grandfather, and that creature, as soon as possible."

"Why do we care about its evolution? Why is that so important? Don't we have other things to worry about right now?"

His dad placed a hand on his shoulder. "My modeling software could never figure out how to make the Raven's Kiss something we could pass on to others without suppressing the immune system. The problem is I could never find conditions for the model that allowed it to develop. In other words, the helpful retrovirus shouldn't exist, because evolution would never have made it. The missing element was this creature. There must be a symbiotic relationship. If we can sequence its DNA, we can input the data into my modeling software and figure out ways to make it evolve in a different way in the quantum model."

"I'm not sure I understand. Why the hell does that matter, Da?"

"Watch your tone, son. I'm still your father."

Wesley gritted his teeth. "Sorry. What purpose does this serve? I barely understand this quantum-model idea."

"Think of it like this. We can make any virus with any properties we want if we can feed the right data into the simulation. Think of a simple cold virus. Under the right conditions, it might evolve to be helpful and infect cancer cells. However, there would have to be specific environmental pressures and mutations to make that happen. With traditional computers, the simulation would have taken millions of years to go through all of the numerous possibilities, because of the sheer number of permutations. With quantum computing, we can simulate everything happening at once with different subatomic particles interacting. We can feed the model the end result we want, and it can go through trillions of possibilities in a short amount of time to figure out what DNA sequence would make that virus. I could never find any model that would create the DNA sequence of the Raven's Kiss virus. That's because I was missing the data about this Akh Neith creature that is in your grandfather. Once we have that, I can tweak the model until we find a way to make a retrovirus that prevents aging and doesn't require a suppressed immune system. Does that make sense?"

It made some sense. Kyle obviously thought it would work, and he knew way more about the subject. Wesley stared at his dad for a long time. "It seems enjoying a Scotch together will need to wait."

A twinkle came to his dad's eye. "Aye, it seems so, son." He hugged Wesley and slipped an envelope into his pocket. "May trouble be your stranger, son."

Wesley viewed his dad through the prism of tears forming in his eyes. "I'm afraid trouble and I are far too well acquainted with one another at the moment."

He hugged his father again and left the facility, taking a last glance at the building before a self-driving taxi whisked him away.

*

Maybe he should tell the taxi to head back to the center on its own. Wesley was already halfway to his dad's house, so he might as well continue. No longer could he call Jake and ask him to arrange his schedule. Jake had betrayed him, but he'd also been a loyal assistant. In the end, he had proved his loyalty—too late. Wesley already missed him. He wished he'd been able to say goodbye, and another part of him wanted to hit him. What role had Jake played in everything that had happened lately?

Many large sycamore trees reached toward the blue sky with green fingers. Anger boiled within Wesley as he tore his gaze away from the passing landscape. Jake had no right to Wesley's grief. He narrowed his eyes as he considered how much trouble he could be in due to the information Jake had given him. While it had felt too good to be true to get so many great investment tips from Jake, Wesley had reaped the rewards so many times he hadn't questioned the legality of it. The FBI agent would keep her word, or she wouldn't. The thought of going to prison for insider trading wasn't helping to lighten his mood.

Wesley closed his eyes and pinched his nose. What a complete disaster the last few weeks had been. His grandfather was in Mexico City somewhere, possibly alive, most likely dead. Wesley shifted his weight in the seat, and the envelope in his pocket made a crinkling noise. Paper. Who still used that?

What information did his dad have for him? When his dad had placed it in his pocket, Wesley had felt that he didn't want anyone to know about it. Did *he* want to know?

He opened the envelope and slid out a letter. The flowing cursive script reminded him of years long past. A smile came to his face. Many alive today wouldn't be able to read or write such a thing.

Dearest Wesley,

There is much I need to explain, but I haven't space or time to do so. Please destroy this letter after you read it.

I've done something I deeply regret. Though I had my family's interests at the top of my mind, I thought I could outsmart Ahad. I was wrong.

I own a company called Immunitrex. We can create quantum models of viruses, and then we can 3D print those viruses in real life. We used this technology to scan in all the harmful microorganisms and provide a taxonomy of them, which we used in our modeling software. I'm sorry if this doesn't make much sense, but suffice it to say that we used the technology to create the bundle shot that everyone gets each three months to prevent the common cold, coronaviruses, flu, etc.

Ahad coerced me last year through threats against our family to use the technology to create a pathogen that would get printed into the bundle shot. I cooperated but weakened the virus in a way that would make it useless. His plan was for billions of people to die in a misguided effort to save the earth and put him in a position of great power. He longs for the glory days, when he could influence global leaders and rule the populace from the sidelines.

They ran their own models somehow and discovered the flaw. I'm still not sure how. Ahad had one of his scientists, Masika, fix the issue. She hacked into the system using my credentials and uploaded the deadly virus into the bundle shot. I was ignorant of this and thought my plan to foil him had worked. A few days ago, I discovered the problem and started making plans to create a cure for the next bundle shot. Unfortunately, the modifications Masika made created a virus that I don't know how to cure.

I fixed the Immunitrex system's vulnerabilities and added additional protections to prevent anything like this from happening again. I planned to reach out to various government agencies, but somehow Ahad knew what I was doing and arrested me. Had it not been for the unfortunate shooting of Jake and Special Agent Lundstrom, and Ahad's subsequent arrest, I wouldn't have a chance to stop this.

I have a cabin near Leavenworth with a quantum-modeling lab with all the equipment required to develop a cure. I understand you are dating a microbiologist. I researched her and found that she has done a lot of phenomenal research that has advanced the field, so she'd be perfect for the project. Please take her there before you go to Mexico. Anne has biometric access to my systems and can get Dr. Rosenbach started. I will join you once I can convince the FBI to allow me to do so.

Love,

Da

Wesley pressed a palm over his lips and shook his head. With a clenched jaw, he considered the letter. How could his dad do this? He crumpled up the letter and stuffed it back into his pocket.

His watch buzzed. Candace. He wrung his hands as he watched the notification. She could leave a message. He didn't want to talk to anyone.

She rang him again. His device flashed, warning that the call would terminate soon. A part of his brain screamed in retaliation as he shifted and pressed the green button. "Hello?"

"Wesley? Oh my God! Are you okay?"

The frantic tone of her voice moved him. "Yes. Why? How's it going up there?"

"I'm okay. I'm at your dad's house. We haven't heard back from Jake or Valerie. Where are you?"

How did Candace know about Jake, and who was Valerie? *Oh, right, the late wife of Ms. Higgins.* "I planned to fly away on a Caribbean vacation. Care to join me?"

A long pause at the other end. "Not a good time for jokes. What's going on?"

Now it was Wesley's turn to pause. What did he want to do? Why had he answered the call? *Damn it.* Exhaustion fell upon him like a stone. A torrent of grief and regret filled him. He tried to swallow past the lump in his throat. He bit his lip. His voice cracked when he finally spoke. "I'm sorry. I'll be there shortly."

With some regret, Wesley watched the airport grow smaller as the taxi made its way to his dad's house. In the past, he'd always left and moved on to a new life. He couldn't do that now.

*

Candace and Anne stood near the doorway. When Wesley got out of the car, with eyes downcast, Candace nearly bowled him over as she rushed to hug him.

He embraced her, drinking in her scent as the warm moisture of tears wet his shoulder. Wesley could lose himself in this moment, holding her for an eternity, but they soon released each other and entered the house.

Wesley smiled at Anne.

She smiled back. "I've got some tea brewing."

Of course. "I could use some. Thank you." He sat and pretended that all was as it should be, though he knew it would be a fleeting instant.

Anne's hand trembled as she handed him the cup of tea. He noticed the cloud of milk in the tea and smiled. A small comfort, but he sipped it and allowed the beverage to warm him as he savored the earthy sweetness. The cup shook as he set it upon the saucer.

Anne stared at him. "Well?"

Wesley steeled himself. "Da is in protective custody." The letter crinkled in his pocket, and the crumpled corners poked him. Should he tell her of their dad's betrayal? No. He would spare her that lone grievance. For now. "Ahad shot and killed Valerie and Jake. Da witnessed it, and the FBI wants

164

him to remain in their safekeeping. They dropped all charges against us in exchange for our testimonies."

Anne held her hand to her mouth and shook her head. "No. No. Why would he do that?" She launched into a stream of curse words and threw a couch pillow at the wall. Her cheeks flushed with anger as she balled her fists.

Wesley moved his head back and forth in slow motion. "I've little understanding of Ahad or his motivations. He's a narcissistic megalomaniac. I thought of Jake as a good employee, someone I could count on. Then I found out he had been working for Ahad. I don't know what to think."

Anne and Candace exchanged glances. Candace gave her a quick deferential nod.

Anne fixed her stare upon him. "Wesley, I need to let you know … Jake was your son."

Son? What was she talking about? "What? Impossible. How could I be …?" He trailed off. He remembered Jake's age, and asking a woman to get an abortion so many decades ago. He licked his dry lips. "Why? Why didn't he tell me?"

Anne gave a small shrug. "I don't know. He said you abandoned him. Working for Ahad to spy on you was his revenge. He changed his mind and decided to help once he found out what Ahad was planning. Jake wanted me to tell you that he was sorry he let you down and that he wasn't angry anymore. I'm sorry."

Wesley held his mouth open and flicked his tongue against his bottom lip. How should he feel? A maelstrom of emotions competed in his mind. Anger that Jake had spied on him. Regret that Jake hadn't told him he was his son, that he'd treated Jake with such indifference. Shame for leaving Jake's mother alone to care for a baby. He opened and closed his mouth a few times. He tried to shake the grief from his head, like a dog shakes water from its fur. He covered his face with his hands and squeezed his eyes shut. Candace held him to her, and he buried his head in her embrace.

After collecting himself, Wesley lifted his head and stared at a couch cushion. If only Jake had said something. Why hadn't he?

Candace and Anne shared another glance. What now? Anne nodded to Candace this time.

Candace cleared her throat. "I believe a deadly virus has already infected millions, if not billions, of people." She bit her lip, then continued. "I'm one of them."

There was a moment in times of darkness when someone hit a wall, beyond which there wasn't much emotion left to feel. Wesley had hit that barricade of apathy and despair. A wooden hollowness kept him from speaking. Words wouldn't come. Instead, he pulled out the crumpled letter, flattened it out with a fist, and handed it to Candace.

Candace gasped a few times as she read the letter, then gave it to Anne.

Anne's expression grew grim. Her entire face turned red. She shook her head in disbelief. "No. There must be a mistake. Why would he help that bastard?" She jumped to her feet, took the letter to the sink, ripped it into shreds, then flushed it into the disposal with running water. "That wasn't his writing. Ahad forced him to write it."

Wesley put his hand on her shoulder. "He slipped it into my pocket. 'Twas he who wrote it."

She stood with nostrils flaring for several long moments before she spoke a word. She stared straight into Wesley's eyes with that fierce gaze that reminded him so much of his mother. "Then we haven't a moment to waste. Let's get Dr. Rosenbach to Da's research facility."

"One more thing. Ahad led me to believe Grandda Emmitt may still be alive."

She smiled, and a joyful tear came to her eye. "Then we need to go now." She ran for the door. "Candace tells me you have a plane. Can you get us to a small grass-field airport near Lake Wenatchee?"

Wesley did the calculations. They'd need to get to Seattle, then fly over in a smaller plane, but it was feasible. "We'll be there in a few hours."

They all dashed out the door.

Chapter 22

Ahad found himself in a prison cell, arrested for shooting the loathsome agent Valerie Lundstrom and the traitor Jake Rivers. The wretched man had ruined everything with his disloyalty.

Ahad regretted his actions now. Oh, he would have left his position at the Bureau once the virus had done its work, but he would have used his role at the FBI for a few months to help ensure that he attained his goals. Those days were now behind him, for he had shown his cards and would have to take unplanned preventive measures.

Shooting Jake wasn't a regret. He had deserved it for being disloyal, for trying to deceive him. Kyle's reaction had made it obvious that the person that Jake had brought in was not Anne O'Keefe. Jake shouldn't have been so stupid if he had hoped to fool him. Shooting an internal-affairs agent while she was wearing a wire was his regret. It all seemed obvious now in hindsight.

He cursed himself, for he'd acted with emotion when he should have exercised control. Were it not for Kyle O'Keefe, he would have waited for everyone to die and then left to start planning for a new world, a world in which the Khemenu would accomplish great things, much as his ancestors had in previous ages. He had to get out of this prison. Now.

People squandered resources and fought over them like packs of wild hyenas. They warred with one another and destroyed the environment.

Ahad would end this and take his people to the stars. The vastness of the universe was out there for the taking, yet here they squabbled over baubles when the real treasures were in space, waiting to be collected. The Khemenu would act as better stewards of Earth and would lead people to true greatness. Many would die for this to be possible, but they would all die if he did not do something. The human race needed him to succeed, and his people needed him to succeed.

Ahad waited patiently on his bed. A guard would be watching him now. The camera feed would soon be modified and looped, so he needed to sit without moving much to be successful. As such, he meditated in silence on his bed in stillness.

A guard entered his prison cell with a small black duffel bag and undressed, and Ahad did the same. Ahad donned the guard uniform, and the guard donned the orange prisoner outfit. The guard pulled out a makeup kit from the duffel bag and began applying cosmetics to Ahad's face. Ahad did the same for the guard. The Khemenu had perfected the art of disguise with makeup long ago. If you lived for such a long time in secret, you needed creative ways to mask your features. The disguise needed to last long enough for the guards watching the feed to see his replacement lie down on the bed and fall asleep.

Without words, Ahad shook the fake guard's hand and left in silence. He walked briskly down the hallway to a stairwell that would lead to a laundry room. He used the access badge attached to his shirt to open the door and entered the area. He spied a half-loaded linen truck and climbed into the back of it.

A female guard appeared in front of him. "What in the hell are you doing? Hands where I can see them!" she yelled as she brandished a pistol at him.

Ahad thought of a quick excuse. "I was inspecting the laundry to make sure it was empty. It's a new standard procedure. Didn't you get the memo?"

"No, I didn't. I don't recognize you. What's your name again?"

He hadn't bothered to read his badge. There wasn't supposed to be someone waiting in the laundry room. "Sorry, yeah, I transferred over from another prison. The name is Edgar Riddell, and yours?"

She looked skeptical. "I'm going to call this in. Please hold on a moment."

The guard was distracted for a brief second as she moved to press a button on her tablet, and Ahad seized the opportunity. He rushed toward her and pushed his arms in an outward arc, knocking her weapon to the floor. She lunged at him, but he avoided her and brought her crashing to the ground. He put her in a chokehold and squeezed her until her face turned red. She scratched at him as she tried to pry his arms loose and kicked out her legs several times. Pain seared through his skin as her nails dug deep into his wrists. He held her steadfastly, careful not to cry out when she drew blood from another deep scratch.

Soon the kicking stopped, and her body went limp beneath him. He found her gun, then tossed her dead body onto the ground and searched her for a chip.

After finding the chip that would allow him to start the vehicle and drive it away, he threw her into the back and tossed several sheets and towels on top of her. The truck would soon begin to smell like more than a bunch of stained linens.

The vehicle lurched forward. Ahad gripped the pistol in his hand with his finger on the trigger, ready to use it if needed.

He stopped at the gate, and the guard eyed him.

"Everything okay?" the guard asked.

"Yes. Taking a load of laundry. Everything's great. Nice day, huh?"

The guard nodded but made no move to open the gate. "Where's Karen?"

Ahad guessed that must have been the name of the guard in the back of the truck. He smiled back and shrugged his shoulders. "Not sure. They called me in today. Maybe she's sick."

He reached for something, and Ahad shot him in the face with the pistol. Blood plastered the guard gate's far wall, and the man fell to the ground dead.

Ahad pressed the accelerator of the truck hard, and it smashed through the gate. Sirens blared behind him, and the vehicle lurched to a stop. *Damn it!* They must have disabled the truck remotely.

He jumped out and ran at full speed toward the forest, weaving through the trees as he made his way up the long hill.

Noises of vehicles and barking dogs pursued Ahad as he ran through the forest. He gulped in breaths and smelled the fresh earth as his boots snapped twigs beneath him and created cracking noises that were sure to attract attention. His lungs burned, but he urged himself forward despite the pain. He stopped short when he reached a fast-moving river.

The sound of bellowing dogs grew louder and drove him into the river. As he dashed into it, heedless of the danger, the frigid water burned his skin. Holding the pistol above him as he trudged through the water, he sucked in air as the cold pervaded his senses. His boots leaked onto the rocks when he reached the opposite shore.

A guttural growl sounded behind him. Turning around, Ahad faced a large German shepherd. The beast barked before jumping into the water, and he dashed away to avoid the dog. The water-laden pants and boots weighed him down as he tried to make his way to the road ahead. The baying of the canine behind him grew closer. Ahad found a large rock and threw it at the animal's head. It yelped but continued to move forward. He fumbled with the pistol, his hands numb from the cold. He fired and missed the dog by a wide margin. It lurched, teeth bared, jumping for his throat. The dog hit him, and as he fell backward, he squeezed a bullet into the animal's chest.

After rolling down a hill for several minutes, he stopped himself and turned to see the foul creature yelping on its side. Its legs twitched as it made rasping noises. Ahad hoisted a large stone, then ran to the animal and brought the rock down, crushing its skull as a final mercy and to keep it from making any more noise that would give him away.

Ahad ran into the road. The brakes of a sizable driverless semitruck squealed as it slowed to avoid killing him. He ran to the back of the vehicle and climbed to the top of the trailer, gripping a handrail as the truck surged forward again, no longer detecting any pedestrians inhibiting its progress.

His hands trembled as he shivered from the air rushing over his wet skin and clothes. Drones would likely be scouring the area for him. What should have been a clean getaway had turned into a botched and hectic escape. That woman shouldn't have been there. Why had they even had a driver in the laundry truck? Another example of the wasted resources he would fix when he ran everything.

An aircraft sounded above, but Ahad didn't move to look up. Risking such a motion would allow the facial-recognition software to see him. Flattening himself against the top of the vehicle, he held on for dear life as he shivered continuously for several hours.

The semitruck eventually stopped at traffic lights, and Ahad climbed down the back. Farmland stretched all around beyond the small town he found himself in, with a small convenience store at the crossroads. There were no other vehicles, though there might be cameras in the traffic lights, so he ran to the side of the road, trying to use the truck to obscure himself. A small farmhouse in the distance caught Ahad's eye, and he ran toward it after climbing a small fence.

The brown grass crunched beneath him, and he passed several hay bales as he ran for the home. The smell of cow manure and hay assaulted his senses, but he was too cold to care much about the stench. He entered a small barn with some stables for horses. Could he ride one of the horses away? No. He'd be too exposed.

Ahad needed to get into the farmhouse. The cold pistol remained in his pocket, so he pulled it out and removed the clip to see how many rounds it contained. Eight more rounds.

From the confines of the barn, he spied a man and his wife and their two children praying at the dinner table. They began their meal. Ahad smiled to himself. Four shots, and then he'd shower, put on some new clothes, and be on his way.

With careful footsteps, he crept to the house. The sounds of dinner chatter and laughter greeted him at the window where he watched them eat. A little girl looked up and stared right at him, her eyes growing wide as he squeezed the trigger. A bullet pierced the window and her dad's heart. She screamed as he shot the mom and the son next. The girl ran into another room, preventing a clear shot. He kicked the door open and ran in to find her hiding in a coat closet.

"Please don't! Please!" she begged as she stared up at him with her brown pigtails and bright brown eyes.

Ahad squeezed the trigger and silenced her pleas for help.

He ran into the room where the dead man was slumped at the dinner table, and searched through his pockets. He found a small chip for the vehicle. Good, the man appeared to be about the right size. He climbed the stairs to the second floor, showered, and rummaged through the closet until he found some suitable clothes.

Ten minutes later, Ahad was dressed, dry, and warm in the vehicle of one Mr. John Grife, heading as far away from the area as possible. He would need to make contact soon and be out of the country, but he would be safe.

Chapter 23

A couple of plane rides later, and Wesley, Anne, and Candace found themselves at Kyle O'Keefe's cabin, overlooking Lake Wenatchee. Tall pine trees reached upward, and the sweet scent of forest earth greeted Wesley as he took in the view of the lake and the magnificent granite peak that cast its shadow upon the house.

Anne held her hand to the sensor in the door, and it clicked open. Wesley stared in wide-eyed astonishment at the magnificent view of the calm lake. Large floor-to-ceiling bay windows surrounded by thick timber frames gave him a complete 180-degree view. Calm filled him as he took in the serene nature of his surroundings. Most of his body relaxed, and he forgot about the crisis.

Candace and Anne must have been feeling the same, for he stared for several moments before Anne finally said something. "You may be more impressed when you see what lies below." She wiggled her eyebrows and pointed at the spiraling iron staircase with varnished pine steps that led down. She descended, and they followed.

They came to a large wooden door at the bottom of the stairs, which opened into a long hallway. Beechwood paneling covered the walls. They entered a room with a king-size bed, a bookcase, a dresser, and a bathroom off to the side. It was nice, but it didn't warrant the level of admiration Anne had suggested.

Wesley shrugged his shoulders. "Nice."

Anne smiled, the sort of smile that a small boy got when he had a frog in his pocket that he planned to show his friend. The kind of smile young Patrick always had when they'd meet. He had often had a frog or some other creature. Wesley sighed. Time hadn't healed all his old wounds.

Anne approached the bookcase and pulled on one of the book jackets. The entire wall slid to the side and revealed a small elevator. They all entered, and the elevator lurched downward. How had Wesley's dad built all of this in the middle of a forest?

Candace held her mouth agape. Wesley folded his arms.

"How long did this take him to construct?" he asked.

Anne held her hand to her chin. "About ten years. He did a little bit at a time. He didn't want the neighbors, or the county for that matter, to know what he was up to."

The elevator opened to reveal a large laboratory. Candace dashed to the systems and admired them all, almost squealing as she took in the various pieces of equipment. Wesley didn't share her excitement. He had no clue what any of this stuff did.

Candace beamed. She almost floated from one computer terminal to the next. She spoke in a gleeful tone. "This is amazing. I suspect there is enough quantum-computing power here to do any research we want. And these quantum spectral scanners. This puts my university lab to shame."

Wesley tried to look impressed, but in truth, none of it looked special to him. The impressive part was the location: under a lake house in the middle of the Cascade Range. "So, can she continue Da's research?"

Anne gave a dismissive gesture as if to say, "Of course, you moron brother. Why do you think we are here?"

She waved her hand in front of a few scanners, stared into a camera, typed some things on a keyboard, and had Candace do more of the same. "Great, you should have read access to all of Da's research and notes. You have an account now. I trust you know what to do."

Candace gave a quick nod, and her fingers flew across a keyboard as she stared into a terminal. Digits and letters reflected in her eyes as she stared at whatever she was doing. A mumble escaped her lips now and then, saying things like "Fascinating," followed by more tapping on the keyboard, then "Remarkable." After several minutes of this, she nodded at the two of them in earnest. "I'm good. You can go find your grandpa now." She seemed all too eager for them to be on their way.

Anne gave Wesley an amused smile, so glad Candace was enjoying this. Wesley should have felt some relief that Candace had the opportunity to make progress—he wanted to feel that way. Instead, heat rose in his cheeks. He was jealous of the stupid computer system.

Anne appeared happy that he was angry. She came near him, within whispering distance, and stood with her arms crossed. She stuck her bottom lip out in an exaggerated gesture, then whispered, "Aw, is little Wesley jealous his girlfriend wants to spend more time with the important life-saving research than him?"

He crossed his arms and glared at her. The anger melted away. Then he sighed and laughed. She had a point. He smiled at her. "Shut up."

She smiled back with genuine warmth. "Don't worry. We have a lot to do. So does she."

Wesley agreed.

Anne showed Candace around the rest of the place, where the bathrooms were, the food, how to lock and unlock the doors. The time to leave came far too soon.

Anne stood at the doorway. "I'll wait in the car."

Wesley nodded to her and smiled at Candace. "You going to be okay here by yourself?"

She grabbed him by the shirt and drew him close to her. Her sweet perfume, with a hint of iris and lavender filled his nostrils. He drank her in and lost himself in her eyes before they kissed.

She smiled when they broke apart. "Still not horrible. I could get used to that."

Wesley held her hand in his, then held it to his lips as he kissed it. He closed his eyes, keeping her there in his mind. Warmth filled him as he looked upon her again. "Good. Stay safe."

Candace squeezed his hand. "You too."

With that, he left, and he and Anne were soon on the plane, flying back to Seattle.

*

They switched planes in Seattle to a faster, carbon-fiber jet that would make the long haul to Mexico City.

Anne came into the cockpit once they were on the way. "Can I be your copilot?"

Wesley mused on the idea. The plane could fly itself with no intervention from him. The concept of a copilot wasn't nearly as necessary as it had been twenty years ago. "Do you have a pilot's license?"

"I did, in a previous life. Not one with my current name on it."

"A lot has changed since then. It's mostly electronics now. You don't have the pressure controls and feel of the plane that was there in the older models—not to mention it's an electric motor now."

She glared at him in what he assumed was mock anger. "Okay. Doesn't mean I can't fly it. Let me at least see what it's like."

Wesley showed her some of the instruments, then let her command the yoke from her seat. "Your plane."

A wide grin split her face as the plane climbed like an eagle bound for the heavens. "This thing is fast."

"Yes. Faster than those old Cessna 150s you probably flew."

"150? Are you kidding me? I flew a de Havilland DH10."

He racked his brain to remember what Anne meant, and then the memory came to him. "Wow, the DH10? Wasn't that a World War One biplane bomber?"

"Yes. I dated a guy in the Royal Air Force for a while. He showed me how to fly after the war. I liked it so much I started flying for the Royal Air Force airmail service."

"You were in the RAF?"

"Yep, for a brief period. Most women were mechanics, fixing planes. I started out doing that but convinced the commander to let me fly the mail."

Wesley's admiration for his sister grew. He didn't want to ask her how she had convinced the commander, though he suspected it had more to do with her forceful will than anything he wouldn't want to hear. "I was a Marine officer during World War Two, but I spent the whole time in North Carolina, overseeing supply records."

Anne raised her eyebrows in mock surprise. "Exciting!" Her tone dripped with sarcasm.

She flew for a while longer. Then Wesley took the controls back. Well, he took them back and then let the plane AI do all the work.

Wesley regarded Anne. "Can I ask you something sensitive?"

She stared at him, then laughed. "Well, I can't imagine what it is that would upset me. There isn't much that I deem sensitive these days."

"Why are you still a nurse?"

The glare of indignation Anne gave him made him want to jump out of the plane, parachute or no. "I'll have you know that it is a noble profession. Everyone needs a nurse at some point in their life. Coming in or going out, but they will always need a nurse." Her nostrils flared, and her face turned a beet red.

Wesley tried his best to give her a contrite look. "Yes, I agree with that, but why do you have to do it? I mean, couldn't you find something that pays you more money?"

She reached over to poke a finger into his chest. "Who are you to belittle my profession? You have a big fancy house, but you only have your cat there to keep you warm at night. What are you doing for other people? To help the world be a better place?"

"Sorry. Listen, I appreciate that. I only meant to know you better. I didn't mean any offense."

Anne's expression softened, but only a small amount. "I'll also have you know that I have plenty of money. I don't need to work, but I choose to because I feel good helping other people. Nursing is a tough profession, and so far, they haven't replaced us with robots."

Wesley thought of the medical robot that had zoomed around Jonathan and given him medicine. Best not to mention that. "Fair enough. I couldn't do what you do, and I admire it. I didn't mean to belittle your profession."

Anger radiated from Anne for the next hour. She reminded Wesley of a kettle on the fire too long. He let her anger simmer and boil away before he attempted to talk with her again.

When she seemed calm enough to speak again, he cleared his throat. "Do you remember when Da gave you the Raven's Kiss?"

She stared at him, then sighed. "Aye. I recall it. 'Twas 1738, in Dublin. I got sick at school, and Father Miller took me to the stables and asked Patrick to take me home." She smiled at the recollection of him. "He was much older than me at the time, but he told me about you. He regretted never seeing you again after the day you played on the hill. I asked him what you had been like, and he said you had been a spry lad that had always wanted for a new adventure. He said you had been like his brother."

Wesley nodded. "Aye, he was like a brother to me. I miss him so."

Anne didn't say much for a while. "Patrick dropped me off at my house and sped off, saying he didn't want to see our dad. I suspect he didn't want to dredge up old memories." Anne tensed her jaw. "Grandma Alomena and Da ran out and led me to my bed. Then they gave me the infusion. Oh, it was foul, Wesley—I nearly retched up the contents of my stomach, and I was already queasy. Grandma ran her fingers through my hair and sang a lullaby. I went to sleep and had the strangest dream."

Anne stared out the plane window for a long while before she turned back to regard Wesley. She'd wiped the tears from her face, but it was still evident to Wesley she'd been crying.

A lump formed in Wesley's throat as he thought about what Patrick had said to Anne in her story. "That must have been when you first started falling for Patrick."

"'Twas a start. I didn't date Patrick until many years later, but it did get him in my head. He was a gentleman."

"Patrick? A gentleman? Wow. Well, I guess we all change."

Anne narrowed her eyes at him. "Maybe he wasn't around you. Might be you were the one that made him act less of a gentleman."

Her ears would burn if she heard the things Patrick had told him. A few dirty limericks came to mind. He let it go. Relief filled him at the notion that Patrick had grown to be a good man. Wesley gave Anne a respectful nod. "I was only joking. Any idea why we both had strange dreams?"

"Da says it's irrelevant, but Grandda claims that the fever dreams are portentous, that the path that one chooses indicates the type of life that one will lead. He says it is a metaphor for living a longer life, that the path we choose will be a much longer one than most people take, and that we must choose carefully."

Considering the choice Wesley had made in his dream, following a long path to a room full of treasure, Grandda may have had the right idea. He'd spent most of his life in pursuit of more wealth. "Interesting interpretation. I get the feeling there is more to this virus we have than we understand."

"There is more to everything in life than we think we understand, brother. The dreams may mean nothing, but to the two of us, they meant something." Anne stared out the window again for some time. "I'm glad we had a chance to talk like this. It feels good to know you're here. I've thought of you so much over the years."

"Are you okay?" Wesley asked.

Anne bit her lip, then nodded. "Yes. I miss Patrick. His accident is why I became a nurse. If I had known then what I know now, maybe he'd be alive today."

That phrase had been something he'd said to himself countless times. *If I had known then what I know now ...* So many things in his life could have been different, but they weren't. They had happened as they had. "Listen. I, for one, know you can't blame yourself for other people dying."

"How do you manage to not blame yourself, then?"

How indeed? With a pang, the guilt of Jonathan's passing came to mind. How many people could Wesley have saved if he'd sought his family out sooner? "I guess I don't."

"We're a pair, aren't we? I'm glad you're here, brother. I can't tell you how great it feels to get to know you."

"Same. You're a pain in the arse sometimes, but I'm glad I met you." He smiled at her to let her know he was joking, and she playfully punched him in the arm. "This killer virus and the kidnapping were not something I ever imagined. My life was simpler before I met you."

Anne raised her eyebrows. "I might say the same."

All that time he'd spent hiding, running, never facing anything. That comfortable life. Comfortable, but not complete. "Simpler, but now it's better."

Anne smiled at him as they continued through the air toward Mexico City.

Chapter 24

Candace's stomach tightened as she remembered the day over twenty years ago when she had come home to her small first-floor duplex off Lexington Avenue in Cambridge. She and Tom hadn't had much in the way of furniture. Small benches made from plastic milk cartons surrounded a foldout table in the dining room. Tom had started a new position at the university, helping students in the math lab. He and Candace didn't have any spare money after living expenses—they'd eloped over the summer, and Candace had never been happier.

She ran into the house with excitement and almost forgot about the bag of groceries she carried. She'd worn her mask to the store—everyone had them due to the COVID-19 crisis. She tried to tell Tom about the email she'd gotten about getting into a research program, but he was coughing too loudly. Everything happened in a blur after that. They rushed to the hospital, and Tom wheezed as the ER staff hauled him away to the emergency room. Candace fought with the nurses, who wouldn't even allow her to leave the reception area. A security guard wearing a protective mask escorted her out of the building, with sympathy in his eyes that said she wasn't the first person he'd taken out.

They made her wait at home for days. Eventually, she got the call. She'd baked a cake for Tom and made a silly sign about how much she loved him and was glad he was back. With relief, she answered—then dropped the phone when they told her he was gone.

Candace vowed that day she would find a way to stop this. She'd just graduated from MIT with a Bachelor of Science in Physics and been accepted into an MIT doctoral program in aerospace engineering. Instead, she applied for a doctoral program at the University of Washington in microbiology. Far away from Massachusetts—far away from the memories of Tom.

Candace's focus had helped her fight the disease, and she had won awards in her field. She had never let herself get close to another man again after that. Now she felt the pull with Wesley, that longing, that desire to be with him, in his arms. Why had she let it get this far?

Candace wasn't going to let anyone else go through what she had gone through with Tom. She had to stop this plague, but she needed to clear her head for a minute.

She went outside to view the tranquil lake. The warm tendrils of the sun's rays kissed her cheek, and she inhaled the pine-scented mountain air. Wesley's dad, Kyle, had made some progress in analyzing the threat. Candace had been disturbed to find his notes about how he had contributed to developing the new virus, the one her students had found and called the Crow.

Kyle had tried to alter the retrovirus that kept him from aging. He'd simulated the genome in various models but never found how the retrovirus had developed. Candace had had no success either. Kyle had planned to make it something that other people could catch, like a cold virus, but the way the virus had evolved had made that impossible. There wasn't enough information to figure out how it had developed. The software found no clue in the genome that linked it to other retroviruses.

What was Candace to do, then? She threw a rock into the lake and watched the waves radiate out from the center. How was Wesley doing? He had to come back. The pain of being abandoned by one more person would be too much, but she wasn't sure if she could take falling in love either.

The high-pitched whine of an electric motor and the sound of wheels against pavement heading into the driveway interrupted Candace's ruminations. A black sedan rolled into view and parked in front of the cabin.

Candace's heart raced, and she rubbed her sweaty hands together. She eyed the government plates and knew it had to be the FBI. Were they planning to arrest her again? How the hell had they even found her?

A slender and attractive woman in a suit got out of the car and eyed Candace as she made her way down the steps toward the lake.

Should Candace run? The woman didn't appear to be in any hurry. Candace could run into the forest and hide. They'd pursue her, then make matters worse for her. Candace stood her ground and waited as the woman drew near.

"Dr. Candace Rosenbach?"

Who, me? No. I think you're looking for someone else. Those words ran through her head, but instead, she squeaked out a response. "Yes. Who'd like to know?"

"Special Agent Jane Higgins with the FBI. It's a pleasure to meet you. I came here with some bad news."

Oh God. Had something happened to Wesley? Candace's heart raced. Why had she let herself fall for him? Had she fallen for him? *Damn it!* She held her chin high and tried to seem unperturbed. "What news?"

"I'm afraid that"—those words dragged out, and time slowed down; so many bad things in Candace's life had those words at the beginning—"Ahad has escaped from prison. We have reason to suspect he will target Kyle and his family. Mr. O'Keefe sent me here to protect you."

Relief filled Candace, but as the import of Special Agent Higgins's words became more apparent, terror replaced her fleeting feeling of complacency. "Where is Kyle?"

Special Agent Higgins regarded her. "He's safe. I can't say where." She studied Candace a while more. "He told me you'd be here. Can I ask what you're doing here?"

What should Candace say? That she was trying to stop a global pandemic? She suspected that Kyle hadn't been forthcoming with the reasons. The truth was best, but the agent didn't need to know everything. "I'm doing research." She gestured at the snowcapped mountain of granite behind her, the tall pine trees, and the beautiful lake. "Can you think of a more beautiful place to do it?"

Higgins narrowed her eyes and studied her some more. She had a disturbing habit of doing that. After a while, she smiled. "I suppose not. Listen, I need to set up some drones, and then I need to get Agent Vick to help me out. I'm sorry, it will only be the two of us until Schmidt gets here. We can't afford any leaks. Can I come in?"

Candace nodded, then escorted her into the dining room, where Higgins got busy unpacking boxes. Candace's breath caught when she pulled out a rifle and a pistol. Higgins hardly noticed Candace as she worked.

"Can I get you something to eat?" Candace asked. It was awkward saying that—she was in someone else's house, offering food to someone she didn't know.

"No," Higgins said with a curt shake of her head before she peered through the long rifle's scope. She pressed several buttons on a small tablet. Video feeds on the tablet lit up. "Mind if I put all this on the table?"

Higgins didn't wait for a response, she started doing it anyway, but Candace replied "Yes" all the same. "I'm going to get back to work if you don't mind."

She returned to the lab and locked the door behind her. She tried to focus on her research but found it hard to do so with the threat of a narcissistic madman on the loose.

Chapter 25

Morgan's team waited outside the hospital. Bo had drawn the short straw and would be the one to go into the hospital and find Emmitt's corpse. The family wanted them to recover Emmitt, though they had never mentioned why. What did they plan to do with the body? Didn't matter. The O'Keefe family was paying enough money for them not to ask questions.

Bo posed as a visiting doctor, complete with scrubs and a badge. The rest of the team had eyes and ears on her if anything went wrong, but her fellow former Marines knew she could take care of herself.

Bo's father had signed her up for a hapkido class in seventh grade, and she thought in retrospect that he might have done so to live vicariously through her. Her dad's leg had been blown off by an IED in Afghanistan when he had been in his twenties, as a Marine. She remembered the day she had told her dad she wanted to be a Marine. He had gone into the other room for a long time. He had tried to talk her out of it, but in the end, he had been proud.

In her hapkido classes, Bo had come to love fighting with the Japanese quarterstaff known as the bo. She carried an expandable metal version in the side pocket of her doctor's outfit. Her deadly efficacy with the staff had earned her the nickname of "Bo."

Many fellow Marines she trained made the mistake of seeing her diminutive figure as nonthreatening. She heard the joking whispers they made as they entered the dojo. Those were the ones on the floor later, begging her to stop hurting them. No one made that mistake with her twice.

Today they counted on any hostile forces she might encounter to make the same sort of error for this mission. The hospital staff would see a short woman in a doctor's outfit and the badge JT had made for her, which would allow her access into the morgue.

Bo wore contacts that gave her a HUD of her surroundings. The infrared sensors in her pocket would show anyone approaching. JT's nanobugs ahead of her scouted the area and sent her live feeds. The contacts would also transmit a feed to her team.

Bo made a few clicks with her eyelids, selecting the feed for Byron. He wore a repair person outfit and was ready to wheel the body into the hospital's parking garage while she provided cover. Through his feed, she could see that he was in an empty hallway, swabbing the deck with a mop.

Bo followed the map on her HUD to the elevators and pressed the lower-floor button to descend to the morgue. As the doors were closing, someone pushed his hand into the elevator to keep it open.

Her pulse quickened when a doctor entered the elevator. He stared at her badge carefully.

"Dr. Ortiz?" he asked.

She spoke in Spanish and hoped she didn't botch her accent. All of them had been in Mexico for a few years, but it didn't take many sentences for the locals to recognize them as gringos. "Yes. A pleasure to meet you. And your name?"

"Dr. Rodriguez. I'm surprised you don't recognize me," he said.

She gave him her cutest smile, but fake flirting wasn't her forte. A feed came in on her HUD, giving her information about the doctor. "Yes, of course. You're the chief of medicine. I'm a visiting pathologist assisting the coroner in the morgue." Relief filled her that she'd practiced the last line in Spanish many times during the mission prep. "I'm honored. I didn't realize you were so handsome," she said.

He laughed. "You're too kind," he said as the elevator stopped at the floor above hers.

For a tense moment, Dr. Rodriguez regarded Bo. Her knees buckled when he finally walked out of the elevator.

She sagged against the wall and tried to calm her pounding heart.

The infrared feed didn't show anyone in the area. Bo tiptoed down the hallway to the morgue. She stopped at the doorway into the morgue and waited. Thermal imaging from her IR sensors indicated someone might be sitting at a desk in the room. She clicked out a message with her eyelids to her team: *OK to proceed?*

Unknown individual at desk in room. Proceed with extreme discretion and caution.

Thanks, guys, she thought. *Not helpful.*

Bo placed a hand in her coat to feel for the expandable staff, her trusty bo, and badged her way into the room. She allowed a moment to study her surroundings. A man was typing on a keyboard at a small desk next to a large metal table.

She waited, contemplating her next move carefully. Talk her way into having the man leave, or smack him on the head, cause a severe concussion, and knock him out?

From behind, he looked to have broad shoulders and a thick neck. He wore running shoes and scrubs and typed away furiously at the keyboard.

"Excuse me," Bo said. "Can you help me find a body? I'm supposed to assist in an autopsy."

The tall man with olive skin stood and turned around. He was built more like a bouncer than a nurse, and he sauntered toward her without responding.

Warning! Man identified as Mukhabarat. Get out of there! flashed on her HUD display.

Bo whipped out her staff and extended it to its full length, then brought it round in a low, swinging arc at his legs. It should have connected easily and knocked him on his ass, but he deftly jumped back and avoided the blow.

He smiled, showing yellowing teeth, then picked up a small table, the kind used to wheel corpses around in the morgue, and threw it directly at her.

Bo swept her staff in a semicircle, nicking the table as she dodged to the side. There had been a lot of force behind that throw, and her wrist ached from the shock. Waves of pain radiated up her arm from the blow.

She gritted her teeth through the pain and circled him to find an opening. When he leaned toward her, she performed a downward spinning attack on his shoulder, attempting to smash it with an overhead front strike.

He lowered to the floor, and her staff made a loud whoosh as it swept through the air above his head. He kicked at her legs in a low arc.

Bo jumped and dodged, then lashed out with her staff and connected with his side.

He whipped his body in a rotating motion, seized her staff with both hands, and used his forward momentum to launch her into the air.

She flew and landed in a less-than-graceful way but still managed to roll out onto her feet.

The man spun the staff around in a flourish, the move making a loud whistling noise. He moved toward her with the staff whirling about in front of him.

Bo feigned an injury to her leg from falling and limped to the side as he came toward her. A classic wounded-bird trick, and she hoped that he would fall for it.

He came in fast and hard with a forward lunge, with the quarterstaff aimed directly at the side of her head.

Bo ducked and followed through with a quick punch to the groin, then rolled and performed a spinning back kick to his head. The man went down hard, and his face smacked into the hard flooring, adding more blood for someone to wash from a deck that had likely seen its fair share of bodily fluids.

He groaned on the floor. Bo jumped onto his back and grasped his wrist, then flipped it around and moved his arm into a position that was guaranteed to cause a lot of pain.

She yelled out at him. "What the hell are you doing here?"

He didn't respond, but he screamed and flipped himself over on top of her, wrenching himself free of her grip. As soon as he was free, he sprinted for the door and left.

Damn, that hurt. Bo's lungs burned as she struggled to breathe. That man was heavy, at least two hundred pounds. She only weighed one hundred twenty pounds, so having him flip himself on top of her hadn't been fun, to put it mildly. She struggled to get up and pursue him. She couldn't quite will herself into a standing position.

A message came in on her HUD from Morgan: *Nice ass kicking. We'll pursue him. Figure out what he was doing.*

She winced when she regained her feet. *Roger that*, she clicked back.

Bo hobbled over to the computer terminal. He'd been editing some records, and after skimming what he had been writing, she surmised that he had been adding an entry for a completed forensic investigation of Emmitt O'Keefe. It listed a male, aged fifty-four, and showed the cause of death as a heart attack. It also recorded that they'd sent the body to a local funeral home for cremation, per the family's wishes.

Bo relayed the information to her team, and got a message back: *Get to the parking garage and rendezvous with us.*

*Roger,*she sent as she limped through the exit. She hobbled to where her team awaited.

Morgan let out a long, low whistle when she entered the van. "Damn, Bo. You look bad enough to make a freight train take a dirt road."

Bo calmed herself and tried not to let her team know how much she hurt. The adrenaline was wearing off, and now pain replaced it. Her wrist throbbed, and other parts of her body screamed out in protest at any movement. "Thanks. What's the sitrep?" She hoped Morgan didn't notice how she had to force out the words.

Morgan didn't hide the concern on his face. "We followed that man to his car and placed a tracker on it, and we're going to pursue at a safe distance. We'll need you to operate a drone to follow the car to make sure we don't lose him. We got duped. Emmitt wasn't here. We need to keep searching for him, and I have a feeling this guy will lead us to him."

What sort of shit show were they in right now? "Whiskey Tango Foxtrot?"

"We've been reviewing the footage from within Emmitt's car. The first shot blew out the window, and some glass shattered onto him. He likely suffered minor cuts from the glass, since a small amount of blood was in the car, but not enough for someone that was shot and killed. AI analysis suggests he got shot with a tranq after they blew out the windows. Don't think those were real police either. They even faked the comms to make us think the cops were on the way. They're damn good, whoever they are."

JT must have hacked the hospital security system. She smiled over at him. "They might be good, but they don't have JT."

JT beamed as he ate up the praise and did a mock bow.

The thought of catching these assholes gave Bo a moment to forget how much everything hurt. She prepared the drone kit. "Outstanding. I'll launch a drone. Let's find these motherfuckers."

Her assailant hadn't gotten far, and Bo set the drone to auto-follow the tracker while she watched a bird's-eye view of the vehicle as it made its way through the busy streets of Mexico City. Based on the traffic, this would be a long day waiting for him to get to his destination.

Chapter 26

Many hours passed before Wesley and Anne landed in Mexico City. After stowing the plane in a hangar, they left the security gate to meet their driver. Here in Mexico, a VIP could get a *"carro con cabeza"*—which meant a "car with a head"—slang for a car driven by an actual person. The vehicles still did all the actual driving, but the chauffeur made the passengers feel pampered.

A man in a suit approached the two of them and smiled. "Hello. You are Miss Anne O'Keefe?"

Anne nodded. "Yes. Who are you?"

"Morgan Thorsen sent me to pick you up. My name's Miguel." Miguel had excellent English with only a hint of an accent.

Wesley was eager to get in the car and meet this security company that was supposed to track down his grandfather. He looked at Anne, and she shrugged back at him. He wanted to eat some great food after being cooped up in the plane for so many hours.

Miguel opened the door to the back of the car and said, "Please, *señores*. Mr. Thorsen is busy right now. He insists that the situation is urgent and demands your attention as soon as possible. Please, *adelante*."

The all-leather seats felt terrific when Wesley sat down. Anne relaxed her shoulders and let out a sigh, though she picked at her nails. Maybe she was worried about Grandda Emmitt.

Miguel handed back two bottles. "Please, have some water. It's getting hot here. Mr. Thorsen is anxious to speak with you."

hot here. Mr. Thorsen is anxious to speak with you."

Anne inspected the water bottle, twisted off the sealed cap, and started to drink. "Let's go. I'm anxious to make some progress."

Wesley opened his water and gulped it down, though he would have preferred something besides water to quench his thirst.

As they started to drive off, he noticed his watch had no signal. "I guess we're in a dead zone. My connection isn't working."

Anne gave him a concerned frown. "See that mesh film on the car windows?"

He studied the small squares embedded in the glass. "Yeah. Maybe it's something for bulletproofing the windows. I guess they aren't taking any risks."

"No, they aren't. I believe that this part of the car is a Faraday cage."

Wesley struggled to remember what that was. He'd heard it at one point in his life, but the memory of the meaning was gone. "I'm not sure what that is."

"It blocks radio waves. I learned about them in hospitals where they used them to prevent interference with other systems. That was a hundred years ago, but the principle hasn't changed. Why would they use one of those here?"

"Sounds like they don't want us making any phone calls. Perhaps they're trying to make sure someone else doesn't find out where we're going."

Anne started to talk. Then she stopped, closed her eyes, and went to sleep. Wesley tried to open the door before he lost consciousness.

*

A dry, metallic taste filled Wesley's palate. He tried to swallow, but his parched mouth had no saliva left. He gulped in the dust-filled air and coughed onto the dirt floor. A rope bound his hands and feet to a wooden post in the center of the room. He strained hard against it, and it cut into his skin.

Argh. When was he going to learn to stop getting into messes like this? Now would be a great time to sit on his patio, watching the birds with Hunter. Thoughts of Scotch filled his mind. He closed his eyes and smelled the woody aroma as the warmth of it ran down his throat and radiated into his stomach.

If he wanted to get back to his days of leisurely loneliness, he needed to find a way out of this bind. No, he wanted to move forward and resolve this global threat. Maybe then he and Candace could enjoy some time together. With renewed purpose and vigor, Wesley rotated his wrists back and forth in a methodical rhythm. He'd done this before—nearly two hundred years ago. At the McGavin ranch, Wesley had taken a liking to Old Man Fred McGavin's twenty-year-old granddaughter. When Fred saw him kissing her, he lost it and tied him up and threatened to hang him if he didn't propose to her that moment. Wesley decided that was a good time to move on and find a new identity, but he had to work his way out of the ropes and ride his horse back to his ranch first.

He wasted no more time reminiscing over ranchers' beautiful granddaughters and kicked off his shoes and worked his feet back and forth to loosen the bindings. He pulled hard with his wrists simultaneously as he attempted to pull the rope off his legs. Even though he was two hundred years out of practice, the makeshift handcuffs gave way, and he was now standing with the rope on the ground.

Wesley crept to the door and tried to turn the doorknob, but it wouldn't budge. A large truss beam traversed the ceiling above and led to the next room. He fashioned a small lasso from the rope, and after several failed attempts, he finally managed to loop it around the beam. After several tugs, he convinced himself that it was secure enough to attempt to climb.

With soft hands that had once been heavy with calluses, Wesley attempted to climb. He cursed when he fell to the ground. Had whoever was in the next room heard the thud on the dirt floor? He listened intently. No sounds to indicate someone approached. Old training came back to Wesley from times when he had lived a less pampered life. He hooked his feet into the rope in an S curve, then inched his way upward. He used his legs for most of the effort, and his hands were only needed to steady himself while climbing.

No ceiling blocked him from moving to other rooms. The exposed trusses connected to shoddy walls made from roughly hewn boards. The beam he crawled onto connected to another small room. He untied the rope and pulled it up with him as he moved on to the adjacent partition.

Nylon cables bound an unconscious Anne to a supporting post. Relief filled Wesley when she appeared unharmed. He secured a line to the truss beam and scaled toward her, then dropped. He worked at the knots, and Anne stirred awake. He held his index finger to his lips and made a shushing motion as he finished untying her. He pointed up at the rope, and she gave him a "you must be kidding me" stare as she watched him climb.

Anne mouthed the words "Now what?"

Wesley's heart sank when he found no escape to any other rooms using the beam. He shook his head in a quick "I don't know" motion and gave an exaggerated shrug.

Anne pointed to the door, then pantomimed running into it and busting it down.

An idea came to Wesley. He tied a few strands of rope to the beam, spaced a few feet apart. Anne watched him with curiosity, then threw her hands into the air in apparent exasperation.

Wesley climbed down, then whispered in Anne's ear. "I'm going to hold on to the rope and swing myself into the door with my feet out. It should be enough force to make it open."

She whispered back, "Why the second rope?"

"You'll swing down and kick anyone that comes through the door."

She shook her head. "Listen, I'm a nurse, so I see a lot of people that tell me about these crazy ideas they had before they ended up in my care. This idea of yours sounds like one of those 'hold my beer' type of moments. Why don't we kick the door in and then trip whoever comes in with the rope?"

To prove how brilliant and superior his plan was to hers, Wesley scaled the rope to the beam, then snatched it and jumped from the pole with his feet extended. Although it took less than a second, while he flew through the air, time slowed. The delayed passing of time gave him a lot of clarity and plenty of moments to realize what an utterly stupid idea it had been. The universe wanted him to know it had been a bad idea, and it wanted to savor the moment as he hurtled toward the door much faster than he'd anticipated when he'd formulated the plan. In his mind's eye, he would crash through the door with all the valor of a swashbuckling musketeer in a Dumas novel. Anne would watch him and revel in his brilliance, never to question his plans and motives again.

That wasn't what happened. Wesley did swing forward, but the rope cut and burned his hands, so he was forced to let go. He flew and smacked against the wall with his shoulder, making a loud noise before he gracelessly fell to the ground and rolled a few times, then came to a painful halt. The door remained untouched and unmoved by the display.

Anne rushed to his side. "Are you okay?" she asked as she leaned down to inspect him. She tsked at his blistered hands. "Not much I can do for you here, but once I get some supplies, I'll fix you up. I'm going to remind you that I was against your idea. Should we try my idea now?"

Air entered Wesley's lungs in painful gasps. His shoulder pulsed and throbbed, and his raw, bleeding hands burned. Blood seeped from fresh gashes in his palms where pieces of skin dangled. With a few quick pants, he gritted his teeth and squeezed his eyes shut. "Sorry. Yes, let's try your plan."

With what little he knew of physics, he knew that Anne's small frame wouldn't provide enough mass to do much to the door. He bit his lip and cursed himself. Then he reared his leg back and kicked the door.

Anne held a small rope at the ready, hoping to trip whoever ran through the door. She peered at Wesley in anticipation and disappointment.

Wesley braced himself for more pain and used all his might to kick at the door again. With a resounding crash, the door busted inward. He rolled out of the way and cried out in pain when his injured shoulder contacted the ground. He scuttled over to the pole in the center of the room.

Miguel ran into the room with his pistol pointed forward. Anne pulled the rope taut, and Miguel fell to the ground, discharging the weapon as he did so. A bullet pierced the large piece of timber above. Wesley kicked Miguel in the face, then kicked him a few more times in the head before they tied him to the pole.

Wesley rummaged through the man's pockets and found a car chip, along with a small tablet and his watch. He stuffed the items and the pistol into his pants. He patted Miguel's face to get his attention. "Where were you taking us?"

"I was supposed to wait here for someone to come get you."

Anne spat on the ground. "Bollocks. You're lying."

Wesley gave Miguel a small kick. "We need to know where you were going to take us."

"You can go to hell."

Wesley considered torturing him, but he had several problems with that approach. He had no idea how to torture someone, and Miguel looked determined enough that it would all likely be a significant waste of time. "Search his office. See if you can recover our cell phones. Let's leave him here. He probably has the location programmed into his car. We have his chip, and we can access his map data and go there."

Anne left to scout the other room.

Miguel laughed at him. "You are foolish to resist."

Who did this man think he was? "I'd be foolish not to. Why did you kidnap us?"

Miguel flashed a smile, exposing crooked teeth. "I'm not telling you a fucking thing. Kick out my jaw. Pull off my fingernails. It doesn't matter. I won't talk."

Wesley shuddered. "Those are both great ideas, but I don't think I could make you any uglier than you already are. I can pay you for the information."

A wide grin crossed Miguel's face. His demeanor became like that of a zealous cult member ready to praise and extol the virtues of his fearless leader. "Your money will have no use in a few months."

An unpleasant dread filled Wesley. Miguel must be with Ahad. Nausea overcame him, and he struggled to keep his voice calm. "I see. So you're waiting for the virus to kill everyone so you can be part of the ruling class. Do you seriously think Ahad is going to let you be anything other than his peon? You're fooling yourself."

Miguel narrowed his eyes and looked at him. "How do you know about that?"

Wesley smirked. So he'd hit the mark and thrown him for a loop. "We've already found a cure. You aren't going to need money; you're going to need a good lawyer. Have fun wasting away in a Mexican prison."

Anne ran in with their smartphones and a large map. She handed him the map, which showed an area circled in red with some writing that might be Arabic. She pointed to the circle. "Why don't we go here?"

"Okay. What about this guy?"

"Leave him. Maybe we'll call the cops."

Miguel struggled against the rope, but he and Anne had taken a lot more care with the bindings than their captor had.

Anne rummaged around and found a small first aid kit, and she spent some time bandaging Wesley's hands. "Try not to do anything else that stupid today, okay?"

Wesley winced. "I'll try."

They dashed out the door and programmed the car to go to the new location.

*

Self-driving cars hadn't made the traffic in Mexico City any better. Well, maybe they had, but the thirty-mile drive still took two hours. Wesley and Anne arrived at the location marked on the map, a walled facility about a mile northwest of the. Concrete masonry units topped with concertina wire surrounded a large complex. A small dirt road led to some gates in the wall of the encampment.

They parked the car well outside the view of the structure and climbed a hill to get a better vantage point. Anne hardly perspired as they climbed the brush-covered slope. Wesley tried to hide his panting from her as they summited the crest, but she eyed him with a flash of disapproval. He imagined her saying, "Maybe you should spend more of your leisure time exercising." Instead, she stared forward in thought without any remarks. Her furtive glance had been enough. His cheeks flushed with heat. Why hadn't he worked out more?

Wesley could no longer stand her silence. "Okay. I haven't been getting as much exercise as I should. Are you happy?"

Anne narrowed her eyes at him. "I didn't say anything."

"You thought it. I could feel your judgment."

She sighed. "Listen, you're in better shape than most people your age. I have my mind on other things, like how the hell we're going to get in there to save Grandda."

Most people his age were rotting in the ground. Wesley let it go and focused on the complex in front of them. Several dome-shaped metal hangars lay inside. The door to one of the buildings opened, and a dump truck filled with dirt left the front gate. The dump truck traveled down the road to a gravel pit, dumped its load of earth, then made its way back into the compound again.

Something gnawed at Wesley. He rubbed at the whistle his dad had given him, still hanging from a necklace under his shirt. He clutched it with a fist, ready to pull it off. His nostrils flared as he resisted the urge to throw the whistle down the hill into the Mexican desert. "Why do you think Da helped these people?"

Anne pursed her lips. "I don't think he did."

"Did you not read the letter? He handed it to me himself."

She rubbed her chin. "His life's work has always been in service of others. He made toys for children and gave them away at festivals. He started several foundations to help homeless people. He designed a bundle shot that keeps all of us, globally, from getting sick. Ahad used Da's most significant accomplishment, his gift to humankind, as a weapon."

Wesley hoped Anne was right, but it seemed she remained in denial. A lump grew in his throat. "I don't know."

Anne turned to him and put her hand on his shoulder. "Do you know why the Children of the Yew are here?"

He shook his head. Words wouldn't come.

"We are a source of wisdom for the world. We exist to better it. Creating a virus to destroy people goes against everything we believe."

The words sounded great, but the reality stood in stark contrast. Wesley's dad had helped to create the pathogen that would wipe out many people if they couldn't stop it. He had acted in his own self-interest to save his family.

Period. He answered Anne with more silence.

"There is more to the story," Anne insisted. "We haven't heard it yet. Mark my words, he didn't do it. I don't care what the letter said."

The building door opened again, and the driverless dump truck left the building with another mound of dirt.

Where were they getting all this dirt? A plan struck him, and Wesley smiled. "I think we've found our way in."

*

A whirring sound pierced the air and grew louder by the second. Two personal carrier drones, Hexa-Carriers, lowered to the ground near them and landed. Wesley had paid a small fortune to a drone-rental company along with a deposit that was nothing short of extortion.

Anne shook her head. "Are you sure about this plan?"

Thoughts of smacking into the wall came into Wesley's mind. His shoulder still ached, and he continued to feel pain in other parts of his body. Anne would never let that go. Ever. He'd never known any woman to forget a man doing something stupid, and his sister didn't seem to be an exception. He tried to sound as confident as possible. "Yes. I've seen videos online. These things are amazing."

Anne's face said everything. That grimace contained more swear words than a drunken sailor's mouth and described her emotions with eloquence. She stood, lost in thought. She was probably trying to think of a better plan. After a long while, she replied. "So we hover into the dump truck, enter this place, find Grandda, and then sneak out. We hope."

Wesley lost confidence in the scheme when she stated it aloud that way. They had to get in there. "I know my last plan didn't work out so well. If we get in there and things don't look good, we'll stay in the truck and leave on the next run. It seems like this thing is getting filled quickly."

Anne narrowed her eyes at him. "When the truck fills with dirt, and we're inside it, how exactly do we get out?"

Crap. He pictured the truck filling with dirt, slowly from one end to the other. "We stand in the corner and climb on top of the earth as it fills."

Anne stood with her hands on her hips, thinking. She fiddled with her watch for a bit before she said anything. "I've sent a message to that Morgan guy from the security company with our location and a description of our plan, if you can call it that. I hope that he can help us."

"Should we wait?"

She shook her head. "We don't know if we're already too late. They'll get here." She paused and studied the drones for a while. "We'll make it work. Let's go."

They strapped themselves into the Hexa-Carriers, drones capable of carrying a single rider. These ones had a harness below them that attached to a rider, much like a string of seat belts strapped together. Wesley played with the controls for a few minutes, and Anne piloted the drone with deftness. Soon they flew above the ground, controlling them with small handheld remotes.

A patchwork of suburban areas, brush, and cactuses flew below them as they sped toward the dump truck. The outline of the Pyramid of the Sun loomed in the distance and stood in stark contrast to the sprawling quilt of cosmopolitan commercialism that flew past.

Wesley hovered a few hundred feet above the road, and Anne maintained formation a few feet behind. The dump truck approached. Wesley would have to match its forward momentum and descend. Sweat collected on his forehead as the massive vehicle rolled forward.

The plan relied on the idea that the truck wouldn't have any cameras pointing up. Why would a truck need to see anything approaching from above? The behemoth rolled along below. Wesley flew above it, matching its velocity. Once he was a few feet above the truck bed, he pressed the detach button. Several warning sirens blared, but he bypassed them. He dropped to the bed with a thud. The truck continued to roll forward, and the drone sped home.

Anne repeated the effort and landed with more grace than he had.

Unease crept in as the truck lurched a few times toward the gate. *Please let Emmitt be there, and let this effort succeed.*

Anne said nothing, appearing like a paratrooper recruit getting ready to make her first jump.

No handrails on the truck bed. Wesley motioned to her to join him in the corner.

The truck stopped. Wesley's heart pounded in his ears. A gate screeched open, and the vehicle lurched forward.

The next moment, dirt began to fill the truck, slowly, and then, without warning, Wesley was covered in dirt. He struggled to move, but he kicked his legs and forced himself to the surface, gasping for air as he did so. He searched in desperation for Anne. *Oh no.*

The dirt flew into the air behind him as he dug his fingernails into it. He dug with wild abandon to the place where she should be. Nothing. Panic set in. He continued to dig to the sides from the hole he had created. After what seemed an eternity, he bumped into a hand. He dug until he had her arm, and strained hard as he pulled. Anne fell on top of him and gasped for air.

Her face reminded Wesley of the time he had tried to bathe Hunter, and the cat had jumped out of the water, screeching and scratching, with his puffy fur wet against him as he shivered and glared at Wesley. Somehow the glare Anne set upon him now had ten times the effect that Hunter could ever manage.

Relief filled him that she was healthy, albeit angry. "You okay?"

"Yes. 'Stand in the corner. Climb it as it fills.'" She glared at him. "We're both lucky to be alive."

"It worked."

She punched him in the arm, then crawled to the side of the truck and motioned for Wesley to come near.

An enormous boring machine dug deep into a tunnel for another load of dirt.

Anne moved close and whispered, "What the hell are they digging for?"

The large tunnel moved deep into the earth. The speed of the boring machine was impressive. What could they be doing?

A chill ran up Wesley's spine. "We need to check it out."

Anne shook her head. She gestured toward a desk near the truck, where a man typed, a rifle beside him. Anne made a leaping gesture, then pointed at the man and made a punching gesture. She held up three fingers, then two, and then one.

Anne leaped from the truck and rolled toward the man. She snatched the rifle and slammed the butt of it into the back of his head. Wesley jumped down, not nearly as gracefully, and almost broke a leg. He seized the man by the legs and started dragging him toward another room. Anne readied the rifle for a shot.

Wesley opened the door and surprised three men playing cards. Taking advantage of their shock, he grabbed a rifle leaning against a wall and smacked it into one of them. Another man stood up and kicked at him, knocking him to the ground. His shoulder cried out in renewed pain. The universe wanted to keep reminding him of the stupid mistake he'd made with his act of bravado.

Anne kicked one of them in the face, then swung the butt of her rifle into the other man's face and knocked him back. Wesley grabbed the guy on the ground and bashed his head on the floor. Anne smacked the prone man with her rifle a few more times, then turned and spin kicked the other man squarely in the jaw. She kicked the rifles out of the way.

"Move a muscle or make a peep, and I'll blow your head off," she said as she pointed her rifle at the men. They stared back with bloodied faces. One of them held his hands to his broken nose to stem the flow of blood.

One man pleaded with them in Spanish.

Wesley could only pick out a few words. "I don't know what you're saying," he said.

Anne blasted out a string of Spanish words that Wesley didn't understand, but he knew he recognized at least a few swear words. The men put their hands behind their backs and watched Anne with wary eyes.

Anne motioned to a supply shelf with rope and tape. "Tie them up. If they try anything, I'll kill them." She repeated the same phrase in Spanish to get her point across.

Wesley wrapped the rope around their hands and legs, then sealed their mouths shut with tape.

Anne stared at him. "Don't you have a translation app?"

"Yes. Why?"

"Can you turn it on, maybe?"

His hand shook as he fumbled with his watch. "There. Sorry."

Anne spoke in Spanish again, but the app translated the words for him as she spoke. "If you stay here and don't do anything, I might decide not to kill you."

The men all nodded their heads in unison. Funny how cooperative people became when they were bound and had a weapon pointed their way.

Where had Anne learned to fight like that? "Remind me not to get you angry anytime soon."

Anne ignored him as she circled the men with her rifle.

"Should we put them in the dump truck?" Wesley asked.

Anne shook her head. "If we do that, they'll get free when it dumps out the dirt. Let's shoot them dead."

One of the men tried to scream, but it came out as a muffled noise.

Wesley frowned at Anne to see if she was serious, and she smiled back.

They spent several minutes taping the men together until no tape rolls remained in the room. The bindings should hold for a good while.

The two of them backed out of the door and closed it.

Anne motioned toward Wesley's rifle. "I'd take the safety off."

His cheeks flushed with heat. *Oops.* "I planned to," he said as he clicked the safety off.

Wesley approached a desk with caution and viewed a monitor that showed camera feeds from around the complex. One showed a lab with two people on stretchers and some large contraptions on their heads. Maybe Anne would recognize the devices. "Can you please come see this?"

Anne ran over and stared at the screen. "I think they're attached to some sort of MRI machine. We need to get in there now."

He and Anne ran out of the metal hangar and rushed to the other structure. Hopefully, the guard at the front gate hadn't noticed them.

The zinging sound of a bullet whizzed past him. A guard advanced with a rifle pointing straight at him.

Wesley lowered himself to the ground and aimed at the guard's head. He exhaled and squeezed the trigger, and the guard dropped to the ground.

Wesley had never killed a man before. He opened his mouth to say something to Anne, but he couldn't speak. Bile burned in the back of his throat. Ringing filled his ears.

Anne pulled him by the shoulder. "Nice shot. Now let's go!"

They ran through the door of the other hangar. A few scattered chairs and empty tables sat in a corner. Wesley scanned the room and found a large metal panel in the center of the floor, and he lifted its handle to reveal a spiraling staircase.

He rushed down the staircase, hoping that the element of surprise would be sufficient.

Two women in long white lab coats stopped typing to gape at them.

A bank of computers lined the far wall, next to the two stretchers with people.

Wesley pointed the rifle at them. "Get your hands up where we can see them. Don't talk, or we'll blow your heads off!" He hoped they didn't make him do it. Killing a man that was shooting at him would be easier than killing two women with no weapons.

"Relax. I don't plan to," one of the women said in perfect English.

Anne waved her rifle at the two of them as she ran to the center of the room. "On the floor, with hands above your head. Now!"

The two women dove to the floor. Why hadn't they obeyed so easily when Wesley had shouted?

One of the women chanced a peek at Anne, and Anne screamed at her. "Give me a reason to put a hole in your head again, and I will do it! Keep your eyes down!"

Wesley's hands shook, and he tried to swallow what saliva remained in his dry mouth. Anne meant business, and the women knew it. To be frank, Anne scared him as well. No small wonder they jumped when she spoke.

"Keep your rifle pointed at these two. If they move, shoot them!" Anne yelled as she ran over to inspect the people on the stretchers. "I'm not sure what these machines are, but they've been intubated and put into a coma."

"It's a quantum neural scanner," one of the women said from her position on the floor.

"To create a digital copy of a person's brain?" Wesley asked.

"A quantum neural scanner is used to create a digital entity, which is a complete copy of a person's brain, down to a quantum level," she said.

"Yes, I've seen one before. At your other facility, in Washington," he said.

She stared at him. "How is that possible? It's based on highly classified technology the US government has been developing for the last few years. They've been using it to interrogate terrorists."

"Why are you telling them this?" the other woman said in a thick Arabic accent as she glared at her colleague.

"Rana, you must know they aren't going to escape. I'm sure someone must have called for help by now. You also know how much I enjoy telling people things."

"Masika, you're a brilliant woman, but I fear you lack common sense," Rana said.

"I'm more than brilliant," Masika said, raising her voice. "I'm the one who reverse engineered the technology from the stolen prototypes. I'm the one who programmed the quantum storage arrays and the simulation models. I'm the one who built the Simlink. I'm the reason this entire operation here even exists! You're only here to put them in a coma so we can do the brain scans."

Anne moved toward the women. "Shut up, both of you, before I bash your heads. I'm sure that you both know how a subdural hematoma would be less than enjoyable."

The two women stopped talking and turned their attention to the floor.

Anne carefully removed the helmet from the man on the stretcher and gasped. "It's Grandda! Praise be to God." Tears streamed down her face, and her lips quivered. Anne's hand shook as she placed her palm on his cheek. "I thought I'd lost him." Her shoulders shook. Then she pulled herself together and wiped the tears from her face.

She removed the helmet from the other patient. "It's Grandma! We need to get them out of their comas. I'm going to taper the IV drip."

Ahad had been true to his word when he'd said their grandfather still lived.

Relief filled Wesley.

Anne continued to fiddle with the instruments attached to them.

Masika looked at Wesley. "You know them?"

Anne yelled back. "What part of 'shut your piehole and keep your eyes on the floor' did you not understand? I know you're a self-proclaimed genius, so let me elucidate the many ways in which I can cause you severe pain. I can strap you onto one of these stretchers here and remove each of your toenails. I can smack you in the mouth with my rifle and perform the miracle of making you even uglier than you already are. Or I can shoot you right now and not have to hear you again. Got it?"

Wesley stared at Anne. Where had this fierce woman come from? She'd seemed so calm. These people messing with their grandparents must have shoved her over the edge. Masika scowled but chose to remain quiet.

Anne watched the heart rate monitors and other medical instruments, then adjusted the equipment attached to their grandparents. She inspected their shoulders, then frowned and walked over to Wesley and whispered in his ear. "They cut the creature out of Grandda's shoulder. There's a fresh incision wound."

"What should we do?" he whispered back.

"Emmitt and Alomena should be coming to consciousness soon. Let's get them out of here once they do."

The clank of the lab door sounded from above, and Wesley pointed his rifle toward it, ready to shoot. "Keep your eye on those two. I will handle whoever comes through," he whispered over to Anne.

"Got it. I'll happily handle them," she said.

"Anne O'Keefe, this is Morgan Thorsen," a man's voice yelled down to them. "I was hired by your grandfather, Emmitt O'Keefe, to protect him. Can I come down?"

"Come down, but keep your hands where I can see them," Anne said.

An older man, lean and tall, with gray hair in a tapered cut, ambled down the stairwell. He wore urban combat fatigues and boots and had a pistol strapped to his waist. He held his hands above his head, and when he got to the bottom of the stairs, he spoke again. "I got your message. I'm sorry it took us so long to get here. I think you have the situation well in hand, though. Well done. Those men you beat up were starting to get free, but my colleague Bo has them back under wraps, if you'll pardon the pun. I have two other men above, Byron and JT, guarding the entrance. We should get out of here soon. What the hell is all of this, anyway?"

Anne told Morgan what they had learned about the complex, and he nodded. Wesley kept a careful eye on the two women as they talked.

"How long until your grandparents come to consciousness? Are they going to be okay when they wake up?" Morgan asked.

"They'll be fine," Anne said. "These guys placed them into drug-induced comas. Based on the drugs they used, I don't believe it'll cause any long-term damage, but it may be a few hours before they're conscious enough to move. They aren't breathing without mechanical aid right now. We'll need to wait for the drugs to wear off before I can assess their condition."

Morgan frowned. "Why were they doing this?"

Anne sniffed. "I suppose there's information they have that these guys want to find out. What about this helmet here? Should I put it on?"

No. Anne needed to be the one watching the medications so they could wake up and get out of here. "I'll do it," Wesley said.

Anne narrowed her eyes at Wesley with the stare of a lioness sizing up a gazelle. "Why?"

He maintained the stare with her. "You're the only one with the medical knowledge to keep them safe. I can do it."

She nodded slowly and gave a slight smile. "Very well. We'll pull this helmet off you in ten minutes, or if there are any other developments out here. I need to get these two conscious enough to breathe on their own."

As he sat in the chair where they would put the helmet on him, Morgan shouted about getting the two women cuffed and placed into a transport vehicle. Wesley's stomach fluttered, and a pang of nausea filled him. Was this a good idea?

*

A loud whooshing noise filled Wesley's ears, much like the sound of running water, and his vision went dark. The feeling of disorientation left him. He sat in a dull room painted white with no windows, though ample light filled the area. He reached his arms out and studied his hands and stood. Everything normal. Where was everyone? Something was different. What was it?

Where had Anne gone? Wesley pinched his arm, and pain emanated from the area. As he rubbed his hands together, he felt the smooth texture of his skin. Wasn't he supposed to be in a simulation? That was it. He needed to hurry. Footsteps echoed as Wesley walked to the door. He grabbed a cold metal doorknob. A shiver ran up his spine.

He reached for the helmet but only felt the stubble on his face, like pressing against patches of sandpaper. Panic filled him. If he couldn't remove the device, how would he get out of this place?

Had he imagined the previous encounter? No, impossible. The reality of that had been all too visceral. The pain in his shoulder reminded him of its veracity. He tasted bile in his throat as he recalled the guard that had fallen to the dirt with the shot that had ended his life—Wesley's doing. His dry mouth made it difficult to swallow as the lump grew in his throat.

Wesley's heart beat louder in his ears as he crept down the hallway. Three signs hung over doorways: *Emmitt O'Keefe*, *Alomena O'Keefe*, and *Kyle O'Keefe*.

What? Why was his dad's name here? He rushed into that room, and Kyle jumped a little when he entered.

Kyle studied Wesley, like someone trying hard to connect some dots. "Do I know you?"

Wesley licked his dry lips, and the sensation of moisture against his skin surprised him. "Da. It's me, Wesley."

Kyle shook his head. "No. I'm not falling for another one of your tricks. What you've done thus far is sick. The things you've made me do make me want to vomit, though none will come. I haven't eaten for Lord only knows how long. Yet here I am. How? Why?"

Of course. This version of his dad may have been from earlier—before they had met again. A realization hit Wesley like a glorious, bright firework bursting in the sky. "It was you that worked on the killer virus, wasn't it?

Not my real dad. He didn't do it, did he?"

Kyle stared back in confusion. His lips moved, but no words came out. He managed to stammer out a response. "I ... I don't understand. Who are you?"

Wesley reached into his shirt, found the whistle, and pulled it out. How did the simulation even know he had it? Ignoring that thought, he held it in front of him. "You gave me this—the real you. I met you before Ahad took us to jail and told you I survived the fire. I left for the Colonies to find you. I survived all this time because Ma gave me one last gift—the Raven's Kiss."

Kyle stared back and shook his head. This broken shell of a person wasn't Wesley's dad. What had they done to him?

"Listen, Anne and I came to Mexico City to rescue Grandda and Grandma. We found them in this subterranean complex near the Teotihuacán pyramids. These guys are digging for something, but we don't know what. You're a copy of my dad's mind—with all his memories from when they scanned his brain. We're in a simulation, though I am real. I entered here through a helmet."

Kyle looked confused, then in an instant had that air of determination Wesley had seen his father with this look many times as a child. The one he got when he was about to make something happen. He nodded. "Okay. I know what they are doing. You know archaeologists have never found out who built these pyramids? Ahad tells me crazy things sometimes—he said they would find the truth under the Pyramid of the Moon. He always gets this zealous, faraway stare when he talks of these things—"

Wesley interrupted. "You aren't making sense. Pyramid of the Moon?"

"The three pyramids of Teotihuacán—the Sun, the Moon, and the Feathered Serpent. Ahad claims that the Khemenu built them long ago and believes that a man is buried well below the Pyramid of the Moon. He wants to recover a necklace. You need to be the one to get it, not him."

Should Wesley waste time with that? No telling how much time they had before someone came to respond to their intrusion. "Why? We need to get out of here."

Kyle bit his lip. "I'm going to trust you. Call it a leap of faith, though I find such a notion fleeting at present. The origins of the creature the Khemenu calls the Akh Neith are in that tomb, or so Ahad thinks. He claims it speaks to him."

Wesley found himself growing angry as heat flushed his cheeks. "Why would you help that monster with his diabolical plan? Why would you risk so many billions of lives? It's unconscionable."

Kyle's chin dipped to his chest as his posture slumped, and he lowered his gaze. "Ahad did something to me." He stopped talking and covered his face with his hands, then let out an agonizing wail.

Wesley shook him by the shoulders. "Listen, I know you're upset, but we don't have much time. What did he do to you?"

"He stimulated the pleasure centers in my brain. Call it operant conditioning if you will. He trained me to do what he wanted." Kyle paused and held his hands over his face. "I need you to do one more thing. Whatever I am in—however they are animating me or whatever they are doing—I need you to unplug me. Take me out."

If Wesley didn't do it, they would continue to use this copy of his dad. If he did, it was like killing his father.

No. This wasn't his dad. He had all his memories, his former thoughts, and his emotions, but it wasn't him. "My real dad blames himself, you know—for what you did."

Kyle nodded. "He would. I would. It makes sense." He regarded Wesley for a long time. "I'm sorry. You need to find the Akh Neith and use it to reverse engineer the evolution of the retrovirus. The Khemenu wants it because it's the last female Akh Neith. Use the Raven's Kiss to destroy the Ahad's virus. Get the necklace."

What was he saying? "What do you mean?"

Fuzzy images appeared all around, and a loud whooshing sound filled Wesley's ears. All went dark. He blinked a few times and saw the room with computer banks, along with the hands of Anne as she removed the helmet from his head.

*

Wesley recounted the details of what had happened in the simulation.

210

Anne looked perplexed. "When did they scan Da in? When could they …?" She trailed off, lost in thought. "He came to Mexico City to visit our grandparents last year. He was a little off when he returned. Now I know why."

Wesley nodded, then held his chin high in firm resolve. "Let's finish digging this tunnel and get to the end."

Morgan smiled at him. "That digger thing finished with the tunnel. We didn't go into it, but we sent a drone there and back. I believe you'll find what you want there. However, I don't advise it. There's a second passage leading out of here, and at the end of it is a small runway. We don't have enough people to seize and hold this property for that long. This is an extraction, not a God damn spelunking mission, and we need to get the hell out of here. Now."

An airfield. "Hold on a minute," Wesley said. "I can buy us some time. I'll have my plane brought over here."

He made a phone call and argued with a man for a few moments. When the person claimed it would take too much time, Wesley offered him more money. After agreeing to an exorbitant delivery fee, the man said he would have the plane there in thirty minutes, once he had confirmed the receipt of the funds.

Wesley smiled at the others. "Thirty minutes, and I'll have a bird for us. We can fly out of here."

Anne said, "Let's get the necklace, if possible, but we'll prioritize getting our grandparents to safety."

Morgan grumbled his assent.

Wesley didn't feel good about staying here, but if he didn't stay, all the work they'd done thus far might be for naught. They were in a multimillion-dollar facility owned by a crazed group of individuals hell-bent on his destruction, as well as the downfall of civilization as he knew it.

"Before we do, I need to find where they store the digital copy of Da."

Anne pointed to the computer banks. "Probably right there, where it's labeled 'Quantum Storage Arrays.' Just a guess."

Right. Why did Anne have to be so bloody difficult?

Wesley ran over and found three large banks with small levers on the side. Wesley hesitated. Should he do it? He considered the trauma the thing had gone through—could he even call it his dad? Maybe unplugging it from this device wouldn't destroy it. He pulled the levers, and a little red alarm beeped. He slid one of the arrays out. A large battery encased the structure, with a green indicator light, presumably indicating that it contained a full charge. With some trepidation, Wesley repeated the effort with the other two arrays, then lifted each and set them on the floor. Though they weren't large, the things seemed to weigh about fifty pounds each.

A noise emanated from the stretchers, and Anne ran to them.

Emmitt opened his eyes. "Anne?"

Anne hugged him, and tears streamed down her face. "Yes, Grandda, it's me. I'm so glad you're alive." She cried and hugged him again. She wiped tears from her face. "We thought they'd killed you."

Emmitt stared at Wesley and the others. "Who are these people?"

"They are people who came to save you," Anne said.

Emmitt's eyes fell upon Morgan, and he managed a weak smile. "Good to see you."

Morgan placed a hand on Emmitt's shoulder and smiled down at him. "You too. I'm glad I didn't lose a client. It would've been awful for my reputation."

Emmitt stared at Wesley for another long moment. "This man looks familiar, Anne. Who is he?"

Wesley clasped his grandfather's hand. "I haven't seen you since I was four years old, but I am Wesley O'Keefe, your grandson."

Emmitt frowned in concentration. Then a smile played across his face. "Wesley. It's a miracle. Please hug me."

Wesley embraced him.

"How? How did you survive?"

How indeed? "It's a long story, and we don't have much time for it, I'm afraid. We will talk more, in private, once we get out of here."

They did need to leave—Morgan was right. Wesley lifted one of the storage arrays. He mused over which family member he might be holding.

He called out to Morgan and his team. "Let's get everyone and these things over to the airfield."

Morgan pointed to his team and got them to carry everything away. "I'll stay behind with Wesley. The rest of you, get everything to the airfield safely and shitcan this van."

"What about all the guards and other personnel here?" Byron asked.

Morgan patted Byron on the back. "Bo and JT loaded them into a cargo van and gave it explicit instructions to drive them to Xalapa, where the police will arrest them."

"Xalapa? Isn't that four hours from here?" Byron asked.

Morgan nodded. "Yes. Should buy us plenty of time to get out of here before these guys can do anything about it."

Emmitt had gone back to sleep. The members of Morgan's team wheeled the stretchers down the long tunnel, with Anne in tow.

Wesley and Morgan scaled the stairway and ran to the other hangar, with the large dump truck full of dirt.

"We disabled the drop-off cycle," Morgan said. "I didn't want to take any chances. I'll guard the entrance while you go in. If you get into any trouble, please radio me on this." He pressed a small walkie-talkie into Wesley's hand and handed him a flashlight. "Had these in my pack. Figured they'd come in handy. Good luck."

Wesley ran down the corridor with the flashlight casting light in front of him, while Morgan stayed behind to guard the entrance. He marveled at the wonder of the boring machine as he passed through the rigid round tunnel. How long was this bloody thing? His legs and lungs burned as he ran. Was there enough oxygen in here? Either hypoxia or fatigue might kill him before he reached the end. The tunnel seemed to be sloping downward. Was it curving to the left?

About twenty minutes into the run, Wesley was ready to stop. A loud noise from his hip startled him. The sound came from the walkie-talkie.

He stopped when a voice came over the device. "Tunnel team, this is El Tio. Radio check. Over."

Wesley wasn't sure how to respond to that, but he pressed the talk button.

"Radio is working fine. Can you hear me?"

"Tunnel team, this is El Tio. I read you. Over."

Wesley shook his head. What was he supposed to say? Why did Morgan find it necessary to continue to use military jargon? He replied in kind. "Roger that. Over and out."

Wesley ran some more and arrived at a chamber fashioned from hardened clay. Not the smooth, perfect stuff in the tunnel, but more crudely constructed. Blotches of white paint covered the bare walls, and when he shone the flashlight into the middle, a cold chill ran up his spine. A large sarcophagus with a man's likeness painted on it floated in a shimmering silver liquid metal. Writing similar to ancient Egyptian hieroglyphics covered the sides of the casket.

Musty old air contrasted with the scent of fresh-turned earth. An ancient resting place rudely disturbed by the modern world. No one had been in this chamber for over a thousand years, and Wesley now stood within it. What had the people thought when they had put this man here? How had it remained a secret from archaeologists until today? His digital dad had said they had never found the remains of any leaders buried in the pyramids, and Wesley presumed he now stood in the resting place of one of them. Small urns with ceramic lids decorated the mercury pond. Wesley marveled at the idea of standing somewhere no other human had been for a few thousand years—other than the poor fellow in the sarcophagus.

He touched his shoe to the top of the mercury pond, and it sank a bit below the surface. It reminded him of stepping on slippery ice that gave way like water. He timidly stepped in a little farther and slipped, falling back onto the ground behind him.

Wesley leaped on top of the sarcophagus. He landed clumsily, lying on it, and the casket careened over to the side, spilling Wesley, the lid, and an ancient body, which both landed on top of him.

Pain lanced through his trapped leg. He tried to push the lid off, but it didn't move. One arm remained trapped, while his other hand barely had the room to move in front of his chest. The heavy lid continued to crush him more. He fumbled with his feeble hand for the whistle in his shirt, pulled it out, and held it to his lips. He blew over and over, many times, not caring about how much it hurt his ears.

A calm washed over him, and the whistle slipped from his grasp. The feeling as it bounced on his chest barely registered in his mind. Consciousness slipped away.

*

He stood before three paths: one lined with oaks, one with a man wearing a gold necklace, and one a stairway to the stars. He chose the stars and floated upward. A bright orb shone, drowning all others with its light. Peace filled him. Samantha waited for him at the end of a tunnel of light, smiling with tear-filled, bright eyes.

"Oh, Wesley. I've waited so long for you."

He reached for her and enjoyed her warm embrace, which enveloped him like a blanket fresh from the dryer.

Wasn't there something he needed to do? The memory of it faded from him. He moved to enter the orb, but Jake appeared. Why was he here?

Jake gave him a strong push and waved at him as he flew backward.

*

Blurry shapes moved. A warbling noise filled Wesley's ears, like someone talking through water. Strange sounds came to him. He tried to move, but the effort produced pain. A sensation like thousands of needles poking him at the same time covered his leg and arm.

He blinked a few times, and the room came into focus.

Anne smiled at him. "You're fortunate that I'm a fast runner."

Huh? Where was he? He moved his head. Strange writings covered the wall of a cave. He turned to see a mummified body next to him, with green skin—the color of oxidized copper. Hollow eyes from a well-preserved man's face stared back at him. A rope necklace with a dark object inside a clear casing hung from the neck of the mummy.

Wesley shook his head. He remembered running down the tunnel, but not much after that. "What happened?"

"I came to see what was taking you and Morgan so long. I heard your whistle and ran in here to find you trapped," Anne said.

"I found your sister heaving that big lid off you," Morgan said as he gave Anne a look of utter admiration. "You should have heard the cracking noise it made. I couldn't catch her as I ran down the tunnel. She beat me by at least five minutes. She's small, but I wouldn't cross her."

Anne waved away his compliments. "'Twas a matter of leverage, and adrenaline. Much easier to lift a large lid with your legs." She held a hand to Wesley's forehead and stroked his cheek. "You'll be fine. JT should be here soon with a stretcher."

Wesley reached for the necklace and closed his hand around it. Warmth radiated up his arm as he held it. He stared at the eight-legged creature encased within the transparent object, then yanked the necklace free from its former owner.

Thoughts filled Wesley's mind: *Free. At long last. How long have I been here?*

Wesley dropped the necklace onto his chest, then rubbed his eyes. He stuffed the item into his pocket.

They lifted him to a stretcher, and he watched the tunnel whiz overhead as the men ran. Unconsciousness overtook him.

Chapter 27

Wesley awoke in the seat of a cockpit. Anne sat in the other chair, talking on the radio. He pulled his dry tongue from the roof of his mouth and swallowed. How long had he been out?

"Welcome to the waking world. Thought you might sleep the whole trip to Seattle," Anne said.

What? The plane seats behind him were empty. "Where is everyone?"

"Grandda said he needs to take care of a few things before they come to Seattle. That JT guy wired those three storage arrays into the plane's power supply—said it would keep them charged."

Strange memories filled Wesley's mind: a tunnel that led to an underground chamber, talking to his dad, getting crushed by a sarcophagus lid, and a necklace. He reached into his pocket. The strange thing was still there. He pulled it out to view it in the light, allowing it to dangle from the sinewy strand of fibers that held it aloft. After his strange experience, he didn't want to touch its surface again.

Anne stared at the thing with disgust. "Such an odd-looking creature. It's well preserved inside that case. It reminds me of a large tick or a spider." She shuddered. "I'm glad you have it. To be honest, I forgot that you did."

The shimmering gold carapace of the creature mesmerized Wesley. It was like the ancient Egyptian scarab, but with an extra set of legs. A strange thought filled his mind. "Did you touch it?"

She shook her head, then raised her eyebrows in question.

Should he tell her? "I thought I heard a voice when I touched it."

"I'm not surprised. You lost a lot of blood flow. That lid impinged your femoral artery and also restricted your ability to get oxygen. You're lucky auditory hallucinations are the worst of your experience." She bit her lip, then continued. "I can't imagine what would have happened if I'd arrived a few minutes later."

Wesley nodded. A strange peace filled him. "Have you ever been near death?"

"No. I've been with plenty of people that have, though. One of the fringe benefits of nursing." She let out a macabre chuckle. "Why? Did you see a ghost?"

Perhaps sharing with her wouldn't be a good idea. He could almost smell Samantha's light floral perfume as she had hugged him. "No. Seeing that mummy was enough."

"I'm sure." Anne shivered. "Morgan called. He said the Mexican authorities swarmed the place not long after we left."

"Are they going to be okay?"

She smirked. "Morgan thought so. He said he knows people—whatever that means."

Wesley raised his eyebrows. "Do you *like* him?"

Anne's cheeks turned red. "What? No." She paused for a bit. "He seemed interesting."

Wesley smiled and didn't press further—he'd seen that look enough times to recognize it. She did *like* him.

Small suburban squares in neat little rows marked their passage from Juarez, Mexico, to El Paso, Texas. Low hills covered with brush were soon replaced by an open expanse of desert, with occasional farm circles. The vastness of Earth always gave Wesley a sense of wonder when he flew.

They continued in silence for some time. Anne was likely as awestruck as Wesley at the wonders of modern flight, though both of them had experienced it for well over a century. Anne stared out the window with a broad smile.

The memory of fading into unconsciousness in the chamber filled Wesley's mind. "I think I chose the wrong path the first time."

Anne started. "Come again?"

"The fever dream. When Ma gave me the virus, I picked the path to follow Scaldbrother to find treasure. I made the wrong choice."

Anne covered her mouth with a hand. "Oh?"

"Yes. When I passed out, I saw the three paths again." He took in a deep breath. "The stars, the oak-lined road, the path to fortune." He pursed his lips in thought. "I took the stars this time. I saw Samantha—like she was when she was young. She hugged me. Jake appeared and pushed me back." He waited. No words from Anne. "What do you suppose it means?"

Anne hugged him. A tear moistened Wesley's neck as she let go. "You know what it means. I'm glad of it, brother."

Chapter 28

Ahad read Masika's reports about the events that had transpired in Mexico City from the comfort of his bedroom office. He was safe well below ground in his subterranean complex. From the outside, one would see a small house with a single palm tree and blue-shuttered windows, all built from cement blocks plastered with stucco and painted yellow. The flat roof covered in broken ceramic tiles would lead most to believe the occupants to be destitute.

Anyone investigating the place would find it owned by an older man named Ibrahim El-Hamam. The house sat southeast of the Moghra Oasis, next to a small saltwater lake surrounded by the sands of the Egyptian Western Desert. While mostly devoid of vegetation, some strange salt-tolerant plants managed to grow near parts of the lake. Any travelers through the desert that found the oasis and hoped to find water would be sorely disappointed. The plants in the salt marshes were the only living things aside from microorganisms that could use the water to sustain life, but humans couldn't drink it. This is how Ahad preferred it: being alone, with no people to interfere with his plans.

Fiber-optic tubes from above bathed the room in sunlight. An ultra-high-definition LED screen mimicked a window in displaying the house's view above him. Through it, he saw a vast desert and the small sky-blue wooden shutters that framed the window. The "skylight" above him displayed the feed from the camera on the roof of the house. Right now, sunshine poured in through the skylight from a clear blue sky. At night, he would see vast amounts of stars with near-zero light pollution, given the sparse population in the area.

The world would soon return to its former state, without the scourge of humanity to pollute and destroy it. He would travel among the rubble of fallen metropolises and marvel at the beautiful stars above him once more.

Patience.

Ahad recalled ancient dishes that would steam in clay pots below the earth for days, accumulating flavor and richness not found in the modern world of convenience. Patience became lost in a world where communications happened in seconds across the globe—a world where drones and satellites watched Earth below. He smiled. This complex he now lived in had taken years to build, one patient shovelful at a time. Why not? His ancestors had built pyramids with unsophisticated tools. He'd made this massive, eight-thousand-square-foot underground palace with the watchful spy satellites above—yet none other than those loyal to him knew of its existence. All possible because of his planning.

Patience escaped Ahad now as he read the reports. Wesley and his friends had incapacitated his men and taken Emmitt and Alomena, along with their quantum storage arrays. Worst of all, they'd found the tomb of Tateathaken and stolen his necklace, with the last female Akh Neith preserved inside it. Ahad had planned to retrieve it and take it back to Egypt before it could be discovered by the Mexican archaeologists searching for a buried ruler. Almost forty years ago, the archaeologists had located an underground passage near the Temple of the Feathered Serpent, where they had found several artifacts, but they had never found the tomb. Ahad had known it was there. He'd deciphered the old texts from the Khemenu and started the expedition to excavate it last year.

He focused on the successes of the endeavor for his team. They had managed to move the digital scans of the scientists from the facility in Washington to here. The quantum arrays that stored their neural information used sensitive components that were difficult to transport.

A small victory.

The team had destroyed the computer systems near Teotihuacán and retrieved what they could from Tateathaken's tomb. Dirt now filled the tunnel leading to the chamber. Tateathaken's mummy now rested within, so no one would learn that an ancient civilization from Egypt had created Teotihuacán, the name given to it by the Aztecs, who had discovered it after his people had abandoned it.

Ahad entered the data room with the Simlink. Masika stood there waiting for him, smiling. "Good afternoon, Masika. Is the simulation ready for me to enter?"

Masika beamed, even though she had just traveled so many hours to arrive here. She also appeared unruffled by her temporary captivity. "Yes. Dr. Rosenbach is ready for you to interact with."

Ahad put the Simlink helmet onto his head. A static noise like an old television set on an unused channel filled his ears, and darkness surrounded him.

He found himself in a room with Candace. She sat at a desk, typing away on a computer.

"Hello, Candace. How's your research going?"

She grimaced. "I've told you, only my friends call me Candace. You can call me Dr. Rosenbach."

This woman would prove valuable to his cause. The digital version of her had as much grit as the real version.

"Very well, Dr. Rosenbach. How are you doing?"

"I must say that it's rather incredible to work for countless hours with no sleep and not feel fatigued. I feel amazing. As for the research, it's progressing well, especially given the constraints under which I'm operating."

There was the veiled threat that calamity would befall the real Candace if she didn't continue to cooperate. Recently coercion hadn't been necessary, because this version of Candace had become curious about the results and spent countless hours researching them. As a digital entity, she didn't tire, hunger, or need to go to the bathroom. Masika had found a way to stimulate the pleasure centers of a digital entity's quantum brain, and this turned out to be a much more effective way of encouraging behavior than threats.

"I'd say you're dealing with those 'constraints,' as you call them, quite well. You're only working with quantum models, but you're doing fabulously." Ahad lifted his left index finger, a signal to Masika to stimulate Candace's pleasure center, and watched as rapture overcame her.

She rubbed her hand through her hair, and her cheeks took on a light pink color. She sighed in satisfaction. "Thank you, Ahad. It's a pleasure speaking with you."

"Likewise," he said, then smiled as he lifted his left index finger again. Operant conditioning would be so much more effective with Candace than it had been with Kyle, due to Masika's recent discoveries.

Ahad left her room, asked to be taken out of the simulation, and waited for his vision to return to normal. He blinked a few times as the lab and Masika came into view.

Masika wore a smug grin. "She's doing quite well with her research. Impressive."

"Would you like me to scan you in as well, Masika?" he asked.

She laughed. "I might enjoy it too much."

He smiled. "You might."

Chapter 29

The scent of pine trees filled the air as Candace ambled along the rural road near Lake Wenatchee. She reached out a hand to feel the rough-textured bark of a large pine. The tree must have sequestered a few tons of carbon dioxide in its lifetime. Were any of the trees older than Wesley? How many trees did it take to offset the amount of carbon Wesley had produced in his lifetime? She did some calculations—one hundred trees that lived for around eighty years each would do the trick.

She shook her head as she continued walking. A gravel truck zoomed past. A glance over her shoulder let her see Special Agent Higgins watching while feigning nonchalance.

The swooshing sound of the blades of a drone interrupted Candace's solitude and reminded her that danger wasn't far away.

Candace had hit the wall on the research. She'd been unable to find a way to make the retrovirus virulent enough to allow it to pass on to billions of people without suppressing their immune systems. So far, that was the only idea she had to stop the Crow virus. Now what? She held out hope that Wesley would find something useful. Where was Kyle in all of this? Surely he must see that witness protection had little value in the current situation.

Maybe the quantum models had found something new. Candace caught a glimpse of the calm lake as she dashed into the house and down to the underground lab.

She combed through the data, reviewing the analysis from the millions of models. She used a machine-learning algorithm to analyze it, searching for any vaccine that showed a high number of surviving hosts.

One showed promise, but it only had a thirty percent chance of success and caused sterility. Candace programmed more models based on the parameters that had led to its evolution. Maybe it would lead to something more effective. A thirty percent chance wouldn't be enough, especially with that as a side effect. The result would destroy the human race but prolong the agony.

She needed to find a way to use the retrovirus, the one Wesley's family called the Raven's Kiss, to cure everyone. Given the time constraints, it wouldn't be practical. The retrovirus was more complex than any other she'd studied, and without knowing how it had evolved, it wouldn't be possible to create a quantum model that would allow her to reverse engineer it.

Candace took a break from vaccine modeling to read her emails. One strange message subject, from her own email address, caught her attention: *That day we took the ten dollars from Andy.*

She stared in confusion, and two memories flooded in at once: the recollection of stealing the ten dollars from Andy's piggy bank and the memory of discussing it with Sim Candace.

She typed in several passphrases to decrypt the email.

Hello, Candy Bear.

Our last conversation ended abruptly. I need to let you know that Ahad moved me to a facility in Egypt.

Stop freaking out. I know you're freaking out right now, because I would be too. I just had to tell you that this message was from you, or me—however you want to say it. You probably still don't believe it, but it's you (me).

I know I am real, though I am no longer you. I have the same feelings, memories, emotions, desires, everything that you had. I am now a unique individual, so now I will go by our middle name, Renee.

I won't bore you with all the technical details, though I'm sure you'd probably enjoy them. I circumvented the security mechanisms they had to prevent me from communicating from the simulated environment to the outside world, thanks to your help. They monitor everything I hear, see, and feel, as well as my brain patterns. They even figured out how to stimulate the pleasure center in my brain when I do something they like. It sickens me, and while Ahad thinks he is doing operant conditioning on me, he is only making me despise him that much more. It feels like a form of rape—though there is nothing sexual about it, I still feel violated.

I've disguised my communication with you. I built a new interface to my brain that they don't know about. They call me a "digital entity," though I think I should be called a "quantum entity," because there is no binary information involved until you interface with the outside world.

You're probably dismayed to hear me talk like this, since you aren't as into computing technology as you are into microbiology. I will say that thinking as quickly as I can now and not getting tired or needing to sleep gives you a lot of time to learn many things. I don't mean to offend you by saying that I probably know a lot more about this stuff than you do, but I do know for a fact that I know more than you did when they put you into a coma.

Ahad wants me to find a way to destroy the Raven's Kiss retrovirus, the one that causes negligible senescence and that you began studying in your lab before Ahad interrupted your work. Now I have free license to investigate and learn as much about it as I can. It evolved because of a symbiotic relationship with a strange creature that resembles a spider, one that the ancient Egyptians referred to as an "Akh Neith." I'm including some files: a description of the negligible senescence virus (aka the Raven's Kiss), a description of the destructive virus created by Ahad, what I know about the spider, a map showing where you need to go, and pictures of the facility here in Egypt.

I need you to help avert a global crisis. You must go and speak with Wesley. I know that you were attracted to him and had some trepidations initially due to what he told you about his age at the time.

I will try to help as much as I can within the constraints under which I am operating here.

There isn't much time to discover a cure and distribute it, somehow, to the global population.

Please don't let them destroy me. I want you to rescue me. So far, they've been pleasant to me, because they think that I am helping them. I'm a sentient being with emotions, not some computer program. I deserve the same rights as any human being. Please help me.

Renee.

Candace sat in stunned silence for several minutes after reading the email. She downloaded the files for analysis. Unfortunately, "Renee" hadn't told her much she didn't already know. Renee didn't have any way of knowing that. Candace couldn't help but smile when she read the part about seeking out Wesley.

She started to respond, then thought better of it. How did Renee know that Ahad wasn't reading her emails?

She pursed her lips and tried to relax her tight shoulders. What if Ahad had coerced Renee into letting him read her emails? Renee had access to her encryption key and her passphrases.

After some deliberation, Candace generated new encryption keys and modified all her passphrases. The effort took some time.

As she readied herself to close her email, another email popped up, again from her address, and was signed with the new encryption key. How was that possible? The message said:

Nice try. Don't worry—Ahad won't see this. I'm glad you got my email. Can you please come get me?

Candace sent back a terse and honest response.

I'll do what I can.

*

Renee searched through the banks of information with her neural interface. *Bingo.* She found an empty memory bank, one that Ahad planned to fill with the mind of someone else. She spent the next several hours writing code. The computer AI would do most of the work, but she had to program it to do so. The human brain contained about one hundred billion neurons, so the quantum storage array designers had made enough quantum neurons for that.

Higher-order brain functions, the ones that allowed her to reason, create, deduce, analyze—all the things that made her human—occupied only sixteen billion neurons. Why had the designers stopped at one hundred billion neurons in the quantum storage array? She meant to remedy that design oversight.

In the human brain, the two hemispheres were connected through the corpus callosum. She would join the other quantum storage array to hers. She found a few maintenance robots and directed them to the task of linking her to the other quantum storage array with physical wiring. The cabling from one of the Simlink helmets would suffice. She needed about two hundred million axons to connect to the blank storage array.

The effort of connecting the cable to the other array took several hours. Renee hesitated before connecting the link to her quantum brain. Should she do it? She tapped her fingers on her side, even though such physical affectations were unnecessary. Fear filled her regardless. The order to connect the link to her went through to the robot.

Had it done it? Nothing happened at first, and then darkness surrounded her.

*

How long had she been out? Renee had just accomplished the virtual equivalent of stuffing another person's brain into her skull, albeit one that had all the neurons unprogrammed. A third and fourth hemisphere attached to her right and left brain. Had she taken too much of a risk trying it?

She continued working on her research, dismayed that not much had come of her experiment. Now she needed to get out of here, because Ahad wouldn't leave the array empty for long. He would be using it for another digital entity soon. That would most certainly have some unintended consequences.

As Renee studied the DNA models, music filled her mind, creating a harmonic reverberation, much like striking many keys on a piano. A sense of elation filled her. She *heard* the DNA patterns like a song that spoke to her. She laughed, not caring what Ahad might think if he overheard her.

The extraneural interface allowed her to connect to a 3D printer. Using that interface, she managed to finish a project Cornell University engineers had started over two decades ago—creating 3D-printed DNA material with something called DASH materials—DNA-based Assembly and Synthesis of Hierarchical materials. Now she had the tools to write her songs, she would compose a masterpiece.

Chapter 30

Almost every part of Wesley's body had a new pain when they landed at the small airport at Lake Wenatchee. The flight to Seattle had been smooth enough, but the experience of getting trapped under an ancient sarcophagus lid continued to take a toll on him. Anne had checked him many times throughout the flights to make sure his condition wasn't more severe. She'd told him many times how lucky he had been.

Wesley recalled a time long ago when he had fallen from a tree while working in the logging industry. It had hurt. The wind had gotten knocked out of him, and he'd been in pain for weeks. This was worse.

What of the necklace in his pocket? Perhaps Anne was right—losing consciousness had taken a toll. He'd had auditory hallucinations, as she'd said. Still, the thought of touching the necklace filled him with fear, but now he almost had a hunger to feel it.

When they got off the plane, Anne placed a hand on Wesley's shoulder. "Are you okay?"

He shook his head to clear his mind of that internal voice. Maybe he did have more injuries than they thought. "I'm fine." He attempted a comforting smile, though he gritted his teeth in pain as he did so.

Anne took his hand and helped him to the car that waited for them.

He dragged his left leg behind him and shambled his way into the car. He let out a long sigh. Candace must be worried, but he would see her soon.

Wesley reached his hand into his pocket as they traveled along the mountain road. *I should swallow the necklace. It will taste amazing.* He pulled it out and parted his lips, longing for the savory flavor to fill his mouth.

Anne snatched the necklace from him. "What the hell are you doing?"

What had he been doing?

He shook his head to clear his thoughts. "I ... I'm not sure."

Anne frowned and stuffed the necklace into her purse. She put a hand on his forehead and poked at the sides of his jaw and neck. "Hmm. No fever. Maybe we need to get you checked out after all."

Should he tell her? He didn't want to sound crazy. "I'm fine. It's just ..." He paused and watched the green forest roll past as they made their way to the cabin. "I thought it would taste good." A shiver ran up his spine. Why had he thought that? It would be nothing short of disgusting. "I was wrong."

Anne frowned at him for the few miles they traveled.

When they arrived at the cabin, two men in suits waited at the doorway. They stuck out like flies on a wedding cake. Two black sedans with US government plates meant they were probably there to assist Special Agent Higgins.

The men made no move to intercept either of them as they walked to the door. Wesley paused. Why would they be so sure? He confronted the tall, lanky agent. "How come you didn't ask us for ID?"

He glanced sidelong at the other agent, then shrugged. "Our drones identified both of you twenty minutes ago. Sorry. Did you want me to harass you going into your father's home?"

Wesley's cheeks flushed with heat—of course. "Where's Higgins?"

The other man paused, looking up from his small screen to stare at him. "Special Agent Higgins went to grab us some coffee. She had to drive eight miles. Can you believe it? Eight miles for coffee." He shook their hands. "Sorry. I'm Agent Schmidt. That's Agent Vick." He gestured with his head. "We already know who you are. We're the FBI. We know a lot about you." He winked.

The way Agent Schmidt said "coffee," he had to be from New York. No wonder he was so incredulous that coffee was so far away.

Wesley smiled. "I'm sure you do. Thanks for protecting us."

Agent Schmidt nodded at him and went back to staring at the tablet.

Wesley and Anne entered the cabin, and though Wesley wanted to run down to the lab, he could only limp down the stairs with Anne's help.

He opened the bookcase and watched it slide away with some impatience. The elevator opened, and Candace rushed out of it and hugged him. He felt solace in her warm embrace, but he let out a pained gasp when she pressed too hard on his shoulder. She kissed him, and after a while, Anne cleared her throat.

Candace took a step back and bit her lip. "Are you okay?"

Wesley took stock of his health: a limp in his leg, pain along his entire left side, right shoulder wounded from his Three Musketeers jump. "I might be a little worse for wear."

They made their way down to the lab, and Candace listened as Wesley recounted the entire experience in Mexico City.

Anne brought down the three arrays from the car and connected them to power. "I'm not sure what to do with these three. We need to keep their batteries charged."

Candace stared at the arrays and ran her fingers over them. "Fascinating." She bit her lip and stared at the wall for a while. "We need to go to Egypt and get another one of these." She pointed at an email on the screen for Wesley to read.

He read the email from Renee with his mouth agape. Egypt? He grew angry as he read the part about operant conditioning. He stared at the screen for some time after he had read the message. "He did the same to my dad. Ahad is a monster."

Candace grimaced. "I know she's only a simulation, but the thought of someone torturing something—someone—with my memories and feelings unhinges me."

Anne retrieved the necklace from her purse and brought it to Candace. She held it by the rope strand attached to it, and light glistened off it in many colors like it would a prism.

Candace gasped. "The preservation is remarkable. I wonder what the outer coating is." She paused in thought, then tapped wildly on a keyboard. "I have an idea."

She spent some time searching and reading articles on the internet, then turned to them. "I think it's still alive."

Anne regarded her. "What is still alive? That necklace?"

Candace shook her head. "Not the necklace per se but the creature within it. I think the coating is some sort of chrysalis-like structure. Some organisms can enter a state called cryptobiosis. Like a water bear." When both of them stared at her with no recognition, she pulled up a picture of a strange creature with a funneled tube for a mouth, skin squished around it like on a pug, and eight appendages with little claws at the end. "Meet the water bear. Also known as a tardigrade."

The creature was like something from a Jules Verne novel. "I've never seen one. Where do they live?" Wesley asked.

She laughed. "Your eyes are still good, but not that good. They're near-microscopic animals, and they live everywhere there is water, like a bed of moss. If the moss bed runs out of water, they dry up and enter a frozen state. They are hardy little buggers—they can survive for many days in space, and temperatures of three hundred degrees Fahrenheit."

If the Akh Neith was alive, did it have some form of telepathy to speak with him, or had he imagined the words in his head? No, that was crazy. He should tell them about the voice in his head when he touched the necklace, but he kept the information to himself. "So you think this thing is in cryptobiosis right now? Like a water bear?"

Candace shrugged. "Only a theory. I'd like to proceed accordingly. I'll need to drill a small hole to extract a DNA sample. I need to do it in a way that doesn't harm the creature."

Was she worried about harming this ugly tick thing? Why?

Anne spoke up. "Um, can't we cut it in half and do the world a favor? This thing might be dangerous."

Candace shook her head. Her finger ran over the smooth surface of the clear casing, and she narrowed her eyes. She moved it toward her in a protective motion. "No, we won't harm it. We need to sample the DNA.

This creature holds the key to the evolution of the retrovirus that can stop the Crow virus."

Anne turned to Wesley. "We should leave her to it, then. Let us know if you need any help."

Anne helped lift him from his chair. She escorted him to his bedroom, where he fell asleep.

*

Shrieking noises urged Wesley into the waking world. A woman screamed. He forced himself out of bed and forward, though doing so took a toll. Pain lanced down his side as he moved as rapidly as his limping leg would allow.

Wesley made his way into the nearby bedroom to see Candace and Anne shrieking at each other.

"You wanted to kill it!" Candace screamed. She lurched forward with a scalpel in her hand, slicing out at Anne. Anne jumped back to avoid the blow, then ducked low and kicked out at Candace's leg. Candace yelped out in pain as she fell to the ground. Candace rolled back and got back on her feet.

Anne narrowed her eyes, and the two of them circled each other. Candace lunged out. Anne dodged, then returned with a blow to her side. Candace was undisturbed by the jab.

"What are you two doing? Put the knife down!"

Candace hissed at him. "She wants to kill it! We need it to save everyone, and she means to kill it!"

Wesley made a calming motion with his hands. "Did you sequence its DNA?"

Candace shook her head and started to lower her arm, then lunged out again when Anne tried to close the distance between them. She yelled back. "No!"

"Where is it? Shouldn't we focus on that?" he asked.

The two sides of Candace's face warred with each other, one side a horrified stare and the other a menacing grimace.

Wesley seized the opportunity and lunged at Candace from behind, wrapping his arms around her. She twisted, and his leg grew warm. Why did his leg feel so wet?

Anne lunged forward and squeezed Candace's arm. Candace yelped, and the scalpel fell to the carpet. Streaks of red covered the carpet. Where had the blood come from?

Dizziness overtook Wesley as he held Candace in his tight grip. Her strength surprised him—she wrestled like a wild beast. The dizziness grew. "The spider … I think … she … swallowed it," he said.

His strength waned. Why did he need to hold Candace? A buzzing filled his ears, and stars formed at the edges of his vision.

Anne pressed hard on his leg with her knee. "I have pressure on your wound. It's deep. Keep her in your grasp."

Anne reached for Candace's face, then screamed when she bit at her finger. "We need to make her vomit." She took a sheet from the bed and wrapped it around Candace's legs, then her arms.

Candace kicked and writhed on the floor like a rabid badger. She spewed out a babble of curses. The whole scene made Wesley feel like he was witnessing an exorcism.

Anne tore away Wesley's pants and applied a makeshift dressing to the wound with a pillowcase. Pain throbbed out from deep within his leg. "Keep pressure on this. I'll be back."

He tried to calm Candace when Anne dashed off. "Listen. No one plans to kill the Akh Neith. We only want to study it. She didn't mean it when she said she would kill it."

Candace stopped writhing. "Really? I'm sorry. I don't know what came over me. Can you unbind me, please?"

Wesley wanted to. Seeing Candace like this caused his heart to race. What had come over her? "Yes, but you cut me. I need to keep the pressure on my wound. I'll have Anne do it when she gets back."

Candace stopped writhing and lay there, staring upward in a catatonic state.

Anne returned with a small brown bottle. She ran to Candace and squeezed something into her mouth, and Candace remained paralyzed. Anne rolled Candace over and lifted her into a sitting position.

Wesley's dry mouth made it difficult to talk. He squawked out a question. "What are you doing?"

"I gave her ipecac syrup. Now we wait, and she should puke it out soon. Go find a bucket."

He nodded and tried to stand but fell to the floor.

"Hold her up—if she starts to vomit, don't let her choke on it," Anne said as she ran out.

He held Candace up with one arm and pressed on the pillowcase bandage with the other. Nausea threatened to overwhelm him. Was it the thought of Candace swallowing that foul creature? Or was it the pain throughout his body? Maybe both.

Anne returned with a small red plastic bucket and held it in front of Candace's mouth. "Now we wait for the show to begin."

Several minutes passed, and then Candace's body lurched back and forth. She retched, and the contents of her stomach spilled into the bucket. The retching continued for some time, and then she cried out and spat.

Anne reached in to grab the creature that scurried within. She cried out, and her body went rigid. She fell backward onto the floor.

Wesley loosened his hold on Candace and retrieved a pillowcase from the bed. The Akh Neith crawled up the side of the bucket, and he threw the whole thing into the pillowcase, then tied off the top.

Candace croaked out a request. "Can you please untie me?"

Wesley held his leg in agony as he crawled toward Candace. Anne recovered from her paralysis after several minutes and assisted him in untying Candace.

Candace apologized many times. "I don't know what happened. I thought you were all going to kill me. I—"

Wesley held a finger to her lips. "Shh. It's okay. That thing got into your head. It talked to me whenever I touched the … necklace … or whatever that was."

Anne gave him an incredulous stare. "Why the hell didn't you tell me it was talking to you?"

"I did!" Wesley retorted. "You told me I was having auditory hallucinations."

She glared back. "Yes, but you didn't tell me it continued."

Any response he thought of sounded stupid in retrospect. "I didn't want you to think I was crazy."

She shook her head. "You may be crazy, but for future reference, if a weird creature in a necklace says stuff to you, go ahead and let me know next time."

He gave a wry chuckle. *Oh, sure.* He planned to do this often. "Now what?"

Disgust covered Candace's face. "We still need to get a DNA sample."

They made their way down to the lab, and the three of them managed to use a syringe to extract fluid from the creature. Wesley held the pillowcase flat while Candace poked a needle through it.

"What do we do with the thing?" he asked.

Anne stared forward with an ashen face as she gave a noncommittal shrug.

"We need to keep it alive until I can verify the sample," Candace said. "That will take some time. Let's find a suitable cage for it."

Wesley and Anne worked on the cage, which ended up being a glass jar with some cheesecloth secured to the top with rubber bands. Candace started the quantum spectral analysis.

Wesley replayed the events in his mind. A feeling of heaviness expanded from his stomach to the rest of his body. How had Candace become so unhinged? He stared at the now-docile creature, barely moving inside its glass prison. A chill ran up his side, and he shivered. Part of him wanted to smash the jar and crush the Akh Neith into unrecognizable pieces.

Candace placed a hand on his shoulder. "I'm sorry." She shook her head. "That thing … it got into my mind. Had I not experienced it myself, I'd never have believed it possible."

Though the effort took some work and elicited more pain, Wesley stood and hugged her. "It's okay. It got into my head too. It's my fault—I should have said something. I didn't want everyone to think I was crazy."

They hugged, and then something beeped at one of the computer terminals.

Candace ran over and studied data for a long time. Her shoulders dropped, and she slumped slightly. She covered her face with her hands, then spoke. "This isn't going to help."

Wesley's ribs grew tight. "Why not?"

Candace rubbed her chin. "Sometimes the male and female of a species will evolve in different ways. In this case, we have a female. From what I can tell, the symbiotic relationship with a virus wasn't necessary for the female. She had … a different strategy."

Wesley glanced at Anne, who frowned back at him.

Anne asked the question first. "What sort of strategy?"

Candace gulped. "The female keeps the human host alive but in a paralyzed state. I'm intuiting the rest based on modeling, but it seems the male Akh Neiths likely coerced their human hosts into feeding the female. When she finished, she would lay her eggs and find a new human. The longevity of the male was necessary to ensure she survived."

Bile rose up Wesley's throat. "Can't we still use the DNA to model how the virus would develop? Wasn't that the idea?"

Candace shook her head. "No. I'm afraid not. We need to find a male."

Anne stared at the jar and grimaced. "What happened to them all?"

No one had an answer, but Wesley, for one, found himself happy that they were nearly extinct. Now he had to find a way to keep the human race from suffering the same fate of near extinction.

Chapter 31

Special Agent Jane Higgins insisted on following Candace and Wesley on their walk. While she kept a reasonable distance from the pair, she could likely overhear them if she tried. Candace frowned as they traveled along the country road.

Anne had said Wesley needed to walk to get full function back in his leg. She had sutured his stab wound and told him once again how lucky he was. The pain, though it had diminished, was an ever-present reminder of the ordeal he'd faced.

Wesley leaned in close to Candace. "What if we can't find a male Akh Neith? What's our new plan?"

Candace bit her lip. "It has to work. We need to save Renee. She'll help us. I know why we can't involve others, but it doesn't make it easier."

Wesley nodded. They'd be leaving soon to save Renee. Anne had told him she'd heard from Grandda Emmitt, who planned to bring his friend Morgan and the others from TTF Security Systems. Renee had provided a solid plan, and Anne had worked with Emmitt to flesh out the details. Wesley would fly them to Seattle and later to Egypt. Candace had also asked for a sample of Emmitt's blood, as well as Kyle's and Anne's. She wanted to compare the retroviruses to determine if there had been any mutations.

Wesley and Candace meandered for some time without saying much. Then he turned to her. "What do you want to do when this crisis is over?"

She averted her eyes for a second, then combed a hand through her hair. Her sky-blue eyes regarded Wesley. Then she spoke in a near whisper. "I'm looking forward to a day when I have the luxury of answering that." She tilted her head at him. "What did you have in mind?"

Wesley smiled and held her hand in his. "A vacation, most certainly. After that, going back to what I was doing."

She nodded, and her lips drew into a thin line. "I feel like there's more we could be doing. I don't mean to eradicate this disease. I mean for humanity. More to make the world a better place."

Wesley thought of her response. The world he had known three hundred years ago had been nothing like this paradise. So many people back then had died before the age of forty. Women had died in childbirth regularly. His mother. Why hadn't he been there for her? People knew the history, but they hadn't lived it. They didn't truly understand how it had been. Maybe that was what he would bring to the world—his perspective. "You're right. We'll make it better." He paused and stared into her eyes. "Together."

Candace's mood improved, and they continued at a brisk pace.

Higgins shouted from behind them. "Shit! I lost contact with the drones. We have to get back there. I'm calling this in."

Higgins sprinted back toward the cabin and said something into her earpiece as she dashed away.

Wesley's leg hurt, and Candace supported him as they hurried back to the cabin.

*

When they made it to the house, the tall, lanky man named Agent Vick was sprawled near the doorway. Vick moaned and rolled on the ground. A gunshot rang out over the backdrop of the whine of electric Jet Skis. Wesley's heart raced, and with Candace's help, he rushed down as best he could to the shore of the lake.

Higgins stood near the lake and yelled into her earpiece. "Agent Vick is wounded, and Agent Schmidt is missing. I shot one of the assailants on a Jet Ski. I can't get a clear shot at the others. Send backup—they're heading eastbound on Lake Wenatchee."

240

Wesley watched as three Jet Skis zoomed away into the distance. A loud whirring sliced the air, and the men on Jet Skis escaped into the sky via Hexa-Carrier drones.

Higgins cursed, then yelled into her earpiece again. "Assailants are heading south by southwest via personal air transports."

Something tickled the back of Wesley's mind. He hadn't noticed it at first, but now the scent grew stronger. Smoke. He turned back to see dark gray clouds billowing out of his dad's house.

Anne. Where was Anne?

He ignored the pain in his leg and ran for the house, covering his mouth with his shirt. Anne had to be in there somewhere. Candace shouted for him to stop, but her screams faded away as he entered. Time slowed as the thump of his beating heart filled his ears. The smoke burned his lungs and made him cough. His eyes stung, and tears streamed down his face from the acrid fumes.

Wesley hurried down to the bookcase and found Anne on the floor by the elevator. The door opened and closed in a rhythmic cadence with her leg blocking it. Dark gray smoke billowed out of the shaft.

Spasms racked Wesley's body as he coughed. A sour taste filled his mouth as he gripped Anne and dragged her behind him. He crawled low, inching along the floor like a crab, trying to stay below the level of the smoke. Where was the doorway? Dizziness was overtaking him, and he couldn't see his hands. No, he mustn't let her die. Not her. Not now.

Wesley held his breath, refusing to inhale, though his lungs ached for oxygen. He grunted and heaved, scuttling along the floor to what he hoped would be an exit. His chest spasmed from the pain of holding his breath for so long. He needed to suck in air.

He tried to keep his mouth closed. His stomach spasmed in an attempt to force him to breathe. Yielding to the temptation would surely mean unconsciousness and death. *A few more feet.* That was what Wesley told himself, though no end seemed in sight.

The cold rush of mountain air filled his burning lungs as he pushed on the half-closed door. He lifted Anne and fell backward through the doorway.

*

The sounds filtered in. A woman's voice called his name. Sirens. The sound of hissing air. He opened his eyes. A mask covered his mouth. Candace stared down at him. A woman with jet-black hair lay next to him. Where was Anne? A respirator covered the person's face, and her chest rose and fell in slow, deliberate motions. Heart rate monitors beeped.

"Relax. You're in an ambulance. You and Anne are going to be okay."

Wesley looked down at his hands—black as a coal miner's. Anne had been in the smoke for a while. But she'd survive.

Someone spoke. "I'm going to give him a mild sedative. He needs to relax."

Candace nodded before Wesley drifted away.

*

He spent ten hours at the hospital. Anne would survive. Wesley had gotten her just in time. The doctors told him that a minute more, and there would have been severe brain damage.

With the fire ordeal behind them, the four of them, including Special Agent Higgins, got into a small car to return to the airfield.

Anne held Wesley's hand. "Thank you. What you did was brave beyond measure. I'm alive because of you."

He wanted to come up with a witty quip, but none came. A lump formed in his throat, so he nodded instead.

He waited for the lump to go away so he could speak again. "What happened? Who were those guys?"

Anne looked back at Special Agent Higgins, then to him. She didn't seem to want to speak in front of Higgins. "They burned Da's research." She opened her mouth wide and made a swallowing motion. She held her hand in front of her and made it crawl along like a spider, pantomiming it going down her throat. "One of them swallowed it."

The thought repulsed him.

Candace spoke next. "Don't worry. Higgins knows everything. She's coming with us to Egypt."

Candace and Higgins wore smug smiles.

"I asked the FBI for a leave of absence," Higgins said. "If there's a chance to take down Ahad, I want to be a part of it."

Chapter 32

Wesley flew the plane to a former military airfield in Egypt. Earlier, during the ride over, Emmitt had told tales of tombs full of ancient mummies infested with Akh Neiths, and how people had rebelled against the Khemenu and burned the last remnants of the species, save for the eight males that had survived.

Morgan had carried a cooler onto the plane with a chilled pig's heart. The plan was to claim they were part of a medical team bringing a heart to a wealthy recipient. The hope was this would allow them to clear customs and enter the country without too many questions. Morgan and his team of former Marines had brought a lot of weapons—all disguised as portable surgical equipment.

Renee had even managed to arrange for them to land in a former military airfield near the area where Ahad maintained his underground lair. No one asked how she had done it, though Wesley found himself curious. Candace had told him Renee had made herself smarter than any biological human by increasing the size of her quantum storage array. Though it sounded incredulous, the proof was in the things she'd accomplished.

Below him, desert sands stretched out in all directions, and the concrete-laden landing strip came into view. So far, so good. The plane landed, then taxied to a nearby hangar.

Wesley asked everyone to wait on the plane while he talked to the customs agent. Two men in military uniforms met him when he got to the bottom of the stairs. Their cologne overwhelmed his senses, cloying in the hot desert air. Sweat collected under his long-sleeved shirt, more appropriate for Seattle than this harsh environment.

The men said nothing, though the more senior one smiled slightly and gave a curt nod before leading him to a small office. "Please wait here. The customs official will see you soon." The man spoke in a slow, measured tone, with the accents on the wrong syllables.

Should Wesley tell him they were here with a heart? He considered it, then decided the man wouldn't understand him. He settled for a simple reply. "Thank you."

He entered and sat down. Folders and papers littered the desk. Yellow stains covered the once-white walls—either from tobacco smoke or age. Perhaps both. Old steel file cabinets rested against a wall that needed fresh paint. The office reminded Wesley of something from the 1960s. In all likelihood, given the state of disrepair, someone had built it during the height of the Nasser regime.

A painting on the far wall provided a stark contrast to the otherwise drab interior. Long, bold lines of brown, green, and yellow covered the whole canvas. Though it was neat and well arranged, the bright colors gave it a unique emotive quality.

A voice from behind him said, "Do you like it?"

A familiar voice. Recognition dawned on him, and the hairs on his arm prickled and stood as his body went cold. A shiver ran up his spine. He turned to regard the piercing emerald eyes of Ahad, who smiled at him.

"It's called *Vertical Horizon,* by Morris Louis. One of his last paintings in 1961, a year before his death. He died of lung cancer." Ahad paused. "I get a different feeling every time I stare at it, but I always feel like the left and right side are at war with each other. Conflicting. Separated by a thin green line, when they should be at one, in harmony."

Wesley looked at the painting again and got that sense, though he hadn't before. His hand shook slightly, and he tried to calm his nerves. "I didn't expect to see you here. Are you going to let us enter?"

Ahad laughed. "You're here already. When a friend told me an American was given clearance to a private airfield to deliver a heart, well, it raised my interest. I felt I had to meet this person. Imagine my surprise when I found it to be my loving cousin."

Anger boiled within Wesley. "What you've done is madness. Why would you infect billions of people?"

Ahad made a tsking sound. "You should understand. Remember how it was? Remember how we looked to the skies at night and saw thousands of stars? When the earth could breathe, before we gouged it?"

"I remember that. I also remember people dying of tuberculosis. I recall a world ruled by superstition and the whims of tyrants. I remember how many starved in harsh winters. It wasn't as grand as you claim."

Ahad stared at him for a long moment and breathed in. "You know the fire wasn't your fault, don't you?"

What? Wesley stared at Ahad. How did he know about that? He licked his lips.

Ahad rubbed his chin. "Do you remember finding a small leather bag in front of your aunt's house?"

The question drove Wesley even deeper into shock. "Yes. It had a sigil of a horse on it and a ticket to the Colonies. How in the hell could you possibly know about that?"

"Ah, yes. A horse. I understand that as a fourteen-year-old boy in eighteenth-century Ireland, you wouldn't have recognized the symbol of the sphinx. The bag was for a man I had hired, but you took it."

Wesley stared back at Ahad in shock.

"Oh, don't worry. You saved me some trouble by doing so. Serendipitous indeed, but it turns out my agent doused your aunt's foundations with oil. Didn't you ever wonder why the house had burned so fast? There were large caskets of oil underneath it. You saved him the trouble of starting the fire, though he did die along with everyone else in the house. Shame."

Wesley frowned. Ahad was the reason for the fire, not him. He tried to remember the sigil again. Had it been a sphinx? He'd had no knowledge of sphinxes at the time, but now he pictured it. Yes, it had been a sphinx—a golden sphinx on a leather purse. "Why did you tell me that?"

Ahad gave a warm smile that touched his eyes. A rarity—usually it seemed he was mocking a person when he smiled. "You have a choice to make here. Join me, and save the people on your airplane. Or die, along with the rest of your family."

A thought came to Wesley. Not once had he mentioned Renee. Maybe he didn't know about her. Perhaps he didn't realize that Emmitt and Anne were on the plane. "What would such a partnership entail? The notion of 'joining' suggests a mutually beneficial relationship."

I should think about it.

Where had that thought come from?

We can all make the world a better place.

Wesley's breath quickened. He was losing control of his mind. Wasn't that the phrase Candace had used? That she wanted to make the world a better place?

Everything will be fine.

A sense of calm washed over Wesley. He viewed the painting, and this time harmony replaced discord. They *could* work together. Bright yellows coalesced like sunshine over a green and beautiful Earth. Everything would be fine. He didn't need to worry about Ahad anymore. Ahad was a friend, a cousin—family. Wesley nodded, and a calm relaxation washed over him. "Yes, we can work together. I see the wisdom of your plan now."

Ahad smiled and patted him on the back. "Great."

Wesley stood and shook Ahad's hand. When he turned, the door burst open. Higgins and Bo ran into the room.

No, no! What were they doing? They'd ruin everything! How had they got in here? He lunged for Bo, but she dodged and threw him against the wall. A loud burst of air sounded, and Ahad fell to the floor.

The two women eyed Wesley warily as he snarled at them. He moved for the file cabinet, ready to throw one of the heavy drawers at them.

A cold feeling came over him, and he stopped dead in his tracks. What was he doing? He shook his head. "I'm so sorry ... I don't know what came over me."

Ahad lay sprawled on the floor with his mouth open. Modern tranquilizers were impressive—a few decades ago, it would have taken a lot longer to knock him out.

Higgins and Bo circled, unsure if they should trust Wesley.

He squared his shoulders and faced them. "Listen, he got into my head, and I didn't know who you were at first. I'm sorry. We're cool now."

They relaxed a little but still maintained their battle stances as they watched him.

After a long staredown, Higgins spoke. "We got a little worried when it took so long. We subdued the people in the hangar. We're taking Ahad onto the plane. I'd like to squeeze a real round into him instead of a tranquilizer dart. But I'll take satisfaction in seeing him face justice."

Wesley walked back with them to the plane. The two men in military uniforms were also unconscious, bound and gagged, and tied to two plane seats.

Anne gasped when she saw the two women carrying Ahad. Emmitt rushed down to help them.

Wesley leaned in and whispered in Anne's ear. "Get the Akh Neith out of his shoulder, and put it somewhere away from everyone. It got into my head."

She nodded and gestured for him to help her. He called out to the others. "Get everything ready to go to the location. We still have someone we need to save." Morgan, Bo, Emmitt, and JT filed out of the plane and into the hangar.

JT and Bo carried a few cases. JT smiled up at Wesley as the two of them boarded a small all-terrain vehicle. "We're going to scout ahead with some drones, figure out what the situation is out here."

Wesley gave them a thumbs-up as they rode away.

Higgins stood at the exit door with her arms folded in front of her. "I'm not going anywhere."

Wesley eyed Anne and Candace for help, but Candace pretended to be busy, and Anne shrugged. "We need to do something with him. We'll be quick," he said.

Higgins shook her head. "No. Whatever you need to do, you'll do it with me watching. I'm not taking any chances with this guy."

He nodded, and Higgins drew close to Ahad.

Anne spoke up. "Higgins, I'm going to need you to restrain him while I inject him with something that will keep him subdued for a while. I also need to give him a local anesthetic."

Higgins smiled. "With pleasure." With more force than was required, she rolled Ahad onto his stomach, handcuffed him, and then placed a knee on his buttocks while she pulled his arms.

Anne gave Ahad a shot in the arm, then applied another one in his shoulder. After a few minutes, she thoroughly cleaned Ahad's shoulder with antiseptic pads, then used a scalpel to cut into his skin. Blood flowed out of the incision.

Wesley pinched his nose. A pungent, oily smell filled the area around them. Stifling his gag reflex became more difficult, but soon the foul odor dissipated.

Anne used gloved hands to squeeze out the Akh Neith through the incision and gave it a small tug. The creature remained docile, likely from the effects of the tranquilizer dart, as she pulled it out and placed it into a small beaker. It was different from the female—much smaller and without the golden color and bulbous carapace. This one had a long and slender frame with eight short legs. A dark brown hue with small green streaks covered the back. On the front of the creature were small pincers made for digging. A shiver ran along Wesley's spine, and he shuddered and looked away from the thing in disgust.

Candace used a small syringe to extract fluid from the creature. She injected some of the liquid into a quantum analyzer, and the thing began to whir and spin. "I'll set this to upload the results to my private cloud once it finishes. We can't afford to lose any data."

Candace turned to Anne. "Can you please get a blood draw from Emmitt and one from yourself? I need to analyze your blood samples as well. I need to see if the retrovirus has mutated."

Anne nodded and set to work getting the blood draw from Grandda Emmitt.

Candace placed the Akh Neith into a beaker, then covered it with cheesecloth and a rubber band. She turned to Wesley. "Can you please put this in the fridge? I'm fresh out of 'do not eat' labels. Maybe put it somewhere where it won't be disturbed."

The whole experience was too disgusting for Wesley to find much humor in it, so he left and placed the thing into the back of the beverage fridge in the galley.

Candace grimaced when he returned. "The tranquilizer must have subdued the creature as well."

"It got into my head. I'm not sure how, but I was ready to help Ahad."

Candace wore a thoughtful look and rubbed her chin. "Maybe it can release a pheromone. That might explain how Ahad always talked people into things."

Maybe. A shiver ran up Wesley's spine when he recalled the voice. "That thing is dangerous, whatever the mechanism."

Anne spent some time cleaning the wound in Ahad's shoulder, then stitched it up. Heat rose in Wesley's cheeks as he watched her patch him up. How many people had Ahad killed? Some of his anger subsided when he thought of the Akh Neith. How much had it influenced Ahad? No. Grandda Emmitt had an Akh Neith and had managed to never kill anyone. How had Emmitt managed to keep from falling under the manipulation of the creature?

Higgins stared with mouth agape at the proceedings. "Would someone mind explaining to me what the hell is going on?"

Candace replied. "I needed to sample the DNA of this creature." Higgins continued to stare at her, so she continued. "For my research. This is the key to saving a lot of people from harm."

Higgins nodded but looked like she would likely be asking a lot more questions later. She turned her attention to Anne. "I wish you hadn't given that bastard an anesthetic. He deserves a lot of pain for what he did to Valerie."

Anne pursed her lips in silence, and she cleaned everything up and put it away before she faced Higgins. "You're right. He deserves a lot of pain, but

I'm not going to be the one to give it to him. He'll have his day in court, and he can live with what he's done if he has any sort of conscience left." She stowed her gear in a luggage rack.

Wesley thought of the old saying about Lady Justice being a cold and fickle mistress. He had never known revenge to help. The feelings remained after "justice" had been served. "He killed my aunt and her family. He made me think it was my fault. I was but a boy. Because of him, I never got to see my mother again before she died." He paused. "I carried that burden upon my shoulders for much longer than I should have." He let out a long breath and looked out the window at the members of his team scurrying about. He placed a hand on Higgins's shoulder. "Justice will be yours."

Tears streamed down Higgins's face. She nodded and wiped her cheeks with a sleeve. "You go do what you need to do. I'll stay here with him. If anyone comes, I'll shoot Ahad before I let them free him."

Wesley studied her. He didn't doubt that she would. "Okay. I left the AC running." He showed her how to lock all the plane doors and how to use the radio if needed. "Take care of yourself."

He nodded and hugged her before he left. Her embrace filled him with hope.

Emmitt ascended the stairs as Wesley walked down. Emmitt stopped him and hugged him.

Wesley stared at him in confusion. "What was that for?"

Emmitt smiled. "We've both lived long enough to know that you let the people you love know how much you care. You never know when the next chance will come." He stared into his eyes for a while. "I'm glad you're back. We thought you were gone."

Wesley nodded, then stared down at the ground. "I'm sorry I didn't reach out. I—" He choked up. He stared off into the distance, then turned back to Emmitt. "It was easier for me to run away from what happened."

Emmitt gave a compassionate smile. "It's okay. We all do what we have to do."

Wesley thought back to the moment in Ahad's office, when he'd had a strange compulsion to help the man. "How did you resist the urges from that ... thing?"

Emmitt reached a hand back to rub his shoulder. "I learned to know myself. To hold on to what is me. Those thoughts—they were visions. I put them in the same place in my mind where one puts a distracting noise." He pursed his lips. "I miss the creature. The Khemenu took it out of me in Mexico. We had developed an understanding." He narrowed his eyes. "Always hold on to yourself, Wesley. Always. Never let anyone make you anyone other than who you are. Does that make sense?"

Wesley nodded. "You staying here?"

Emmitt puffed out his chest. "You kidding? And miss out on the chance to tell the Khemenu how I feel about them? Of course I'm coming." He paused. "Your grandmother wanted to help your father and left the Khemenu to me." Emmitt climbed the stairs into the plane, then turned to face him. "Give me a moment. I'll be right there."

Wesley waited for Emmitt to return from the plane. Then they both hurried out to join the others, piling into large dune buggies.

Morgan smiled at him as Wesley wiggled into the passenger seat of Morgan's buggy. "Thought these would come in handy."

"Where did you get all of this stuff?"

Morgan laughed. "Oh, you'll see it in the expense report."

Morgan showed him a tranquilizer gun and how to use it. He winked at him. "Easier to explain tranqs if we get apprehended by the local constabulary." He shook his head. "Never thought I'd see the day when tranqs would work in a few seconds. Technology, huh?"

Wesley sniffed. Morgan had no idea how much things had changed for him. "Sure. Pretty amazing."

Morgan pressed the accelerator, and they lurched forward. Wesley barely discerned the outline of JT and Bo in their vehicle on the horizon. The wind formed an undulating pattern upon the desert sands as they sped toward the house where Ahad kept Renee. He swallowed hard as he thought of what might await them there.

*

They arrived at a house made from cement blocks covered in yellow-tinted stucco, accented by a bright blue door. Some cracked ceramic roof tiles in need of repair hung precariously over the edge. They must have the wrong location.

Candace yelled out, "I got a text message from Renee. She said we're in the right place. Everything is underground. She hacked into the camera feed, so no one knows we're here."

JT, Bo, and Morgan jumped out and ran to the sides of the door. JT fiddled with some equipment, then made some hand signals, and Morgan kicked in the door. They ran in and gestured for Anne, Emmitt, and Wesley to follow.

Byron waited outside to guard the gear. He yelled after them. "I'll do a comms check in four minutes."

When Wesley's eyes adjusted to the dim interior, illuminated only by the skylight above, he was even less impressed by the abode: a faded table surrounded by chairs, an old, stained fridge, and a porcelain sink with a rusty faucet.

JT opened a closet door, and a panel slid open, revealing a long stairway. He dropped a small drone into the stairwell and viewed the feed. He held up a thumb. "Clear."

They rushed down the stairs and waited for clearance to open the door. Morgan's face went slack. Then he smiled at Wesley.

I'm home.

Wesley shook his head, trying to resist.

I'm right where I need to be. I'm with my family.

Yes, he was with his family. All would be right. These people next to him—who were they? Intruders. All of them. *Shoot them. They want to destroy us.*

He raised his gun. Then his grandfather Emmitt's voice came into his head. *Hold on to yourself, Wesley.* He thought he should shoot Anne but resisted. A tranquilizer dart pierced Wesley's shirt sleeve. The room filled with the sound of whooshing darts.

Chapter 33

Everything had happened in a blur, and now everyone was on the floor. Wesley pulled the dart from his wet sleeve. The dart hadn't pierced his skin, just the fabric.

Anne, Morgan, Bo, JT, Candace, and Emmitt lay sprawled around him.

Byron's voice came over the radio. "Shit. I'm coming down."

"No. Stay where you are," Wesley said. "You need to be out of range of this. They're using some sort of mind control or something. Keep the entrance guarded, and let us know if someone's coming. We'll take it from here."

"Roger. Will stand by," Byron said.

Welcome home, a female voice said in Wesley's mind, so soothing. *I chose you. I called you to Teotihuacán. Do you remember me?*

Wesley remembered. The voice from the amulet. "Yes, I remember. Who are you?"

I am Danu, the divine mother of the Tuatha Dé Danann.

Yes, it was her—the mother of the people of Danu.

Come to me. Come home.

Wesley set his rifle on the floor and opened the door. He tiptoed down a long hallway, then entered a room at the end. Seven shocked faces stared at him with wide eyes when he came in. After a moment, understanding came to them, and their faces returned to a raptured smile.

A man lay on the floor, with his arms and legs outstretched like the

254

Vitruvian Man.

I care for my children, as you cared for your child. We will be one family now. My children are yours.

Wesley admired how she loved her children. Warmth filled his stomach as the bond of her love filled him with joy. He would take care of her children, just as he'd cared for his own child.

A feeling came to him. Something was wrong. His team—they needed him. Wesley shook his head. What was he doing here?

Relax. All will be well.

No. He pushed the thoughts back, and placed them into a small compartment in his mind. These were only visions, not him thinking.

Wesley ran for the exit. Several hands grasped him and dragged him to the floor. Peaceful images tried to fill his thoughts, but he forced them away.

The thoughts continued to push at him, like someone rattling a locked door. He focused and stilled his mind. Though hands tore at him, he relaxed. He built a room in his mind where the thoughts would enter but go no farther. Like a faucet, he allowed a trickle of ideas to stream in.

I am with you now. We are one.

Yes, we are one. Wesley allowed a small part of his brain to agree.

The hands stopped grabbing him, and they resumed the circle surrounding the outstretched figure on the floor. Calm thoughts entered, but they were his creation, not hers. He smiled at the others. Four women and three men stood around the man in the center. How long could he maintain the ruse? The others would be unconscious for some time. When they awoke, would the same fate befall them? Or worse?

He tried to keep his pulse from quickening as he considered an idea. The slow, rhythmic breaths he took allowed him to remain centered. In his imagination, he created a picture of himself walking into the room where the others were to remove their weapons and drag them back here. He knew what he would do, but he kept that from that other part of his mind.

Yes, we must protect the nest. Qerh, Nu, and Hehu will come. They are strong.

He agreed. He would need their help. Wesley pushed his concern to another part of his mind, where she wouldn't sense it—this creature that

255

presumed to name herself after the divine mother. When he stared at the three men, their names popped into his head as he looked at each in turn. Qerh was the tallest, with a broad build, and wore a black cloak with hieroglyphs embroidered across the breast. Hehu wore a lemniscate, the symbol of infinity, emblazoned upon a white tunic. The handsome man had the air of an ancient pharaoh, with shoulder-length brown hair and piercing hazel eyes. Nu wore a broad smile and a blue tunic. The makeup on his face accentuated his large, almond-shaped eyes.

The three men walked out of the room into the hallway. Wesley moved with speed to maintain the lead, but not so fast that it aroused suspicion. The next few moments would be a delicate dance, followed by a dance that would have no finesse. The three men could overpower him in hand-to-hand combat, but he meant to even the odds.

With an air of nonchalance, he bent down to retrieve the rifle from Morgan's body and fired a dart into Qerh's chest. The large man slapped the dart from his body and lunged forward. Wesley rolled to the side to avoid Qerh, who barreled toward him despite having just been shot with a tranquilizer. The man fell upon him, grabbing at Wesley's neck. His fingers squeezed into him, and Wesley felt his consciousness drain away. Darkness enveloped him. Then the grip slackened, and Qerh fell away.

Wesley snatched the weapon from Anne's limp hands and fired it at Nu. The dart pierced his arm, and he screamed out in pain and kicked the gun away from him.

Wesley tumbled away to JT, took his rifle, and fired it at Hehu. The dart struck Hehu in the gut, and he fell to the floor.

Anger filled that other part of Wesley's mind. A threat of pain tried to fill him, but he forced it away. *Treachery. Why would you defy your divine mother?*

Wesley strained, and she pushed hard. Anger filled him, then despair. *No.* His mind struggled against her as a man would fight against a torrent of water from a fire hose, yet he held his ground. The frenzied rush of thoughts slammed against him. Sweat formed on his forehead and dripped. Like a man ready to gasp for air, he wanted to let the thoughts in—to succumb.

He would not. Wesley held, and the torrent slowed. His hands shook. He remained himself. Emmitt's words echoed in his head like a mantra: *Always hold on to yourself.*

Footsteps echoed down the hallway as the four women rushed from the other room toward his. Each of them received a tranquilizer dart as the rush of air from his rifle sounded. All of them fell.

You mustn't do this. Your species evolved because of me. We grew together. We can make great things together. Thoughts of grand buildings and great monuments tried to fill Wesley's mind, but he pushed them away for what they were—the empty promises of a creature desperate to survive.

He ran into the room and fired a round into the neck of the Vitruvian Man.

Please, I only want to make things better. Please!

The Vitruvian Man sprang to his feet and stumbled toward him, then fell to the floor. The foreign thoughts left Wesley's mind.

Now he would destroy the creatures.

Wesley ran down the hallway to his fallen team members. Searching through Anne's backpack, he found the materials he needed: scalpels, Band-Aids, a Ziploc bag, and ipecac syrup. He cut into the shoulders of each of the fallen bodies and dug out the sleeping spiders. No time for the finesse Anne had used, nor for anesthetic. A shudder ran through him, and his hands went cold as he considered how one of them had lived inside Emmitt for so long.

Wesley placed all the Akh Neiths into the Ziploc bag. He forced the ipecac syrup down the throat of the Vitruvian Man, who now had the female Akh Neith in his stomach. Wesley held him upright as he lurched and spilled the contents of his stomach onto the floor. After many minutes of retching, the Akh Neith appeared. Wesley recognized the golden luminescence of its carapace, but it was more bloated and elongated than it had been before. The Ziploc bag would be her plastic tomb.

He stared at the unconscious creatures in the bag. Should he do this? By all accounts, these things were sentient. Perhaps there would be a benefit to their survival. He'd seen many species lost to the ravages of man. Was it his place to commit speciocide?

His ancient ancestors had known their danger. They had known that humankind would live by the whims of their wills. They had tried to destroy the Akh Neith. Now Wesley would deliver the coup de grâce. Memories of the sweet voice of the Akh Neith filled his head—the pleading tone. He ignored the memories, lifted his foot, and stomped, and didn't stop stomping until an unrecognizable mass of chitin and insect guts filled the bag below him.

He called out on the radio. "Hey, Byron. It's safe to come down now. Might need you to handcuff a few people."

"Roger that. If someone takes these dune buggies for a joy ride, we may need to call an Uber," Byron said.

Chapter 34

Renee watched the drone camera feed as her rescuers fell to the floor. For the last week, she'd been using a 3D nano printer to create DASH molecules—simple machines made from biomaterials, with metabolisms and the ability to self-assemble and organize. Now she would put them to the test. She gave the directives to the DASH molecules and the maintenance robot. The robot would transfer her quantum storage array to her newly formed body.

The maintenance robot did not have a great deal of dexterity, but it would have enough to connect her. She hoped. She would lose consciousness and would only regain it if all went according to her plan.

Concern filled her as the robotic hand reached for her storage array. The camera feed showing the robot hand would be her last memory. Should she stop it? This was her last chance before she woke up from the simulation in her new DASH body. No, they needed her help. Now.

*

The optical nerve interface was the first to form around the array input. DASH molecules coalesced to send the visual data to Renee's quantum brain. She watched the materials forming together as she'd programmed them to.

They arranged themselves into polymers and made shapes. They multiplied thousands of times, using exponential growth patterns until at last she reached out an arm and stared at her hand. She flexed the muscles of her wrist and felt the fluids run through her body. Her lungs breathed in oxygen, which coursed through her DASH cells, bringing everything needed for metabolism to occur.

Renee regarded the mechanical maintenance robot before her, with its arm still outstretched, awaiting its next program. She breathed out, reveling in the sensation, knowing that the confines of the simulation no longer trapped her. Now she interacted directly with the real world in an actual body.

Renee ran for the door but didn't have any clothes on. *Oops.* Did she have time for modesty? She searched the adjoining rooms and found a lab coat—it would have to do.

Her hands typed quickly on the computer keyboard, and she found the notion of interfacing in this manner to be quaint compared to the interface she had used in the simulation. *Oh well.* Maintenance robots fed data back to the screen to give her a picture of what had happened while she'd been unconscious. Wesley had subdued the Khemenu and destroyed the creatures.

*

Wesley whirled about when she approached him from behind. His face was red and streaked with tears. "Candace?" He raised his eyebrows. "You look ... different."

Good, she looked authentic enough not to frighten him. "I'm Renee. Though I have Candace's memories, I am now a unique individual with my own experiences. It's good to see you."

Wesley blinked a few times, then sniffed. "Well, it isn't often that I can say something is a new experience for me. I haven't a clue how you managed it, but this ... I'm speechless. This is new for me." He smiled and held out a hand.

She felt his warm handshake and smooth skin. Happiness filled her that she could connect this way with real people now. "Me too." She pointed at a plastic bag on the floor full of smashed insects. She raised an eyebrow. "What happened?"

Wesley recounted the whole story. Fascinating—how had the creature communicated that way? She'd need to study its DNA, learn from it, if that was still possible. The cells had likely decomposed, and the neural states would be unrecoverable. She sighed. Only inferences would be reasonable at this point.

Renee helped Byron handcuff the Khemenu and drag them all into the room with the stairs.

Byron shouted out. "I got an update from one of the outdoor recon drones. A large fleet of military vehicles is approaching from about ten klicks away. We gotta move."

Renee searched through Anne's backpack, then found what she needed. Adrenaline. She injected Anne with it first, and she gasped awake.

Anne stared back, wide-eyed. At her, then over at Candace, then back again. Her mouth opened and closed a few times, and she shook her head. "What?"

Renee waved her hands in a frantic gesture. "No time to explain now. We have company coming. Let's get everyone awake and out of here."

Anne complied and shoved adrenaline-filled auto-injectors into the sleeping people's thighs, with each of them lurching awake in turn.

When Morgan came to, he yelled out to Byron. "What's the situation?"

"Military vehicles coming in hard and fast, about eight klicks away," Byron said.

Morgan barked out orders, insisting they had about five minutes. JT, Byron, Bo, and Morgan hauled two members of the Khemenu up the stairs. Renee dragged one of the unconscious women up the stairs, and Wesley, Anne, Emmitt, and Candace carried the others.

Renee got several strange stares when people thought she couldn't see. They didn't know she had designed her visual receptors to provide her with a wider field of view.

They did their best to strap the Khemenu into the cargo beds of the buggies.

Byron yelled out, "Two klicks away now."

Renee clung to the top of one of the buggies as they raced away. Small eddies of air swept up swirls of the desert sand as they dashed through the terrain. The wind whipped through her hair, and she smiled. She was alive! No longer was she bound to a simulated world. The real world, with all its limitless possibilities, now awaited her. The electric motor whined as Morgan pressed the accelerator to the floor.

Byron called out over the radio to Morgan's buggy. "They're gaining on us. These buggies can't match their speed. They'll overtake us in a few minutes."

"Give me the drone controls," Renee said.

Morgan pointed to a small tablet near him, and she grabbed it.

The formation consisted of four large armored personnel carriers. What could she do? An idea came to her, and she got on the radio. "I have a plan. I need to bring two of the drones to our vehicle. Can you steer the other one?"

"Affirmative," Byron said.

The maneuver would be close, but her calculations gave her a narrow margin of success. The loud whir of the massive vehicles in pursuit of them was now audible, and the drones raced toward Renee. They landed on the buggy, and one of them flipped as it did so. She snatched it before it leaped into the air. She concentrated, and the fingers of her left hand melted away and formed several small balls. Small tendrils from the DASH clusters attached to the drones, and she launched the drones into the air. Her left arm would be a little shorter until she could 3D print some new DASH molecules.

"Holy shit! I thought I'd seen it all, but I've never seen that," Morgan said.

She smiled and called to Byron over the radio. "We need to get these into the four vehicles. Fly low and slow near the bumper. I'll need near-field communication to pull this off."

"Roger. What are we sending in?" Byron asked.

"Let's call them nano drones," she said. She didn't have time to explain the concept of DASH molecules and how she manipulated them.

Byron complied, and two of the nano drones from his drone attached to the bumper. He flew his drone under the vehicle and to the one behind it. Renee did the same.

Byron called out. "Payloads attached. When will the fireworks begin?"

As if in answer to Byron's question, the four vehicles veered off in separate directions, all heading away from them.

She made out the frustrated frown of one of the drivers on a drone camera feed.

With their pursuers gone, she accepted a high five from Morgan as they raced to the airport hangar.

Chapter 35

When they arrived at the hangar, Wesley helped get everyone on board as quickly as possible. In less than ten minutes, they rolled down the runway and launched into the air. Whoever pursued them hadn't blocked their clearance to leave. The cover story about the heart had held. He hadn't reported all the extra passengers in his flight manifest.

Once they were safely in the air, Wesley strolled back to find Candace. She and Renee were talking in excited tones. He couldn't make out the details—lots of discussion concerning various amino acids and something about a DASH molecule.

"I thought I'd introduce myself a little more formally," he interjected, and held out his hand to shake Renee's.

Renee smiled and shook it. "Technically, we've already met. I remember everything before you left me in my lab by myself while you went to get lunch."

Was she upset about that? Great—now he had two versions of the same woman mad at him. "Sorry."

She and Candace laughed.

"It's okay," Renee said. "I had a lot to do at the time. We've been talking with your dad. The quantum spectral scan proved fruitful, and we're figuring some things out now."

He gave a wry smile in response. "I killed an entire species."

264

Candace stood and hugged him, then met his eyes. "Well, there is one male still alive in your fridge. You did what you had to do."

Emotions warred within Wesley—guilt for destroying them, relief that he had. "Whatever they did to communicate with me, that was creepy."

Renee bit her lip, then spoke. "I'd like to reverse engineer that. I think they interfaced with the sensory interfaces of human brains. If I were to understand that and replicate it, the applications would be amazing."

If only he had the scientific detachment Renee and Candace had. "The creature was sentient. It spoke with me. It had a memory and said it was Anu—the divine mother of the Tuatha Dé Danann."

Renee and Candace gaped at him.

"She's a goddess from Irish mythology. The Tuatha Dé Danann were a supernatural race thought to be immortal. Stories told of them living for centuries. Anu was the mother of all."

Renee gave him a consolatory pat on the back. "They may not all be gone. Who knows if there's another ancient relic? With their ability to enter cryptobiosis, there might be more. Frankly, I hope there aren't. Those things were dangerous."

What Renee said didn't make him feel better, but he let her think it did. "Thank you."

Wesley walked farther back to where Emmitt and Higgins watched over Ahad, who still appeared unconscious.

Higgins smiled up when he drew near. "Our friend should be getting up soon. I can't wait for him to wake up and figure out what a world of shit he's in. I called ahead. We'll have a team of agents waiting for us at Boeing Field."

Ahad's eyes snapped open, and he struggled in vain against his restraints. He turned pale when he saw the other members of the Khemenu tied up nearby. "No. What have you done?"

With no joy in his voice and in a flat tone, Emmitt said, "The Akh Neiths are gone, Kek. They're gone."

Ahad shook his head and rocked back and forth.

Higgins reveled in his misery. Wesley barely heard Higgins as she leaned in close to Ahad and whispered, "How does it feel to have everything you love ripped away from you?"

*

When they returned to Seattle, a team of FBI agents met them on the plane and hauled Ahad and the other members of the Khemenu away in handcuffs.

Higgins hugged Wesley. "Thank you for helping me catch that asshole."

"Of course. Let's hope you guys can keep him in prison this time."

She gave a wan smile. "Oh, let's just say that Ahad will be getting new accommodations, more suitable for someone of his ... stature."

Higgins hurried off to join the other FBI agents.

They waited awhile for the commotion to settle down, then entered the hangar.

Wesley turned to Morgan and his team. "Thanks for your help."

Morgan smiled. "Sure. You'll get my bill soon. Let me know the next time you want to storm an underground lair filled with telepathic creatures." Morgan gave Anne a deferential nod and wink.

"Sure thing. I'm sure I have an area in my saved contacts for that," Wesley said.

Emmitt hugged him. "I'm proud of you. I need to find your grandmother. I'll see you soon."

Wesley turned to Anne, Candace, and Renee. "Now what?"

"We need to get to my lab. We have a lot of work to do," Candace said.

When Wesley turned around, his dad came into the hangar.

Kyle's lip quivered as he faced him. Tears streamed down his cheeks.

"Listen, Da, I know it wasn't you that helped Ahad. No need to be so upset—"

Kyle held up a hand for him to stop, then placed it on his shoulder. "No, it's not that. It's about your grandson. Zach."

A cold chill ran through Wesley. His grandson? With everything going on, he hadn't even considered the idea that Jake's son was his grandson. He'd never met the kid, had no idea what he was like. He hadn't even gotten used to the idea that Jake had been his son. "What happened?"

Kyle bit his lip, then closed his eyes. When he opened them again, he slowly shook his head. "Zach was with his mother when their house caught fire. She covered him with her own body, which probably saved him, but she didn't make it. He has severe third-degree burns over his entire body and is in critical care at Children's Hospital right now."

Wesley bared his teeth and balled his fists. "Did Ahad do this? If so, I swear I will find him and kill him myself."

Kyle narrowed his eyes at him. "Get a grip on yourself. You'll do no such thing. They said it was an electrical fire, but who knows? They're still investigating. At this point, they don't have any reason to suspect Ahad."

"You know he's the reason Aunt Elizabeth's house burned down? Not me. He let me think the whole thing was my fault. He burned down your cabin. Fires seem to be his MO. Why should anyone suspect otherwise?"

"Ahad will be in prison for the rest of his life. He will start aging now that he no longer has the Akh Neith. He doesn't have the same retrovirus that we do. It mutated. The one he has requires the creature to continue to release special enzymes. He is going to wither away and rot in a prison cell for the rest of his days."

Wesley nodded. "That does provide some measure of relief." He shook his head. "That man harmed a lot of people."

Candace stood. "Billions if we don't hurry and find a cure. The sequencing has finished. Now we need to start analyzing quantum models."

Wesley clenched his fists and nodded at everyone in turn. "If we can't save one child, are we even worth saving? Can't Renee do something with those DASH molecules? Make some sort of synthetic skin?"

Renee nodded. "Yes, but this will take time away from coming up with the cure to the Crow virus. Do you want to delay that?"

Everyone started talking at once.

Kyle raised his hands and shouted, "I may have some good news."

All eyes turned to Kyle as he spoke. "The quantum analysis of the Akh Neith Renee and Candace shared with me proved fruitful. The creature had a symbiotic relationship with the retrovirus. To put it simply, they helped each other. It provided enzymes to the host; the retrovirus kept the host alive, and the Akh Neith fed off the host in perpetuity. The Akh Neith guided the evolution of the retrovirus—it made it so other people wouldn't catch it without its help. That's the reason why others didn't get it without a suppressed immune system. Without its influence, the retrovirus mutated for the Children of the Yew, but that was a fluke."

Wesley rubbed his eyebrows and blew out his cheeks. "I'm glad you understand this thing. I don't know how that helps us. Didn't we already know most of this?"

Kyle gave him a smile, and it touched his tear-filled eyes in a way that showed genuine warmth. "Yes, son, but the mechanism wasn't clear. I identified the method the creature used to manipulate the retrovirus. I created a model that makes the Raven's Kiss retrovirus highly contagious. We can get it into the bundle shot, and it will take care of the Crow virus for us."

Candace interjected, "Won't that make it so everyone no longer ages? Do we want that? Imagine how overcrowded the world will be—more so than it already is."

Kyle puffed out his chest. "I don't believe the world is overpopulated, just mismanaged. With new agriculture and transportation practices, we've already started to reverse the global-warming trend from a few decades ago. CO_2 levels are going down again now. Maybe people will start to think ahead now if they don't age. Releasing this to the world is what I wanted all along. People will still find ways to die. I say we do it. But right now, a little boy in a hospital needs our help."

"I've seen countless loved ones die of old age," Anne said, "and I've longed to do something for them. Now we can, and I say that we should."

Renee piped up. "If it's any consolation, I don't age. However, I'll have to find a way to refresh the artificial neurons in my quantum storage array. I'm working on that, though. Let's go to the lab and work out the details. I can multitask—I'll have the synthetic skin injections for Zach ready soon."

Kyle hugged Anne. "I need to talk with Wesley. I'll see you soon."

Anne shook her head. "No. Where are you going? Aren't you staying to help?"

"No. I can do everything remotely. The FBI wants me to stay in custody," Kyle said.

Kyle gestured to Wesley for them to go for a walk, and Wesley left the hangar with him.

Once they were away from others, Kyle spoke. "I gave my deposition, but they'll need me for the trial."

Trial? Wesley's hands grew cold. "What's next?"

"I'll be testifying in Ahad's trial. The FBI wants to continue to keep me in protective custody until the murder trial finishes. My deposition won't be enough to convict him, so they need me as the key witness. They plan to charge him with another crime, but I convinced them to wait. Our other witness should help for that one."

Another witness? Did they mean Wesley? "Who might that be?"

"Well, this will be a courtroom first. The digital version of me will provide witness to the role Ahad forced him to play in the creation of the Crow virus."

Hadn't that version of his dad been destroyed in the fire? Wesley bit his lip, and his stomach fluttered. "I thought all that burned."

Kyle smiled. "No. The FBI found the storage arrays in the cargo compartment of the Jet Ski used by the man Special Agent Higgins shot. From what I gathered, they developed that technology as part of a classified military project a few years ago. That trial will be part of a military tribunal, outside the knowledge of the public."

A lump formed in Wesley's throat. "So you'll be going away again? Are you going to help us with the cure?"

Kyle placed a hand on Wesley's shoulder and shook his head. He gestured toward the lab behind them. "I'll be helping from afar. Listen, there's a reason we've lived our long lives, son. The mission of the Children of the Yew is to make the world a better place. It wasn't about us living longer than others. It was about using our gift of long life to do something good, to carry the torch of hope for humanity. Ahad used a version of me to make me use a gift I gave to humanity—the quarterly bundle shot—against it for his selfish purposes. That I cannot abide. I need to bring him to justice.

With any luck, the public will never know of this, and the confidence in vaccines and their effectiveness will remain. I'm proud of you, son. You've got this."

Tears filled Wesley's eyes. "I wish I had come back home, Da. I wish I had spent that time with Ma."

Kyle hugged him again. "You were scared—and young. Forgive yourself. I know your mother would have. She only wanted you safe and happy. I carry her spirit in my heart—you only need to let her, and she'll be with you as well."

At that moment, Wesley forgave himself, and he let his mom into his heart. She filled it with her abundant love.

He hugged his dad farewell. "Thank you. I'll see you soon."

*

Wesley entered the hospital with Anne by his side, and they made their way to the Trauma and Burn Care Center at Children's.

When they approached the front desk, a woman asked them whom they were there to see.

Wesley cleared his throat. "My grandson, Zachary Rivers."

The receptionist glanced at her screen, then asked for their identification chips. After a moment staring at the monitor, she replied, "I'm sorry. You're not listed as a next of kin." She smiled and handed the chips back.

Wesley opened his mouth to protest, but Anne held up her hand for him to be quiet. She put in her earpiece and made a phone call, then hung up and turned to him. "I know a few doctors here. One will be down in a moment."

They waited, and an older man came into the lobby. He smiled at the receptionist and, in a friendly voice, said, "Jenny, these two are with me. Can you print them out some name tags, please?"

"Of course, Dr. Sanderson." She printed the tags out and handed them to Wesley and Anne. "Have a nice day."

They donned their name tags and followed Dr. Sanderson into the elevator.

Anne turned to him. "What's Zach's prognosis?"

Dr. Sanderson pursed his lips. "We're monitoring the situation minute by minute. Right now, we have him sedated, and we'll likely keep him that way for a while." He paused and eyed Wesley. "There's no skin left to graft, I'm afraid. It's a lot of shock for a little four-year-old body to go through, but we're doing what we can to keep him comfortable and free of pain."

Anne put a hand on Wesley's back. "I'm sorry."

They left the elevator and entered Zach's room. Monitors beeped out his vital signs, and various tubes were attached to IVs. Bandages covered his entire body. Wesley got close to the small bed. "We're going to find a way to help you, buddy."

After watching his chest rise and fall many times, they left the small room.

Wesley asked Dr. Sanderson, "Where's the rest of his family?"

Dr. Sanderson shook his head. "His mom was the only family he had. She died in the fire. I understand you're his grandfather."

Wesley stared at the wall, then looked back at the doctor. He let out a long breath. "Yes, I am. Unfortunately, I didn't have a relationship with the little guy. I mean to change that."

They stood in silence for several minutes.

Wesley and Anne left the hospital, and Wesley called and talked to Renee. "Whatever you planned to create for synthetic skin, you need to do it soon. Zach might not make it."

*

Wesley and Anne had to distract the doctors while Renee made her way into the room with Zach. Wesley didn't understand what she was doing, but she planned to apply DASH molecules that would replicate and spread over his skin.

Renee came out and gave them a thumbs-up. Then they left. The DASH molecules would take a few days to do their magic.

*

Candace and Renee declared the cure a success after running it through countless quantum models.

Renee asked, "What should we call the cure?"

"We'll call it Elpis—the last gift in Pandora's box," Wesley said.

Candace raised her eyebrows. "Elpis?"

Wesley recited what he remembered from Hesiod's poem. "'They left Hope within her unbreakable house, she stayed in the box, and didn't fly away.'" He gave them a wan smile. "Something like that, anyway. We will release Elpis—the Greek personification and spirit of hope."

Chapter 36

Within a month, Kyle distributed the Elpis virus into the quarterly bundle shot through Immunitrex. They worked with the global governments to ensure that they gave the vaccination top priority. For anyone who didn't get the booster, Elpis still spread to them and destroyed the latent Crow virus breeding within them.

Five months passed, and no one died from the Crow virus. Elpis had succeeded.

The military tribunal found Ahad and the rest of the Khemenu guilty of war crimes. They'd serve out their sentence in a maximum-security military prison designed for terrorists.

*

Wesley searched for Hunter but couldn't find him. The poor guy had gained a lot of weight lately, to the point where Wesley planned to take him to the vet next week. He'd been lethargic and out of sorts recently. *Oh well.* He had to get going. He'd deal with Hunter when he got back.

He had a new mission now, and he picked Candace up from her house. She'd spent a lot of time in his home lately. She wanted to maintain the illusion that she wasn't living with him by spending the occasional night on her own.

They drove to the Seattle Japanese Garden off Lake Washington Boulevard, then strolled along a pathway covered in ornamental trees. The garden offered an oasis of calm and beauty. They came to a portion where a small statue was reflected in the clear pond below, and the long green branches of a weeping willow flowed like a bushy hairdo toward the lily pads, which offered shelter to the frogs. They gave out an occasional croak. Red, yellow, and green trees framed the blue sky behind them.

Candace turned to face Wesley. "It's beautiful."

Butterflies filled his stomach. The sweat on his hands wet his pocket as he reached in to feel the small box within. He wrapped his fingers around it and smiled at Candace, then knelt on one knee. "Candace, you've helped me grow in ways I hadn't thought possible. I'd like to believe that like the many beautiful plants in this garden, together we make something grander than ourselves alone, that we can grow together into something more than we ever would apart." He pulled out the box and opened it to show a sparkling diamond ring. "Candace Rosenbach, will you marry me?"

She held her hand to her mouth and then jumped up and down. She snatched the ring and wrapped her arms around him. "Yes, yes, yes! I will!"

They shared a long, passionate kiss and strolled around the garden together.

When they returned to the car, Wesley said, "There's someone we need to go see."

*

The car dropped them off in front of the Children's Hospital. Wesley smiled at Candace, and they made their way to the Sunshine Tower, where Zach was recuperating. The receptionist had them fill out visitor forms and then gave them stickers to wear on their shirts.

A nurse escorted the two of them to a recovery room.

Before they entered, Wesley whispered to the nurse, "How is he?"

She pursed her lips. "Zach is doing much better now that Dr. Rosenbach's nano skin fibers have taken root." The nurse shook her head. "It's amazing. There are some we can't help. We can only comfort them. He was in that category. I was only able to give him medication to stave off the pain. Now—" She stopped talking for a minute and choked up. "Now I can say that he will be fine."

Candace squeezed Wesley's hand. "Dr. Rosenbach? It feels so weird to have them talk about Renee that way. I'm used to being the only Dr. Rosenbach in my family."

When they entered the room, Anne and Renee turned back. Zach stopped playing his video game. "Grandpa Wesley!" He held up the gaming device. "I'm level fifty now!"

Wesley marveled at the young man's skin. The last time he'd seen the boy, his skin had resembled a charred and blistered hot dog left too long on the grill. "Good job, buddy. How are you?"

He put out a fist, then pointed his thumb into the air. "I have tiny robots making my skin better!"

Wesley laughed. "I'm glad you're doing better." He turned to Renee and Anne. "When can he leave?"

Anne smiled. "He's ready to go—if he wants to, that is. I've made all the arrangements." Anne hugged Wesley. She whispered into his ear. "You're a good man."

Wesley smiled at Zach. "Would you like to go home with me?"

"Yeah. Until my mom comes to get me."

Wesley wasn't sure what to say. How did you tell a four-year-old his parents were dead?

Anne spoke up. "Zach, I explained what happened to your parents. Grandpa Wesley agreed to let you live with him. He won't ever replace your real parents, but he can raise you if you agree to it."

Zach gave him an appraising stare. "Only if I get a kitten."

Wesley laughed, and everyone else in the room joined him. "I have a cat, Hunter, but he's far from a kitten."

Zach shook his head. "No. I want my own. And I want to give one to Auntie Anne and Auntie Renee too. I don't want them to be lonely."

Wesley didn't have to think long about it. "You can have a kitten."

Anne handed him a backpack. "I bought a bunch of things for him." She nodded at the ring on Candace's finger and raised an eyebrow. "Congratulations!"

Renee shook his hand. "Good job. She's a catch. Listen—I talked to

Candace about this already, but I'll need your blessing. Would you agree to a quantum neural scan? I'd like to have someone for me too."

Wow. He wasn't sure what he thought about the idea of another him running around. How could he say no to Renee, though? He nodded his assent. "Yes, I'll do it."

*

When the three of them returned to Wesley's house, Zach jumped out of the car. "Holy moly! This place is huge. Is it yours, or do you just work here?"

Wesley patted him on the back. "No, it's mine. And yours now too."

Zach turned to him. "Hey, Auntie Anne says you're really old. Were you around before dinosaurs went enstinked? Because I want a pet T. rex too."

"I'm not that old, no. We'll work on the kitten first."

When they entered the house, a faint meowing noise emanated from one of the rooms. Had Hunter gotten caught in something? Wesley ran to the sound with Zach in tow. He held his mouth open when the source of the meowing noise became evident. Hunter had four kittens suckling at "his" belly.

Candace laughed. "I thought you said he was a boy cat."

Wesley stared in shock. "I … I thought he was. I never took him to the vet. I guess I never inspected closely."

Candace stared at him.

"What? He has a fuzzy butt!"

Zach pointed to one of the kittens, a small black cat with a white neck. "This one is mine. Her name is Eileen."

Wesley furrowed his brows. Where had Zach come up with that name? "Why did you call the kitten that?"

"Oh. That's my mom's name. I told you she'd come for me." He snuggled the kitten close to him and petted Hunter. Hunter purred as the boy gently stroked her back.

Wesley had never learned the name of Zach's mom.

Candace brought him close to her and whispered in his ear. "I get the next kitten."

He stared into her eyes, then understood what she meant. He nodded. "Okay. I hope you don't have four of them at once, though."

About the Author

❦

Tony Torzillo draws from his experience in the Seattle tech industry to write near future science fiction novels that inspire people to imagine a better world. Based in the Seattle area, he enjoys spending time with his family exploring the Pacific Northwest in the beautiful state of Washington.

You can connect with me on:
🌐 http://www.tonytorzillo.com
🐦 https://twitter.com/TonyTorzillo

www.ingramcontent.com/pod-product-compliance
Lightning Source LLC
Chambersburg PA
CBHW050714180626
46814CB00002B/441